C000231672

BLUE ANGEL
CONFESSIONS

BLUE ANGEL NIGHTS

Foreword by the translator

This remarkable novel by Margarete von Falkensee was first published in 1931 in a small edition by OBUS Verlag of Berlin, the original title being *The Pleasure Garden*. It is set in Berlin in the late 1920s.

Satire to the point of indecency was a well-established form of social comment in Berlin, the cartoons of George Grosz being a well-known example, while cabaret artists such as Werner Finck became notorious for their outspoken performances. In this tradition Margarete von Falkensee outdoes anything previously seen in print in her presentation of the politics of the Weimar Republic in terms of sexual activity in a group of people broadly representative of the times.

Some of the topical allusions in the novel have lost their meaning with time but the interest remains in a picture of a collapsing society and some of the characters are still easily recognised. Jutta von Loschingen, for example, is a caricature of the old aristocracy and Hildegard Buschendorf of the German middle-class zeal for authority. Magda Nebel symbolises a new menace, the emerging authoritarianism of National Socialism. It is needless here to categorise all the women in the novel; the reader will recognise them.

Two chapters may be referred to briefly as central to the author's thinking. In one, the elections of May 1928 are represented as a visit to a brothel and a choice between prostitutes. In the other, an account of an orgy in a Turkish

Bath, the religion of the times is mocked in a highly indecent way.

Those of a literary turn of mind may see some resemblance between the main character of the novel, Manfred von Klausenberg, and Voltaire's hero Candide. There is also a possible comparison with Kafka's hero in *The Trial* and *The Castle*, these two novels being published in Berlin only a few years before *The Pleasure Garden* was written. But whereas Candide withdraws from a world he finds unacceptable and Kafka's hero succumbs to forces he does not understand, Klausenberg fumbles his way towards an alliance with wholly unpredictable results. Whether the author was seriously proposing this as a solution to Germany's political and social problems is impossible to say. This is a novel, not a tract, however symbolic.

The years from 1924 to 1929 were regarded by most Berliners as the Golden Twenties, but this was a superficial view. The Republic founded in 1918 had survived Communist and Fascist attempts at revolution and it had survived the crippling hyper-inflation of the early 1920s. By 1925 the currency was stable, industrial production rising and employment growing. It was a time of dawning hopes and expectations, but events soon proved that there was no secure foundation under the new prosperity and no stability in the democratic system. The world recession heralded by the Wall Street stock market crash of 1929 brought bankruptcy and intolerable unemployment to Germany. The moderate centre in politics was eclipsed by the extremists and the National Socialist Party increased its representation in the Reichstag. In 1933 its leader, Adolf Hitler, was appointed Chancellor and the long night of barbarism fell on Germany.

Although this novel is set in 1928 it did not appear until 1931 and the delay killed off any prospect of success it might have had. It is very probable that the author had difficulty in finding a publisher, given the uncompromising nature of the content. OBUS Verlag was a small publishing house founded by the Hartmann brothers at the end of the

1914–1918 War and had a reputation for avant-garde work, Willi Klar, Gerd Fischer and Ursula Strauss being among its authors. By the beginning of the early 1930s OBUS Verlag was on its way to bankruptcy, its authors being more acclaimed than bought and by the time *The Pleasure Garden* came out Germany was in financial collapse and deep social turmoil. The catastrophe had happened and no further warning was required; *The Pleasure Garden* passed almost unnoticed.

Margarete von Falkensee was born in Potsdam in 1896 and was the daughter of a civil servant. After some experience in the theatre she worked in the film industry after 1924. Like many other writers, directors and performers, she emigrated to America when the Nazi Party took office. Her efforts to establish herself as a screen-writer in Hollywood met with only limited success, though her name can occasionally be seen in the credits of old black and white films. She died in a road accident in San Diego in 1948.

This English edition of *The Pleasure Garden* has been retitled *Blue Angel Nights* for reasons which may require some little explanation. Heinrich Mann's novel *Professor Unrat* was based on the same basic theme as Margarete von Falkensee's – sexual corruption as an image of the destruction of social values. It was filmed as *The Blue Angel* by Josef von Sternberg, with Marlene Dietrich as Lola and first shown in 1930. It treated the theme as tragedy, but Margarete von Falkensee treated it as vicious comedy. The new title for the English edition will, it is hoped, give it some of the flavour of those long-gone days and serve as an advertisement to the reader of what to expect.

It is not only the times that are long gone; the Berlin of this novel has also gone forever. Allied bombing reduced large parts of the city to rubble and Russian artillery and tanks destroyed much of the rest in 1945. Some of the sites in which the action of the novel takes place have vanished and some have been rebuilt; some lie on the far side of the Berlin Wall. Margarete von Falkensee's Berlin has disap-

7

peared from the earth as surely as ancient Babylon, but some of its spirit lives on in these pages.

Egon Haas,
Munich, 1985

The Birthday Party

On the morning after his twenty-third birthday party Manfred von Klausenberg woke with an aching head and a queasy stomach. The curtains were drawn and the room dim, for which he was grateful. He could hear the sound of quiet breathing beside him and there was a warm bare thigh over his waist. He slid out of bed cautiously, so as not to waken his partner, whoever she might be, and found that he was wearing only a sadly crumpled evening shirt and black silk socks. He stepped on an empty champagne bottle lying on its side on the floor and almost fell. The bottle skidded away under the bed, while Manfred stripped off his shirt and made his way to the bathroom.

Plenty of cold water on his face and the back of his neck helped to revive him a little. There was a bright red evening frock and one silk stocking draped over the side of the bath – the property of the woman asleep in his bed, he reasoned. He couldn't at that moment remember who she was. In fact, he couldn't remember going to bed at all. His head needed aspirin, but his stomach refused to accept it.

Naked but for his black socks, he padded round the apartment. The drawing-room was in semi-darkness and stank of tobacco smoke, stale drink and perfume. A man and a woman lay asleep in each other's arms on the zebra-skin sofa, the man without his trousers. *Poor Dieter, he never had much style*, Manfred thought, when he saw who the woman was. In an armchair two women slept together, Ulrika with her hand between the other woman's thighs. All the other guests seemed to have gone. The indications

9

were that the party had been a resounding success. About fifty friends had been invited and they had brought others with them so that it had been impossible to keep track of who was there – not that anyone tried. There had been a seemingly endless procession of pretty women and well-dressed men, talking, dancing and, above all, drinking.

He went back quietly to his bedroom for trousers, shoes and a thick ski-pullover and then out for a walk in the cold March sunshine to clear his head. He walked at random, trying not to be sick and hardly aware of his surroundings, his head throbbing unmercifully whenever a tram rattled past or a car hooted. Memories of the night before started to reassemble themselves, though chaotic and incomplete.

There had been a long and comic wrangle between Horst Lederer and Max Schroeder about Horst's style of painting. According to Max, it was outmoded, socially irrelevant and intellectually dangerous. Horst retaliated by insisting that the work of modern Expressionist artists was trash, the work of timid men who needed to distort reality before they could bear to look at it. Things livened up when Horst, as genially drunk as the rest of them, told his girl to show her backside to Max. Without demur she turned round, bent over and flipped up her frock to display a big fleshy bottom that was innocent of underwear. Horst patted it affectionately.

'There's reality for you,' he said, 'Rosa's backside. There's more life and truth in that than in all the rubbishy smears you pretend to admire.'

The little group of friends standing round to listen to the disagreement laughed. One of them prodded Max in the ribs and demanded to know how he answered that.

'Horst has a very *fundamental* view of art. He is the sole survivor of the peasant school of painting,' Max retorted.

'And I am proud to be so,' said Horst, 'it is the only school that will survive. Manfred – you're rich enough to buy pictures – what would you spend your money on – Rosa's backside or the degenerate daubs which Max promotes?'

10

'Give me Rosa any day! You have only to look about my walls to see that I never buy these modern problem-pictures to give myself bad dreams.'

Max threw up his hands in mock despair.

'I've looked at all your pictures, Manfred, and I am thoroughly depressed by your taste. Flat Prussian landscapes and family portraits! The plight of the intellectual has never been made plainer. We are trapped between the upper millstone of aristocratic ignorance and the lower millstone of bourgeois stupidity. Deep down in their hearts aristocrats and bourgeois are equally peasants.'

'I suppose that makes me a peasant too,' Rosa complained, her head still down near her knees.

'Yes,' said Max and Horst together.

'You can kiss my arse!' she replied, forgetting as she used the common expression what it was that she was showing.

Max and Horst grinned at each other and both bent over to plant a smacking kiss on the pink cheeks of Rosa's bottom, to the vast amusement and applause of the bystanders.

'As it is futile to discuss art with you, Horst,' said Max. 'Perhaps I may have the pleasure of discussing it with Fraulein Rosa.'

'By all means,' said Horst with a sly grin, 'if you kiss her backside enough times you'll come round to my way of thinking.'

There was another curious argument later on with Werner Schiele, which did not have so amusing an outcome. Werner was holding forth to two very pretty women in a corner by the piano.

'It is our moral duty to ourselves and to history to demolish this ugly city, this monument to militarism. We must destroy the Brandenburg Gate, the Royal Palace and all the relics of the shameful past.'

'I hope you'll leave the Opera,' said Manfred, 'I like that.'

Werner did not even pause for breath.

'When we have reduced to rubble these hideous monuments to barbarism, we shall build a new and modern city, shining and glorious, a symbol of the new Germany.'

'What sort of city, Werner?' one of the women asked.

'A wonderful city of glass and concrete. Walter Gropius is showing us the way to a new and magnificent expression of our national genius.'

'What about the Kranzler Cafe?' Manfred asked anxiously. 'There's no better place for a drink on the terrace while you watch the girls saunter past on a warm afternoon. I hope you're not going to knock that down.'

'You are a dinosaur!' said Werner fiercely, 'a fossil from a dead age. You will be swept away with the rubbish of the past.'

'What you overlook is that most Berliners like their city as it is. They won't thank you for knocking it down and building it in a different style.'

'The people are ignorant,' said Werner, 'they will be taught to respect the future instead of venerating the past.'

'He's mad,' said the woman who had spoken before, 'come away, Manfred, it might be infectious.'

'You are right,' said Manfred, taking her arm, 'against stupidity the Gods themselves struggle in vain.'

'Really? Who said that?'

'Schiller. Let me get you another drink.'

'You'll see!' Werner called after them, his tone angry.

Some time later, or perhaps it was earlier, for the sense of time was totally confused in Manfred's mind, he found himself perched on the arm of a chair in which two of his friends had become involved with each other. Nina was sitting on Konrad's lap, his hand was down the front of her low-cut evening frock and he was talking to her about politics.

'We lost our Emperor and became a Republic. But after ten years of this political comedy it must be obvious to everyone that we do not want democracy. It was forced upon us at bayonet-point by the Allies in 1918. The German

12

spirit is not naturally democratic. What is democracy but the rule of the ignorant mob?'

'My husband would agree with you,' said Nina, 'but should you be doing this to me in front of him?'

'Manfred is not your husband. I know for certain that he is not married.'

'Not Manfred. That's my husband over there, dancing with the red-head.'

'The one with the monocle? Is he a jealous man?'

'I've never yet found out.'

'Manfred,' said Konrad, 'is this dear lady's husband a jealous person?'

Inside her frock his hand was moving slowly over Nina's breasts.

'I don't know either,' Manfred answered, 'he doesn't seem to object when Nina comes here to visit me. But then, she and I have known each other for many years and perhaps he thinks that we discuss books together. Do you tell him what we do together, Nina?'

'Idiot!'

'On the other hand,' Manfred continued, 'if you look closely at Gottfried von Behrendorf, my dear Konrad, you will notice that he has a duelling-scar on his cheek, from which we may deduce that he understands how to use a sabre. He also hunts wild boar whenever he gets the chance, so he is no stranger to fire-arms. Before you move your hand from Nina's charming breasts to an even more fascinating part of her delightful body, you have a difficult decision to make.'

'Nina, this is a matter we must talk about in private, away from this neutral fool,' Konrad declared.

The two of them got up and made their way between the dancers and out of the room.

'Poor Konrad,' said Manfred to no one in particular, 'Nina will drain him dry and then Gottfried will butcher him. Life is tragic sometimes.'

Then there was the American girl. Not that he knew she was an American at first; his attention was caught by the

13

way she was dressed. She wore a man's evening-suit, stiff collar, white tie, tails, the complete ensemble. Some of the smarter lesbians about town had been affecting this style since a well-known actress appeared on stage in it a year or two before. This girl, moving with great poise through the noisy party guests, was exceptionally beautiful. She had jet-black hair and an expression of disdain. Manfred bowed, kissed her hand and introduced himself, wondering who had brought her. They danced together and, though her German was fluent, her accent was foreign and he learned that she was from New York.

Manfred was as well-disposed towards Americans as most, and for good reason. American money had refloated German industry and stabilised the country. American bankers were very welcome in Berlin, especially if they had beautiful daughters. But how terrible, Manfred thought, that so wonderfully attractive a girl should be interested only in other girls. What a loss to men! What a loss to himself! *'Life is tragic sometimes'*, he repeated aloud.

She thought he was talking to her.

'Only if you laugh,' she answered mysteriously.

She drifted away from him after the dance. A girl dressed in shiny white satin rose from between two men on a sofa and flung herself into Manfred's arms, bursting into tears.

'Make them stop, Manfred! I can't stand it!'

'Good God, what are they doing to you?'

'Nothing. I've been sitting there with my skirt up to my belly-button for twenty minutes and neither of them has even looked at my legs. All they do is argue about books.'

'They're strange creatures, the intelligentsia. I'll save you from them.'

In his fuddled state he was not sure what to do next. Instinct propelled him towards the bedrooms, the tearful girl clinging to his arm. He pushed a door open a little and peered round it, wondering what he would find. The room was in darkness but there was enough light round the door to reveal two couples making use of the bed. Across the middle he could see a bare and hairy bottom pumping up

14

and down in full spate. At the bottom of the bed a pair of silk-stockinged legs pointed straight up in the air, their thighs clamped round the head of a man kneeling on the floor.

'I know those legs,' said Manfred, 'they're Nina's. In you go, my dear, someone will take care of you.'

He pushed her towards the bed, backed out and closed the door silently, feeling that he had done his duty as a host.

After walking for an hour in the streets, Manfred found that his headache was gone and his stomach settled. He was in Friedrichstrasse, surrounded by window-shoppers. The other side of the street looked less crowded and he dodged across two lanes of cars and took refuge on a central island. Eventually he reached the other side and kept going until he came to the railway station.

A small comic scene was being enacted there. Two men were collecting money outside the station for their political movements. One wore the brown military uniform, the jack-boots and swastika armband of the National Socialist Party. The other wore a shabby overcoat and a workman's cloth cap and held a placard on which was lettered *RED FRONT*. Both were shaking their collecting-boxes aggressively at passers-by. They stood about five metres apart and ignored each other ostentatiously.

Manfred was hungry. He walked past the collectors, giving each of them the same glare of disapproval, and went into the station restaurant. It was warm and comfortable after the chill of the streets and smelt pleasantly of food. After pig's knuckles and sauerkraut and a glass or two of cold beer he felt much better and decided to take a taxi home.

It was well after midday when he let himself into his apartment. The married couple who looked after him and cooked and cleaned had done their work well. The rooms had been aired out, the mess removed and the furniture put back into place. Frau Geiger was in the kitchen, washing up glasses and plates.

15

'Good day, Herr Manfred. Did you enjoy your party?'

'It was very good. I've been out for some fresh air. No problems?'

'Nothing serious. We waited till ten o'clock, as you said, before we came in to clear up. There were two people asleep on the sofa in the drawing-room and I made coffee for them before they went. My husband found a young lady in the dining-room, asleep under the table, and put her in a taxi. He lent her one of your overcoats.'

'Why was that?'

'She was stark naked and we couldn't find her clothes anywhere.'

'Was she pretty?'

'If you like thin redheads. My husband couldn't keep his eyes off her. She said her name was Schwabe and that she'd send your coat back.'

'Yes, I know her. Where's your husband now?'

'Getting rid of the empty bottles. Will you dine in this evening, Herr Manfred?'

'I don't know yet. I'm going to shave and have a long soak in the bath.'

The telephone calls began about three that afternoon. The first caller was Nina von Behrendorf to thank him for a marvellous party and to congratulate him.

'I'm glad you enjoyed the party, Nina. I noticed that you and Konrad continued the political discussion in my bedroom. Evidently he has a persuasive tongue. But why the congratulations? My birthday was yesterday.'

'Congratulations on your engagement, darling, what else.'

'Engagement? What do you mean?'

'I'm sure you'll be blissfully happy together, just like Gottfried and me. Must rush now. Auf wiedersehen.'

She hasn't sobered up yet, Manfred thought. Engagement indeed! But in the next hour more friends telephoned to offer their congratulations and he became completely bewildered. He telephoned Wolfgang, whom he trusted, to

16

find out what was going on, but there was no answer. Eventually he managed to extract some sense from Konrad.

'You mean you don't remember?' said Konrad in open disbelief. 'You couldn't have been that drunk. You've got cold feet and want to call it off.'

'Konrad – who am I supposed to be engaged to?'

'Mitzi, of course, you made a big enough scene of the announcement.'

'But I don't know anyone called Mitzi.'

'As you wish. But it's a damned strange way to behave. The girl will be broken-hearted by such callousness.'

'But who is she?'

'I don't know. I'd never seen her before last night. But she is very pretty.'

'Who brought her to the party – do you know that much?'

'No idea. I was a bit drunk and didn't take everything in.'

'You managed to take Nina in – or part of her, at least.'

'Whatever passed between her and me was in private. Your performance was both public and vulgar.'

'What do you mean?'

Konrad chuckled.

'No one will forget that engagement in a hurry. After all, you stripped your fiancée naked in front of us all and danced a tango with her.'

'Oh my God!'

'Then you dragged her off to the bedroom and that was the last we saw of you. Didn't she remind you of all this when you woke up together this morning?'

'There has been a dreadful mistake, Konrad. I must speak to this young lady at once. Do you know where I can find her?'

'She's your fiancée, not mine.'

'But did you see her with anyone last night who might know her?'

'I hardly noticed her before you played your big scene. I was too busy with Nina. After you'd paraded her naked round the room everyone wanted to talk to her – but you

17

rushed her off to bed. Wait a minute, though, I think I saw her in the dining-room earlier on having something to eat with Werner. But I wouldn't swear to it.'

Manfred cut him off with a brief 'thank-you' and telephoned Werner Schiele.

'Werner – do you know a girl called Mitzi?'

'That's good, coming from you! I've half a mind to come round there and punch your thick head. Of all the cheap stunts to get her away from me!'

'Werner, there's been a misunderstanding. We can punch each other some other time. Just give me her telephone number.'

'Were you too ashamed to ask her this morning? My God, when I think what you put that poor girl through – you ought to be flogged in public!'

'We can go into that later. Just give me the number.'

'She's not on the telephone.'

'Then where does she live?'

'You couldn't be bothered to take her home? You'll tell me next you forgot to ask her name. What a cheap and rotten trick to get a girl into bed!'

'Everything will be explained eventually. What is her name and address? I must talk to her at once.'

In tones of high indignation Werner at last gave him what he wanted. Manfred consulted a street-guide and drove himself to the address. It was in a far from fashionable part of Berlin, a grey and shabby apartment building in an unknown street of grey and shabby buildings. The caretaker informed him that Fraulein Genscher lived on the first floor. In fact, when Manfred walked up the unswept stairs, he found that she had a room in a large old apartment. A landlady in a worn and shiny black frock opened the door and showed him the room he wanted, knocked for him and ushered him in.

It was a fair-sized room, but filled with heavy oldfashioned furniture and a divan-bed half-hidden beyond a wardrobe. Three young women sat at a table, drinking coffee and eating little cakes. They looked up at Manfred's entrance, smiled, and the middle one came quickly across the thin carpet to throw her arms about him and kiss him on both cheeks.

'Darling! I didn't expect you until later. I was telling my friends about the wonderful news. Come and meet them. You already know Rosa Vogel – and this is Ilse Kleiber.'

Manfred bowed over their hands. He remembered Rosa as the plump and jolly model who had been with Horst at the party. She was pretty, in a fleshy way, and so was the other woman, Ilse. Mitzi herself was easily the best-looking of the three, a tall, yellow-haired beauty in her early twenties, with a round, doll-like face and a complexion like fine porcelain.

'Let me present my fiancé,' she said in breathless pride, 'Herr Manfred von Klausenberg.'

'Ladies,' said Manfred, bowing again.

Mitzi took his hat and overcoat and asked him to sit down.

'He is so handsome,' said Rosa, 'isn't he, Ilse?'

'So distinguished,' said Ilse, a tinge of envy in her voice.

'And so rich,' Rosa added, 'you should see his apartment!'

Manfred was out of his depth. He took the cup of coffee he was offered and sat in silence, trying to look pleasant.

'Mitzi has been telling us all about the party,' said Ilse, 'it is like a fairy-tale come true.'

'The guests were so elegant,' said Mitzi, 'I was in my old red frock that I've had since before Christmas. I felt terribly out of place, as you can imagine. Then, out of the blue, Manfred took me in his arms and said the most charming things to me.'

'So romantic,' Ilse sighed, 'and you were there to see it, Rosa.'

'What made it even more romantic,' said Rosa, 'was something very common that happened earlier on. That mad Horst made me show the whole company my backside and kissed it. And one of his friends!'

That was something which Manfred definitely remembered from the chaos of the night before.

'I think it must have been that which gave Herr Manfred the idea for what he did later on,' Rosa continued. 'Of course, being a gentleman, what he did wasn't common at all.'

'Tell me,' said Ilse breathlessly.

Mitzi took up the tale.

'His strong arms held me and I trembled like a little girl. I looked into his handsome face and it was like a dream. Then it happened, the most wonderful moment of my life.'

'What happened?' Ilse asked quickly.

'He called for silence in a great ringing voice and announced to all his friends that he had fallen passionately in love with me.'

'Fantastic!' said Ilse.

'He took this ring from his finger and put it on mine as a token of love until he could buy me the biggest diamond in Berlin.'

She held out her hand. With a sinking heart Manfred recognised his heavy gold signet ring, engraved with the family coat of arms. Until that moment he had not missed it.

'Ah, and then came the best part of all,' said Rosa, 'the dance!'

'The dance,' said Mitzi, 'even now I can hardly believe it happened.'

'He made her strip off,' Rosa said solemnly, 'every stitch! They danced a tango with all of us looking on. You should have seen the men staring at Mitzi. Their eyes were sticking out on stalks. You could hear trouser-buttons popping right round the room.'

'Rosa!' said Mitzi in reproof. 'You make it sound like a cheap cabaret act. It was supremely romantic. I felt like a goddess floating in the arms of some great hero of old. Love had transformed us and put us beyond shame or modesty at that moment. We were in love – and we were divine!'

20

She smiled lovingly at Manfred, who sat appalled at these revelations.

'I could refuse you nothing,' she told him proudly, 'you swept me into your bedroom and showered me with kisses.'

'And the rest,' said Rosa.

'Fiancés have their rights,' said Ilse, her face pink with emotion.

'Mitzi, I must talk to you alone,' said Manfred awkwardly, 'if these ladies will graciously permit?'

'Come on, Ilse,' Rosa said at once, 'these two have private matters to discuss.'

'Yes, you must leave now,' Mitzi agreed, her pale blue eyes aglow, 'my fiancé wants to be alone with me.'

'And we can guess why,' said Rosa with a giggle.

Manfred stood up and bowed as Mitzi's friends left. He had no idea of how to extricate himself from the predicament in which he found himself without being brutally discourteous. He must have been insane last night!

He was still on his feet when Mitzi closed the door and came back to him. To his amazement she flung herself at his feet, wound her arms round his thighs and pressed her face to his belly.

'Darling! I am so pleased you are here. I have been longing to see you all day.'

'The thing is,' he began uncertainly, 'you and I have something of importance to sort out between us.'

'So many things,' she agreed, 'so many arrangements to make for the wedding. But first . . .'

Her fingers were busy with his trouser-buttons and before he had time to say more, her hand was into the slit of his underpants and held his dangler.

'I think I must be going mad!' he exclaimed piteously.

'Yes, mad with passion, like last night,' she said, her warm hand fondling what it held, 'three times you drove me to the madness of ecstasy before you let me sleep.'

'Three times – did I really?'

'You were magnificent. When I woke up this morning

in your bed I felt that I was already a bride on her honeymoon. But I was alone. Where were you, my darling?'

'I needed air. I went for a walk.'

'Do you want another walk now? Or do you want something else?' she teased him.

Manfred's stem stuck out of his trousers like a steel rod. He took Mitzi under the arms and raised her to her feet. She was tall, nearly as tall as he was, and strongly built. He snatched at her dove-grey frock and pulled it over her head. Her satin slip went the same way, flung across the room, and she was naked except for her stockings. In Manfred's circle the smart young women had given up wearing underclothes years before and it came as no surprise to find Mitzi without, even though she was very obviously from a different social level.

'Ah,' he said in appreciation.

Her body was strong and well-proportioned, very pleasing to the eye. And also to the hand, he confirmed, as he ran his palms over her weighty breasts and down over the very smooth skin of her sides and hips. He looked into her eyes and saw an expression of eagerness.

'Mitzi . . .' he began, and stopped.

He wanted to explain that what had happened at the party was no more than a drunken frolic, for which he now felt ashamed and apologetic. He also wanted to make love to her now that the delights of her naked body were open to him. Desire struggled with shame and he wavered.

'Manfred, I am yours,' she whispered, 'do what you like with me.'

His mind urged him to stop before he became involved deeper in an absurd misunderstanding, but the part of him sticking out impudently lower down insisted that he should go on.

'You were not so hesitant last night,' Mitzi told him, 'did you over-exert yourself? Can't you do it again yet?'

'Three times you said?'

'If you can't decide, I will!'

She whirled away from him, very light on her feet for a

22

large woman, and seated herself on a low stool upholstered in faded red plush. Her feet were together, the heels of her white shoes touching, and her knees wide apart. The hair between her legs was almost the same yellow colour as the hair on her head. Manfred regarded it in silence, admiring its aesthetic appeal.

'It's yours to do as you please with,' she said, and ran her middle finger up between the pink-brown lips to open them.

'Dear God!' Manfred breathed and threw himself to his knees, though not in prayer.

Mitzi's feet moved apart, her hand reached for his stiffness and tugged him towards her, he shuffling on his knees until she had him at the right spot. He held her by the thighs, up above her gartered stockings, and pushed slowly into her. His eyes were on her round doll-face, enjoying her expression of simple adoration.

'So big and strong!' she murmured, 'I can feel you right up inside me.'

Her legs were round the small of his back and her arms about his neck. To maintain her precarious balance on the stool Manfred put his arms round her waist and supported her. He bestirred himself with slow deliberation.

This was not a pleasure to hurry through, he thought. Explanations could come later and, when they did, that would be the end of it, with hard words and tears. But until then, this marvellous life-size blonde doll was his to enjoy.

Her responses were keener than his own, he shortly discovered. His stately stroke was not long established before her legs tightened round him like a vice, her body shook in his arms and she gasped out 'Oh, oh, oh!' Manfred maintained his rhythm unbroken. He could not recall when he had last enjoyed making love so consciously as now and it was far too good to spoil. Before long Mitzi cried out again in another crisis and half-choked him by the grip of her arms round his neck.

He felt the heat of her body right through his clothes.

The part of him inside her experienced her warmth and softness even more directly and revelled in it, like a king in his castle. The moment came when Manfred could restrain himself no longer. His steady thrusting became a frenzy of short strokes and he poured his passionate offering into her. Through his own ecstasy he heard her gasping and moaning.

'Darling,' she said when she could speak rationally again, 'do you truly love me? I want to hear you say it.'

The horrible moment had arrived and could be evaded no longer. Manfred held her closely to him, to restrain any violent reaction to his words and, still embedded in her wonderful body, made his confession.

'There has been a most unfortunate misunderstanding, Mitzi. The fact is that I was too drunk last night to know what I was doing. I must apologise to you for the distress I have caused by my regrettable behaviour. It is not possible for us to be engaged.'

'What?' she exclaimed shrilly. 'You take advantage of my good nature and then tell me you were drunk when you asked me to marry you? I've never been so insulted in my life – never! Don't think you can slide out of it that easily – I've got witnesses.'

'I don't doubt it. But what did they witness?' Manfred asked reasonably. 'A drunken frolic at a party, that's all. And perhaps the witnesses were drunk too. Listen to me, Mitzi, I think that everyone was confused about what happened last night. You're a very nice person but I don't love you and not for one moment do I believe that you love me. Would it not be more sensible to let the matter end like that, with a suitable present from me to you as a token of respect?'

'Am I a whore to take money for letting you make love to me!' she said in outrage.

'Certainly not. I would not insult you by offering money after the tender exchange that has just taken place between us. What I had in mind was a fur coat.'

To his surprise she began to laugh. She laughed so hard

that his now limp affair was ejected from its warm hiding-place by the constriction of her muscles. He felt it safe to let go of her now that her rage had subsided and sat back on his heels, still fascinated by her big naked body.

'A fur coat,' she said cheerfully, 'I like that very much. Though to be fair to you, it seems a lot for one quick go.'

'And the three times last night, of course.'

'Last night you were so drunk when they carried you to bed that you were past it,' she informed him, 'I tried to rouse you but you were dead to the world.'

Manfred grinned at her. She was a good-natured woman, as he had thought.

'It's too late to go shopping today,' he said, 'I will call for you tomorrow morning at eleven, if that is convenient.'

'You really mean it, don't you?' Mitzi said, half-surprised.

'You have my word. And I would like you to return my signet ring when I come for you tomorrow.'

'Take it now – I trust you.'

'Thank you,' and he accepted it from her and slipped it back on to his little finger.

Mitzi sat up straight on the stool, knees together, and looked at him seriously.

'There is one thing,' she said.

'And what is that?'

'Until I am wearing the fur coat you promised I have every right to regard you as my fiancé.'

'If you choose,' he answered, wondering what she intended.

'Fiancés have privileges. You heard my friend say so.'

Manfred stared at her big and beautiful breasts.

'Fraulein Ilse was correct,' he said, 'since our engagement will be a very short one, I ought to make full use of my rights while I have them.'

'It would be a pity not to,' Mitzi agreed.

She rose from her stool, offered him her hand to rise and led him to the divan-bed by the wall.

* * *

25

Punctually at eleven the next day Manfred called for her in his impressive maroon-coloured Mercedes tourer and took her shopping along the Kurfurstendamm. Her pleasure in being taken seriously in expensive shops was so engaging that Manfred let her indulge it to the full. He sat quietly smoking cigarettes in shop after shop while assistants brought coats for Mitzi to look at and try on. It occurred to him eventually that he had never in his life given any woman so much pleasure as Mitzi was experiencing in trying on coats and staring at herself in long mirrors and twirling round in front of him to let him see the effect and give his opinion.

Eventually she chose a red fox coat, magnificent in appearance, which set off her blonde colouring admirably. Her old cloth coat with the rabbit-skin collar was neatly folded and wrapped by a smirking shop-assistant who knew all about men buying fur coats for pretty young women. Manfred tucked the parcel under his arm, led Mitzi to his car and decided to take her for a light lunch to Kranzler's Cafe. He was in an extremely good mood and ordered champagne as soon as they were seated.

'A toast, Mitzi. A brief engagement but a happy one.'

'That's worth drinking to. If only all engagements could be like that!'

'Tell me what happened at my party. It's still a blank to me.'

'About two in the morning you were blind drunk. You danced with me and you were muttering to yourself. I couldn't make out what, but you were unhappy about a woman. I felt sorry for you – you were really suffering – so I tried to be nice to you. Then you decided that you were madly in love with me and told everybody. You didn't even know who I was and I don't suppose it made any difference, the state you were in.'

'Who had made me unhappy? Did I say?'

'No, but I guessed later. You asked me to undress and I was drunk enough to do it and we danced together. It was a sensation – your friends were clapping and shouting.

26

In the middle of the dance you passed out and half a dozen of the men put you to bed. After that they put their heads together, a few of them, and dreamed up this story. You were supposed to wake up with me in bed and find out that we were engaged. Then they'd confirm the story. Only it nearly went wrong when you got up and vanished while I was still asleep. So they did it the other way round by telephoning you and letting you come to find me. Understand?'

'My God – they really put one over on me. All of them who telephoned me were in on it – Konrad, Nina, Werner – and Rosa, of course. Whose idea was it?'

'The lady.'

'Nina von Behrendorf, you mean?'

'She was hanging on to that Konrad and she wanted to get at you. And she was the one you were unhappy about, I think, when we were dancing. Something went wrong between you, that was obvious.'

'Nina and I were in love for a long time, but she married that idiot Gottfried. It was my fault, I suppose. We were happy as we were and I saw no reason to change things by getting married. So she married him to spite me. Then at the party Konrad was making up to her and I didn't take her away from him, which is what she wanted. I let them go off to the bedroom together.'

'Why? If you love her and she loves you, why are you trying to hurt each other? It doesn't make sense. She marries another man to hurt you and then you let somebody else drag her off to bed when you want her yourself, so that you can hurt her. It's too complicated for me. Are you sure you were in love with her?'

'To distraction! We had wonderful times together and we did marvellous and crazy things. The winter before last, we were skating one afternoon on the little pond in the Tiergarten. It was just getting dark and there was hardly anyone about. Shall I tell you what Nina did? She stripped off and skated naked to please me. She was so beautiful in just her tall fur hat. Her body was the colour of mother-

27

of-pearl – my heart was beating so fast that I had to stand still and watch her. Then a nurse-maid came by with three children and the woman shouted to the children to come away at once, as if the sight of so much beauty would harm them! And an old man with a big moustache rushed out on the ice waving a walking-stick at Nina, and he slipped and went sliding across the pond on his backside. His indignation was incredibly comical – I was aching with laughter. Nina skated a circle round him as he sat there croaking at her. Then she came to me and kissed me and I wanted to throw her down on the snow and grass and make love to her.'

Mitzi smiled and reached across the table to stroke his hand.

'You should have married her, Manfred.'

'Maybe. What about you, though – Werner brought you to the party but he didn't mind having you go to bed with me as part of the joke.'

'He'd had enough of me. I knew that before he did. There was only one thing he wanted from me, and he didn't want that for long. He told me that you were soft-hearted enough to see me right if I made you believe the story they cooked up about being engaged.'

'Something must be done about Werner,' said Manfred. 'He meant that I'm soft in the head, not the heart. And the coat you're wearing is proof of that.'

'Look,' said Mitzi, 'it was only a joke for me. I didn't know about the ill-feeling or I'd never have agreed to it. Take the coat back to the shop and get your money back. I don't want it now I know how I was used.'

'No, you keep it, Mitzi. I like you and you've been honest with me. Besides, it suits you and every woman should have a fur-coat.'

'If we're talking about honesty, there's something you don't know about me.'

'I'm sure there are many things I don't know about you. But it's not important and you don't have to tell me.'

'You've been straight with me and I want to be the same

28

with you. You see, even if you'd fallen for the joke and really believed that we were engaged, it wouldn't have meant anything. I'm married already.'

'But you don't wear a ring.'

'I pawned it ages ago. My husband is in prison, the dirty pig.'

'What did he do?'

'He's a cheap swindler. They caught him selling dud insurance policies to old women. He went inside and left me penniless. That was two years ago and I was twenty.'

'How have you survived since then?'

'As best I can. Once or twice I've found a job for a few months, but I'm not really any good at anything and sooner or later the boss starts feeling my backside, so I move on. Most of the time I find a nice young man who wants to pay the rent and take me out. I'm not a whore, you know, but there is one thing I'm good at.'

'Have there been many before Werner?' Manfred asked sympathetically.

'Five or six since I've been on my own. This will make you laugh – the first one was my husband's brother. He couldn't wait to get his hands on me. That was all right – I liked him – but his wife found out that he was keeping me and that was that. I thought my troubles were over with Werner. I mean, he's got plenty of money and lives the way he wants to. It's all parties and dancing and nice restaurants. He took care of the rent, but he was too mean to buy me any clothes, except now and then.'

'What will you do now?'

Mitzi winked at him across the table.

'Someone else is interested in me,' she said happily. 'He's been after me since he saw me strip off at your party. He's biding his time till the engagement joke is over. That's now, I suppose.'

'So it is, dear Mitzi. And while my best friends may be laughing at me behind my back, the truth is that I've enjoyed the joke more than they have.'

'Have you?'

She stared at him, her pale blue eyes shining with amusement, a little grin on her doll's face.

'Oh yes – the thing that you are good at, as you put it, you are very good at. Shall I tell you what I'd like to do this afternoon?'

'Go on, then.'

'I'd like to take you back to your room and take all your clothes off and kiss you from head to toe.'

'We're not engaged now, you know,' she said, her grin getting wider.

'Then I'd ask you to put your new fur-coat on, so that the silk lining is against your naked body, and the fur against my naked body, and then I'd roll you around on your bed until we both go nearly crazy with sensation and I'd open the coat and throw myself on top of you and make love to you like a madman, time after time. What do you think of that?'

'Why are we sitting here talking?' Mitzi asked, 'Let's go!'

Backstage at the Theatre

To celebrate the successful first night of Oskar Brandenstein's new comedy *Three in a Bed* there was the usual
glittering party back-stage. Oskar, a burly man in his mid-
forties played the impressario most convincingly, accepted
congratulations with an air of world-weary politeness and
told everyone about the even more sensational new comedy
he intended to put on in the autumn. Actresses and actors
flitted about, kissing each other repeatedly, and assuring
each other that their performances had been marvellous.
Oskar's backers and the other non-theatrical guests drank
champagne and tried to look important.

In this heady atmosphere of euphoria and bright promise,
Manfred von Klausenberg circulated happily. He told
everyone who would listen that Oskar would soon displace
Max Reinhardt as the leading figure in the theatre.
Everyone agreed enthusiastically, especially Oskar himself,
who clasped Manfred's hand in both of his own and almost
shed tears of joy. The only person who did no. agree was
the young American lady who had appeared at Manfred's
birthday party.

'Oskar has talent,' she informed Manfred, 'he would do
well on Broadway. But Reinhardt has genius. There is a
difference.'

Her name was Jenny Montrose, Manfred ascertained, for
he couldn't recall asking her name the first time he met
her. She was more conventionally dressed for Oskar's party,
in an elegant frock of cerise taffeta that left her arms and
shoulders and much of her bosom bare.

31

'I don't see your fiancée,' she said brightly, 'Isn't she here?'

'I have no fiancée, Miss Montrose. That was a silly joke by some of my friends.'

'But it was you who ripped the girl's clothes off and danced with her.'

'That was a different sort of joke,' he said uneasily.

'What a strange sense of humour you Germans have.'

Her companion was the star of Oskar's play, Hugo Klostermann, a handsome matinée idol over whom young girls and middle-aged matrons had been swooning for years. The story told about him, as Manfred knew well, was that unless he made love at least every four hours he developed a raging head-ache. Perhaps it was no more than a publicity story, but in theatrical circles it was open gossip that he invariably had a woman visit him in his dressing-room half an hour before the curtain went up. If none of his countless girl-friends turned up to oblige, the female members of the cast took the duty in rotation.

Manfred saw that his first impressions of Miss Montrose must be revised. The male evening dress she had worn at his party could have been no more than affectation, for she and Klostermann were clearly on the best of terms. It was to be seen in the way he touched her arm as he talked and the way she smiled at him. Her taste was for men, after all, and with the actor that taste was surely being indulged to the full.

Manfred had been brought to the back-stage party by an actress who played a minor role in *Three in a Bed* and who had of late been playing a leading role in Manfred's own bed. But sometime after midnight, when large amounts of champagne had been consumed, the allegiances of many of those present began to shift. It dawned upon Manfred that Anna had deserted him. She was sitting on Oskar's lap, stroking his bald patch and evidently auditioning for her next role. Manfred shrugged and grinned. He wished her well in her career now that he had, when all was said, fairly well exhausted her repertoire.

So it was that he cultivated the acquaintance of another of Oskar's minor players, Magda Nebel. She was in conversation with a fat old man who looked like a financier and probably was. It proved easy enough to detach her from him, so easy in fact that Manfred concluded that she had been instructed by Oskar to be nice to the money-man and had no relish for the task.

She was about twenty-five, dark-haired, and wore a short evening frock of bright green with little tassels round the hem. Her hair was cut dramatically short and brushed back from her forehead and ears, but her most striking feature was her sulky mouth. Manfred found her charming. As simple logic indicated that Anna was not likely to accompany him home that night, being too deeply engrossed with Oskar and her future on the stage, he applied himself to making a good impression on Magda. He was flattered to find that she already knew who he was and pleased to observe that she gave every sign of being well-disposed towards him. When the party began to lose its interest for both of them, Magda accepted his offer to drive her home. Even better, when they got there she invited him in for a drink.

Her apartment was not large, but modern in its furnishings and colours. Manfred settled himself in a square arm-chair upholstered in oyster-satin, a glass of brandy in his hand, while Magda left him for a few minutes. He was well content. More than that, he anticipated a rewarding night, which might perhaps prove to be the start of an interesting new friendship.

His heart bounded when Magda returned. She had changed into a short négligé of white lace and, from the glimpses of pink flesh it afforded through its open pattern, she was obviously naked inside it. In addition to his heart, another part of him bounded when she took a chair opposite him and tucked her bare legs under her.

'I suppose you think I brought you here to make love to me,' she said casually.

'Dear Magda, no such presumptuous thought entered my head.'

Her thighs were very smooth where the short négligé parted a little to reveal them. She stared at him thoughtfully.

'Why not? Don't you find me attractive?'

'Of course I do! You have a dark and sultry beauty which I find irresistible.'

'Is that so? You seem to be resisting very well.'

The hint was clear enough. Manfred moved across to the arm of her chair and kissed her. Her mouth was passive, even when he slipped a hand down her négligé to cup a soft breast.

'It takes a lot more than that to get me started,' she told him, 'and when I do – look out! There aren't many men who can cope with me.'

'I've never yet met a woman I couldn't please. Nor one I couldn't arouse.'

Her fingers touched his trousers to ascertain his condition and then pinched hard through the cloth.

'Men know nothing about women,' she observed, 'they think that if they grope about for five minutes any woman will open her legs and beg them to stick it in her.'

She sounded almost angry and there was no point in arguing with her. Although Manfred was still fondling her breast with an expert touch, its bud remained soft and unresponsive to his attentions.

'There is a mystery here to be solved,' he said, 'you have a secret which I cannot even guess at. Yet I feel that if you were to allow me to share your secret, the experience would be exceptionally enjoyable for both of us.'

'It might be more than you bargained for.'

'That makes me even more interested.'

'Don't say that I didn't warn you. Come with me.'

She led him into her bed-room. It was square, white-walled and had a low divan-bed. The only note of colour in the room was a dark wolf-pelt spread over the bed itself. Without a word she removed her lace négligé and stood,

34

hands on hips, for Manfred to look at. Her expression was beyond him to define, part defiant, part sulky, and part something for which no adequate word occurred to him just then. It was easier to stare at her heavy breasts, her narrow belly and the small triangle of curls between her thighs. These features at least presented no complications and required no elaborate interpretation.

'You are superb,' he praised her, 'provocative and dangerous!'

Magda cupped her breasts in her long-fingered hands and pushed them upwards. The reddish-brown halos around her buds were larger than on most women and contrasted sharply with her clear skin tones.

'The other girls at the theatre say they are too big for the style today,' she remarked, 'do you think they're too big?'

'Not at all. I like women who look like women and not like boys. I think your breasts are luscious, Magda. Let me see your bottom too.'

She turned about to display a pair of round cheeks, well-proportioned and very appetising.

'Are you sure you don't prefer boys?' she asked. 'Is my bottom good enough for you?'

'Perfection!'

Before he had time to give her bottom a fond squeeze, she walked across to a white-painted wardrobe, opened it and rummaged inside. When she turned back towards him she held a coil of crimson cord, of the kind used for bell-pulls in old-fashioned houses.

'There!' she said almost fiercely. 'My secret. Do you understand it?'

Manfred's imagination raced as he stared at the coil. This was a new bedroom game for him. He nodded, words failing him, and Magda held the coil out to him.

'Prove it,' she said sharply, 'what kind of man stands dumb-struck with a naked woman and does nothing about it?'

He seized the heavy coil with enthusiasm, weighed it in his hands, found one end of the cord and tested it. It was smooth and supple and probably almost unbreakable. Before Magda could taunt him again he spun her away from him, pulled her arms behind her back and tied her wrists together.

'NO!' she cried out when her wrists were securely bound, 'Let me go!'

He had no experience of tying up naked women, but the idea had a certain appeal. Improvising as he went, he looped the crimson cord from her wrists over one shoulder, under one breast and back over the other shoulder. Interest and ingenuity made up for lack of experience and in a minute or two he had Magda on her knees on the fluffy white rug, the cord between her legs and pulled tight, her ankles bound and a length of cord round her waist and cutting into her belly. Through it all she struggled and complained and, when he stepped back to view his handiwork, she said with every appearance of anger that unless he released her at once she would scream for the police.

Manfred smiled and flicked the silk handkerchief from his breast-pocket to gag her.

'Scream all you like. No one will hear you except me.'

The criss-cross of the crimson cord over her pale flesh was very exciting to see, as was the way in which she squirmed against her bonds. Manfred sat on the rug and felt her trussed breasts to his heart's content and Magda made hoarse noises through the silken gag. Her buds were standing very hard now and had flushed a darker red. On a sudden inspiration he gripped her by the shoulders and put his mouth to the nearest breast to suck at the swollen tip.

'So, it seems that I have succeeded in getting you going, dear Magda. As for satisfying you, I see no problem there.'

He rolled her on to her back, the bonds keeping her knees up towards her belly, and examined her between the thighs with feverish intensity. Under the dark curls the lips had been forced apart by the cord between her legs. He moved the cord sideways into her groin and forced his middle finger inside her to tickle her pink nub. It was very

36

slippery and it needed only a little stimulation to set her belly twitching.

The game had aroused Manfred as much as it had her. He rolled her over on to her knees as if she were a big parcel, her face down on the rug and her bottom in the air It was the work of a moment to kneel behind her and open his trousers.

'Now comes the moment you dread, Magda! You are about to be savagely raped and you are helpless to move or to beg for mercy. What a nightmare of torment for you!'

He pressed the ball of his thumb against the little knot of muscle between the cheeks of her behind and his finger into the lips lower down.

'Two warm little holes,' he teased her. 'Which one of them is to be violated? Something hard and brutal will force itself into one or the other. Do I prefer boys or girls, you asked me. This is when you will find out.'

He heard her gurgle through the gag as he touched the tip of his swollen stem to the tight little entrance in her bottom, let her tremble in fear for some moments, pretending to be pushing into it. Then with his thumbs he pried open the proper entrance and slid in quickly.

'You are relieved that I prefer girls,' he gasped, 'But your relief is only temporary. I am going to treat you viciously.'

With his hands on her hips to steady himself, he plunged briskly in and out. It was no time for tenderness – Magda had shown that rough handling excited her. He intended to give her enough of it to satisfy her.

She had left the wardrobe open and it had a long mirror on the inside of the door. Manfred could see his own reflection and could hardly believe what he was seeing. He was still in his elegant evening clothes, black bow-tie perfectly in place and a white carnation in his button-hole. Magda's bare rump, on which he was mounted, was in full sight, but her head, down on the rug, was out of sight in the mirror. Manfred grinned at the image of his own face and the image grinned back, red with excitement and exertion. So bizarre a view of himself spurred him on to harder endeavours, which brought louder gurglings from Magda and an explosion in his own belly that flung an ecstatic stream into her. He pounded away until at last the pleasure faded and left him panting for breath.

When he was calm again he released Magda from her bonds and lifted her on to the bed. Her skin was marked where the cords had constricted it.

'Brandy?' he asked.

She nodded, her eyes closed and her legs still trembling. He fetched the bottle and glasses from the sitting-room, exhilarated by the grotesque game in which he had taken part. On his return he found her sitting cross-legged on the wolf-pelt, rubbing her breasts upwards.

'Do they hurt still?' he asked, pouring brandy for her.

'No, they feel good. I like stroking them. I do it all the time when I'm alone.'

Manfred sat on the bed, facing her, and poured brandy for himself. The night still had a long way to run.

'Did I do it right?' he asked.

'You're a fast learner, if that was the first time.'

'It was the first time I've tied a woman up.'

'Did you like it?'

He raised his glass to her in salutation.

'It was fantastic.'

Magda emptied her glass and put it down. Her hand went between her legs to pluck at the dark curls there.

'Now you know what it takes to get me started. But you still don't know what it takes to finish me off.'

'I think I can guess.'

'You think you're clever, don't you? But you may be in for a surprise.'

Manfred was fascinated by the way in which she was stroking the dark-haired lips between her thighs. She saw the direction of his glance and grinned wickedly.

'Do you like my Fotze?' she asked him.

'It's a beauty – and very hospitable.'

'Then you have no objection if it welcomes you again?'

38

'Far from it – I shall insist on another visit when I've finished my brandy.'

'Finish it then. I'll show you a different game to keep your interest up. It wouldn't do for your attention to slacken halfway through. Why don't you take your clothes off?'

Manfred stood up to undress. He had guessed that Magda would want to reverse roles and bind him this time. The prospect was amusing and strange enough to be exciting.

'Kneel on the floor and let me tie your hands,' she said when he was naked.

She bound his wrists behind his back with the skill of long practise. She did not truss his body, as he expected, but linked his wrists to one ankle. And that, he realised, was all that was needed to make him helpless, for he was unable to get to his feet or free himself. Magda stood back to stare at him, her head tilted to one side and her hand still caressing between her legs.

'Good,' she said, 'now for the surprise.'

He watched with keen interest as she went to the open wardrobe and bent over to reach into the bottom of it. Her rump was thrust towards him and, between her spread thighs, he could see the dark-curled mound he had ravaged. Its long pink slit was agape and the impression the sight made on him was so lubricious that his limp stem stirred again. His interest turned to surprise, as Magda had promised, when he saw her pull on black knee-length riding-boots. Surprise became astonishment when she buckled round her narrow waist a black leather belt, complete with pistol-holster on one hip. And finally, astonishment was overwhelmed by incredulity when he saw her put on a military helmet with a badge on the front and a spike on the top.

Attired in this incongruous manner, she posed before him, a long and thin riding-crop in one hand. She stood arrogantly, legs apart, head back and her fists on her hips, glaring down at him.

'Now, you swine – it's time you found out what happens

39

to scum like you! Straighten your back! Stop drooping like a bag of rubbish!'

Her voice was harsh, her expression cold. Manfred knelt up straight, intrigued by her change of personality and wondering how this version of the game was played.

'Look at you!' she said, 'good for nothing! What use are you to a woman with a shrivelled little thing like that?'

'You found it useful enough a little while ago.'

'Silence!'

She reached down to prod him between the legs with the end of her riding-crop, none too gently.

'As much use as a punctured balloon.'

'It's resting,' Manfred told her, 'like a boxer between rounds.'

'Boxer! That miserable thing couldn't punch its way through a paper bag. One quick sneeze and it's done for! I've seen better on six-year-old boys.'

She poked the end of her crop under his limp equipment and started to flick it upwards as she harangued him.

'Up with it! I'll have no laziness here. Do you think I brought you here to doze off?'

The rough jerking had its effect. Manfred's disabled limb began to grow strong again.

'About time too,' Magda commented brutally, 'I thought it had died of shock after its little performance.'

Manfred gazed down fondly at his growing stiffness. His pleasure was cut short by Magda flicking at it hard with her crop.

'That hurts!' he complained.

'Hurts! My God, what a weakling!'

She flicked repeatedly at his uprisen projection, cutting at it from each side in turn. Manfred twisted his body to escape the stinging little blows, but in the end the only way to protect himself was to bend forward, his head down on his knees. At once Magda changed tactics and flicked him across his upraised bottom.

'Kiss my boots,' she ordered, 'quick – or I'll really lay into you.'

She planted one jack-booted foot on his bent knee so that Manfred could kiss the shiny black leather.

'Now the other.'

She changed feet and he obeyed her meekly.

'Now you know who is in control here,' she said heavily.

Manfred raised his head slowly, his gaze travelling up her booted legs to her smooth thighs and at last to the dark triangle of curls where her legs joined. She resumed her former pose, feet apart, back straight and hands on hips.

'Yes, stare at my Fotze,' she said scornfully, 'that's all men ever think about – how to get their miserable length of gristle between a woman's legs. You're all the same! No sense of decency, no dignity, no higher emotions, no sensitivity, no culture! You've got nothing but a silly prong sticking out in front.'

Kneeling up straight again, Manfred found his face on the level of her groins. Magda moved closer, twined her fingers in his hair and pulled his face to within a hand's-breadth of her curly fleece.

'As you're only interested in what happens below the belly-button, now's your chance to get a good look. That's what you want, isn't it? Let me tell you something, you brainless rapist – what you see there between my legs is far too good for you.'

'You forget that I've tried it out already. It was nice but no more than that.'

'It's the most beautiful thing in the world,' she said furiously, 'kiss it!'

Her clenched fingers tightened painfully in his hair and he had no choice but to press his mouth to the warm lips between her straddled legs.

'That's all you're good for,' she said contemptuously, 'that's all any man is good for. Lick me!'

This new version of Magda's game had aroused Manfred sharply and the scent of her hot eroticism drove him further. He forced his tongue between the pouting lips and found her slippery nub.

41

'You swine!' she gasped. 'How dare you try to excite me like that!'

All the same, she kept his face clamped to her. Manfred's tongue flickered and in a surprisingly short time she screamed thinly and her legs shook until she almost fell.

'More, more!' she moaned, her finger-nails digging into his scalp.

Her orgasmic throes passed quickly and Manfred found his cheek pressed against her perspiring belly and the big metal buckle of her leather belt.

'So fast!' He murmured, proud of himself.

'Too fast,' she answered weakly, tremors still running through her belly, 'you spoiled my game with your clumsiness. You're going to pay for that.'

Manfred was thoroughly into the spirit of the game. He knew now that what excited her so quickly was not the physical stimulation alone but the sense of domination she experienced from having him at her mercy, bound and unable to escape from her. And perhaps not domination alone, but the contempt for her partner that sprang from it. He set out to provoke her.

'You talk of culture and higher emotions,' he said with a laugh, 'what higher emotions were you feeling when my tongue was in you? Was it a high aesthetic experience? Did it promote a philosophical insight?'

Magda pushed his head away from her belly and glared down at him. Her mouth was beautiful, he thought, sulky and dangerous.

'The philosophical insight was mine,' he continued, 'while you were squealing and shaking I remembered what the great Schopenhauer said about women. Shall I tell you?'

'What is it to me what some crazy old professor said?'

'He said that only a man whose mind is clouded by sexual desire would think that women are beautiful, for in reality they are undersized, narrow-shouldered and broad-hipped.'

'So!' she hissed. 'You insult me! Suddenly you've got your courage back.'

'My mind is not clouded by desire,' he taunted her, 'I

see nothing special about the little slit you call your Fotze. I've seen plenty of them and you can take it from me, dear Magda, yours is no different from any other.'

'You're brave now because you saw me in a moment when my body betrayed me into weakness,' she said with awful and menacing deliberation. 'You blockhead – that was nothing to do with you. It was an accident.'

'A cultural accident,' Manfred sneered, 'the sort of accident you arrange for yourself three times a day. The only culture you understand is a *prong* in you.'

Magda's face turned dark red with rage. She put one booted foot against his upright stem and pressed it hard against his belly.

'Be very careful what you say to me or I'll tread it flat!'

Manfred looked down from her furious face to the join of her thighs and the dark-furred entrance he was becoming desperate to get into.

'You needn't look at me there,' she said angrily, 'you'll never touch that again.'

'No great loss,' he answered calmly, 'it was boring when you had your bottom up in the air and I was thumping away to give you satisfaction. I almost got up and left, but I thought I ought to be polite.'

'I'll show you what's boring,' she shouted hoarsely.

She raised her boot to his chest and pushed hard. He toppled over backwards on his tied hands and lay awkwardly. Magda, a monstrous sight in her spiked helmet, dumped herself down on his belly and her bent knees clamped into his ribs.

'In case you are too ignorant to know,' she said icily, 'these are cavalry boots I'm wearing and this is a cavalry helmet.'

He winced as her hand groped for his hard stem and forced it between her legs. She sat down abruptly on it, driving it in deep.

'Untrained colts have to be broken,' she said. 'Trot!'

To her own command she rose and fell on him at a controlled pace, flicking at his nipples with her riding-crop.

43

Manfred stared up at her flushed face and saw that below the metal edge of the helmet her dark-brown eyes were glinting with the emotions of power.

'Follow my movements,' she ordered.

He obeyed willingly, pushing upwards to her rhythm as far as his constricted position would permit. The feeling was so agreeable that he was soon moving faster than she intended.

'Halt!' and she pinned him to the rug with all her weight.

'Magda – don't stop!'

'What do you think you're doing?' she roared. 'You're here to learn, not to enjoy yourself. One more twitch out of you and I'll thrash you until you bleed.'

'I can't control myself – it's too exciting!'

'I'm controlling you. Lie absolutely still. Understand?'

'Yes," he whispered, sensation swirling in his belly.

'You will now be taught how to canter.'

She bounced up and down on him, faster than before. Manfred clenched his fists behind his back and willed himself to lie still. It would take very little more of this to finish him off.

'That's better, you're learning,' Magda gasped, 'don't move a muscle. We're going to gallop now.'

With bulging eyes Manfred stared up at her big breasts bobbing up and down to her rhythm. Her eyes were only half-open and her breathing was loud and ragged as she pounded at him hard and fast. But the gallop was a short one. Manfred felt his belly contract and with a loud cry he jolted his essence into her, not feeling in his delirium the riding-crop slashing across his chest, nor hearing Magda's scream of 'No!'

His spasms lasted a long time, but at last he lay still and opened his eyes to see her staring down at him with an expression on her face that made him shiver. She looked so cruel that he wondered, for the first time, just how far the game might go.

'Poor little horse,' she whispered thinly, 'he was beginning to learn his lesson but he tripped and fell. His leg is

44

broken and he's done for. There's nothing for it but to put him out of his misery.'

She threw away her riding-crop and unbuttoned the flap of the holster on her belt. Little tremors ran over the skin of her belly and thighs, Manfred saw, the tips of her breasts were hard dark-red points. It was obvious that she had not shared his violent ecstasy.

The pistol she pulled out of the holster was large and looked dangerous. With the end of the long barrel she tickled her nipples, one after the other, smiling thinly.

'When this one fires his shot,' she said, her voice distant, 'you really know about it. It's not just a quick squib for him, it's a great roaring fiery burst.'

'Magda, put that pistol away!'

'Poor little horse, he's whimpering in pain. I must do my duty.'

Manfred stared in real alarm as she cocked the pistol, gripped it with both hands and leaned forward to press the cold muzzle to his temple.

'Magda, for God's sake!'

'Goodbye, little horse,' she said shakily.

'No!' he shouted in terror as her finger tightened on the trigger.

The pistol clicked emptily and Magda writhed on him in a stupendous orgasm, her bottom grinding into him and the grip of her knees almost cracking his ribs.

'Ah, ah, ah!' she was screaming.

It went on and on. The heavy pistol fell from her hands and almost broke Manfred's nose before it slid off his cheek to the carpet. Still she rocked and squirmed, her finger-nails clawing at her own breasts. Then without warning, she pitched forward and Manfred twisted his head out of the way to dodge the heavy steel helmet. Even so, he got a hard knock on the corner of the jaw that made him swear. Magda lay heavily on him, very still, hardly breathing. The sheer force of her climactic release had overloaded her nervous system and she had fainted.

Trapped in this ridiculous position, there was little that

45

Manfred could do. He heaved his shoulders to try to roll her off, but with his hands bound behind him her weight was too much for him to move. He shouted her name in her ear, again and again, but it seemed a long time before she twitched and began to recover her senses.

'Magda,' he said in relief. 'Are you all right?'

'Oh yes . . . that was incredible. I passed out.'

She took his face between her hands and kissed his mouth, his eyes and his temples, telling him between kisses that she could easily fall in love with him. The prospect made him shudder, but he kept his voice cheerful.

'That's the nicest thing any woman has said to me for a long time. Untie me and let's have a glass of brandy. We both deserve it.'

She climbed off him and hauled him to a sitting position to free his hands. They got into bed together, under the wolf-skin, and Manfred drank a whole glass of brandy in one swallow.

'Did you enjoy the game?' she asked affectionately.

'You certainly kept your promise to surprise me.'

'The look of fear on your face was so convincing that it did for me instantly.'

'I didn't know whether the pistol was loaded or not.'

'Nor did I. I thought I'd unloaded it but I couldn't really remember. That's what made it so interesting.'

Manfred thought it over and decided it was time to leave her.

'No, don't go,' she cajoled him, stroking his bare chest, 'Stay here tonight. I know another game we can play when we wake up.'

'With the pistol?'

'No, it's completely different. You'll love it. I'd show you now but I'm finished for tonight after what you've just done to me.'

'I had the impression that you were doing it to me. If I stay, promise there'll be no weapons tomorrow.'

'No weapons and no rope, I promise.'

'What then?' he asked, yawning, 'I can't imagine that you'll want to lie on your back and do it the usual way.'

'I can't get excited like that,' she said sleepily, 'I'll give you a hint. I've got a lovely little leather restraint harness that fits round the waist and controls your pink tail when it starts to stand up.'

Manfred was already asleep, the results of strong emotions and brandy, and he missed her description of the delights to come in the morning.

He was enjoying a light breakfast, two days later, when Oskar Brandenstein telephoned him. Oskar sounded hoarse.

'How is that little actress friend of yours,' the producer asked after they had exchanged greetings.

'Which one do you mean?' Manfred asked cautiously.

'Anna Kindt. Is she well?'

The question was puzzling and Manfred thought quickly before he gave an answer.

'She's in your play, Oskar, you must know better than I do how she is.'

'I'm in bed with a wretched cold – have been ever since the first-night party. I haven't been to the theatre.'

'I haven't seen her since the party either. I spoke to her on the telephone yesterday, but that's all.'

'How did she sound?'

'Oskar, what is this? I have no doubt you took her home after the party. If you haven't heard from her since, then perhaps your style of entertainment failed to please her.'

Oskar chuckled.

'I was asleep when she left and so I had no opportunity of asking her.'

'Who needs to ask?'

'To tell you the truth, Manfred, I got very drunk and I have only hazy recollections. But I think it was all right. I woke up stark naked in my own bath and I've had this awful cold ever since.'

Manfred laughed.

'It's time I had visitors,' said Oskar grandly. 'Come round and see me after lunch. I'm beginning to feel lonely without someone to talk to. Bring me grapes and chocolates to make me feel better.'

About the middle of the afternoon Manfred drove to Oskar's apartment in Mohrenstrasse, behind the State Theatre. He was taken by surprise when the door was opened not by a servant but by Magda Nebel. She was oddly dressed in a short skirt of chamois leather dyed scarlet and a coloured shawl round her bare shoulders.

'Magda dear, my apologies. I've obviously arrived at an inconvenient time. I see that you're playing games with Oskar. Tell him I'll come back tomorrow.'

'Don't be silly,' she said, her smile welcoming him, 'you haven't interrupted anything. I'm helping Oskar read new scripts, that's all. Come in, he's expecting you.'

Manfred stepped inside, closed the door behind him and took Magda in his arms to kiss her warmly. His questing hands confirmed his impression that she was naked above her skirt and had put the shawl round her shoulders only to answer the door-bell.

'But you're dressed to play games,' he said, squeezing her bare breasts.

'You're wrong.'

The bedroom was hot and stuffy. Oskar, his nose red and swollen, lay in a vast modern bed that had a framed oval mirror as head-board. In black silk pyjamas he looked like a beached whale. Half a dozen manuscripts bound in cardboard covers lay scattered about the bed.

'Manfred, my dear friend, how good of you to visit me on my bed of pain. Don't come too close -- I should never forgive myself if you caught my cold. Magda, give him a drink. I find schnaps very good for colds.'

Without going close enough to shake hands, Manfred took a chair and accepted a glass of schnaps from Magda. She at least had no fear of catching Oskar's cold, for she discarded her shawl and sat on the bed with her back to the big mirror, so that Oskar could rest his head comfortably on her bare bosom.

'A man needs his comforts at a time like this,' said Oskar, 'have you ever heard of Karl Kessel?'

'No, who is he?'

'I'd never heard of him myself until the other day, but he writes plays and it seems he's had some success in Munich. Not in the real theatre, or I'd know about him. Probably in a beer-cellar or students' club. He's sent me a play to read and it's very funny.'

'Good enough for you to produce?'

'Well, it couldn't be put on in Munich and it may be too obscene even for the Berlin stage.'

'I never thought to hear *you* say that. What's it about?'

'Little girls, mostly. I think the man's a pervert. I'll outline the plot so that you can judge for yourself.'

Manfred tried to concentrate his thoughts on what Oskar was saying, but his eyes were drawn to Magda's big bare breasts and his thought followed in the same direction. He remembered all too clearly her black leather restraining harness which buckled tightly round his waist and held his wrists strapped to his sides and another part of him strapped tightly at a right-angle to his body, with a thin steel chain that ran between his legs and various metal loops and fasteners sewn into the leather that enabled Magda to create curious sensations and ecstatic results. Oskar droned on, sniffling every now and then, and Manfred crossed his legs to hide the reaction in his trousers to the sight of Magda's breasts and his own memories of their violent games together.

He had no doubt that Oskar had deliberately planned this scene to get his own back. Magda too was enjoying his discomfiture – she was smiling cruelly at him and her hand moved lightly and slowly over the soft leather of her skirt, exactly above the object of his desire.

An idea struck him. Magda's pleasure lay in humiliating men, as he knew from first-hand experience of her games. By her standards Oskar's little revenge was hardly amusing

49

at all. If it were possible to reverse the roles and get her to turn her attention towards Oskar, that might be far more interesting. He waited patiently for the summary of Kessel's comedy to end.

'I see what you mean, Oskar. It would not be easy to find little girls to do that on stage. Perhaps with grown-up girls? Would that work, dramatically?'

'Stupid question, my boy! The whole essence of the comedy is that the girls are all under twelve years old.'

'But how exhilarating to see dear Magda on stage doing those things. What a lucky man you are, Oskar, to have her as your friend. She is enchanting and has great talent. She's easily the best actress in *Three in a Bed*.'

The surest way to make Oskar disagree was to praise anyone else.

'Magda? She's a good enough little bitch,' said Oskar dismissively, 'I've trained her personally, you understand, otherwise she would be nothing.'

'I disagree totally. Without her the play would be nothing – a farrago of semi-humorous dialogue, a patch-work plot and a cast of not very inspiring actors. Hugo Klostermann is dreadful, of course. The only part he can play is himself – the idol of elderly ladies and schoolgirls. No, you have to agree that Magda brings life and piquancy to the play. She makes it work.'

'Nonsense!' said Oskar. 'It's a first-class comedy. Magda is nothing – I gave her the part out of charity. Without me she would be just another little whore of a would-be actress with no future.'

His puffy face screwed up as he sneezed loudly into his handkerchief. While he was so occupied, Manfred stared into Magda's dark eyes and gave her a hard grin. She returned his stare, took the handkerchief from Oskar and wiped his nose tenderly, kissed him on the bald spot on his head and slid a hand into his black pyjama jacket to stroke his chest.

'Another little whore of a would-be actress,' Manfred said slowly, 'those are cruel words, Oskar. I can only think that your cold has made you feverish and you don't know what you are saying.'

'Of course I know what I'm saying. I know all about would-be actresses. Every little whore in Berlin thinks she has only to open her legs for me and I'll make her a star. As if I cared whether they open their legs or keep them together! I have no interest in that, have I, Magda?'

'Certainly not, darling Oskar,' she answered, her bare arm further down inside his pyjamas, obviously stroking his paunchy belly, 'that's for fools who know nothing about the real pleasures that you enjoy.'

'You are one of the few women who understand me. Well no, no one can really understand the complexities of my personality, but you have some faint glimmering.'

Oskar's voice was shaky, perhaps from the effects of his cold. Or perhaps, thought Manfred with gentle malice, from the effects of what Magda was doing to him under the silk sheet. It was moving in a manner which made it all too obvious which part of him she was now stroking.

'Shall I ever understand you, Oskar?' she asked.

'As much as anyone else – perhaps more than most. I am not an ordinary person who can be diverted by the tedious acts which ordinary people regard as pleasures. At least you understand that much about me.'

Manfred found it difficult not to smile openly at Oskar's discomfiture now that Magda was using him as the object of her game. He almost laughed aloud when Oskar exclaimed in a quavering voice:

'Give Manfred another drink.'

'Yes,' she said at once, continuing her secret massage, 'Is the schnaps to your liking, Manfred, or would you prefer something else?'

'Let me think,' he said, playing along with her, 'it is very good schnaps, no question of that. But how much of it should one drink in the afternoon, that is another matter.'

Oskar's face had turned a dull red. He grabbed at Magda's arm to stop its movement, but she had a firm grasp on him and continued what she was doing inside his silk pyjamas.

'For Oskar's cold, schnaps is an excellent medicine,' Manfred said slowly, 'But as for me, I do not have a cold and it may not be the appropriate drink. There is much to consider here.'

'Magda, stop it!' Oskar groaned.

'Is something wrong, Oskar?' she asked calmly. 'Has your temperature gone up again? Perhaps I should fetch the thermometer and check. Maybe I should telephone Dr Feinberg. You are looking very hot and flushed, my poor darling. How do you feel? Tell me.'

The outburst she had been provoking took place. Oskar's bulk heaved upwards under the bedclothes and he gave a gurgling cry.

'Oskar, what is it?' she exclaimed, her arm moving in short and fast jerks.

'Uh, uh, uh . . .' he gurgled.

'Manfred's visit has been too much for you,' she said, withdrawing her arm from the bed. 'You are over-tired and you must rest. I'll see him out while you try to sleep.'

She eased herself from under his head and settled him on the pillows. His eyes were closed and he was breathing heavily.

'Auf wiedersehen, Oskar,' said Manfred.

Magda made no attempt to cover herself with the shawl as she led Manfred out of the bedroom, bare-foot and in only her red leather skirt. The moment the door was closed, Manfred stepped close behind her and put his arms about her to take hold of her heavy breasts.

'You really turned the tables on the old devil,' he said admiringly.

'There's something hard against my bottom,' she said, pressing back against him, 'I wish I had my harness here to restrain that wicked thing of yours.'

'It doesn't need restraint just now – it needs freedom.'

Her hands moved between their bodies, between her

skirt and his trousers, to undo his buttons and pull out his hard stem.

'So it has freedom,' she said, 'but restraint is more amusing.'

Her hands moved away and Manfred pressed against the soft chamois leather of her skirt. The sensation was extraordinary. He clasped her closer and rubbed himself slowly against the leather.

'Be very careful, little pig,' she warned him, 'I don't want stains on this skirt.'

They were still standing outside Oskar's bedroom door.

'Where shall we go?' Manfred whispered in her ear.

'The servants are in the kitchen. Don't make too much noise, unless you want an audience. Come with me.'

He followed her into the dining-room. There was a table big enough to seat a dozen, made of highly polished syca-more. Magda pushed aside one of the chairs and turned to face Manfred, her bottom resting on the edge of the table. She grasped him by his conveniently uncovered handle and pulled him to her.

'You're just like Oskar – one feel of my balloons and *this* is sticking out like a crow-bar. His was standing up for hours because I took my blouse off. It didn't take much to finish him off. As for you, if I had my riding-crop with me a few smart cuts would soften it for you.'

'But as you haven't,' Manfred countered, his hands busy fondling her *balloons*, 'we must find some other way, dear Magda.'

He winced as her red-painted finger-nails scraped along his out-thrust stem.

'What awkward things men have,' she said contemptu-ously, 'hard and swollen -- very ugly. When did you ever see a statue of a man with his tail standing up stiff? Never. No artist would give himself the embarrassment of depicting it. But in great art no part of a woman's body is hidden. That's because every part of a woman is beautiful.'

The touch of her nails on his flesh had ceased to be slightly painful and had become pleasurable.

'Some women have very beautiful bodies,' Manfred agreed.

'Especially the part between their legs,' she informed him.

The words took him back to the first time he had entered into her games, when he knelt before her and she had made him kiss her between the legs. Was she repeating herself already – were there no more variations she could devise? She let go of him and used both hands to wriggle her skirt up her thighs so high that he saw she wore no underwear. No doubt Oskar had amused himself by resting his head on her dark curls while he read his scripts.

She knocked Manfred's hand away roughly.

'You are allowed to admire my Fotze,' she said coldly. 'You have no permission to touch it. Keep your hands to yourself. My God, such disrespect!'

It was much the same game as before, but without the crimson cord, Manfred decided. She was goading him and herself into a fury that would end in cataclysmic release. He fell into the role required of him, put a hand on each of her bare thighs and forced them apart, his fingers digging deeply into her flesh.

'What am I to admire?' he sneered. 'A slit with brown hair round it. A few Marks will buy me one as good as that on any street corner.'

'You swine! How dare you insult me like that!'

He moved in closer, his legs between her knees to keep her accessible while he steered the tip of his stem to the pink lips and pushed slowly. Magda's nails clawed at his face, but he managed to catch her wrists before she could scratch his cheeks more than once. He used his strength to force her arms behind her back and hold them there.

'I won't let you do it to me!'

'You have no choice whether to let me or not. It's for me to decide if this toy you prize so highly is interesting enough to make me want to use it. Tell me what is so special about it, Magda.'

'Let go of me! I refuse to be raped by that long ugly thing. Take it away!'

'Refuse as much as you like – the decision is mine. And as I can see nothing exceptional about your dearest possession, I must explore further.'

He pushed forward, in spite of her struggles, until he was settled comfortably inside her.

'It feels like any other,' he told her. 'Lie on your back.'

'No!'

He took the risk of letting go of her wrists long enough to put his hands on her bare shoulders and force her backwards. Her feet left the floor and her hands struck at nothing as she went over on her back on the dining-table. He took her under the knees and flung her legs up and over his shoulders and held them there tightly to stop her kicking his face.

'You never expected to be flat on your back with something hard inside you, did you? Do you find the position ordinary and boring?'

'I forbid you to do it!' she said through gritted teeth.

'Consider this – the next time Oskar has a dinner-party here you can entertain his guests by telling them what happened to you right here on the table.'

'You're raping me!' Magda gasped, her face mottled red with anger.

'That's right,' and Manfred stabbed hard and fast.

His deliberately brutal pounding at her body fired her anger to incandescence. Her mouth opened in a soundless scream of mad rage as her violent emotions exploded into shuddering ecstasy. For Manfred it was as if he had been struck by lightening and his high excitement discharged itself in a cloud-burst of passion.

When at last, after a long time, he disengaged himself from her, she sat up on the table and dried his limp part on his shirt-tail for him before tucking it back into his trousers.

'I really like you, Manfred. You play so well. You understand me.'

'In the same way you understand Oskar?'

'Him? There's nothing to understand. He can't do it properly with a woman. His only pleasure is to be shamed. He's pathetic.'

'You shamed him thoroughly this afternoon. He won't want to see me again after that.'

'Don't be an idiot. That was probably his wildest dream coming true. Now that he's been humiliated in front of you, he'll be your friend for life.'

To be a part of Magda's sexual fantasies was strange enough, but to find himself included in Oskar's was simply ridiculous. Manfred burst out laughing.

Madame Filipov

It started for Manfred as an evening at home, a pleasant pause in the round of dining out, theatre-going, taking girls to dance and the other amusements that made up much of his life. On this one fine evening in May he planned to relax at home and go to bed early and alone. Frau Geiger prepared an excellent light dinner for him: a soup with croutons, followed by chicken breasts stuffed with melted butter lightly seasoned with garlic, with golden sliced potatoes and red-currant jelly. After that there was a dish of black cherries with vanilla ice-cream, with a dash of Kirsch over it. Geiger waited at table, in his black suit and white cotton gloves, bringing in his wife's cooking and serving it expertly to Manfred, who sat at one end of the long table, his glass constantly replenished with a good white wine from the Rheinland.

Afterwards, in his gold brocade smoking-jacket with green velvet lapels, Manfred reclined on the chaise-longue in the drawing-room, coffee and brandy on a low table at his side, and set himself to read until bed-time. His domestic idyll was not fated to last. Soon after nine o'clock Geiger announced the arrival of Herr Schroeder. Max was elegantly attired in a new dinner-jacket, a flower in his button-hole. He sat down and accepted the brandy Geiger poured for him.

'To what do I owe this unexpected pleasure, Max?'

'There is no particular reason. I had arranged to take someone out to dinner, but she cancelled at the last moment. I ate alone and thought I'd come here and see if you were at home.'

'You were lucky. I'm hardly ever at home in the evening.'

'I was passing the end of the street anyway, so I took a chance and told the taxi to drop me here. What are you reading?'

Manfred passed him the book.

'Collette,' said Max, 'amusing, but no substance. There never is in French novels.'

'I wasn't looking for substance. We have more than enough of that in our own novelists – misery, suffering, symbolism, social purpose – all that rot. Did you know that Ernst's new novel is to be published in the autumn? It will be dreadful. I prefer a little frivolity in a book.'

'For you life is a frivolous affair,' said Max with a smile, 'but for many it is a long and losing struggle.'

'I'm sure you mean well, but I can't feel guilty about the state of Germany today, Max. It wasn't my doing – or yours. You and I were still in short trousers when the War started and still at school when it ended and the Republic appeared out of nowhere.'

'But don't you feel any responsibility for changing things?'

'That's for the politicians. It's their trade.'

'Politicians!' said Max scornfully. 'What do they know?'

'Democracy means that every idiot has the right to vote for whichever idiot he prefers. That is our new system,' said Manfred, bored by the turn of conversation. 'You said you were passing by – that means that you were going from one fixed point to another fixed point and I am somewhere between.'

'Your logic is faultless. Since the young lady I invited to dinner did not appear, I had it in mind to visit Madame Filipov.'

'Who is she? I've never heard of the lady.'

'For good reason – she remains anonymous to all but a select band of admirers.'

'That conjures up a great many possibilities. How select is her band of admirers?'

Max grinned.

'Her talent lies in the organisation of unmentionable depravities – does that answer your question?'

'You mean she keeps a brothel?'

'That is a very crude description of what she does. A brothel is a place where you hand over your money and a fat young whore lies on her back for you. Madame Filipov does things very differently.'

'But Max, you know plenty of girls – why go to a brothel? There's a telephone in the hall – all you have to do is ring any one of a dozen or score of girls we both know. One of them will be at home. Have you been with Magda Nebel? She'll show you new ways of doing it, if it's a change you need.'

'That's not the problem. Listen, do you ever get bored by going to bed with the sort of women we know?'

'What a strange question! Let me fill your glass for you – I see that the girl who let you down tonight has made you thoroughly miserable. Who was it? Anyone I know?'

'Jenny Montrose.'

'The beautiful American!'

'We've been going out together the past few weeks, since Oskar's first-night. I thought she was a lesbian, but when I saw her with Hugo Klostermann I knew she couldn't be. So I called on her the next day and invited her to dinner and we went dancing afterwards, and so on.'

' "And so on" means that you have made love to her, I suppose.'

'Naturally.'

'Is it the same as with a German girl?'

'She's very strange in bed. She is very beautiful when she takes her clothes off and she has a sharp appetite – I could almost say greedy. But somehow she isn't there.'

'What on earth do you mean?'

'I find it hard to explain. Even in the wildest moments, the impression she gives is that her spirit, her inner self, has withdrawn to some secret hiding-place. From its secure place it watches her body shake with pleasure, but never takes part in the enjoyment. Do you understand what I mean?'

'You are too imaginative, my dear Max. Some women are noisy in their passion and some go very quiet at the big moment, though they enjoy it as much as those who scream and bite. Obviously Jenny is one of the silent ones, that's all. There's no mystery about that.'

'You're wrong. I've been with silent women and I know the difference. In a way I cannot define, Jenny is still a virgin in spirit, whatever her body has experienced.'

'How morbid you are tonight, Max. Are you feeling well?'

'I'm perfectly healthy, but I'm not very pleased with life. Tell me something – when you walk along a street, do you notice how many people look thin and hopeless? Do you really look at them, or do you just rush on to the next restaurant or bar as if they were just a part of the scenery? They're real people too, you know, and their lives are lived in abject poverty and despair.'

Manfred was becoming alarmed by his friend's pessimism.

'What can any of us do about it?' he asked. 'We can only go on electing idiots because there is no one else.'

'I don't know what we can do and that is what worries me.'

'Look here, Max, this won't do. What you need is a visit to this fancy whore-house you mentioned. A bottle or two of champagne and a frolic with a girl and tomorrow you'll see that the world isn't such a bad place after all.'

'If only it were that simple!'

'It's a damned sight better than turning Bolshevik or marching with those thugs in the brown uniforms. Tell me what's so special about Madame Filipov's house. The women are young and pretty, I suppose.'

'More than that. It's a place where you can do anything you like with a woman. Or two or three, for that matter, all at the same time. Everything is possible, nothing is forbidden.'

'My imagination recoils in horror from the nameless depravities we might commit there,' Manfred said with a cheerful grin.

'I wish I had your eagerness. The truth is that even nameless depravities become wearisome after a time, believe me.'

Manfred was on his feet, determined to rescue Max from his black mood.

'Pour yourself more brandy. It won't take me more than a minute or two to change and we'll be off. You must introduce me to this remarkable place.'

'As you wish,' said Max, with no enthusiasm. 'Bring plenty of money with you.'

Ten minutes later they were in Manfred's car and on their way, across the city centre and west along Stralauerstrasse.

'Turn right at the next corner,' Max instructed him, 'Then the second left and look for number 19.'

The entrance to number 19 looked like the entrance to any large family home. The door-keeper who opened the door when Max rang was plainly-dressed, like any servant, though his height and the bulge of muscles under the shoulders of his black jacket suggested that he had duties beyond those of an ordinary servant. His nose had been broken and had set crooked. He bowed to Max and addressed him ironically as 'Your Excellency', obviously recognising him, but he stared hard at Manfred.

'The gentleman is with me,' said Max.

They went upstairs and into a large room, very dimly lit by small shaded lights on the walls. It was furnished with a number of ottomans and low tables and about half a dozen men and rather more young women sat and drank together. No sooner had Max and Manfred taken seats on an unoccupied ottoman than a tail-coated waiter, elderly and frail, placed an ice-bucket with a bottle of champagne on their table.

'The drink of the house,' Max explained, 'there is no point in asking for anything else.'

'Where is Madame Filipov?' Manfred asked.

'She never makes her entrance before midnight. But there will be other company.'

The words were scarcely out of his mouth before three young women detached themselves from a group on the other side of the room and sat down uninvited, one between the two men and one on either side of them. Without a word said, the waiter set glasses for them and poured champagne.

'Good evening, dear ladies,' said Manfred.

'Bring another bottle,' Max said to the waiter, 'that one's done for.'

The woman on Manfred's right was fair-haired and had a prominent bosom. She might be eighteen at most, he thought, though the dim lighting was deceptive. She sat half-facing him, one bare arm along his shoulders while she sipped champagne and told him that her name was Trudi. The woman on the other side of him was no older. She was very slender, dark-haired, and tiny pointed breasts made twin peaks in her frock. She too sat close to Manfred, resting a fragile-boned hand on his thigh while she chatted as chirpily as a bird. Her name, he learned, was Frieda.

Manfred lay back comfortably on the big cushions covering the ottoman and let things take their course. So far it was not very different from other expensive brothels he had visited and he could not imagine how Max's promise could be fulfilled. Trudi pressed her fat breasts against his face and his hand found itself under Frieda's frock to rest on her furry mound.

'That's what he likes,' said Frieda approvingly, 'his hand up a girl's clothes. But what does he want next? That's the big question. What do you think, Trudi?'

'He's a handsome boy,' said Trudi. 'He must have had his hand up plenty of girls' clothes before. He's come here for something he can't find anywhere else.'

'But what might that be?' Manfred asked, looking from Frieda to Trudi and back again.

He felt fingers glide over his trouser-front.

'This says you're ready for something new,' Frieda told him, 'and this part of a man never lies. There was a gentleman who came to visit us last week – he looked something like you, except that he had a moustache as soft as silk. You remember him, Trudi – the one who was so bored lying on top of girls that he'd even tried it with boys. But he didn't like that.'

'And he discovered something new here?' Manfred asked, wondering if she was telling him the truth or whether it was just a story to arouse his interest.

'Everybody finds what he's looking for here,' said Frieda with a giggle.

'There's a gentleman who comes here very regularly,' said Trudi, 'And he always asks for me. Do you know why? Because he thinks that I look like his daughter. He brings a little suitcase with him, with some of her clothes in it. We go up to one of the private rooms and I put the clothes on – very stylish, I can tell you! He calls me Gerda – that's his daughter's name you see.'

'Wicked old man!' said Manfred with a chuckle. 'But at least it keeps him out of trouble.'

'The things that man wants to do to his daughter!' said Trudi, chuckling too. 'You wouldn't believe it. I call him Papa and play with his thing and suck it. Then he . . .'

'Spare me the details, please,' said Manfred, 'Family life is not to my taste.'

'Do you know what he gives me when he leaves?'

'A suitable token of his gratitude, I'm sure.'

'A thousand Marks!' she said triumphantly. 'And always a box of chocolates. What do you think of that?'

'I've been given that much, more than once,' said Frieda immediately.

'For special services, of course,' said Manfred.

'Very special. The last time was only a day or two ago.

63

There was a gentleman from Munich who wanted to make use of both entrances.'

'But hardly at the same time.'

'One after the other,' she said, wriggling her warm and furry mound against his hand, 'face up and then face down. I think he was an Army officer, though he wore civilian clothes.'

'If you had been old enough to be here five or six years ago, when you were still at school,' said Manfred, 'he would have given you thousands of millions of Marks – and it wouldn't have bought you a new pair of shoes.'

'Don't talk about those times,' she said at once, 'they're gone, 'My mother was a widow with four children to feed. All we ever had to eat was potatoes, and not much of that. Give me another drink, for God's sake – you've given me the shivers.'

As Manfred sat up to fill her glass, there was a muted wail from the other side of the room. In the dimness he saw a man in a dinner-jacket jerk suddenly upright from the cushions, like a steel spring released, clutching at his trousers with both hands. The girl who had been lying beside him burst out laughing and the two girls with Manfred giggled.

'That stupid Maria!' said Trudi, 'She didn't even get him upstairs. He won't want to pay after that and there'll be a row.'

'What could she have said to him to bring that on?' Manfred asked.

'Some men are like that,' said Trudi, settling beside him again, 'As soon as they whisper their really secret wishes into your ear and you touch them a bit to make them feel good, it's too much for them. They just go off pop in their trousers. It's telling a sympathetic girl what he's kept hidden for years that does it. He'll be all right the next time he visits us – Maria will get him straight upstairs and he'll be doing it instead of talking about it.'

Before the threatened row could develop, a short and stocky woman waddled into the room, summoned by some

64

mysterious system of signals. Her hair was cropped as short as a man's and her arms were as thick as thighs. She took in the scene at a glance and made straight for the unfortunate man, now complaining loudly. She stood pugnaciously in front of him, hands on her hips and silenced him with a glare. The girl with him stopped laughing and looked uncomfortable.

'Come with me,' she said to the man, took him by the arm and hauled him to his feet and out of the room.

'She'll make sure he pays the house, even if Maria gets nothing,' said Trudi. 'Shall I tell you about a foreign gentleman who was here not long ago and what he wanted me to do?'

'Other men's dreams and needs are not mine,' said Manfred, 'let's get another bottle from the waiter. Max, old friend, you are curiously silent – how are you now? Better pleased with life?'

Max was on his back on the cushions, his girl half on top of him, one of her legs between his, her mouth close to his ear to whisper to him.

'Life is a nightmare,' said Max, 'one day I shall wake up from it.'

'But until then?'

'Until then there are worse ways of passing the hours than lying here with this young lady, who has been telling me the most extraordinary things about herself.'

That squat woman with the cropped hair came back and clapped her hands together for attention.

'Gentlemen, Madame Filipov is ready to receive those who wish to pay their respects to her.'

The announcement surprised Manfred, who had assumed that the muscular woman was Madame Filipov herself. He removed his hand from between Frieda's legs and leaned across her thin body to tap Max on the shoulder.

'What do you think, Max, you know the rules of the house.'

'You should go,' said Max, 'Madame puts on quite a show.'

'And you?'

'I have reached an arrangement with this charming Oriental blossom and intend to accompany her to a private room.'

'She doesn't look Oriental to me.'

'She tells me that she was born in China, where her father was a Lutheran missionary. You would be amazed by what she has told me of the antics they practice in the East. You go and pay your respects to Madame and I'll see you back here later – much later.'

'If you will excuse me, ladies,' said Manfred to the girls on either side of him, 'I have the honour to attend on Madame Filipov.'

They both smiled at him.

'We'll be waiting for you,' said Frieda.

With two other men Manfred followed the short-haired woman along a passage towards the rear of the house, through a door panelled in faded red leather, which clearly marked the division between the public and the private parts of the building. Like Manfred, the other men wore dinner-jackets and were well-groomed and presentable. One was not much older than Manfred himself, a slenderly-built young man with narrow shoulders and a pale over-refined face. The other man was in his forties, heavily-made, with lines on his face and grey in his hair. He seemed to be embarrassed and his face was shiny with perspiration.

'Courage, my dear man,' said the narrow-shouldered one, 'we have been here before.'

The other man glared at him and made no reply.

'Not I,' said Manfred cheerfully, 'this is my first visit to Madame.'

They were ushered into an elegantly decorated room in which the main piece of furniture was a dressing-table with a large mirror. A chair stood close to it and, behind that, three other chairs, at about arm's length from each other.

'Madame will be with you shortly. Please sit down,' said their guide.

'Thank you, Fraulein Dunke,' said the pale young man courteously.

They selected seats and Manfred took a cigarette from his gold case and lit it. The older man pulled out a leather cigar-case and chose one. No one spoke, for it hardly seemed a moment for light conversation. In a few minutes the door opened and in swept Madame Filipov, followed by a girl dressed as a maid in black frock and starched white apron and cap. The men rose to their feet and bowed.

Madame Filipov was perhaps forty years old, of middle height and with raven-black hair worn long and piled up on top of her head in a very old-fashioned style. Her face was smooth and attractive still, not with the prettiness of youth, but with character and a touch of humour. She wore a long silk négligé in blush-pink, with a trim of marabou feathers round the neckline. Altogether a formidable woman, Manfred thought, when it was his turn to kiss her hand.

She addressed the other young man first, evidently knowing him well.

'Baron von Stettin – how nice to see you again so soon. You are always a most welcome guest. And Herr Krill, your business has brought you back to Berlin again. I am most pleased to see you.'

She smiled at Manfred.

'You are very welcome, Herr . . .?'

'Manfred von Klausenberg, Madame,' he said, bowing again.

'It is such a pleasure to make new friends. I have been informed by my staff that there was an unfortunate disturbance earlier. I apologise, gentlemen.'

'There is no need to apologise, Madame,' said the Baron quickly, 'the fellow was an ill-bred boor who should have been thrown downstairs, neck and crop.'

'Thank you, your words make me feel better. What exactly did happen? I was given only the vaguest account.'

Manfred was amused by Madame Filipov's poise, and impressed by it. She conducted herself as if she were a

Grand-Duchess receiving members of the aristocracy and the contrast between that and the reality was very piquant. Seeing the Baron and Herr Krill hesitate to put into words that would be acceptable to Madame the ridiculous affair of ten minutes ago, he took it upon himself to answer and, by doing so, show that he could match her style.

'A wretched-looking fellow in a ready-made suit was in conversation with Fraulein Maria,' he said, 'and as is often the way with such people, he allowed his enthusiasm to overcome his sense of propriety and finally disgraced himself by doing what is not done in polite company.'

Madame Filipov nodded graciously and looked at him with a new interest. She knew very well what had happened in the drawing-room and was using the incident to cause a tingle along their nerves.

'We must make allowances,' she said, 'I believe that it was the gentleman's first visit. The conversation of Fraulein Maria can be very stimulating to those unfamiliar with it.'

'It is also my first visit,' Manfred reminded her.

'The first of many, I hope. Perhaps you should converse with Fraulein Maria and learn to appreciate her style of sympathetic understanding.'

'Do you think so, Madame?' he asked, smiling at her boldly.

She fluttered her hands in an appealing little gesture.

'To speak truly, Herr von Klausenberg, it would surprise me to learn that Fraulein Maria's conversation was of much interest to a superior person like you. But who can say? Please sit down, gentlemen.'

They waited until she seated herself on the chair at the dressing-table, her back towards them, before resuming their own seats. Any one of them could have reached out to place a hand on Madame Filipov's silk-clad shoulder, but such a familiarity was unthinkable. The little maid-servant stood at Madame's side and handed her a crystal jar from the array on the dressing-table. Madame applied a thin layer of face-cream to her cheeks and forehead and stroked it in lightly with her finger-tips.

'Tell me what important affairs of business you have been engaged in, Herr Krill, since you were last here,' she said conversationally.

Herr Krill launched on a lengthy and tedious account of his dealings, his lined face shinier than ever with perspiration as he watched Madame Filipov making herself up. Indeed, both Krill and the Baron appeared to be utterly fascinated by what she was doing and had eyes for nothing else. Manfred found as much diversion in watching the two men as in watching Madame. While Krill rambled on, talking of deals, loans, contracts, hundreds of thousands of Marks, competition, imports, exports and other rubbish dear to the heart of his sort, Madame Filipov casually opened her pink silk négligé, threw it back from her white shoulders and applied face-cream to her neck. In the mirror Manfred had a perfect view of her uncovered breasts, as did the other men, and as she intended they should. He liked what he saw – they were still firm and well-separated and their rosettes were small and red-brown.

He caught her eye in the mirror. She saw his little grin and pouted at him. When she had creamed her neck to her satisfaction, she leaned back in her chair, her long-fingered hands resting on its padded arms, for the maid to apply a fine apricot-coloured powder to face, neck and breasts, with a big and fluffy powder-puff.

Krill broke off his recital to watch in adoring silence. Baron Stettin exclaimed nervously:

'Madame is exquisite!'

'It is sweet of you to say so, my dear Baron. But the words are mere flattery and not from the heart, I fear.'

'I swear I spoke from the heart! If it were permitted, the greatest honour in the world would be to kiss your adorable little slipper – I dare not say your foot!'

'So delicate an emotion deserves its reward,' she answered in a coquettish tone.

The little maid put down the powder-puff, took the silk slipper from the foot Madame raised and conveyed it to the Baron, holding it on the out-stretched palm of her hand.

The Baron received it as if it were an objet-d'art of enormous value and pressed it to his lips with reverence. Madame Filipov watched him in her mirror.

'Ah, Baron, you are one of my dearest friends,' she said fondly, 'I miss you when you stay away from me. And you, Herr von Klausenberg, do you also wish to kiss my foot?'

'That goes without saying, Madame,' he answered lightly, 'but I must tell you that we Klausenbergs are by tradition more inclined towards conquest than acts of homage.'

'The old Prussian spirit,' she said with a broad smile, 'how exciting to meet it again! I thought it had been lost forever in these modern times.'

Baron von Stettin was lost in rapture, stroking the pink silk slipper with his finger-tips and pressing a kiss on it from time to time. Manfred concluded that he was deranged in his wits and looked away to meet Madame Filipov's eyes in the mirror again.

'No, you are not likely to kiss my foot,' she said, 'but I am sure that my dear friend Herr Krill is dying to.'

'Yes,' the man answered hoarsely.

'Then do it!' she said, her voice sharp and commanding.

Krill rose from his chair to kneel at her side and take her bare foot in his clumsy hands.

'Kiss it!' she ordered him.

He bowed his head low and pressed his mouth to her foot.

'Herr Krill is from Lubeck,' she said for Manfred's benefit, 'but his spiritual home is here in Berlin, in my house. It is only here that he can cast off the restraints of his provincial and family life and indulge himself in the pleasures for which his soul is hungry. But you, Herr von Klausenberg, you seek something else from me, I think.'

Manfred was enjoying the play-acting.

'It would be an honour to drink a toast to you in champagne from your slipper,' he said.

'Of course!' she answered, her eyes glowing, 'it is far too many years since a handsome young gentleman did that.'

With her bare toes she kicked at the face of the man at her feet and spoke harshly to him.

'We need champagne, Herr Krill, so that the gentleman can drink a toast to me. Am I to be kept waiting?'

Krill scrambled up awkwardly and pressed a bell-push on the wall by the door. In a very short time the elderly waiter appeared.

'Champagne!' Krill ordered brusquely. 'And fast!'

At once he was back on his knees, caressing Madame Filipov's foot and kissing it.

'This tradition you spoke of,' she said to Manfred, 'I would like to hear more of it. It brings back pleasant memories of how things were once, before all this modern nonsense ruined Germany. You have a large family estate, I suppose?'

'The estate is very considerable, Madame, but it is not mine. My brother lives there with his wife and children. And my mother. I idle my time away in Berlin.'

'And why is that?'

'In the words of Goethe, "*Two souls dwell, alas, in my breast.*" '

The waiter returned with the champagne. He ignored Krill at Madame's feet, opened the bottle and filled a glass for her. The maid removed the tiny slipper from Madame's other foot and held it for the waiter. He filled it without the flicker of an eyelid, looked doubtfully at the Baron, who was lost in his dream, set the bottle in its silver ice-bucket on the dressing-table and took his leave.

The maid carried the slipper to Manfred, holding it in both hands so as not to spill a drop of the contents. Manfred stood up to take it from her, called out 'To you, Madame!' and poured the champagne down his throat in one. She raised her glass to him in the mirror and inclined her head gracefully.

'You must explain what Goethe's words mean to you,' she said, leaning towards the mirror to apply scarlet lipstick.

'Half of me is of the old stock. Like you, that part

respects our great national traditions and history. But the other half of me is drawn towards the new Germany that is emerging. Alas, the two halves do not fit comfortably together.'

The look of interest on Madame Filipov's face vanished abruptly as she glared down at Krill.

'Enough!' she said angrily. 'You go too far! I gave you permission to kiss my foot. I did not reprove you when I felt your lips touching my knee. It seems that I am too soft-hearted with you.'

'Forgive me!' Krill gasped, his face flushed dark red.

'Your manners are deplorable,' she answered coldly, 'God knows what you would have tried next! Your crude attempt on my modesty is shameful and unforgivable. Gretchen – bring me the stick!'

'I try to overcome my failings,' Krill moaned, 'you know how hard I try . . . but to be allowed to approach you so closely is more than I can bear without becoming desperate for a small sign of your esteem . . .'

'You shall have a sign of my esteem,' she said, her tone languidly cruel.

She got up and turned her back towards him while she opened her négligé fully and removed the only other garment she wore – a pair of silk knickers cut in the French style, with an edging of lace round the wide legs. Manfred was treated to a view of her body, breasts, belly and the patch of dark hair between her pale-skinned thighs. Meanwhile the maid had pulled out from behind the dressing-table a long and flexible cane. Madame Filipov dropped the silk underwear she had taken off on to the seat of her chair and turned to take the cane from her maid.

'Now Herr Krill, since you are so anxious to obtain a token of my regard and because I am a good-natured and obliging person, there before you lies something of mine – something more intimate than you dared to hope for.'

Krill shuffled on his knees to the chair and put his face down on to the silk garment.

'Oh!' he moaned loudly, 'I can feel the warmth of your body, Madame!'

Presented with so easy a target, Madame Filipov swung her stick and laid it with a crack across the seat of his trousers. To Manfred it sounded most painful, but he had not the least doubt that Krill was enjoying it. The energetic way in which Madame Filipov applied herself to thrashing her admirer's broad backside made her open négligé swirl about her and showed off her naked body to Manfred and the Baron to very fine advantage.

'Oh . . .' the Baron whispered, hugging the silk slipper to his heart, 'the delight of this stern Amazon destroying her victim . . . I shall faint with the joy of it . . .'

Herr Krill bore his punishment in silence, only his heavy body jerking slightly at each crack of the stick on his rump. Eventually Madame Filipov tired of beating him.

'There! That will improve your manners, Herr Krill. Whenever you are here I take a great deal of trouble with you and one day you will be truly grateful to me.'

'I am, I am,' he babbled, raising his purple-flushed face from the chair.

'I am pleased to hear it. You may take your leave of me and go to the room where Fraulein Ellie is waiting for you. She will soothe your pain with her cool hand and relieve your distress in ways that suit you.'

He kissed both of her bare feet, rose and bowed stiffly, her silk knickers in his hand, and hurried out of the room. Madame handed the cane to her maid and resumed her seat, to examine her hair in the mirror in case it had been disarranged by her vigorous exercise.

'He's a dear man,' she said, 'so devoted to me! His visits here are the high points of his life, you know.'

Baron von Stettin spoke in a quavering voice.

'I would die if you beat me like that!'

'You, my dear Baron? What a terrible idea! You must put it right out of your mind. Herr Krill requires very firm treatment – it is the only thing he understands. But you are a high-born and sensitive person and you could never forget your manners. Isn't that right, Gretchen?'

'The Baron is a most correct gentleman,' said the maid.

'Of course he is. His blood is very different from the coarse peasant blood of our dear Herr Krill. Therefore he deserves our respect and consideration. For him we reserve our tenderest concern.'

'Oh Madame, you are too kind,' he replied in so soft a voice that Manfred could only just hear the words.

'I must show you how dearly I admire and cherish you,' said Madame Filipov, 'Gretchen, let the Baron see how completely devoted to him I am.'

How many times, Manfred wondered, had this little comedy been played with the anaemic Baron and the dreadful Krill? Evidently Madame Filipov knew the most furtive wishes of her clients and indulged them at a price, while remaining to all appearances a gracious lady.

Gretchen seated herself on the Baron's lap and Madame continued with her make-up.

'If the Baron will permit,' said the maid and without waiting for a reply she unbuttoned his evening trousers and pulled out his stiff stem. She took the little silk slipper he was clutching and fitted it over his fleshy projection. When Manfred saw her agitating the one inside the other, he turned away from the scene to stare at Madame Filipov's face in the mirror.

'There, dear Baron, dear kind friend,' she cooed over her shoulder, 'I hope that this expression of my highest respect and admiration for you is not unpleasing.'

'Oh Madame, the delicacy of your sentiments is . . .' came the Baron's soft murmur and Manfred missed the last word.

As if nothing out of the ordinary were taking place behind her back, Madame Filipov turned her attention to Manfred.

'So you are torn between past and present, Herr von Klausenberg?'

She took a large crystal bottle from her dressing-table and was perfuming herself. She dabbed it behind her ears and under her chin, then parted her négligé wide to perfume her skin between her breasts.

'I am not torn between them,' said Manfred, 'I am trying to enjoy the best of both worlds.'

She spread her négligé wider and stroked perfume into her groins with her finger-tips and then behind her knees.

'The past has gone forever,' she observed, 'the future may be terrible. Only the present is of any importance.'

'In that I cannot agree with you. There are some ideals from the past which are worth maintaining in the present.'

'For example?'

'Philosophy in the boudoir,' said Manfred with a chuckle.

The sight of her body naked and in violent action as she swung her stick at Krill's backside had excited him. Her deliberately langorous movements as she perfumed herself added to his arousal. This she knew, of course, and now she sat still, négligé undone, to give him a full view of her breasts in the mirror. His stem jerked inside his trousers when she took up her lip-stick again and carefully tinted her nipples scarlet with it.

The Baron whimpered '*Oh, oh, oh!*' but Manfred kept his eyes on the mirror.

'One thing my father told me,' said Manfred, 'horses and women like a rider with a strong knee-grip.'

She nodded and smiled and spoke to her maid without looking round.

'Is the Baron satisfied with my demonstration of respect, Gretchen?'

'Yes, Madame, I believe he is.'

With this assurance, Madame Filipov spoke to Baron von Stettin in tones of warm friendship.

'I am so pleased that you were able to visit me this evening, Baron. I look forward to your visits, as you know. I hope it will not be long before you are here again. Friends should see each other often, to keep their friendship growing.'

The Baron was on his feet, his trousers decently fastened by the maid. He kissed Madame's hand, bowed slightly towards Manfred, and left. The maid flopped the spoiled slipper into a gilt-painted wicker waste-basket beside the dressing-table, collected the other one from which Manfred had drunk his toast and disposed of it in the same way. *On the Baron's bill*, Manfred thought. In the mirror he saw Madame Filipov looking at him thoughtfully.

'The next time you are here I shall know how to please you,' she said.

'How so, Madame?'

She laughed and told her maid to give him a proper glass of champagne. That done and the maid back beside her, Madame leaned back in her chair and studied her reflection. She was pleased with what she saw and smiled at herself appreciatively.

'The visit of my dear friends has made me quite agitated,' she said, 'you must attend to me, Gretchen.'

The maid knelt between Madame Filipov's parted legs, folded back her négligé with great care to expose her body completely, and kissed the tuft of dark hair where her thighs met.

'Good girl,' said Madame lazily, 'I become so flustered by the whims of my visitors that I don't know what I would do without you to soothe me.'

How will you know what pleases me if I come to see you again?' Manfred persisted.

'Unless you are as cold-blooded as a fish you will not leave my house before you have had a private interview with one of my young ladies. They are very clever, dear Herr von Klausenberg, in fact they are selected for their skill in pleasing gentlemen in unusual ways. You will be able to express yourself fully, even if your way of doing so is eccentric.'

Between Madame Filipov's thighs, the maid's head with its little starched cap bobbed busily up and down.

'Whichever young lady you converse with, I shall hear about it,' Madame continued, her words soft and interspersed with little sighs, 'so when you are here next time,

I shall know better than you do yourself what will truly please you.'

'Not everyone who comes to your house has the honour of being received personally,' said Manfred, 'most of them are content with your young ladies, I imagine.'

'As you say, only a few attend upon me. Herr Krill . . . I guessed what his secret desire was after he had been with one of my staff a few times. He still goes to her, but he calls upon me first . . . our meeting raises his spirits so he can enter fully into the conversation with Fraulein Ellie.'

'And the Baron, of course.'

'He is a dear, sweet, gentle person . . . too much so for his own happiness . . . he would find it impossible to approach a woman in the way most men do . . . but delicacy and tenderness and a proper regard for the proprieties – these are what he responds to . . .'

'With me there is no need for these roundabout methods,' said Manfred, hotly excited by what he saw the maid doing to Madame Filipov, 'I will tell you in plain words what I want.'

'Ah, a man who is not afraid of his secret desires . . . tell me – whatever it is . . . I will arrange it for you at once . . .'

He got up, stood behind her chair and reached over her shoulders to take hold of her bare breasts.

'I want *you*. Little games like those you played for Krill and the Baron may be amusing sometimes, but at this moment I want to make love to you in the simple old-fashioned way.'

Her eyes were half-closed in enjoyment of the emotions rippling through her body from the maid's busy tongue between her thighs.

'This is outrageous,' she murmured, 'I am not at the disposal of anyone who walks into my house.'

'You said that whatever I wanted would be arranged for me at once.'

'Oh, Gretchen . . . faster!'

He gripped her breasts tighter as her body writhed on

77

the chair in hot release. The maid ceased her attentions and her face turned up to grin lewdly at Manfred.

'Madame is satisfied?' she asked.

Without waiting for an answer, she took a bottle of caude-Cologne from the dressing-table, soaked a soft pad and gently wiped over Madame's belly to cool her and remove the faint sheen of perspiration.

'With the gentleman's permission,' she said, and pushed Manfred's hands away to wipe under Madame's breasts and up between them.

'Thank you, Gretchen,' said Madame Filipov faintly. 'It seems that I made a promise without thinking. Are you so inconsiderate of my feelings, Herr von Klausenberg, to hold me to it?'

'I am determined,' he answered.

'You understand that to converse with me is a more serious matter than a private interview with one of my young ladies?'

He understood well enough what she meant – it would cost him more to enjoy her than one of her employees. He answered equally obliquely so as to preserve her pretence of gentility.

'Believe me, Madame, when a Klausenberg makes up his mind, nothing deters him, not blows, blood or gold.'

'There speaks the rider with the strong knee-grip! Gretchen, prepare the bed.'

The little maid scrambled up and trotted out of the room. Madame Filipov leaned further back in her chair and rested her head against Manfred. He put his hands over her shoulders again and stroked her cool breasts.

'How old are you?' she asked.

'Twenty-three. My birthday was in March.'

'A good age to be! I wish I were twenty-three again.'

'If I may ask, what were you doing when you were twenty-three?'

'I was married and travelled with my husband. We lived in Paris sometimes and in St Petersburg. But the War and the Bolsheviks finished all that.'

'And your husband?'

She laughed briefly, but did not reply. Manfred thought it better not to enquire further, in case he was told that Filipov lived up in the attic and counted the takings.

'Come with me,' she said, smiling at him in the mirror.

Her long négligé wrapped around her, she took him into the next room. Manfred thought it very elegant, decorated in the style of the French Empire, with pale walls, gilt mirrors and bow-legged furniture. The bed was magnificent, an antique piece of taste and value. From a gold-embossed plaque set high on the wall, ivory silk drapery descended in soft swags to form a canopy round the carved bed-head.

Gretchen had already turned back the cover to reveal sheets of silk the same colour as the drapery. Hands folded in front of her, she stood at the foot of the bed, the very picture of the attentive servant. Madame Filipov dropped her négligé casually to the honey-coloured parquet floor and arranged herself seductively on the bed, one knee raised, as if in modesty, to hide what lay between her cream-skinned thighs.

'Assist the gentleman, Gretchen,' she ordered.

The maid helped Manfred to undress. She took his jacket and then went down on one knee to unbutton his trousers, while he pulled at the ends of his bow-tie to undo it. She helped him out of his shirt, knelt again to remove his shoes and socks and grinned up at him as he stood in only his silk underpants, his stem sticking out rigidly. She took hold of the waist-band and divested him of his final garment, stood up and clasped his protuberance firmly, as if to assess it.

'The gentleman is ready for you, Madame.'

By now Manfred was very excited indeed. He jumped on to the broad bed and used Madame Filipov with vigour. He rolled her about in his arms, rubbed himself against her, handled her breasts and bottom so firmly that she soon sighed and scratched at his chest with her finger-nails. He put his hand between her thighs and explored her slippery

79

entrance briskly and she gasped and sank her teeth into his shoulder. In short, it more resembled a wrestling-match than an act of love, but that was the mood that her games had put him in. Wise in the ways of men, she went along with his mood. It was not long before he rolled her on to her back, spread her knees and was on her and in her. She clasped her hands on the back of his neck and urged him on with cries and thrusts of her own hips and Manfred rode her as if he were galloping a good horse over the countryside of his boyhood. Madame Filipov moaned and heaved, her movements growing wilder in time with his, till everything dissolved in ecstatic convulsions that rocked the bed.

It took her some time to recover herself after so energetic a bout. Manfred lay beside her and smoked a Turkish cigarette he found in a Sevres porcelain box on the bedside table. It was only then that it occurred to him that Gretchen had remained in the room throughout, sitting on a gilt chair by the door, her hands folded in her lap, a silent witness to Madame's passionate interlude.

In another minute or two Gretchen came to the bedside with a very large bottle of eau-de-Cologne and refreshed Madame by wiping the cooling spirit lightly over her entire body, round her neck, down between her breasts and over her belly and down the insides of her thighs, much as she had done earlier, this evidently being a regular part of her duties.

'Thank you, Gretchen,' Madame Filipov murmured, her eyes opening slowly, 'and thank you too, Herr von Klausenberg – you made me feel myself twenty-three again.'

The maid had finished with her mistress. She moved round the bed and with her little palm smoothed eau-de-Cologne over Manfred's chest and belly. The sensation was most pleasant and the effect was cooling, but the touch of her hand in his groins had an unintended result. Manfred's limp stem quivered and began to grow longer again. Gretchen grinned at him and stroked the insides of his thighs upwards.

'The gentleman is ready again, Madame,' she announced.

'Great God!' Madame Filipov exclaimed, turning her head on the silk pillow to stare at him, 'you are determined to kill me with your brutal Prussian ways. No, it is out of the question!'

'I remember a certain promise,' said Manfred, amused by her response.

Privately he wondered how many times the girls of the house were expected to entertain clients each night, while Madame cried off after once.

'Promises are sacred,' said Madame, 'you must help me, Gretchen.'

The maid stood at the foot of the great bed and faced them while she took off her starched cap, her apron and black frock, her stockings and cheap underwear. She clambered on to the bed and crept up between Manfred and Madame Filipov, lying on her back with her arms at her sides. Madame put an arm under the girl's thin shoulders and, with her other hand, caressed her slack little breasts.

'She is such a good girl,' said Madame, 'so loyal!'

Manfred raised himself on one elbow to look at the girl and stroked her thin legs, up past the pink marks her garters had left on her thighs, to the few wisps of mouse-brown hair that decorated the surprisingly well-developed and protruding lips of her sex.

'Has she been in your service long, Madame?' he asked.

'Five or six years now. She was a wretched orphan of fourteen when I found her in the street selling herself to drunks for the price of a crust of bread. I am sure you remember the hungry years well enough, though you never went without food or new clothes. I took pity on little Gretchen and saved her from disease and death, and she loves me for that and takes care of me.'

A sly smile appeared on the little maid's face as Manfred stroked between her parted legs, his finger exploring between the warm lips there.

'Do you like that, Gretchen?' he asked.

'Yes, it's very nice,' and she opened her legs wider for him.

81

'She is almost like a daughter to me,' said Madame Filipov fondly, 'I have never let her become one of my young ladies and converse with gentlemen who have eccentric tastes. She attends upon me and she is the best lady's-maid I have ever had in my life.'

'Her duties seem more comprehensive than those of the average lady's-maid, Madame. For instance, the service she performed for you earlier on, when you were agitated. And at this moment too.'

'The gentleman is ready, Gretchen,' said Madame Filipov firmly.

The maid turned on her side to face Manfred and threw her leg over his hips, her hand reaching for his stem to tease it with nervous little tweaks. Not knowing what to expect in this extraordinary household, Manfred slid towards her until he was close enough for her to steer his stiffness into her fleshy little socket. He pushed and wriggled closer and embedded himself comfortably in her until his belly touched hers.

Madame Filipov also turned on to her side and was close up to the maid's thin back. Her hands gripped Gretchen's hips and held her firmly against Manfred's slow thrusts.

'Oh Madame!' the maid murmured. 'He is so strong!'

'Oh Gretchen!' Madame gasped. 'So strong!'

As Manfred grew more excited he became unsure of which of the women he was doing it to, the mistress or the maid. His arm was over Gretchen and his hand was squeezing Madame Filipov's warm breast; Madame's hand was over the girl to stroke his face and push her thumb into his mouth. Her belly was bumping against the maid's bottom, to make her respond to his thrusts, and both women were sighing and moaning. When he discharged his turbulent passion, both women cried out at the same moment.

After a pause, the maid eased herself away from him and slid down to the foot of the bed and off it. Manfred was left gazing at Madame Filipov's face on the pillow.

'It has been a great pleasure to make your acquaintance,

Herr von Klausenberg,' she said, 'I hope to see you again before very long. But now I must ask you to excuse me – I have matters to attend to. Please stay here with Gretchen if you wish, for as long as you like. Now that I know you I have no hesitation in entrusting her to you.'

'Thank you, Madame, but I must take my leave.'

She remained on the bed, posing gracefully, while Gretchen assisted him to dress. She was expert as any valet, even to tying his bow-tie neatly, and her nakedness added a certain pleasure to the proceedings.

'Auf wiedersehen, Madame,' he said, bowing politely towards the bed.

'Auf wiedersehen, Herr von Klausenberg. When you come to see me again I shall have a very special way of pleasing you.'

Gretchen opened the bedroom door for him. He patted her bare bottom and gave her five hundred Marks, being in a generous mood. She smiled and curtseyed, her bare breasts bobbing in a way that was faintly comic.

Outside, beyond the red-panelled door, he found the squat and short-haired woman waiting for him and he learned from her that the services of Madame Filipov cost him very much more than the gratuity he had given her maid.

Ulrika's Celebration

'Thank you for inviting me, dear Ulrika,' said Manfred into the telephone, "but surely you don't want men there. What would be the point?'

'I'm asking a few men friends so that they can see what they're missing.'

'You mean that you want to tantalise us with forbidden fruit. Anyway, what are you celebrating? it isn't your birthday until October.'

'I'm celebrating being me – what better reason? Will you come and help me to celebrate that? After all, I came to your birthday party and watched pretty young girls being pawed by men. Now it's your turn to suffer a little.'

'Ulrika, you did not suffer at my party. I saw you the next morning asleep in one of my armchairs with your hand up a girl's skirt. Don't pretend that nothing happened before you fell asleep.'

'That was a little flirtation,' said Ulrika with a laugh. 'She came home with me and stayed a couple of days but after that she became boring and I sent her back to her regular girl-friend.'

'There you are – you found her boring! How do you know I won't find your celebration boring?'

'It won't bore you to be surrounded by naked women, even if you can't touch them.'

'How so, naked?' he asked with more interest.

'Because I'm having my celebration in a Steam-bath.'

'That's very original. It will be like a visit to a Turkish harem.'

'And there will be slaves on guard to stop any unauthorised interference with the women of my harem.'

'I can see it now! Frustrated men wandering about with huge projections sticking out under their bath-towels and your girl-friends laughing at them. It sounds more like a torture-chamber than a harem.'

'I wouldn't be so unkind to you, Manfred. I've invited some other women – the sort who prefer men, though God knows why. And you can bring a girl of your own.'

'Thank you, but if I brought a girl, you'd eat her alive.'

'As you wish. There'll be enough others to keep you happy.'

Even with that assurance, it was with mixed feelings that Manfred arrived at the Steam-bath on the evening of the celebration. Ulrika Heuss was a cousin of his, five or six years older than himself, and he had known her all his life. He liked her – her parties were a different matter.

A large notice fixed to the door of the Steam-bath said CLOSED TO THE PUBLIC. Ulrika's money had talked. Inside, a muscular male attendant checked names against a list before passing anyone through – there were to be no gate-crashers, which was not in the least surprising. Five minutes later, his clothes stowed away safely in a wooden locker, Manfred strolled into the main room of the Steam-bath, wearing only a towel round his waist. There were at least thirty women in the hot and steamy room, some with towels round them, some completely naked, glasses in their hands and chatting away as if they were at an ordinary party and wearing their most elegant clothes. There were one or two men in the throng, all sporting bath-towels like himself, he noted with some relief.

'Manfred darling – at last!' Ulrika called to him.

As befitted her reputation for caring about nothing. Ulrika was stark naked, though she had a long string of matched pearls round her neck – so long that it looped down to her belly-button. She kissed Manfred on both cheeks and told one of the young women hanging round her to get him a glass of champagne. Manfred had never

85

had the honour of seeing his cousin naked before and was taken by her elegance of form. She had kept her body slim and supple and, though approaching thirty, her breasts were pointed and firm. What was very striking about her was that the light brown hair between her thighs was neatly trimmed into a heart-shape.

'There's lots of people here you know,' she said, 'and your dear friend Nina is coming later.'

'And her husband?'

'Don't be silly. Gottfried is too boring for words. Did I ever tell you that he offered Vicki Schwabe a thousand Marks at your birthday party?'

But why? Vicki does it for nothing.'

'She doesn't do what he wanted, the filthy beast! It proves what I've always said about him. Why do you have that ridiculous towel round you, Manfred? You're not ashamed of anything, are you? Take if off – this is a celebration, not a prayer-meeting.'

Manfred had drunk a bottle of wine with his dinner and a good quantity of brandy afterwards. Consequently he felt no qualm about unwrapping the towel from his waist and handing it to the girl who at that moment came back with a glass of chilled champagne for him. She looked startled.

'Don't be afraid, Gerda,' said Ulrika with a wicked grin, 'you're not about to be raped. At least, not by Manfred. I'm the one you should worry about – I might drag you into a corner and ravage you until you scream.'

'Oh Ulrika!' the girl murmured, her eyes down-cast and a smile on her pretty mouth.

Manfred raised his glass.

'I celebrate *you*, dear Ulrika. May you never change!'

'You may rely on it. I'm glad you decided to come – you know I have a soft spot for you.'

He was conscious of her gaze, particularly on that part of him for which she had no use.

'You've grown up to be a very handsome man. And well-equipped too. It's grown a lot since you and I played together when we were children. It was a tiny little thing then.'

'I don't remember that. Are you sure it was me?'

'One summer in the country. You were about four. That was before I found out what really interested me.'

'Such a shame,' he said, smiling at her, 'you are a beautiful woman and if you had any interest in men, I'd take you to bed for a week. Did you really play with my dingle-dangle when I was a child?'

Ulrika laughed at him and padded away on bare feet to greet more guests. Manfred looked round for more champagne and poured himself another glass. Over on that side of the room two girls sat on a long wooden bench, both pretty and neither more than eighteen. They were giggling, exhilarated by what they had been drinking, and in a mood for anything. But even as he strolled towards them, the plumper of the two began to stroke the other girl's bare breasts and he knew that he was wasting his time. All the same, it was interesting to watch them. The plump girl lifted a leg over the bench and straddled it, exposing her brown thatch, and her friend turned to face her and put her legs round her waist. Manfred's stem stood to attention at the sight of their loving caresses and he turned away, to find himself face to face with Werner Schiele and Vicki Schwabe. Werner had a bath-towel round his waist, with a bulge under it. Vicki wore nothing, and the sight of her bouncy little breasts and reddish-ginger tuft was not only entrancing but probably accounted for Werner's condition.

'I got my clothes back after your party,' she said brightly, 'it was that idiot Dieter who took them. He said it was a joke, but I'm not so sure. Maybe he wanted to try them on.'

'Anything is possible with Dieter,' said Manfred, 'he has no style.'

'You should find yourself a towel,' Werner advised him, 'you are indecent like that.'

'Shame is for little minds,' Manfred retorted grandly. 'Have you seen Mitzi lately?'

'Your fiancée,' said Werner, with a malicious grin, 'No, not I.'

'I'm relieved to hear it. She seemed to me a very nice person, far too good for you.'

'If that were for me,' said Vicki, staring at Manfred's out-thrust limb, 'I'd take it as a compliment. But as you're alone, a swim might help to reduce the swelling.'

Manfred nodded and headed for the pool. Vicki followed him, leaving Werner dumbfounded. On the edge of the pool, Manfred stood with arms raised, in addition to what else was raised, curled his toes round the tiles and dived. He surfaced gasping for breath in the very cold water, just in time to see Vicki leap in, bottom first and legs flying. They splashed around for a while, flicking water at each other, until Vicki said she was freezing. They climbed out together and went into the hottest room, shivering as the water trickled down their skin.

They found a marble slab and lay side by side, warming up. They could hear voices in the room but caught only occasional glimpses of anything at all through the billowing steam.

'Look over there!' said Vicki.

Manfred raised himself on an elbow and saw, across the room, a tableau which made him chuckle. There was Werner, flat on his back on another marble slab, his towel discarded to let his meaty flag-pole point skywards. There was a woman with him, massaging his belly with both hands.

'He's lost no time, has he?' Manfred asked.

As the steam-clouds drifted across to conceal the scene, he saw the woman squat over Werner's face and lower herself on to his mouth.

'Anita Lenz – the slut!' said Vicki.

'Of course – I didn't recognise her now that she's bleached her hair.'

'Pity she didn't bleach her tuft while she was about it. It looks silly being blonde on top and mud-brown below.'

'Werner doesn't seem to object to the colour, and he has the closest view.'

'He's an artichoke-eater,' said Vicki, a note of hostility in her voice.

'I'm sorry,' said Manfred, 'is there something between you and him?'

'If there was, it's just evaporated. We've been going about together for a few weeks, that's all. He's nothing special.'

She turned on her side towards Manfred and put a hand on his thigh.

'He's a joker, Vicki. I owe him something for that little affair he arranged at my birthday party, when I thought I had got myself engaged to Mitzi. All in all, I am not very fond of Werner.'

'Nor am I. I'd rather be with you.'

Her hand closed round his stem.

'The cold water didn't cool you down for long. When we got out of the pool this was so small and shrivelled like a baby radish. Now look at it!'

'I can think of a good use to put it to,' he said, pleased that he'd got her away from Werner.

'I can think of ten good uses at least,' she answered.

Manfred fondled her breasts. Their pink tips became firm almost as soon as he touched them, which bore out all that he had been told about Vicki by friends who knew her better than he did. He put a hand between her thighs and found how warm it was there.

'The problem is,' she said, 'that this slab we're on is so hard that I'll be covered in bruises.'

He had to admit that she was right. She was slender to the point of thinness and the lines of her ribs were discernible below her breasts. Her hips were angular and were made even more prominent by the narrowness of her waist. He ran his hand along her pale-skinned thigh and felt her bottom. The cheeks were small and taut.

'You don't have much flesh on your bones, Vicki. Do you eat properly or do you diet to stay slim?'

89

'I eat like a wolf and it has no effect at all. It's because I am so energetic.'

'You like sport?'

'Only one sport, but I play it a lot.'

'We mustn't let you be bruised. Everyone would think I'd been beating you.'

'Some of them would find that amusing. You don't beat women, do you?'

'Hardly ever,' he answered, grinning at a sudden recollection of Magda's games with ropes and harness. 'Now if you were to get up on your hands and knees . . .'

'Do it like dogs in the street? That's disgraceful!'

'Or like a stallion and a mare in a field,' he suggested.

'Or like parrots in a cage,' she giggled, and positioned herself as he had proposed.

'Parrots! What do they know about it?' he asked, grinning.

From behind her rump he surveyed the ginger-flossed peach she was presenting to him, split it with his thumbs and pushed his stem into it swiftly. From all accounts this delectable part of her had been used more than was usual for a woman of twenty-two, but this was his first encounter with it.

The temperature was very high in the hot-room. Vicki's back was slippery with perspiration as he lay along it and tried out his new toy. His hands were under her to stroke her breasts, and they too were slippery. Quite soon he learned something which no one had bothered to mention to him – Vicki was a noisy lover.

As her excitement grew with his, she started to sob loudly in pleasure. Not that Manfred cared – it tickled him to know that she was enjoying what he was doing to her. He carried on with great enthusiasm and, when the critical moment arrived, his delight was magnified by Vicki's ear-splitting shrieks of ecstasy.

An instant later, while his belly was still convulsing and she was still screeching, all the delight was spoiled by a sneering voice close by. It was Werner.

'So! You've stolen another girl from me! First it was Mitzi and then, as if that wasn't enough, I find you sticking it up Vicki! This is getting to be a habit with you – a bad habit! I shall have to put a stop to it.'

Manfred turned his head to glare at Werner, who was standing within arm's-reach of him, staring and grinning unpleasantly. Anita was beside him and she too was grinning. Werner's flag-pole was down and Anita looked flushed.

'The fact is that women prefer me to you,' said Manfred, not wanting to start a quarrel, 'Leave Anita here when you go, there's a good fellow.'

'They can't like you for your style,' said Werner, 'I thought it very unimaginative – crude, in fact. Of course, Vicki is easily pleased, but even so, I think it must be your money they prefer. Someone told me that Mitzi got a fur coat out of you. Will Vicki get the same, or does she do it for less?'

Manfred was strongly inclined to pull free from Vicki and punch Werner in the face. Before he had time to translate the thought into action, Vicki spoke up.

'Go away, Werner, or I'll tell everyone about that little episode with the beer bottle. You didn't demonstrate much style yourself then.'

Werner's face turned a dull red. He seized Anita by the hand and dragged her away. Manfred freed himself from Vicki and turned her round to kiss her.

'What about a beer-bottle? What did he do with it?'

'If I tell you, everyone will know and I'll have nothing to threaten him with if he starts being tiresome again.'

'He's always tiresome.'

'I know,' she agreed. 'How about a cold shower together?'

Some time later, back in the big room, Manfred spotted the beautiful American, Jenny Montrose. But beautiful was an inadequate word, he thought; she was heart-stopping! She was naked and she gave no sign of embarrassment as she talked to Ulrika. Manfred stared at her as if to photo-

91

graph her on his memory – and with good reason. Jenny
was long-legged, round of hip, with a neat black tuft where
her thighs joined. Her breasts were perfect, but most
ravishing of all was her face, long, patrician and with an
expression of slight disdain. She wore diamond ear-clips
which shone against her jet-black hair like stars in the night-
sky.

Manfred started towards her, only to be stopped in his
tracks by the sight of Ulrika putting an arm round her waist
and kissing her on the mouth. It did not seem much like
the ordinary friendly kiss with which women greet each
other – at least, not on Ulrika's part. Yet Max had made
love to Jenny – he had said so, and Manfred did not doubt
his word. But Max had also said, he recalled, that she was
strange in bed, as if her spirit was elsewhere.

The two women turned away and walked slowly towards
the massage-room, each with an arm about the other's
waist. Manfred stared at two long and elegant backs
retreating from him and he saw that Ulrika was stroking
the American's bottom.

Damnation! Manfred swore aloud, and if Werner had
been in sight at that moment, he would have beat him to
a pulp to relieve his frustrated emotions.

Over by the wall, on the wooden bench, the two girls he
had seen earlier were still caressing each other slowly. The
plump girl was lying full length, legs astride and her feet
on the tiled floor. The other girl sat with her knees up,
tickling her friend between the legs with her big toe.

'Isn't that sweet!' said a well-known voice behind him.
'Someone should photograph it and make it into a Christmas card for Ulrika.'

Manfred turned to smile at Nina von Behrendorf.

Naturally, Nina was naked to show off her charms. Not
quite naked, she had knotted a pale orange chiffon scarf
round her waist, the loose ends floating in front. The
chiffon was transparent enough for her triangle of brown
curls to show through and the effect was more provocative

than if she had worn nothing at all. Konrad Zeitz was with her, a bath-towel round his waist.

'There's an old friend I haven't seen for a long time,' said Nina, reaching out to touch Manfred's hanging part briefly, 'is this an invitation?'

Konrad looked displeased.

'Manfred's an exhibitionist,' he said, 'it would not surprise me to hear that he visits nudist clubs and parades himself around among the fresh air fanatics.'

'Better to wear nothing than a worn-out towel with someone else's name on it,' Manfred replied. 'What are you hiding, Konrad?'

'Yes, why are you hiding it, darling?' Nina asked, 'You've nothing to be ashamed of.'

'I'm sure you know,' said Manfred, 'I'm glad you're both here at last. There's less than a dozen of us who support the traditional method. All the rest are wild women chasing each other round the swimming-pool.'

'Each to his own – or her own,' said Konrad, 'so long as they don't try to include Nina in their frolics.'

'Surely that's Nina's choice,' said Manfred.

Konrad scowled, Nina laughed and patted his cheek.

'Don't look so angry – I'm a supporter of what Manfred called the traditional method. What I don't understand is why Ulrika invited us.'

'She gets a thrill from flaunting herself and her little friends,' said Manfred.

'Where is she?'

'Around somewhere, amusing herself – the champagne is over there.'

They drifted away and Manfred was free to go in pursuit of Ulrika and Jenny. Why he wished to do that he was not entirely sure. He told himself that it was an opportunity to settle the question of whether the American girl was a lesbian or not, but why that should be important to him he had no idea. He searched through the whole Steam-bath, witnessing scenes of love taking many forms, and at last tried the only place left – the store-room. There were voices inside, so he opened the door quietly and slipped round it, to conceal himself behind a cupboard against the wall. There were seven women in the room, including Ulrika and Jenny, and there Ulrika's celebration of herself was well advanced.

She lay on a wooden table, cushioned by dozens of folded bath-towels, her legs apart and her head pillowed on Jenny's thighs. Olga Pfaff, a very pretty blonde woman with whom Manfred had once been on terms of intimacy for a few weeks without discovering her interest in other women, lay cross-legged between Ulrika's raised knees. The other women stood around the table, close up to it, engrossed in what was going on. All attention was concentrated on the heart-shaped tuft of light-brown hair between Ulrika's thighs. It graced a plump mound, split by fleshy lips, with a little bud at the top from which the opening descended vertically until it disappeared into the shadow below.

Blonde Olga was leaning forward, her red-nailed hands busy with Ulrika's exposed treasure, stroking it upwards again and again with deliberate slowness. Ulrika's thighs were trembling and her head rolled restlessly on Jenny's bare thighs. As the finger stirred her emotions, the women standing round the table uttered tiny sighs and drew in their breath swiftly. Ulrika was in seventh heaven, revelling in sensation and in the total exposure of herself to her little congregation of friends, hiding nothing, pretending nothing, joyously celebrating being herself.

'Darlings!' she said, speaking to no one in particular, to all who could hear and to herself, 'this is my body, my beautiful living body, given freely for you. Whenever two or three of you are gathered together, do this in remembrance of me.'

Her gleaming belly contracted when Olga's finger probed deeper and touched something of special interest. Ten or a dozen upward caresses caused the fleshy lips to open by themselves within the heart-shaped brown fur, to expose the pink skin within. Ulrika's breathing quickened and her breasts rose and fell to the rhythm, her long rope of pearls sliding over her moving flesh. Olga brushed blonde hair from her forehead with the back of her free hand and leaned closer to stare into the tender pink vestibule in which her fingers were playing.

'Look at me closely, little ones,' Ulrika breathed, 'feast your eyes on my secret and sacred heart.'

Her raised knees parted wider, descending in opposite directions towards the table on which she lay, their movement pulling her open to the full. Her head rolled a little on Jenny's naked thigh and Jenny smoothed her hand over Ulrika's flushed cheeks.

The other women standing round the table to observe Ulrika's long act of surrender and triumph were fondling each other, hands squeezed breasts, palms stroked bellies, fingers caressed between thighs. On each face was the same rapt expression. Now that Ulrika was open for all to see, Olga concentrated her attentions on the tiny pink bud that stood revealed. Her finger-tips touched it delicately and Ulrika's sighs grew loud and insistent.

'There is a great and lasting love for every one of you in this secret heart of mine,' she murmured, 'you know that – you have all touched it! You know what it is to be in my arms and to be loved by me. You have felt the true ecstasy that I give to those I love . . .'

All of them, Manfred thought feverishly, his stem straining at full stretch. That included Jenny. He tried to imagine her in Ulrika's arms, their naked bodies pressed close together, their breasts flattened against each other's breasts, their mouths joined in a long kiss and Ulrika's hand between Jenny's long legs, inducing ecstatic sensations.

'Oh Ulrika, I love you!' Olga moaned, her fingers fluttering between the spread thighs, 'I love you, darling! Give yourself to me!'

'And I love you,' Ulrika answered, her voice shaky with emotion, 'as I love all of you.'

'Give yourself to me!' Olga cried, almost hysterically.

'Freely!' Ulrika gasped.

In a flash Olga's legs were uncrossed and her body twisted about until she lay face-down, her blonde head between Ulrika's thighs. Her wet pink tongue flickered over Ulrika's little bud. Manfred, concealed behind the cupboard, bit his knuckles hard to top himself from crying out. He saw Ulrika's legs shake to the urgent swelling of delight in her and then her fingers clutched at her own breasts, plucking at the upstanding nipples. The little group of women seemed to have crept in closer around the table, arms tight about each other, the sound of their breathing harsh as they waited for Ulrika's moment to arrive.

Manfred's stem was so swollen that he thought it might squirt involuntarily. Trickles of sweat ran down his forehead and chest, his legs trembled. Then Ulrika announced the moment of consummation with a long shriek of joy, her mouth wide open to show her teeth and her body bouncing up and down on the scattered bath-towels. Olga's arms were tight around Ulrika's thighs, her face pressed deep into the heart-shaped tuft.

Manfred could stand no more. Before Ulrika's cry of triumph died away, he backed quickly out of the storeroom, leaving the door open, and ran, holding his raging stem in his hand to stop it from shaking painfully about as he raced through the large room where the drinks were, scattering young women left and right without even seeing them. He was looking for Nina and he found her in the massage-room. She lay on one of the massage-tables, her chiffon scarf pulled to one side so that the knot was on her hip and her tuft was uncovered. Konrad was not with her.

'Nina – help me!'

'My poor Manfred, what has happened to you?'

There was no time to explain. Manfred flung himself on her, but her legs closed at once, denying his desperate need.

'What are you doing?' She demanded. 'Konrad will be back in a minute. He's gone to get me a glass of champagne.'

By then Manfred had her soft breasts in his hands, the balls of his thumbs tickling her buds and it was like the old times again, when he and she had been lovers. Nina's blue eyes stared up at him, amused, and her legs parted in welcome. One fast push took him deep into the flesh he knew so well and before he had time to realise that the deliciously wet and velvety feel of it was due to Konrad's ministrations, the raging torrent inside him burst its banks and he was gasping and jolting in release.

'My God, that was quick,' said Nina.

'Thank you, Nina, thank you, thank you . . .'

'Does this mean that we are good friends again?'

'We shall always be good friends,' he said, recovering himself.

'That's not what I mean, as you know very well.'

'Why are you with that dreadful Konrad?'

'Are you jealous? That's a good sign. But until you make your mind up whether you and I are close friends again, you'd better get off me before he sees you.'

Manfred rolled off her and lay at her side, to stroke the soft skin of her shoulder. Her legs moved close together and she adjusted her scarf to bring the knot into the middle, just below her belly-button, and the trailing ends covering her tuft of curls.

'You shouldn't have married Gottfried. That spoiled everything.'

Before she could reply, there was a shout from the doorway. Konrad was back, carrying two glasses of champagne.

'What's going on?' he demanded, 'I leave you alone for two minutes to get you something cold to drink and I find this Casanova making up to you.'

Manfred rolled off the table and stood up, his deflating stem hidden by the table itself.

'Konrad, you've been hours getting me a drink,' said Nina, unruffled. 'We were talking about the old days.'

Konrad glared suspiciously at Manfred.

'The old days are over,' he said. 'Go and find yourself a girl somewhere. There's plenty of them about, running round without a stitch on. Nina is with me – understand?'

'I enjoyed our little reminiscence of the old days,' Manfred said to Nina with a broad grin. 'We must talk again like that sometime when this bad-tempered fellow isn't with you.'

An hour or more later Manfred was lying on the tiled floor of the big room, his head resting across the thighs of Anita Lenz, who sat half-asleep and propped against the wall. He was in the process of persuading Anita to accompany him into the massage-room, to spite Werner, but she had drunk a little too much and was disinclined to make the effort, though she gave him to understand that she had no objection in principle. Vicki Schwabe appeared, sat beside him and rested her head on his shoulder.

'You look very pleased about something, Vicki,' said Manfred. 'Who have you found to join in your favourite sport this time?'

'This party is a bore. Most of the women are groping each other and the few men there are have had so many offers that they're worn out.'

'I'm not worn out. Let's find a comfortable place and I'll prove it.'

'I knew I could rely on you, Manfred. But not just yet – I don't want to miss what's going to happen.'

'What is going to happen?'

'Wait and see,' she answered mysteriously.

It was very comforting to lie with his head on Anita's lap and stroke Vicki's belly. Manfred thought he might doze for a while until Vicki was ready to accept his invitation. Or perhaps Anita would come to life again and then he would try to get both women with him in some secluded corner and really pay Werner back for his rudeness. With these pleasant possibilities in his mind, he drifted into a light sleep, to be awoken by a noisy and violent commotion. He could hear men's voices shouting in anger and women's voices raised in alarm.

'Come on – there's a fight!' Vicki exclaimed, jumping up.

Manfred followed her at a more leisurely pace. The noise was coming from the pool. Gottfried von Behrendorf, in a grey suit and a homburg hat, confronted a naked Werner Schiele and, but for the two men holding him back, would have been at Werner's throat. Around them were a dozen naked men and women, including Nina, adding their cries to the hubbub.

'What's going on?' Manfred asked the woman nearest him.

'I don't know. This madman rushed in and tried to murder Werner.'

One of the men restraining Gottfried was Konrad, his face red with the struggle. The tumult subsided when Ulrika strode in, her hair untidy from whatever she had been doing, but still magnificently in control.

'Gottfried! What are you doing here? You were not invited.'

'How dare you ask my wife to a disgusting affair like this where she is molested by a degenerate!' Gottfried raved.

Manfred grinned at that. Whatever molestation Nina had been subjected to was by her whole-hearted consent. Konrad had molested her, that was sure, besides himself. How Werner came to be accused was a mystery, but a highly enjoyable one. Fortunately for her, Nina was still wearing the chiffon scarf round her waist and she was the only person present to wear anything at all, jewellery not counting.

'Nothing disgusting is going on here,' Ulrika said forcefully, 'this is a celebration of health and beauty for a few friends. I must insist that you leave at once.'

'Nina, put your clothes on,' Gottfried said sharply, 'We're leaving.'

Without a word Nina walked towards the changing-room, making certain that her little scarf did not flutter as she went and expose anything which might further infuriate her husband.

'As for you,' Gottfried snarled at Werner, 'you haven't heard the last of this. You are a despicable swine.'

'But you've got it all wrong,' Werner protested hotly. 'It was a mistake – I thought she was someone else.'

Gottfried stared at him as if he were a particularly unpleasant insect who had just emerged from under a stone and Werner, trembling visibly, made things worse.

'I thought she was Anita, I swear!'

'Who did you think was me?' asked a voice at Manfred's side.

It was Anita, who had woken up and at last joined the crowd by the pool.

'Anyway,' she continued innocently, 'I've been sitting out there for ages talking to Manfred.'

'That's true,' said Vicki Schwabe with a touch of malice, 'the three of us were together.'

'So!' Gottfried shouted, his eyes popping from his head, 'you are a dirtier swine than I thought! You try to lie your way out of the consequences. I shall deal with you. Goodnight, Ulrika, I apologise for interrupting your health and beauty assembly.'

The men holding him released him and he turned on his heel and marched out. Vicki linked her bare arm with Manfred's and led him towards the massage-room.

'I don't understand any of this,' he told her, 'what brought Gottfried here unexpectedly and why did he find Nina with Werner instead of Konrad?'

'How do I know. I was with you.'

'Not all the time. I suppose you telephoned Gottfried and told him that his wife's honour was in danger. But the rest of it?'

'Who knows? Strange things can happen at parties like this – you should know that. And that fool Werner has been hot for Nina for ages.'

The massage-room was fully occupied, each rubbing-table bearing a couple uninterested in the affray by the pool. And all the couples were women.

'This is a bigger bore than I thought,' said Vicki, 'let's go home.'

'Your apartment or mine?'

'Mine. Believe it or not, I like to wake up in my own bed.'

In the dressing-room they found Werner putting his clothes on, his expression one of utter dejection.

'Going so soon, Werner?' Manfred asked, with a grin.

'I hardly touched her and that lunatic ran in and half-strangled me. And she started to scream, the bitch, to make herself look innocent in front of him. What a mess!'

'It may be worse than you think,' said Manfred, delighted by the chance of getting his own back, 'in fact, it could be very serious indeed for you.'

'What do you mean – he won't make a complaint to the police, will he?'

'No, that's not his style. I think you will find his seconds calling on you in a few hours' time. Take my advice and choose swords.'

'My God – this can't be real?'

'Gottfried can be very old-fashioned about things like honour and all that rot. I don't suppose he'll kill you, but he'll certainly maim you. That's why I suggest you insist on sabres – he'll only slice an ear off. But with pistols it might be much worse. If he aims at your knee you'll be crippled for the rest of your life. And if he became really vicious and aimed higher – at the part you intended to use on Nina . . . Well, you wouldn't want to lose that. So make it swords.'

'What shall I do!' Werner exclaimed desperately.

'There is nothing you can do except stand up boldly and take what's coming to you.'

'Suppose I went and explained that it was with Nina's consent? Then he'd see there was no point in going on with this murderous farce.'

Manfred finished dressing and stared thoughtfully at Werner.

'My dear man, you don't seem to understand the code of conduct of decent people,' he said, tongue in cheek, 'if you even hinted at any such thing Gottfried would divorce Nina and kill you for certain. Leave things as they are.

With luck it will only amount to a week or two in hospital. Then he'll be ready to shake hands and forget the whole thing.'

'There's only one thing for it! I'll pack a bag and get a taxi to the railway station before daylight. Perhaps if I stay away from Berlin for a few months it will blow over. What do you think?'

'Everyone will know that you're a coward, but you'll have a whole skin. Auf wiedersehen, Werner.'

He and Vicki laughed so much in the car on the way to her apartment that the driving was very erratic. They almost collided with a taxi as they passed the Kaiser Wilhelm Memorial Church but not even the driver's tirade of abuse sobered them. Manfred put his foot down hard and they soon left the shouting behind as they sped across the sleeping city. Vicki lived in an unfashionable part of Berlin, on the borderline between acceptable middle-class apartments and workers' tenements. She worked for a magazine, Manfred knew, but obviously she was not very well-paid.

They went into the kitchen to make coffee and lace it with brandy. Manfred noticed that one window had its roller-blind up and the other had it pulled three-quarters down. He looked out of the unscreened window to a narrow courtyard two floors below and, across that, the dark windows of the block opposite.

'It's only about two o'clock and everyone is in bed,' he said, 'you must have hardworking neighbours who need their sleep.'

He pulled the roller-blind down to shut out the unprepossessing view and would have pulled the part-closed one down too, but Vicki stopped him.

'Leave that one – it's my private peep-show.'

'What on earth can there be to look at out there?'

'I don't do the peeping – it's the man in the apartment across the yard.'

'Do you know him?'

'No, he's a little fat man, nearly bald. He started to make

102

a nuisance of himself the day I moved in. He was always at his window, leering and waving at me.'

Manfred sat on a corner of the kitchen-table and lit a cigarette.

'That seems a good reason to keep the blinds down,' he said.

'You don't understand – I'm teaching him a lesson.'

'How?'

'The idea came to me in a flash one morning after I'd been to a party. It was about seven when I got in and I came into the kitchen for a glass of water before I went to bed. And there he was, across the way, grinning and waving at me, the conceited pig. I pulled the blind down and it stuck like that, with a gap at the bottom. That was when the idea came to me. I stripped naked and moved about a bit close to the window. See what I mean? I'll show you.'

She slipped off her short evening frock and passed slowly in front of the window in her white silk stockings and high-heeled shoes. Her gingery-red tuft was at the right height to be seen below the partly-drawn blind.

'That must have cheered up his morning,' said Manfred, 'but what were you trying to achieve?'

'I suppose I wanted to make him feel bad by showing him something he'd never in his life get his hands on. Anyway, that's how it started. I turned round from time to time, to let him see my bottom, and then back to face the window so that he'd get a good eyeful. After a while I hid behind the wall and just peeped with one eye round the side of the blind to see if he was still there.'

'I'm sure he was. No bald little fat man would leave a show like that.'

'You're right. He'd opened his window to get a better view and he was holding a drying-up cloth in front of him with one hand. You can guess what he was doing with the other hand behind the cloth!'

She handed Manfred a cup of black coffee well-laced with brandy.

'Did that make you laugh or did it make you angry?' he asked.

'Neither. I thought to myself *Got you*! and I strolled about again in front of the blind till I thought he'd had long enough. Then I peeped round again.'

'And?'

'Then I laughed. He was slumped on his arms on the window-sill. His head was hanging down and he looked shattered, so I knew he'd done it.'

'I wonder what excuse he invented for being late at work that day?'

'That was only the beginning. Seven in the morning is no time for me to be giving free exhibitions, so I had to think of something else to keep the squeeze on him. He gets home from his work about six in the evening, when I'm getting ready to go out for the evening. So I started to put the same show on for him every evening as soon as I saw him in his apartment.'

'With the same result?'

'It never fails. The moment he spots my red fur-coat below the blind he's ready with his towel.'

'How long has this been going on?' Manfred asked in amusement.

'Nearly every day now for about three months. And I had another brain-wave. It was the time of the month when I couldn't give him his little thrill by showing myself off, so I bought the fanciest pair of knickers I could find – a bright red silk with lace and embroidery – the sort of thing you'd expect a French whore to wear. I put those out on the sill and watched from behind the other blind.'

'Did he take the bait?'

'He certainly did! I watched the whole performance from start to finish. His face got redder and redder as he played with himself behind the cloth and when he'd finished he slumped over with his bald spot pointing at me, just as if his whole body was a big pink thing going limp. That really made me laugh.'

'So what is the lesson you have taught him?' Manfred asked.

'He's still learning it. When he gets home in the evenings I give him a personal exhibition through the window below that blind. And before I go to bed, I put the fancy knickers out on the sill to get him going in the early morning before I'm awake.'

'The poor idiot must be a nervous wreck by now.'

Vicki smiled sweetly.

'I passed him in the street the other day – Sunday, it was. He looked terrible. He's lost weight and he's got dark rings round his eyes. When he recognised me coming towards him he turned away and crossed the road. So I think that he's learning his lesson.'

'Which is?'

'Not to get ideas above his station. No grubby little pig is going to think he can make eyes at *me*.'

Manfred put his cup down and pulled Vicki close enough to him to stroke the ginger tuft between her very slender thighs.

'And how long will you continue this lesson? Until he can't do it anymore?'

'Longer. He's still enjoying himself, even though it's wearing him out now it's twice a day. When he can't do it anymore, that's when the lesson will really sink in. He'll stand there at his window staring at my red-fox and his thing will be limp in his hand and useless. I'll be laughing and he'll be crying. Then he won't come to the window to stare at me and I'll have won.'

'Cruel girl! But leaving aside his dreadful manners, I can understand his fascination with this pretty thing,' said Manfred, stroking her ginger curls, 'as soon as I saw it at Ulrika's absurd party, I knew that I had to become better acquainted with you.'

'And your idea of getting better acquainted was to have me on my hands and knees on a marble slab.'

'Better than parrots in a cage,' he said, remembering her words, 'or is it? I don't know how parrots go about it.'

105

'I do. When I was a child my father kept a pair of parrots.'

The coffee with brandy had raised Manfred's spirits and the touch of her warm flesh was a delight.

'Tell me!'

'It's easier to show you than explain. Come into the bedroom and I'll demonstrate.'

Manfred picked her up. She was slender and weighed little. He kissed her breasts and carried her to the door.

'Which is the bed-room?'

'Second door on the right,' she said, her arms tightly round his neck. 'Wait a minute – I must put out my whore's knickers for the man opposite.'

'Give him a morning off,' said Manfred, 'you and I have more interesting games to play than that.'

Consequences

It was in early July, only a week or so after Ulrika's celebration, that Mitzi Genscher telephoned Manfred to say that she wanted to talk to him. His first thought was that she was between boyfriends and was offering to resume relations with him. The thought was not without a certain attraction – his recollections of their brief *engagement* was pleasurable enough. But he was involved with red-headed Vicki just then and her interest in the variations of sexual enjoyment was absorbing his time and energy.

'Meet me at the Café Schon for lunch,' he suggested.

'No, I want to talk to you about something very serious. I'll come to your apartment this afternoon.'

'Not this afternoon, I shall be out.'

'This evening then,' she persisted, 'it's very important.'

'I'm afraid that's not possible either.'

Nor was it. He had already arranged to pick up Vicki at seven to take her to dinner and dancing afterwards.

'Tomorrow then,' said Mitzi, 'ten o'clock in the morning.'

After a night with Vicki he expected to be sleeping most of the morning.

'Make it after lunch, Mitzi. Let's say three o'clock. What do you want to talk about?'

'I'll tell you when I see you.'

She rang off and Manfred put the telephone down. Her persistence puzzled him. Surely she could have taken the hint that he was not available and turned her attention to some other man. The answer could only be that she was

107

short of money for the rent and food. He didn't mind helping her with that, if it was an emergency. Of course, he thought, she would then show her gratitude in the only way she could. The prospect of an afternoon of Mitzi's gratitude was not unwelcome. Mitzi with her clothes off was a big blonde doll to play with. She offered her pink and white body to her partner's desires and thoroughly enjoyed whatever was done to her – it was that which had endeared her to him. The contrast between her warm, soft and slow yielding and Vicki's demanding temperament was very marked. Vicki's physical thinness belied her wiry energy and her inventiveness in bed was astonishing – as was her insatiability. There had been nights with her when Manfred felt much like her neighbour across the courtyard – wrung-out and still trying to respond long after his body told him that it needed rest.

That being so, perhaps it was time to stop seeing Vicki and slide for a while into a more restful arrangement with Mitzi. The more he thought about it, the more pleasing a prospect it became. He conjured up a vision in his memory of the last time he made love to Mitzi, the day he had bought her the fur-coat. After lunch he took her back to her apartment and the landlady, after one look at the red-fox Mitzi was wearing, addressed Manfred as *Baron* and insisted on serving tea and little cakes in Mitzi's room. The tea went cold on the table while Manfred and Mitzi made love on the bed, she naked but wearing her new fur-coat so that the fur rubbed against his skin and the silk lining against her own. It was a long and delightful afternoon and one well worth repeating.

With these thoughts in his mind, the evening with Vicki proved less enchanting than usual. They danced and drank until about two in the morning and when they got back to her apartment, his intention was not to stay too long – just long enough for honour to be satisfied. Vicki had thought of a new twist to her cruel little game with her neighbour. She wanted Manfred to stay until seven in the morning and then make love to her in the kitchen, close to the partly-drawn roller-blind, standing up and sideways on, so that the poor tormented man opposite would be incited to overstrain himself.

Manfred refused and told her he had no intention of performing in public.

'But it was public enough at Ulrika's party,' she said, 'it didn't bother you to make love to me on the marble slab with other people in the room.'

'That was different. That was for my pleasure and your pleasure. This wouldn't be. I'd never be able to do it for thinking of the man opposite staring at me the whole time.'

She grinned at him.

'I tell you what, I've got another idea. We'll stand by the blind naked when he comes to the window. He can only see a bit of you below the blind and you won't be able to see him at all. So there's no reason to be shy.'

'What then?' he asked cautiously.

'We'll just stand there, so that he sees my fox-fur and your lovely big tail, so that he knows someone else is getting what he can't get. And I'll play with you slowly – I'll make your tail stand up like a broom-stick handle and stroke it till you squirt all over my belly. That should really finish my peeping-tom off – with any luck he'll jump out of the window and break his bones.'

'Dear Vicki, what unnatural ideas you have!' he said, wondering if she could be entirely sane.

He gave her the hardest night of her life, deliberately holding back so that his energy would not be sapped, but making certain that she went all the way, time after time. He did it to her on her back, on her hands and knees, facedown and every other way that occurred to him, until her body was shiny with sweat and her red hair was plastered to her forehead and her face was thin and drawn with exhaustion. About five in the morning, with broad daylight coming in through the bed-room windows, she lay sprawled across the rumpled bed, only part-conscious. Manfred pulled her thin legs apart and spread himself over her.

'No, please,' she whispered, 'not again – I'm done for. Let me sleep.'

He thrust into her without mercy and rode her hard, ignoring her whimpering, and released his passion for the first and only time that night. When he rolled off her she lay with her eyes closed and did not move a muscle. He put his hand on her belly and her skin was cold to the touch. She was deeply unconscious.

Manfred dressed and left, determined to have no more to do with her. He was home and in bed before six and up and bathed and dressed in time for lunch. He thought it sensible to give the Geigers the afternoon off. If things worked out the way he expected with Mitzi, it would be inconvenient to have the servants in the apartment and he could take her out to dinner to show his gratitude for her gratitude.

At three the bell rang, he opened the door, and there was Mitzi and beside her stood her friend Ilse Kleiber. Manfred's heart sank at the sight of Mitzi's protruding belly under her thin summer frock. Nevertheless, he greeted the two women courteously and took them into his drawing-room. Mitzi and Ilse sat side by side on the zebra-skin sofa, gloved hands in their laps, looking at him silently from under their small summer hats.

'My dear Mitzi,' he began, 'I am not sure whether congratulations are in order or not.'

'Congratulations on what?' she said sulkily.

'On your happy condition.'

'Happy! Is that what you call it?' she said shrilly, 'What do you think this is – a cushion under my clothes?'

She was on her feet suddenly, her frock hoisted up to her bosom, to display her bulging belly under thin white knickers.

'Look what you've done to me!'

Frock held high with one hand, she pulled her knickers down with the other, right down until the patch of fair hair between her thighs, so that all of her pale-skinned and swollen belly was bared to his sight. Her obvious distress,

110

however theatrical its expression, moved Manfred to sympathy. He was off his chair and beside her in an instant, an arm round her shoulders to comfort her.

'Don't be upset, Mitzi – let us talk about this calmly.'

For some reason he did not try to explain to himself, his free hand was on her big belly, stroking it in a soothing manner. She turned her tear-stained face towards him.

'Sit down,' he suggested, 'we must discuss this. There are few problems which cannot be resolved with good will and good sense.'

'It was her good will and your lack of sense that put her in this state,' Ilse Kleiber observed acidly.

They sat down on the sofa, Ilse making room for them, and Mitzi huddled against him.

'How could this happen?' Manfred asked gently.

But it was Ilse who answered him.

'How? Have you forgotten? I'll tell you how it happened – she lay on her back and opened her legs and you got on top of her and . . .'

'You know what I mean,' Manfred interrupted.

'I don't know,' said Mitzi miserably, 'I've always been so careful. Oh Manfred, what am I going to do?'

She had dropped her frock when they sat down together but his hand was still under it, stroking the dome of her belly.

'My God!' Ilse exclaimed. 'What are you doing – trying to seduce her? Haven't you done enough damage already?'

'Shut up, Ilse!' said Mitzi. 'He has every right to stroke my belly if he wants to.'

'That's true,' said Ilse. 'After all, there's something of his inside it. The question is, what's he going to do about it, besides giving it a good feel?'

Mitzi's round and doll-like face turned to Manfred with a smile of complete trust.

'You will help me, won't you?'

The taut skin of her belly was smooth and warm and to stroke it was a pleasure that diverted Manfred's attention

111

from the immediate problem. His hand slid down below the curve to touch the curls between her legs.

'What do you think is the best thing to do?' he asked.

'Marry her,' said Ilse immediately.

'Impossible.'

'Isn't she good enough for you?' asked Ilse sharply. 'Girls like us are all right for a quick bang but not for the gentry to marry, is that it? It would have been a different story if you'd put your friend Nina in the family way when she was dropping her knickers for you.'

'You don't know what you're talking about,' Manfred replied angrily, 'Mitzi is married already. The question doesn't arise.'

'Manfred, please don't be angry with me. Ilse means well.'

Under her loose frock her legs had moved apart on the sofa and Manfred's hand was well between them, inside her half-off underwear. Her pale blue eyes stared at him fondly.

'That's nice,' she whispered. 'It's been so long since anyone touched me.'

'Why? Didn't you want to?'

'I've been so miserable and scared since I found out. But it's all right again with you.'

'Never mind all that now,' said Ilse, 'is he going to look after you?'

'Of course he is,' said Mitzi happily.

'He hasn't said so.'

'You'll need money,' said Manfred, 'you can rely on me for that.'

'That's all right then,' said Ilse, 'I'm her witness.'

'She doesn't need a witness. My word is sacrosanct. Did I treat you badly when you helped them play that joke on me, Mitzi?'

'You were very nice to me,' she murmured, quivering with emotion as his fingers caressed the soft lips between her legs.

Ilse sat with her legs crossed tightly, as if she were experiencing the same interesting sensations between her legs as Mitzi. Her pretty face was flushed a light pink.

'You're not thinking of trying to make love to her?' she exclaimed. 'Not in her condition – four months gone!'

'That's for Mitzi to decide.'

'But in front of me!' Ilse protested, her voice jerky with emotion.

'You can wait outside.'

'But I'm her witness!'

'Then be a witness.'

'Manfred, I'm dying for it,' said Mitzi.

She pushed her white knickers down her legs and kicked them away.

'Move out of the way, Ilse,' she said quickly, 'go for a walk or something.'

No sooner was Ilse off the sofa than Mitzi spread herself along it, her back to Manfred and her frock pulled up again to her arm-pits. He understood at once and lay on his side behind her, to undo his trouser-buttons and let his hard stem emerge. Mitzi pulled her knees up towards her domed belly, a little manoeuvring found the right angle and Manfred pushed slowly into her until his belly was pressed firmly to her bottom.

'Oh yes,' she breathed, 'that's wonderful!'

He reached over her to clasp a breast while he thrust slowly and carefully with his loins. Behind him somewhere he heard Ilse gasping and fidgeting, then his attention was captured by the waves of pleasure that spread through him from his probing stem. Mitzi sighed and gurgled happily, evidently making up for lost time, but he kept himself on a tight rein so as not to discommode her in any way. His remembrance of Mitzi was that she responded very quickly and enjoyed two or three crises to his one. But that was all changed, he found, either by her physical condition or her mental state, and it was a long time before she shuddered and cried out in release. By then Manfred was clinging to his last remnant of self-control by his finger-nails almost and with a gasp of relief he jabbed quickly and discharged his passion quickly.

When he disengaged himself from her and rolled on to his back, Mitzi stayed curled up, her sighs of content almost those of the regular and slow breathing of a sleeper. It was obvious that his promise and his actions had removed a great nervous tension and she was at last resting easily.

Manfred turned his head to look for Ilse. She was sitting in an arm-chair and her skirt was pulled up high enough to show her bare thighs above her stockings. Her hand was down the front of her blue knickers and was moving busily. She caught Manfred's eye and stared glassily at him, her mouth hanging open.

'Yes, Ilse,' he said, 'do it!'

She tried to say something, but the words were blurred.

'I want to see you do it,' said Manfred, 'show me!'

Her free hand dragged her knickers down below her knees, her legs spread wider, and he saw the little patch of light brown hair between her thighs. With two joined fingers she was rubbing quickly between the parted folds of flesh there. He glanced up to her flushed face and her bulging eyes, then down again to her fluttering fingers.

'Yes, Ilse,' he said firmly. 'Yes, yes, yes! Do it for me!'

Her body convulsed in the chair, lifting her bottom off the seat as she uttered a wailing cry of garbled words and sobs. Slowly it faded to silence and stillness.

'You devil!' she said, staring at him, 'I don't know what it is, but seeing you with Mitzi gets me going every time.'

'Every time? But this is the first time you've ever seen me with her.'

'The first time I've actually seen you do it to her, maybe, but there was that time you were in her room – when Rosa and I were there.'

'What of it? You both left before anything happened.'

'Mitzi told us how you'd made her dance naked with you and I made a joke about fiancés having their rights.'

'I don't remember that.'

'You wouldn't – your only thought was to get Rosa and me out of the room so that you could make love to Mitzi.'

'It wasn't like that at all – you're romanticising the situation. I wanted to talk to her about the silly engagement business.'

'That's what you say now, but we were hardly out of the room before you had her clothes off and were at it. You can't deny that!'

'She told you that?'

'She didn't have to. My room is next to hers. I could hear her moaning and crying out through the wall. And it wasn't just once!'

'Dear Ilse,' said Manfred, grinning at her, 'you must have heard similar sounds through the wall many times when Mitzi was entertaining her men friends.'

'Plenty of times, but it never bothered me before. It was different that time. I couldn't get out of my mind the thought of you on top of her, bumping away. It drove me so frantic that I had to do what you've just seen me do. I know I shouldn't be telling you this – it will make you big-headed. You did it to her three times that evening and I had to play with myself three times to stop myself going crazy. I was a wreck the next day.'

'Ilse – I am amazed to think that I could possibly have such an effect on any woman, least of all a clever and experienced one like you.'

'Well, now you know. You must think I'm an idiot, especially after catching me at it this time.'

'Not at all. It was enchanting to watch you – and very exciting. Come here.'

Ilse was off the chair at once but, hobbled by her knickers below her knees, tripped and almost fell in her haste. She kicked her shoes off and trampled the blue underwear over her feet and was on her knees beside him. Her hands snatched at his shirt-front and underpants to bare him from chest to groins so that she could kiss his hot belly again and again. Her hand held his risen stem in a tight grasp and she mumbled words of endearment, almost to herself.

Manfred reached down over the edge of the zebra-skin sofa to feel between her legs and slide his fingers into her slippery depths.

'I can never resist a wet one,' he murmured.

Ilse shook and kissed his stem as if it were an object of adoration, her clenched hand moving up and down it in a frantic rhythm and, in response to her stimulation, his fingers rubbed faster in her moistness and he too was gasping as violently as she was and it was far too late to consider a change of position. Manfred's belly contracted and he spouted ecstatically into Ilse's sucking mouth. She gurgled and shuddered wildly, thrusting herself hard against his embedded fingers.

Mitzi stirred herself and rolled over carefully to face them. Ilse's head lay on Manfred's belly and his hand, removed from beneath her skirt now, rested on the back of her neck.

'I wasn't asleep you know,' said Mitzi, 'I was only resting. I knew what you were doing, but I don't mind. I know you've been hot for Manfred since the day you met him.'

'He knows that now,' Ilse answered dreamily, her tongue tickling inside his belly-button.

'You were good enough to tell me that you entertained a certain attachment for me,' said Manfred, who felt very pleased with himself, 'and however surprising I found that at first, your demonstration of affection has convinced me.'

'You devil!' said Ilse fondly.

'Isn't he wonderful!' said Mitzi proudly.

'Dear ladies, our expressions of mutual affection have resulted in a degree of disorder on so hot an afternoon. I suggest that we go to the bath-room and repair the ravages of love.'

They crowded naked together in the shower cubicle and let the warm water splash over them to take away the perspiration from their bodies. Manfred soaped his hands and began to wash Mitzi. She raised her arms and he saw that she had let the hair grow in her armpits and it was the

116

same blonde floss as between her legs. He washed her breasts, unable to make up his mind whether they were bigger now than four months ago or whether the pink buds were getting darker in colour. He washed over her bulging belly with great care and down between her smooth thighs. Ilse, meanwhile, was scrubbing Mitzi's back vigorously, especially the round cheeks of her bottom.

'Don't get me wrong,' she said, 'but I've sometimes wondered what it's like to be a man and make love to a woman. Have you, Mitzi?'

'That's a strange idea!' said Mitzi with a giggle, 'I'm happy with things as they are.'

'You've wondered but you've never tried it?' Manfred asked, smiling at Ilse over Mitzi's wet shoulder.

'Not really. I had a friend at school who was that way inclined and sometimes we'd kiss and feel each other a bit. You know – schoolgirl stuff. Once or twice she went all the way when I had my hand in her knickers, but I never did when she played with me. Then I met a boy who couldn't keep his hands off me and before I knew it I was opening my legs for him.'

'And you've had them open ever since,' said Mitzi.

'Look who's talking,' Ilse retorted, good-naturedly. 'What I meant was not just playing about with another girl but being a man and having a great pink thing to stick in her. How does it feel, Manfred? You're the only one here who knows.'

'It feels very nice, but I don't suppose it's any nicer than being a girl and having a little slot to receive it.'

'But it must feel different, and that's what interests me.'

'I am not at all sure how your curiosity can be satisfied, Ilse, but I'll give the matter some thought,' he said with a grin.

When it was Ilse's turn to be washed she stood with her back to Manfred and leaned her wet body against him. He reached round to soap and stroke her breasts, smaller than Mitzi's and already a little slack, young as she was. By slow stages he worked his way down to her flat belly.

'Lower down,' she breathed.

He teased her by lathering her tuft and just above it.

'Lower!' she repeated.

Mitzi was smiling at her friend's eagerness. She put her own hand between Ilse's spread thighs and winked at Manfred.

'You want to know what it's like to be a man,' she said, 'but have you wondered what it's like to be made love to by another woman?'

'I want Manfred's hand there, not yours.'

'Close your eyes and see if you can tell the difference,' Manfred suggested.

'Stop it, you slut!' said Ilse, wriggling to get away from Mitzi's hand. Manfred tightened his hold, pinning her arms to her body and Mitzi grinned and took advantage of Ilse's predicament.

'Mitzi – I know why you're doing this,' she exclaimed, 'it's because of what I did to Manfred after he'd made love to you. But you said you didn't mind.'

'That's right. So why should you mind what I'm doing to you?'

'Mitzi, leave off! You'll make me do it!'

'Which is more than your school friend ever did.'

'What will Manfred think of us?'

'That you are an adorable pair of sluts,' he said, kissing her wet ear.

At that her protests stopped. Her wet body relaxed against him and in a short time Mitzi's attentions brought her to the critical moments and she cried out in pleasurable release. Manfred stroked her belly lightly to soothe her and soon she was herself again.

'You devils – both of you!' she declared, 'I'll pay you back for that when I get the chance.'

The two of them washed Manfred with great attention and thoroughness. For him it was pure delight to stand beneath the cascading water and feel four hands moving over his body, touching, stroking, rubbing. His stem stood rigidly to attention, making the women laugh at the sight.

118

They covered it with scented soap-suds and washed the suds off, but they were very careful not to precipitate a crisis.

They dried each other and moved into the main bedroom. Manfred lay with an arm round each of them, feeling like an Oriental despot in his harem. The afternoon had turned out very much better than he feared when he first opened the door and observed Mitzi's condition. The moment seemed right now that both women had softened towards him to tell them what was in his mind. Each hand cupped round a warm breast, he began.

'Now, my dears, we must discuss the situation in which Mitzi finds herself. I have already promised that she can look to me for help, but there are things we should all understand.'

'What things?' Mitzi asked.

'The truth of the matter is this, Mitzi – there is no certainty that it is I who am responsible for your condition.'

Both women would have sat up to protest, but his firm grip on them held them close to him while he continued.

'We shall examine the facts, my darlings. When I met you at my birthday party, you were with Werner Schiele. I find it impossible to believe that he had not availed himself of your good-nature. Indeed, you told me that you had been with him for some time when we had lunch together after we went shopping. I made love to you for two days, no more. After that I am sure that you found someone else quickly enough. After all, you are a very attractive woman.'

'What are you saying?' Mitzi asked timorously.

He squeezed the breast he was holding affectionately.

'I am saying that there is only a one in three chance that I am responsible. Isn't that so?'

'I'm sure it was you, Manfred. Women know these things.'

'Easy enough to say, dear Mitzi, but you cannot be sure either. What is happening in your belly may just as well be Werner's doing as mine, or the man after me. Who was he?'

119

'Dieter Bruckner. He was at your party.'

'Of course, he saw you dancing naked with me – that would certainly interest him. Does he know about the problem?'

'He threw her out weeks ago when he found out,' said Ilse. 'He's a pig.'

'And Werner, have you told him?'

'He's vanished and I can't find him.'

'That only leaves you,' said Ilse, trying to take over the negotiations again. 'You can see why we had to come here.'

'I'm not blaming you. But I don't want you to think that I'm a complete fool.'

'I was desperate,' said Mitzi. 'Please forgive me.'

'Werner Schiele is in hiding,' said Manfred, 'and I can guess where.'

'Who is he hiding from – the police?'

'He thinks he's going to be murdered by an outraged husband, but it was only a joke, I'm sure he's in Vienna. I'll be able to get hold of him through friends. I'll offer to make peace for him with Nina's husband if he'll give you a decent amount of money. He'll be miserable away from Berlin, so there's every chance he'll agree.'

'And Dieter?' Ilse asked.

'Leave him to me. I've known him long enough to be able to squeeze something out of him. There are certain private activities he keeps very quiet about in case his father finds out. So there you are – three possible fathers, three contributors towards your maintenance.'

'Oh, Manfred! What can I say,' Mitzi murmured.

'You're cleverer than I thought,' Ilse added.

'Then that's settled, dear ladies.'

'We're not ladies,' said Ilse, 'we're sluts – that's what you said.'

'Adorable sluts,' he corrected her.

She put her hand on his thigh and stroked slowly upwards.

'Being treated like a slut is more enjoyable than being treated like a lady,' she said, 'at least, I think so.'

'Why, how do you imagine ladies like to be treated?'

'How do I know? They always look so elegant that it's hard to imagine them without their clothes on. I mean – what grand lady would finger me in the shower the way Mitzi did?'

'My cousin Ulrika would take great pleasure in doing that to you while I held you fast.'

'She must be the exception to the rule then. You'd never get a grand lady to do what I did to you on the sofa. I'm sure that if one of them ever touched this thing of yours she'd keep her gloves on. And as for kissing it – never!'

'Dear Ilse, how wrong you are. This thing of mine, as you call it, has had the pleasure of being kissed very thoroughly by several Baronesses.'

'Did they know what to do?' she asked incredulously.

'The grand ladies you think so highly of behave exactly as you do when their clothes are off, I assure you.'

'Do you hear that, Mitzi? What do you think – you've been taken to parties where grand people go – do they carry on the way Manfred says?'

'All I know about ladies is that they go out with no knickers on.'

'No, they don't!' said Ilse, 'What a ridiculous idea! They wear expensive knickers made of silk with lace and embroidery. I've seen them in the shops.'

'The young ladies I have the honour of knowing wear no underwear,' Manfred informed her, highly amused by the conversation, 'it went out of fashion years ago.'

'Dirty little whores!' Ilse exclaimed. 'So who wears the fancy knickers in the shops?'

'Adorable little sluts like you, of course. I'll buy you half a dozen pairs each.'

'They won't fit me,' said Mitzi ruefully, but Ilse was much captivated by the suggestion and stroked his hard stem in gratitude.

'Will you watch me try them on?'

'I doubt if any of the shops would permit that.'

'I suppose not. But at least you'll help me choose them –

121

then I shall know what colours you like best. And afterwards you can have a private exhibition, just like you did with Mitzi in her fur-coat.'

'I didn't say I didn't want them,' said Mitzi, 'I only said they won't fit me just now. But in a few months' time they will.'

By then Ilse's attention was focussed on what she held and its possibilities.

'What *is* it like to be a man and make love to a woman with this?' she asked softly. 'Can't you explain it to me at all?'

'There's no way of describing sensations in words. But I have an idea that may help you to understand,' he said, greatly excited by her fondling.

He pulled Ilse on top of him and parted his legs so that hers were between his.

'I don't mind being on top,' she said, 'but it doesn't answer my question. I've made love like this before, you know.'

'This time will be different.'

He put his hands down between their bellies to open her and guide his stem into her.

'Raise yourself on your arms, Ilse.'

She put her hands on the bed and lifted her upper body clear of him, and only their loins were pressed together.

'Now, close your eyes and don't move,' he murmured, 'this is the time for your imagination to take over. Imagine that you're a man and that you're lying on top of a woman. You are Manfred and you're going to make love to Ilse with that strong thing you've pushed inside me. I'm Ilse lying under you and my legs are open for you and I can feel your stem inside me.'

'Ah,' she whispered, her hot belly wriggling on his.

'Bend your neck and look down between us to where we are joined – don't look anywhere else at all, just there.'

She did as he said, dropping her head before she opened her eyes. He too stared down the length of his body. Where their bellies met there were two patches of very light-brown

122

hair, his and hers, not much different in shade, linked by the short section of his column that was now inside her.

'Keep looking at that,' he said very quietly, 'you can see how your stem is going into me.'

'Oh yes!' she moaned.

'Make love to me with it – I want you to.'

Her loins began to thrust against him in short hard stabs.

'I can see it going into you!' she gasped, 'I'm making love to you, Ilse! Can you feel me inside you?'

'Yes, yes! It's so long and thick and hard – do it to me, Manfred!' he moaned, 'I want all of you in me – all of you!'

She slammed herself harder and faster against him, groaning with pleasure.

'I'm going to do it!' she shrieked, 'I'm going to fill you full!'

The crisis swept through them both at the same instant. Ilse cried out again and again as she pounded against him and he cried out with her in his pleasure and for seconds that seemed an eternity they lost their identities and neither knew which was doing it to the other.

At long last Ilse's arms gave way and she collapsed on to him and lay panting. Manfred put his arms round her and held her close.

'My God – you nearly had me off the bed with your jolting,' said Mitzi, forgotten beside them.

But neither paid any attention to her. Ilse was kissing Manfred's face and he was stroking the cheeks of her bottom to soothe and calm her.

'You're utterly fantastic,' she said, 'you really made me believe that I was making love to you! I could see myself sliding into you.'

'And is your question answered now?'

'In a way, but . . .'

Her words trailed off.

'There's no pleasing you!' said Mitzi sharply, 'He's done his best for you, so be content with that. If God had wanted you to be a man He wouldn't have given you a slit between your legs. Not that it matters, but the telephone is ringing.'

'Let it ring,' said Manfred, 'we're not at home to anyone.'

'It might be important. Get off him, Ilse, and let him answer the telephone.'

Manfred recognised the signs of jealousy and eased Ilse off.

'There is something far more important at this moment then answering casual telephone calls,' he said, 'come here in the middle, Mitzi, so that your two very good friends can put their arms round you and cuddle you.'

'Cuddle me! A lot of good that will do me now she's drained you dry with her silly curiosity.'

All the same, she clambered awkwardly over Manfred and lay in the middle.

'Mitzi is feeling left out of things,' he said, stroking her breasts lightly, 'She is passing through a difficult time in her life and she needs all the love and comfort her friends can give her.'

'Poor Mitzi,' said Ilse, stroking her friend's domed belly, 'I know you've got your troubles, but you have to be brave. We'll look after you, you know that. And Frau Brubecker will let you keep your room now you've got the money to pay her. So there's nothing to worry about.'

'Yes, there is!' said Mitzi, sounding as if she was about to break into tears, 'I can't make love properly any more and seeing you doing it made me realise what I was missing.'

'Only for a few months,' Ilse comforted her, 'then you'll be at it twice a night again, just like before.'

'And look what I got for it!' Mitzi complained.

Manfred put his hand between her legs and tickled her.

'That afternoon when you and I made love on the fur-coat was one of the nicest of my life,' he told her.'

'Was it?' she asked doubtfully. 'After what you said about Baronesses kissing you all over I wouldn't think that making love to me was anything special for you.'

'But you're wrong. We really liked each other, you and I, and that made all the difference. You know yourself how much better it is to make love with a man you like a lot

124

than one you like a little. The physical sensations may be the same, but the satisfaction is on another level entirely.

'It was nice with you every time, even when it was only for a joke,' she answered, mollified by his words and by his touch between her legs.

Manfred nodded to Ilse, who understood his intention and slid her hand up to Mitzi's breasts to caress them softly.

'That damned telephone is ringing again,' said Mitzi with a sigh.

'A wrong number,' Manfred assured her, his finger-tip finding her secret bud, 'pay no attention to it and it will soon stop.'

Ilse's thumbs were flicking over Mitzi's nipples, teasing them to firmness.

'It's your bell that's going to ring,' said Manfred.

The Twins

Manfred's elder brother rarely visited Berlin and even more rarely brought his wife with him when he did. This relieved Manfred of the decent dullness such a visit would otherwise have entailed. On this visit they dined with the Behrendorfs one evening, as Sigmund liked Gottfried and generally invited him to stay with him in the country for the shooting. Nina played the hostess impeccably and by all impressions had been forgiven for the unfortunate incident at Ulrika's celebration. Needless to say, there was no mention of it at all. There were two other married couples present, not very interesting people in Manfred's opinion, and Nina's unmarried sister and a widowed sister of Gottfried's, to even up the numbers.

On another day they visited cousin Ulrika for five o'clock tea. She wore a pretty afternoon frock and looked remarkably demure, though she offended Gottfried once or twice by the frankness of her conversation. Manfred took Sigmund to see Oskar's production of *Three in a Bed* and that went down well enough. And on the last night of Sigmund's stay, Manfred took him to the White Mouse cabaret after dinner.

It was expensive, hot and crowded, the main attraction being its nude dancers. For himself Manfred did not find it stimulating to watch a young woman wearing only red shoes twirl about a stage, but Sigmund did. For most of the time he was cut off from entertainment of that kind, his only diversions being field sports with horses, guns and dogs, the charms of his placid wife, and whatever he could arrange in the way of discreet adultery with his neighbours' wives. For this reason, Manfred considered, it was necessary to make allowances for Sigmund when he came to Berlin and let him indulge himself.

The nude dancer twirled as gracefully as she could, her breasts rolling about to her gyrations, and she must have made a marked impression on Sigmund for, when two women of the house sat down uninvited at the table, he made them welcome and ordered another bottle of champagne at once.

The *hostesses* were pretty enough in their way, but Manfred felt no urgent desire to pay for their services. With Sigmund it was otherwise. He took a liking to the fair-haired one, chatted to her confidentially and kept filling her glass. In short, he gave every indication of wishing to make her closer acquaintance. Manfred was not surprised in the least when, after a whispered conversation with her, Sigmund turned to ask him a question.

'This young lady has graciously invited me to her apartment,' he confided, 'What do you think – is it safe to go with her?'

'She won't rob you or let her pimp murder you, Sigmund, if that's what you mean. And if you ask to see her police book, you'll know when she had her last medical inspection.'

Sigmund had by then had a fair amount to drink and brushed aside such unromantic considerations.

'Then if you have no objections, little brother, I'll be off and leave you with the other young lady.'

And off he swaggered, the blonde on his arm, leaving Manfred to pay the bill. It was not much after eleven, according to Manfred's wrist-watch, but the evening was over. Sigmund had found what he wanted and Manfred was left with half a bottle of champagne and a young woman in a tight green frock. She obviously expected him to follow his brother's lead and her hand was on his thigh to encourage him.

'Not tonight, my dear. I'm tired and I'm going home.'

127

'It's your loss. You'd soon be frisky if you came with me.'

'Some other time perhaps.

But however good his intentions were, fate had ordained that he would not sleep in his own bed that night. As he left the White Mouse he collided by accident with a girl in a little wrap and her hand-bag was knocked from her hand and spilled its contents on the ground.

'A thousand pardons, Fraulein. That was very clumsy of me.'

He squatted on his haunches to help her retrieve the multiplicity of small objects -- a lipstick in a silver case, a powder compact that had burst open and scattered its powder widely, keys, rouge, a folded bundle of bank-notes, a tiny lace handkerchief and all the other paraphernalia that women carry. As she squatted beside him, Manfred saw her legs and was impressed. Her skirt had ridden up to show slender and shapely thighs in gossamer thin silk stockings. He looked at her face and found that she was very pretty and not more than about eighteen. She had a small mouth painted scarlet, eyebrows plucked to a thin arch over large blue eyes, a soft little chin – and her hair was straw-blonde and arranged in a profusion of tiny curls.

He helped her to her feet.

'May I find you a taxi?'

'Thank you, yes. I'm not going far but I'm nervous about being alone on the streets at this time of night.'

'Naturally – one reads such dreadful things in the newspapers.'

His words were from politeness only. Young women who strolled the streets at night were not usually nervous.

'I have my car here,' he said, intrigued by the girl, 'may I have the pleasure of driving you home?'

She hesitated at that and looked him over very carefully before committing herself. She must have liked what she saw, because she accepted his offer. Manfred took her arm and walked her to where he had parked, introducing himself as they went. She told him that her name was Tania

Kessler and, without being asked, explained how she came to be alone outside the cabaret. She had been there with a friend, had quarrelled with him and walked out.

As they drove off Manfred turned his charm on her, in the hope that the evening would not be such a fiasco as he had thought.

'This friend – he let you go off on your own? He must be a fool to let so beautiful a young lady walk away from him.'

'I told him I never wanted to see him again. But what about you – why were you in there? Were you looking for a woman?'

Manfred told her about his brother's visit and how he had been deserted.

'How disappointing,' she said cheerfully. 'What do you suppose your brother is doing now?'

'I can guess exactly what he is doing but I would not dare to describe it to you.'

'Do you think I'm a virgin?' she teased him. 'Tell me – what is your brother doing at this moment?'

The conversation had taken a turn which Manfred found promising.

'By now he is in bed with the woman he left with.'

'And?'

'He's not very imaginative. He'll be sprawled on her, thumping away. Unless she has shown him another possibility, of course.'

'Are you imaginative?'

Her hand touched his on the steering-wheel and he knew that the night was not over by a long way.

'I try to approach these matters in a spirit of adventure, Fraulein Tania. There is much more to making love than my brother will ever know.'

'How true that is,' she sighed. 'Do you find me attractive, Manfred?'

'You know that I do. Are you going to invite me in?'

'Wait and see.'

He parked the car outside her apartment building and

assisted her out. Standing there in the street he put his arms about her and kissed her. Her perfume was exciting and her little red mouth was soft under his. Her responsiveness emboldened him to slip a hand under her wrap and lightly clasp a small breast through the thin silk of her frock.

'Are you sure you want to come in with me?' she asked somewhat archly.

'Can there be any doubt?'

She led him up to an apartment on the second floor. The lights were out and she did not switch them on, but Manfred was able to make out that the apartment was well decorated and furnished. Either her family was well-to-do or, more probably, the friend with whom she had quarrelled had been keeping her in good style. Once in her bed-room, she switched on a bed-side lamp which cast a warm and dim glow through the room, discarded her wrap and invited him to sit beside her on a pink chaise-longue which stood by the wall opposite the bed.

Manfred kissed her at length and would have caressed her breasts again, but she stopped him and became coquettish.

'I invited you into my apartment. I didn't invite you to make love to me.'

'As far as it goes, what you say is perfectly true. But there is an unspoken understanding when a pretty girl asks a man to her bed-room late at night. A virgin might not know that – she might think that he was with her to discuss poetry or politics or Patagonia. But as you were so good as to inform me that you are not a virgin, I can only conclude that you are familiar with the conventions of meetings of this sort, young as you are.'

Tania giggled and put her hand on his thigh. It was a long and narrow hand with finger-nails lacquered scarlet to match her lipstick.

'You have a persuasive tongue,' she said. 'Before I know what's happening I'll find myself beneath you and you thumping away like your brother with his whore. That's not my idea of making love.'

130

'I'm pleased to hear it. You must tell me what pleases you.'

Her long fingers unbuttoned his trousers slowly.

'I like to know what I'm being offered before I accept it.'

'Dear Tania, you make me feel like a fruit on a market-stall being squeezed by a housewife before she buys it,' he said, enjoying the touch of her hand on his upright stem.

She put the tip of her tongue in his ear and then whispered to him.

'It's so big and hot! I'm afraid it's going to explode in my hand.'

'Not in your hand – not until we find a cosier place for it than that.'

'You promise?'

Her fingers played with him very skilfully. Her pretty face had a most serious expression on it as she observed what she was doing to him and the tip of her wet tongue played over her top lip. Manfred put his hand on her thigh, under her frock and moved it upwards, over the fine silk of her stocking and to the warm flesh above the stocking-top, where a suspender gripped. His fingers touched the lace edge of loose-legged knickers and he remembered what he had told Ilse about women who wore underwear like that. .

Tania's legs parted for him and he felt higher, seeking her furry mound, only to encounter another and very tight-fitting garment inside her knickers. This puzzled him and he reached higher still until his hand closed on a long and hard bulge held firmly against her belly by what felt like a silk cache-sexe.

Instantly he wrenched his hand away and jerked Tania's skirt up to her waist with one hand while, with the other, he ripped down her underwear. He stared in disbelief at what he had exposed – a thin and hard stem rising from between her thighs! Tania was unmistakably a young man.

'Damn it to hell!' Manfred roared. 'What the devil do you think you're playing at!'

His outrage was such that he swung his arm at the creature's blonde-curled head and knocked him from the chaise-
longue to the carpet.

'Of all the dirty, disgusting, swinish tricks!' he shouted,
up on his feet in blind fury, 'I'll kill you!'

The boy who pretended to be a girl had landed face-
down and was covering his head with his arms to protect
it. Manfred, who hardly knew what he was doing, kicked
him in the side.

'Horrible little pervert!'

'Don't hurt me,' the boy whimpered.

He scrambled up on his hands and knees to escape and
squealed loudly when Manfred landed a hearty kick on his
bottom. How long the violence would have continued
before Manfred regained control of himself, who can say?
Fortunately for the victim, the door opened so fast that it
slammed against the wall and a figure in pink silk pyjamas
rushed in.

'For God's sake leave him alone! You'll kill him!'

'Yes I will!' Manfred shouted back. 'He led me on, the
little swine! I thought he was a girl!'

He rolled *Tania* over roughly with his foot while fending
Silk Pyjamas off with one arm. Tania's frock was up round
his waist and the ruins of his torn underwear hung round
his slender thighs. There stood the unambiguous emblem
of his masculinity, rising from hairless groins.

'Filthy little pig!' Manfred snarled. 'Is that a girl? I ask
you!'

'Come away,' Silk Pyjamas shrilled. 'Leave him alone.'

Manfred's anger was waning. He let himself be hustled
out of the room, and into another bed-room across the
passage, grumbling as he went.

'Sit there,' said Silk Pyjamas, pointing to a chair, 'I'll get
you a drink while you calm down.'

'Who are you?' he growled.

'I'm Ludwig's sister. You can't really have thought he
was a girl – he usually brings his own kind home. Where
did you meet him – in the Eldorado Bar?'

'Certainly not! I don't go to places like that where the men all dress up as women. He was in the *White Mouse*.'

'Albert must have taken him there as a joke. But are you sure you thought he was a girl? I mean, some men are not very honest about their amusements. They do one thing and pretend another.'

'He had breasts! I touched them.'

'You're easily fooled. They're made of soft rubber.'

Manfred took the class of brandy he was offered and thought things over. Now that his anger had dissipated the whole episode seemed ridiculous.

'You're right – I'm a complete idiot. He took me in completely. He's as pretty as any girl and the make-up was perfect. You're his sister, you said?'

'We're twins. I'm Helga and he's Ludwig, but he calls himself Tania when he dresses up as a girl.'

Manfred surveyed his companion carefully. The same size and shape as the other one, the same pale blonde hair, though straight instead of curled.

'You look remarkably alike. Please accept my apologies for disturbing you. I hope I haven't hurt him too badly.'

'There's no need for apologies. This is not the first time I've had to rescue him. Some of the men he brings home are very dangerous.'

'It must be difficult to have a brother like that.'

'He's a nice person really, and very intelligent. But when he goes out dressed as Tania, anything can happen. What's your name?'

'Manfred von Klausenberg.'

'I seem to know a lot about you, Manfred, even though we've just met.'

'Really? What do you know about me?'

'I know that you prefer girls to boys, that you like brandy, that you can afford very elegant evening clothes – and that you've got a fine-looking tail. That's four things already.'

Manfred glanced down at her words and saw that his trousers were still undone, as Ludwig had left them, and

133

that his limp *tail* was hanging out. He hurriedly made himself decent and apologised. Helga laughed and she sounded so much like *Tania* that a suspicion entered his mind.

'You say that you are Ludwig's sister?'

'His twin sister.'

'How do I know that you're not his twin brother? I've been deceived once tonight.'

Helga laughed and she sounded even more like Tania. She ran her hands downwards over her silk pyjama jacket to outline her small breasts.

'Now do you believe me?'

'They might be rubber, for all I know.'

'They might be, but they're not,' and she unbuttoned her jacket and let it hang loosely open so that he could see her small and pointed breasts.

'Now do you believe me?'

'They might be artificial ones, stuck on. How do I know?'

She stood up from the bed and untied the cord of her pyjama trousers so that they slipped down her legs and he saw her light-brown tuft and no sign of anything that should not be there.

'Well?' she asked.

'You're his sister.'

'I'm glad we've got that settled,' said Helga, running her fingers through the curls she had revealed. 'You came here expecting to find one of these and you found one like your own instead. What a disappointment for you.'

'It was the worst shock I've ever had in my life, I assure you.'

'Would it be cruel to send you home disappointed now that you know that the real thing is available, I wonder?'

Manfred needed no further invitation. He discarded his jacket and sat on the bed with her, to kiss her and fondle her breasts inside her open pyjamas. They were authentic, no question about that.

'You look so much like each other,' he said, 'it's unnerving.'

'That's because he dresses and makes himself up to look like me. I'm the genuine one and he's the fake.'

There was a bump somewhere in the apartment.

'Is he all right?' Manfred asked. 'I only kicked his backside a few times.'

'Don't worry about him,' she said, pulling his hand down between her thighs, 'he likes to be beaten up. It's part of his fantasy of being a girl.'

'Surely not!'

'You wouldn't believe half of it if I told you.'

'Try me.'

'There was one night when Albert was staying with me and we were in the middle of you know what when we heard screams from Ludwig's room. I knew what it was and ran in to save him and there was this man punching him all round the room. He wasn't trying to knock him down, just hurt him. Some of them are like that – they get their thrill from beating each other or being beaten.'

'Surely this person had been given a nasty shock, as I was, and was retaliating in the same way,' said Manfred, stroking between her legs.

'It wasn't like that. They were both stark naked and they'd done it already. And while Ludwig went reeling round the room, with this man hitting him, his pecker jerked up again with every punch, till it stuck out like a handle. Every time a punch landed on him it jerked up in the air – you've never seen anything like it!'

'Incredible,' said Manfred, his fingers stirring inside Helga's warm and authentic affair.

'The fists landed on his face and body with a great slapping noise and his sticker jumped every time as if it were on a string – smack, jump, smack, jump, just like that. I grabbed the man round the waist from behind to try to stop him but he was too strong for me. He gave Ludwig a punch in the belly that doubled him over and brought him to his knees – and would you believe it – he squibbed off, halfway across the room! There was I, without a stitch on, hanging on to this gorilla to stop him hitting Ludwig – and

135

there was dear Ludwig down on his knees enjoying the thrill! Then Albert came in, having wasted all this time getting into his trousers, and he threw the man out and his clothes after him. Ah, Manfred!'

She writhed and shook and Manfred wondered how much of her sudden ecstasy was due to his fondling and how much to the story she had told him. It was clear that there was a most unusual rivalry between Helga and her twin brother and he guessed that being invited into her bed was some form of revenge on Ludwig.

When she was quiet again, he undressed and got into bed with her. Her arms closed round him, she rubbed her slender young body against his, and they embarked on a memorable night of love-making. Her climaxes came easily and she gave him little pause between them before her hands were playing with him again to rouse him to renew his attentions to her. It was only when his soldier refused to stand to attention again that she at last reluctantly let him go to sleep, her arms tightly round him as if she feared he might run away. He woke in the morning to the pleasant sensation of her hand stroking his refreshed soldier, now ready to do his duty again and this time Helga lay on top of him and did all the work, as if she were greedy for whatever affection she believed he was offering her.

Later on, they were in the kitchen, drinking coffee, when Ludwig put in an appearance. He was wearing trousers and a pullover and seemed no worse the wear for what had happened. Nor was he in the least embarrassed to find Manfred at the table with Helga, his evening jacket over the back of his chair.

'You're still here,' Ludwig said, smiling pleasantly. 'Did you sleep well?'

'Well, but not long.'

It was after ten o'clock and neither of the twins appeared to be in any hurry to go anywhere. Manfred sat and talked and listened and learned. They were runaways, as he had guessed, and had come to Berlin less than a year before from an unhappy home in Magdeburg. What they lived on was not explained to him and he did not ask. Whatever it was, it enabled them to live well, for by daylight Manfred saw that the apartment was a good one and well-furnished.

Ludwig proved to be an interesting conversationalist. He made no reference to the antics of the previous night, but talked sensibly and was obviously a well-educated young man. As for Helga, Manfred liked her. She was very pretty, well-spoken and, as he had ascertained, accomplished in bed. She gave every impression of liking Manfred, but whether that was to irk her brother was impossible to say on such short acquaintance. The resemblance between the twins was remarkable when the two sat side by side – the same pretty face, the same eyes, the same build. Their hair was the same shade of straw, though Helga's was straight and Ludwig had his in little curls – the result of long and frequent labours with curlers and hot irons, no doubt. And there was one other important difference at breakfast – under his striped pullover Ludwig's chest was flat, while Helga's little breasts pushed out the front of her pink silk dressing-gown.

After the drama of that first meeting Manfred saw Helga as often as she would let him, which was not very often. He came to understand that the Albert she had mentioned who had thrown Ludwig's friend out on his ear was keeping her. It surprised him at first that she would accept invitations to dinner and to go dancing and to sleep with him when she was financially dependent on another man, but before long he became aware that she did not like Albert much at all and would be pleased if Manfred offered to replace him as paymaster. But Manfred had no wish for a commitment like that. It seemed to him more sensible to entertain her, take her shopping from time to time for frocks and other fripperies and enjoy her company in bed whenever he could, while the mysterious Albert took care of the rest.

In these weeks he also got to know Ludwig well and found him sufficiently amusing to ask along sometimes when he took Helga to the theatre or to lunch. Ludwig often talked about freedom and insisted that it was the driving need of every aware person to break free from the bonds of the past, otherwise that person's life was no more meaningful than that of a prisoner. In this he was referring to far more than his flight with Helga from their home to Berlin. The drive towards freedom was to be seen, said Ludwig, in literature and in the theatre and in painting. Liberated spirits were creating new visions of truth for those who could understand them. The first time he and Helga visited Manfred's apartment, he turned up his nose at the pictures on the walls, exactly as Max Schroeder had done on the unforgettable evening of the birthday party. Ludwig had familiarised himself with the work of modern German painters and admired them indiscriminately. He was so persuasive on this subject that he succeeded in dragging Manfred to an art-dealer on the Kurfurstendamm. Manfred stared in total incomprehension at canvases daubed with garish swathes of colour and pictures of oddly distorted people doing inexplicable things. All this, he was sure, was the outcome of a conspiracy between dealers and artists to foist rubbish on the public at high prices.

Nevertheless, Ludwig's enthusiasm and the skill of the dealer won him over and he bought the least offensive painting in the gallery. At the very least it might be a good investment, he considered.

The painting showed two naked and grossly fat women sitting at a small round table, flanking a middle-aged man who resembled a pig in evening clothes. A bottle and two empty glasses stood on the table, and an ash-tray that held a stubbed-out cigar. The colours were hideous, the complexions of the women being greenish and that of the man a muddy purple. What the significance of it might be was beyond Manfred, though he guessed that the artist, whose signature in the corner looked like Glitz, had seen some of the paintings of Toulouse-Lautrec but wasn't up to the same standard. He asked Helga what she thought of it and she was deferential towards her brother for once, saying that if Ludwig said it was a master-piece, then it must be so.

Manfred paid for it, thinking that he would have preferred to have bought one of Horst's studies of Rosa nude. At least Horst painted women any man would be pleased to get hold of, not Glitz's ghastly creatures with sharks' jaws and breasts sagging down to their bellies. For that matter, he would have preferred a nude portrait of Helga by Horst. But he was half-inclined to believe the dealer when he said that the painting would appreciate greatly in value as Glitz's reputation grew to European status and then in due course to international acclaim. There were, Manfred thought, enough rich idiots in the world to bring the dealer's words true.

After he had completed the arrangements to have the painting delivered and hung, he took the twins to the Café Schon on Unter den Linden, it being late in the afternoon and Manfred feeling a need for alcoholic sustenance after spending so much money on something he didn't like. They found a table on the terrace where they could watch the passers-by on the avenue. They had been talking about painting over their drinks for perhaps ten minutes when Jenny Montrose turned into the terrace. She looked wonderfully elegant and attractive in a summer jacket and skirt of tan shantung. Manfred's heart soared as he rose to his feet to greet her.

His mouth opened wide in surprise when her companion, a short man, appeared from behind her. He was a negro with a shiny coal-black face and grinning white teeth. He was dressed in a striped blazer and a straw boater-hat.

'This is Eddie Jones,' said Jenny. 'He's from Philadelphia and he's a trumpet player. Perhaps you have heard him?'

Manfred introduced Helga and Ludwig and invited Jenny to join them. Eddie spoke almost no German at all and sat quietly with his drink while Manfred made himself pleasant to Jenny. American jazz-players had been hugely popular for the past year or two, ever since the *Chocolate Kiddies* revue had been staged in Berlin, but Manfred had never before met a negro socially and was not entirely certain how to proceed. Nor did he understand why some of his intellectual friends accorded jazz some sort of cultural importance. For him it was useful to liven up a party, but not really music in any real sense.

Apart from that, there was in his mind a hazy picture of Jenny and Eddie making love. It was hard to imagine the beautiful body he had seen at Ulrika's celebration lying alongside the shiny black body of the musician, his dark hands on her white breasts. And beyond that – when he lay on her . . . presumably his stem was as black-skinned as the rest of him, and that was a strange thought.

The truth was, Manfred admitted to himself, that he was jealous. He wanted Jenny for himself and to this end he set out to be charming, not caring whether Helga was listening or not. But to his invitations to lunches, dinners, dances, theatres, Jenny was polite and friendly and regretted that she was unable to accept. Eddie, in ignorance of what was being said, grinned happily across the table at Helga. Manfred saw that he was wasting his breath – Jenny was much too involved with her fellow-countryman at present to become interested in anyone else. So he abandoned his pursuit and talked cheerfully of other things. When Jenny left, with Eddie tagging along behind, Helga gave Manfred a furious look and did not speak to him for the next half-hour. But that night, in bed, she was particularly tender and attentive towards him, as if fearing that he would disappear from her life as suddenly as he had entered it.

There was an afternoon when Manfred called at the apartment in Auguststrasse by arrangement to take Helga out. Ludwig let him in and explained that Albert had arrived unexpectedly and taken his sister to lunch.

'Then I will be on my way. Please ask her to telephone me when she returns.'

'I'm sure she'll be back soon. Stay and talk. Albert never has time for her in the afternoon.'

Manfred sat down opposite Ludwig, who was neatly dressed in an open-necked white shirt and grey trousers. It seemed a useful opportunity to find out a little more about Helga's benefactor.

'This Albert – what is his other name?'

'Grutz – Albert Grutz. He's tremendously rich, you know. He made a fortune in the big inflation, though I don't know how.'

'What sort of man is he?'

'He's very generous. To look at he's big and heavy and has a thick old-fashioned moustache. He's about fifty, I suppose. He has a big house in Grunewald Forest, though we've never seen it. I mean, he can't invite us there like you do to your apartment because he's married and has five children. The oldest son is older than I am.'

The picture of Albert that emerged was not much to Manfred's taste, even though Ludwig seemed to like him and Helga obviously found him tolerable, for reasons of her own.

'Is he liberated?' Manfred asked with a smile, referring to Ludwig's usual preoccupation.

'No, he's a prisoner of his own past. He'd like to break free but he's too old to take such a big step.'

'Do you know anyone at all who is free, in the way you mean it?'

'I am,' said Ludwig proudly.

'How so?'

'Because I can become Tania whenever I want to. When I'm Tania I can do whatever I like.'

'You are suggesting that women are in some way more free than men? I don't believe that for one moment.'

'You haven't understood me. When I put on women's clothes and become Tania, it is a spiritual experience. It is to cut the bonds with the past and to see the world in a new way.'

'But changing your clothes does not change the essential *you*, Ludwig. There are women who put on men's evening clothes, but they are still women under the starched shirt-front. The American lady we met the other day – Fraulein Montrose – I have seen her in men's clothes. But it doesn't mean anything. It is like going to a fancy-dress party in disguise. You may be dressed as Frederick the .Great or Julius Caesar, but you are still yourself.'

Ludwig began to describe what happened to him spiritually when he put on women's clothes, arguing that Manfred was wrong and that the personality underwent a change in accordance with the attire. Eventually he offered to prove his point if Manfred would agree to an experiment. Totally unconvinced, Manfred followed Ludwig into his bed-room, feeling slightly foolish but ready to settle the point.

Ludwig opened a wardrobe and showed him a dozen frocks hanging there, colourful, beautiful and expensive.

'Just for a moment try to imagine yourself wearing one of those instead of your suit. Touch the material and feel its delicacy – silk, satin, chiffon!'

'I cannot imagine wearing anything like that.'

'That's because you're shackled to the past, to old ideas and worn-out conventions. You have notions of what is right and what is wrong that have been taught to you by people who never tried to think for themselves. Where in nature does it say that men must wear trousers and women must wear skirts? There are countries in the world where the men wear long robes instead of trousers, and countries where the women wear tight trousers instead of frocks – you must have seen pictures of them.'

'But these are backward countries. They do not have our cultural heritage or history.'

'In the old days, our German ancestors in their forests wore tunics – the men, I mean – and what is a tunic but a short frock? And two hundred years ago, rich gentlemen wore clothes made of silk, embroidered and edged with brocade, with lace at their cuffs. You have a portrait of one of your own ancestors dressed like that – I've seen it in your apartment. Was he less a man for his silks and laces?'

'Why no – he was a military commander of great distinction. But what are you trying to prove?'

'I am trying to show you that you are a prisoner,

142

Manfred. Have you the courage to break out of your prison?'

Courage was a quality which Manfred did not lack.

'We will try this experiment in spiritual freedom,' he said, 'but don't get any odd ideas about me – remember the night when we met and what happened then.'

'I won't forget. Take your clothes off while I find something suitable for you.'

Manfred stripped down to his underpants, still feeling foolish.

'You have a good strong body,' said Ludwig. 'What a pity you are not interested in me.'

'So long as you understand that fact we shall remain friends.'

Ludwig took from the wardrobe a long evening frock of mauve satin.

'No,' he said, holding it against Manfred, 'That won't fit. You're so much bigger than I am. What else have I got . . . you'll have to take your underpants off, you know.'

Manfred removed them, wondering what on earth he was doing.

'Put this on,' and Ludwig handed him a small silk triangle with elastic straps, 'it keeps everything up out of the way.'

Manfred pulled the posing-pouch up his legs until it fitted tightly over his limp equipment and held it close against his belly. He felt better then because it stopped Ludwig from staring at that part of him.

'Good,' said Ludwig with a grin, 'now these.'

These were a pair of pale blue knickers with a band of lace round the loose legs and a pattern embroidered at the waist. Manfred struggled into them, finding them small for him, and stared at his own reflection in the long mirror.

'Now for stockings – sit on the bed.'

He sat and fumbled with the unfamiliar task. Skilled though he was in assisting young women remove their stockings, he had never attempted to help one put them back on afterwards.

143

'I'll show you,' said Ludwig.

Before Manfred could object, he was kneeling by him to smooth the fine silk stockings up his legs and then to slide garters with pink rosebuds up to his thighs to hold the stockings in place.

'Your legs are covered with fine blonde hair,' Ludwig observed, 'I shave my legs so that nothing shows through my stockings when I am Tania.'

'And you shave under the arms,' Manfred recalled.

'And somewhere else as well,' Ludwig added with a smile, 'did you notice that when we first met and you had your hand up my frock?'

'Why do you do that?' Manfred asked. 'Women have hair between their legs too.'

'But the shape is different,' said Ludwig, 'women's hair grows in a straight line across the top.'

'I know one who has it cut in a heart-shape,' Manfred told him, but Ludwig was not impressed.

'None of my clothes will fit you,' he said. 'What can we do? Let me think. Stand up for a moment.'

He produced from a drawer of his dressing-table an object which had led Manfred astray – a white satin brassiere with cups which were filled with soft rubber. He strapped it on Manfred's chest and it fitted extremely tightly, even with the straps adjusted to the maximum. The embarrassment Manfred had experienced at the beginning had by now vanished. Was this the start of spiritual liberation? he asked himself.

Ludwig brought out the wrap he had worn on the evening they had first met. He fixed it round Manfred's chest, under his arms, and pinned it at the back.

'That's the best I can do,' Ludwig sighed. 'Walk about slowly and get the feel of the clothes.'

Manfred took a few steps and the assortment of clothes he was wearing slid over his skin in a way that gave him strange sensations. He was glad to be wearing the tight silk pouch at that moment, to conceal an unnecessary stiffness that was making itself apparent.

'Well?' Ludwig asked. 'What do you think of our little experiment?'

'I'm not sure. There is an effect, but I find it hard to understand.'

'Don't confuse yourself by trying to understand.'

Manfred stopped before the long mirror and stared at his reflection. The wrap fixed round his body outlined pointed little breasts and lower down there were frilly blue knickers and silk stockings. The mirror said that this was an over-sized woman, but the head said that it was a man. The total impression was that of an outlandish creature of inde-terminate sexuality and unknown potential.

'How do you feel?' Ludwig asked softly.

'I don't know,' Manfred answered, engrossed by what he saw in the mirror.

The silk pouch inside the knickers seemed to be getting tighter and tighter. He was, he had to admit, sexually aroused, though the reason eluded him. To put on women's clothes seemed hardly reason enough to evoke feelings of langorous pleasure.

'This is only a start,' Ludwig's voice said persuasively from somewhere behind him. 'The real moment of freedom comes when you show yourself dressed as a woman in public – not to stupid people who cannot overcome their own prejudices – but to friends who know what it is to be free and who hold out their hand to you in friendship and understanding.'

'The Eldorado Bar, you mean?'

'I have many friends there . . . but even that is only a prelude to the moment when you break the shackles that hold you to the past.'

'How is that done?'

'Can't you guess?'

Ludwig was beside him, so that both images were in the mirror together. Manfred felt a hand rest on his bare back, above the blue knickers, and then a knuckle ran thrillingly along his spine.

145

'Freedom springs from sacrificing your old self in an act of love,' he said very softly.

'Ludwig!' a voice called from behind the two of them. 'Did Manfred call?'

Manfred whirled round, his face red, to see Helga standing at the bed-room door, still wearing her hat and gloves. She stared at him in silence for some moments and then smiled crookedly.

'There you are, Manfred. I never expected to find you playing games with Ludwig.

'It's an experiment,' he answered awkwardly.

'I'm sure it is, though I've never heard it called that before. Is the experiment still in progress?'

'It's finished.'

She walked slowly across the room towards him, the crooked smile still on her face.

'Are you sure? From what I can see inside your knickers there's some way to go yet.'

'Helga, you're spoiling everything!' Ludwig protested angrily.

'Am I spoiling your fun? How often have you spoiled mine?'

Manfred stood paralysed by shame as she approached him.

'Blue knickers! Are they really your style, Manfred?' she asked.

Her gloved hand pressed against the silk.

'Finished, you said? Only just started, I would say, from the feel of this.'

'Helga,' he said hoarsely.

'Tell me something,' she said, 'would you rather have my hand or Ludwig's hand touching you?'

With shame Manfred remembered that on the evening he had been in this room with *Tania*, Ludwig's hand had indeed stroked him where Helga was touching him now.

'Lost for words?' she asked. 'If I hadn't come home just now it would be Ludwig's hand rubbing you now.'

'It would not!' he said sharply.

The tightness of the silk pouch seemed to be making Manfred light-headed. He reached out to put his hands on Helga's breasts through her summer frock, hoping to make her crooked smile go away.

'That's something Ludwig can't offer you,' she said, 'his are made of rubber. Mine are the real thing – you should know that – you've played with them often enough.'

'And kissed them!' he mumbled.

Ludwig snorted in disgust and walked away from them. In the mirror Manfred saw that he had thrown himself on his bed and was lying there with a sulky expression on his face.

Helga turned her head to speak to her brother.

'Ludwig – clear out!'

'I won't! This is my room.'

'Please yourself,' she said.

Her eyes stared into Manfred's and their expression was cold as she jerked his silk knickers down to his knees, to be followed by the pouch.

'Ludwig has been telling you about spiritual liberation,' she said, 'he always goes on about it. Do you know what he means? I'll tell you – he wants to get hold of *this!*'

She was gripping Manfred's upright stem so hard that he winced.

'Isn't that true, Ludwig?' she asked over her shoulder. 'This is what you were after – take a good look at it now it's on show because that's as near to it as you'll get while I'm here.'

'You're a bitch!' said Ludwig angrily, 'The only thing you know about is lying on your back for men. You're stuck in the past – you'll never be free.'

'If you're free, I don't want to be.'

'You don't say that when Albert's here,' said Ludwig viciously.

'I thought you'd drag him into it sooner or later. Perhaps Manfred would like to know why Albert pays for this apartment and keeps us both.'

Her grip on Manfred's swollen stem was fierce but not

147

unpleasant. She tugged at it to keep his attention. Manfred shook his head in answer to her question about Albert, silently cursing himself for being drawn into this quarrel between the twins. Helga smiled at him chillingly.

'Dear Albert does all this for us because he likes us both,' she said. 'Sometimes he takes me out to dinner and sometimes he takes Tania. Understand? Sometimes he sleeps with me and sometimes he sleeps with Tania. When dear Albert is in bed he doesn't care which hand is holding his spike. And you know who Tania is because you put your hand up her skirts.'

'Shut up!' said Ludwig, 'I won't let you do this!'

'How will you stop me, *Tania*? You wanted to stay, so stay and watch. You'll see Manfred ruin a new pair of gloves in a minute.'

Indeed, her hold on Manfred was threatening to make him fire his volley.

'I won't look!' Ludwig shrilled.

'I don't care whether you look or not. He's going to do it and I'm the one he'll do it for, not you.'

'But this is my room!'

'That's why.'

Manfred growled in his throat, angry at being in so ridiculous a position. He seized Helga by the waist, took three or four steps and threw her, kicking and squealing on to the bed alongside her brother. He flipped her frock up to her waist and laughed bitterly to see that she was wearing blue silk knickers almost like those that hobbled his legs. He hooked his fingers into the waistband and ripped the flimsy material from top to bottom. Helga screamed and brought up her knees sharply to protect herself. Manfred grabbed her shins and forced her bent legs up to her breasts and then fell on her with all his weight. She screamed again when he thrust hard into her exposed entrance.

'Stop it!'

'Do it to her!' Ludwig cried in malicious glee.

Both outcries were lost in a roar of triumph from Manfred

as his raging stem spat its fury into Helga, only moments after he had penetrated her.

He got off her quickly and she rolled over to hide her face, her arms over her head. Manfred ripped off the wrap he was wearing, hearing the pins tear the material, the knickers and stockings and hurled them at Ludwig, no longer caring whether that one saw him naked or not. He put his own clothes on as fast as he could, saying not a word. Helga and Ludwig were both silent, and Manfred turned his back to them so that he would not have to see them.

Fully dressed at last, he went to the door, determined to have done with the twins forever. He turned, the door-knob in his hand, to inform them that he wanted no more to do with them. Helga still lay face-down on the bed, her gloved hands over her head. Ludwig had moved close to her and was comforting her, whispering close to her ear and stroking her bare bottom delicately, where the remnants of blue silk hung about her thighs. And in that instant Manfred realised that the twins were not only rivals, they were lovers.

Ludwig looked up and fixed Manfred with a look of pure hatred.

'Go away,' he said, his voice clear, 'go away! We don't need you!'

The Book

Ernst Tillich's novel was published in September and according to the reviewers it was the most important cultural event of the year. Even without the acclaim, Manfred would have bought a copy, simply because he knew Ernst, but he found it hard work to read it. In essence it was a tale of a cruel father who beat his children, tore up their books and made their lives so miserable that the eldest boy went out one dark night and drowned himself in the River Spree. This shocked the other children, two more boys and two girls, into open rebellion against their tyrannical father and provoked a scene of brawling confrontation which ended only when they pushed him out of the apartment window. The odious parent fell three floors, cursing his children, until he smashed into the pavement below and lay broken and dying in Kaiserstrasse, within sight of police headquarters. An elderly lady walking her dog fainted at the horrid sight and, as the leash slipped from her nerveless fingers, the dachshund trotted up to the dying man, cocked its leg and urinated on his blood-stained face.

Manfred's view was that the novel was melodramatic rubbish. Nor did it strike him as original – he was fairly sure he had seen much the same story produced as a play in the theatre, some years before, though he could not recall the author's name or whether it ended in the same way. Even so, in the face of widespread praise in the progressive newspapers, he decided to keep his views to himself and go to Ernst's celebration party.

From experience he knew that the standards of hospitality of intellectuals were not the same as his own. He therefore delayed his arrival until the party had been in full swing for some hours and took a bottle of good brandy with him. His hope was that the more tedious of Ernst's literary friends would have talked themselves to a standstill by the time he got there, but in this he was wrong. Ernst's drab and uncomfortable apartment was crowded with people talking at the top of their voices and the only drink left was beer.

Manfred pushed his way through the mob to congratulate Ernst, who was speechless, drunk and happy. He threw his arms round Manfred, thumped him on the back and had to be helped into a chair before he fell down.

Manfred was soon deep in conversation with someone he knew well, Kurt Niemoller, a literary critic of some renown. Kurt was a little unsteady on his feet but still talking hard about Ernst's achievement.

'The symbolism is astonishing,' he informed Manfred. 'The father dying in sight of police headquarters, a symbol of a repressive social order which, at the crucial moment, is powerless to save him! That is a master-stroke! And the dog which gives the final gesture of contempt – wonderful! There has been nothing like this since Thomas Mann's *Magic Mountain*.'

'Ernst is an old friend but I find it an exaggeration to compare his work with that of Mann.'

'You know nothing about literature,' said Kurt rudely, 'but that is to be expected – you are not engaged in the struggle.'

'What struggle?'

'The artistic struggle to create a new Germany! My God, we are living in the middle of a German Renaissance and you haven't even noticed it!'

'There's Oskar,' said Manfred, waving at the impressario to join them, 'he's deeply committed to your struggle, Kurt.'

Oskar forced his way through the crowd, dragging Magda

151

in his wake, like a small boat towed behind a steam-ship. Manfred kissed her hand and then her cheek in an affectionate manner. She was dressed in dramatic style for Ernst's intellectual party, in a short black frock with a large circular hole in the front to display her belly-button.

'I heard my name mentioned,' said Oskar, beaming at Manfred. 'Were you saying something nice about me?'

'I was explaining to Kurt that you are in the forefront of his struggle against the forces of reaction.'

'What nonsense!' said Kurt sharply. 'The plays he puts on are a disgrace. They are flimsy pretexts to get half-naked women on the stage to titillate the bourgeoisie. *Three in a Bed* was rubbish, with no artistic or social merit whatsoever, and no discernible political stance.'

Oskar's face turned slowly red with anger and Manfred stirred things up further.

'Your judgement is superficial, Kurt. *Three in a Bed* was a satire with an important social message which you missed completely. And as for political stance, surely that was obvious enough.'

Kurt stared at him suspiciously and uncertainly, wondering if he had missed something.

'Evidently the symbolism was too subtle for you,' Manfred continued. 'You need a dog to piss in your face before you understand the message. Oskar does it more cleverly and with greater intellectual depth.'

Kurt was now staring at Oskar with a puzzled expression.

'I shall speak to your editor tomorrow,' Oskar said vindictively, 'my name carries some influence. It is beyond me how he can employ the services of someone as totally imperceptive as you.'

Kurt began to make gobbling noises.

'There is the question of Oskar's next production,' said Manfred, 'it will amaze you, Kurt, if you succeed in understanding it. The symbolism lies in a group of twelve year old school-girls . . . but no, I must not give too much away.'

'I refuse to believe what you say,' said Kurt, fairly sure

at last that Manfred was making a fool of him. 'This man produces nothing but salacious and trivial spectacles for the stupid and insensitive. That was what I wrote about his last production and from what you tell me it will be equally true of his next.'

'Do you know how many people paid to see *Three in a Bed*?' Oskar demanded furiously.

Manfred winked at Magda and moved imperceptibly away from what promised to be a lengthy wrangle. She followed him and, once out of ear-shot of Oskar, she burst into laughter.

'Manfred – what a sadist you are! Oskar will lose his temper with Kurt eventually and punch him.'

They found a relatively uncrowded corner of the room, slightly shielded from the din by a large book-case. Manfred was unable to resist putting his hand on the round cut-out in Magda's frock and rubbing her bare belly.

'You are still attending to Oskar's little requirements, dear Magda?'

'Why not? He treats me very well because he is grateful. But who is attending to your requirements, Manfred? It seems a very long time since you came to visit me.'

'It's not that I do not find your games amusing, but they are very strenuous.'

'You are young and strong, not flabby like poor Oskar. If you put your hand down through the hole in my frock you will find out what I am wearing underneath.'

'You never wear anything underneath. It would be no surprise.'

'It's surprises you want, is it? I have just the thing for you – a wonderful new device that stretches you out on a frame with steel chains holding your ankles and wrists and leaving every part of you, front and back, exposed to attentions of all kinds, some of them very severe.'

'How very interesting! Has Oskar tried it?'

'He paid for it. It was designed by a person of exceptional imagination and can be used to produce some very curious results. After his first little session with it Oskar was so wrung-out that he's afraid to use it again. So it stands idle and waiting for you.'

'I am tempted to investigate this new toy of yours, Magda, but I would much prefer to see you chained and helpless in it while I do unspeakable things to you.'

She took his wrist and pushed his hand down through the cut-out of her frock. His fingers closed on a furry mound that promised unknown delights.

'Tomorrow evening,' she suggested, 'Oskar won't want to see me for a day or two after tonight. He will need to recover his strength.'

Manfred withdrew his hand quickly as Oskar bustled through the crowd towards them, his face puce and his voice raised in a bellow.

'That idiot! He knows nothing about the theatre and he dares to insult me! Come along, Magda, we're leaving before I kill him.'

'Culture is a controversial subject,' said Manfred pleasantly.

'What? Yes, you're right. Thank you for trying to set that blockhead straight, even if he's too stupid to see what's in front of his nose.'

He dragged Magda away and Manfred felt someone poke him in the back. He turned to find himself facing a woman of about forty, square-headed and neckless, thick-bodied and waistless. She wore an unbecoming frock of emerald green and was flanked by two sturdy young men. Neither was older than Manfred himself, both had short and bristly hair that gave them the look of convicts. Each had on a cheap suit in dark blue and neither wore a tie.

'You're no writer,' said the woman who had poked him in the back to get his attention. 'You look too well-off to have any talent. What are you doing here?'

'I've known Ernst for years, Madame, and he invited me to his party.'

He thought it unnecessary to tell her that Ernst was the son of the village school-teacher on the Klausenburg estate,

154

or that he had borrowed the fare to Berlin from Manfred himself.

'You're some sort of capitalist,' said the woman. 'We won't need your sort forever. In the well-run society the State will pay writers a salary while they create their works, and then distribute them free.'

'Even then you will still need me, Madame.'

'For God's sake stop calling me Madame. My name's Schreker. Why will anyone need you when the State is run by the people and not by money-lenders?'

'You will need people like me to read your books, otherwise there will be no point in writing them.'

'The workers will read our books!' she declared.

'They are incapable of it.'

'We shall educate them.'

'That will take fifty years. In the meantime the only people who will read your books are other writers, after you have abolished people like me. And you're all too jealous of each other to be a satisfactory audience. I suggest that you retain me until you have educated the proletariat sufficiently to want to read books like Ernst's latest.'

'Have *you* read it?' she demanded.

'Certainly.'

'And what is your opinion of it?'

'Ernst is an old friend. Look at him over there – drunk and happy. He feels himself superior because his book has been noticed and because it will make money for him. He will be able to move to a better apartment and enjoy himself more expensively, eat in good restaurants and find more amusing girlfriends than the scrawny little creatures he finds in bookshops. All this is good. Therefore his book is a good book.'

The woman stared at him in disbelief. Her two companions, looking bored, drifted away to look for more drink. Manfred gestured at their retreating backs.

'Are they writers? They look shabby enough.'

To his surprise Fraulein Schreker chuckled at his insult.

'They couldn't write a laundry-list between them. But they are a great help to me in writing my books.'

'In what way, if I may ask.'

'They've got strong backs and the animal vigour of youth. That shocks your bourgeois morality, no doubt.'

'No, but why two of them? Do you need so much help with your writing?'

'Two's better than one. I never know when the mood will take me.'

'Do you pay them?'

Fraulein Schreker was so set in her frankness that she did not take the question as an insult at all, as any other woman would.

'I give them room and board and some pocket-money.'

'You are to be congratulated on your arrangements. I have met older women who have arrangements with young men for the same purpose and find it expensive.'

'That's not the same!' she said sharply, insulted at last. 'You mean rich and bored women to try to buy the illusion of love. I want no such thing from my boys. Love is total nonsense. What I ask for is physical relief so that I can get on with my work, and the quicker the better.'

'I see that you are deeply committed to the struggle to create a new Germany,' said Manfred, straight-faced as he quoted Kurt Niemoller's words to her. 'You are taking part in the new German Renaissance – a great destiny for a writer.'

'How right you are, comrade,' she answered, obviously stirred to the depths by his words, 'there is not a moment to lose!'

'May I ask about your particular working methods? They say that Marcel Proust wrote the whole of *Remembrance of Things Past* in bed.'

'Decadent French queer!' Fraulein Schreker snorted, 'I get up every morning of the week at six o'clock, put on my old dressing-gown, drink a cup of coffee and start to work. I have long bouts of intense concentration, perhaps for hours at a time. Then suddenly I am physically and mentally drained and can't write another word. My wrist and arm ache from writing and my back aches from crouching over my table, so I lie flat on the floor – did you know that's good for an aching back? Josef or Hans, whichever one is at hand, squats down beside me to massage my legs.'

Beneath the hem of her ugly green frock Manfred saw that she had unusually strong calves and ankles. She saw the direction of his glance and hitched up her skirt to show her legs off better.

'I've always had good strong legs,' she said with satisfaction, 'I did a lot of walking in the countryside when I was a girl. Nowadays I spend so much time sitting at my writing-table that I've developed a broad backside. Not that it's of any importance. Women who worry over their appearance are stupid. What matters is what goes on in here,' and she tapped her forehead.

'I agree that what goes on in the head is tremendously important. On the other hand, what goes on lower down is not without a certain interest, even to a person of your stern principles. A moment ago you described yourself lying on the floor with one of your assistants massaging your legs.'

'The body has a stultifying effect on the mind unless action is taken to prevent it,' she said ponderously. 'A few minutes of massage takes away my fatigue, especially when the thigh muscles are massaged firmly.'

'Quite so,' Manfred agreed solemnly, 'I have noticed more than once that women whose thighs I massage become very lively. And when the hands go higher, they become positively frisky.'

'I never waste time like that. One word from me and the boy has my dressing-gown and night-dress up and is on top of me – and in a minute or two at most I get the physical relief I need. Then my mind is bursting with ideas and I go back to my table and start again.'

'You have matters very well organised,' said Manfred, appalled by what he had heard. 'Do you need this relief frequently?'

'Two or three times a day is usually enough. If I work right through the night, as I sometimes do, then the boys take it in turn.'

'And the books that you produce in this interesting way – are they at all popular? Do they sell well?'

She stared at him in sudden fury.

'Don't you know who I am, you ignorant idiot?'

'I regret, Madame, that I rarely read modern novels, though I made an exception for Ernst. I prefer our great writers of the last generation – Thomas Mann, for example. Are your books anything like his?'

He had found the perfect insult. Fraulein Schreker turned purple with rage, swivelled on her heel and marched away. Manfred grinned and eased himself through the crowd to speak to Max Schroeder.

'What did you say to that awful woman to upset her so badly?' Max asked.

'Nothing at all. I asked her about her method of writing. Did I tell you that I've bought a grotesque painting by Glitz? You must come and tell me what you think of it.'

'There's hope for you yet. But you will find that you have a problem now, Manfred. Glitz will so overshadow those landscapes of yours and your family portraits that you will have to get rid of them.'

'Maybe, but I like those landscapes. I don't like the new picture at all. I may send it to London to be sold – a dealer told me they will pay high prices there for any modernistic rubbish.'

Max had his arm round, of all people, Rosa, the well-fleshed model who normally went about with Horst Lederer. From the way in which she cuddled herself against him, Manfred assumed that they had become close friends.

'Are you thinking of becoming a painter yourself, Max, instead of an art-critic, now that you have acquired a model?'

'A man has other uses for a fine young woman when she takes her clothes off besides painting her portrait,' he answered, and Rosa nodded in agreement.

'Max is a gentleman,' she said, 'not a lout like Horst, even if he is a good artist.'

'The fact is,' Max confided, 'I fell in love with Rosa when I kissed her bottom at your birthday party. It was a turning-point in my life.'

'As I remember, you were far from happy when you and I visited Madame Filipov. I thought you were going to hang yourself that evening.'

'That was because I would not give in to my great urge to simplify my life and thinking. I saw everything in intellectual terms and did not listen to my own heart. With Rosa everything is simple, easy and pleasant. She has a heart of gold and a well-disposed nature.'

'And a magnificent body,' said Manfred, smiling at Rosa. 'I keep meaning to drive round to Horst's studio and buy one of his paintings of her, if he has one left. I want to hang it next to Glitz's horror and see which conquers the other.'

'An interesting experiment,' said Max. 'Of course, now that I've got Rosa herself, I don't need a painting of her. She poses for me, as if for Horst, on a bed or a chair, and I can sit for hours and admire the tones of her skin, the way the light falls on her hair, the curves and planes of her body – it is better than looking at paintings, I assure you.'

'I hope that all this silent admiration leads to some bolder expression of your emotions.'

'I make sure of that,' said Rosa, 'otherwise I'd be standing about naked all day for nothing. He hasn't changed really – he only thinks he has.'

'Max – have you heard from Werner lately?'

'I had a postcard only last week from Vienna. It was a picture of the Johann Strauss memorial.'

'Did he say anything about coming back?'

'He said he would be away for Christmas. Gottfried really frightened him that night, from what I've been told. I wish I'd been there to see it. I must cultivate the acquaintance of your cousin Ulrika and get myself invited to her next orgy.'

159

'Did Werner give an address?'

'Yes – do you want it?'

'I want to get in touch with him urgently. I have news for him.'

'I'll telephone you tomorrow and give you the address on the postcard.'

'And I'll invite you to lunch with Ulrika. Bring Rosa with you and you'll be in her good books right away. Who else is here tonight that we know besides Oskar?'

'They're mostly struggling writers and the like. No one of importance. The American girl is here, of course.'

'Jenny? Where – I haven't seen her?'

'I saw her going into Ernst's bed-room hours ago.'

Manfred's heart sank.

'With whom?' he asked.

'They're smoking opium in there. I'm sure they won't mind if you join them. They're probably all unconscious by now.'

Manfred found his way to the bed-room. It was almost in darkness, the curtains drawn across the window and the only light from a small bedside lamp over which a woman's slip had been draped to dim it. The room was full of smoke and the sweet and heavy smell of opium. On the floor lay a cheap metal tray with a tiny glass spirit-lamp and a long-handled spoon with a small bowl. Jenny lay on the bed, naked except for her silk stockings, and a naked man lay beside her, his head on her shoulder. Two other couples, also undressed, lay on the carpet. One of the couples lay like spoons, the woman's back to the man and his arms round her, while the other couple lay at an angle to each other, the woman's head on the man's belly. Everyone appeared to be asleep.

Manfred stood at the bedside and stared down at Jenny. A strand of black hair had fallen untidily across her face. Her face was expressionless, her eyes half open and blank, a dribble of saliva from a corner of her red-painted mouth. She was exceptionally beautiful, he thought, her body a masterpiece of curves and hollows, made for love and tenderness. He had seen her naked once before, at Ulrika's celebration, bent over Ulrika and whispering fondly to her while Olga Pfaff played with her. Even in those circumstances Jenny had looked proud and brimming with restrained energy. Lying here, stretched out on her back on Ernst's bed, she looked lost and vulnerable – and in some strange way, innocent. Yet she was far from innocent, Manfred told himself. She was stupefied by drugs, in wretched surroundings, throwing herself away on God knows what dirty tramps of so-called intellectuals. The thought so complicated his emotions that he wanted to weep for her and to shout in anger at the same time.

She sighed gently, her mouth open a little. Her perfectly round breasts rose and fell to her quiet breathing and Manfred's emotions became so painful that he wanted to kiss her and beat her savagely, tell her that he adored her and drag her out of the apartment by her hair.

'Stupid little cow!' he said aloud. 'To do this to yourself! You've let that disgusting and hairy swine put his grubby hands all over you! And you've opened your legs for that shrivelled monstrosity of his!'

He touched her shoulder mournfully, his finger-tips feeling the satin texture of her skin. After that it was impossible to resist trailing his fingers down over her breasts, soft and cushiony, to her pink buds.

'I would kiss them for hours if you would let me,' he said to the unconscious girl, 'But you have always been interested in someone else.'

He ran his trembling hand down to her smooth belly. She wore a narrow suspender-belt decorated with fine lace and it concealed her belly-button. He pulled the elastic belt down a little to see for himself and was pleased beyond belief by the soft oval indentation he found. He touched her tuft of jet-black hair and it was like stroking the finest astrakhan. Her thighs were slightly apart and his questing fingers touched the long lips between them. Their moistness was testimony enough to what had happened earlier before she and her companion had passed out.

'I want you more than I have ever wanted any woman before,' Manfred said softly, 'yet I hate you and despise you.'

He heard her sigh faintly again as he touched her between the thighs. He looked at her face, to see her lips move slowly, and he bent over to hear what she was saying.

'Erwin darling, do it again,' she whispered very slowly, and her long beautiful legs slid wider apart on the bed.

Manfred almost choked on his curious and painful emotions. He went round to the other side of the bed, stepping over a sleeping couple on the way. Both partners were unconscious, but the man's loins were moving in a slow rhythm against the girl's bottom, as if he dreamed that he was still making love to her.

Erwin was heavy to lift off the bed and put on the floor. At close quarters he smelled none too clean and on the forearm that had been hidden under him, there was tattooed a dagger with a snake round it. He did not wake as Manfred rolled him under the bed.

'Dirty pig,' Manfred growled. 'Sleep it off under there.'

Two souls certainly dwelled in Manfred's breast at that moment – one urging him to retreat as fast as he could from this unsavoury scene and the other encouraging him to take the revenge open to him. Emotion vanquished reason and in seconds he had his clothes off and was alongside Jenny on the lumpy bed. He stroke her breasts very lightly so as not to disturb her drugged sleep. His stem lay hard against her thigh.

'Yes . . .' she murmured, 'that's nice . . .'

Her eyes were closed and her body limp to his touch. She was in another dimension, where time had slowed down and the mind had ceased to function. But eventually her pink buds grew to firmness under his fingers and her lethargic breathing speeded up just a little. Manfred caressed her belly for a long time and then between her thighs. Her loins made tiny jerking movements and her legs slid further apart until he could find and tease the wet little bud within.

The time had come for decision – leave her or go all the

way. It needed no agony of mind for him to choose. He positioned himself over her with extreme care, his weight on his knees and an elbow, while he guided his leaping stem to the slippery entrance waiting for it. He loathed Jenny, he desired her, he despised her and he loved her – the conflicting passions were too much for him to either understand or deal with. But his body knew what to do.

His belly lay lightly on hers as he slid all the way into her. He kept his weight off her and stayed still – Jenny was doing everything that was necessary. Her loins lifted and fell in a slow rhythm, giving him exquisite sensations. Whether this strange love-making was pleasurable or not, he hardly knew. To Jenny it obviously was – in some remote drug-hazy recess of her mind the sensations were being felt and enjoyed, for her breathing became irregular after a time and the automatic lifting of her loins speeded up fractionally.

How long it lasted, this trance-like act of love, it would be impossible to say. Manfred's mind had lost touch with his body, as if he were drugged himself. In his mind there was a maelstrom of confusion, a mingling of guilt and desire, which tormented him. But his body was isolated from these considerations and was an automaton which was waiting for the switch to be thrown that would cause it to perform its function. Manfred was in heaven and in hell at the same time.

It was as if a bolt of lightning struck him when his body discharged its passion and his seething emotions were blotted out. He groaned and jerked while the fury spent itself in Jenny's slowly heaving body, his mouth pressed to hers and tears trickling down his own face.

She trembled under him for a very long time, her orgasmic pleasure extended by the effect of the opium far beyond the normal. Manfred waited for her to go limp again before he eased himself off her and put on his clothes. He had done what he wanted to do, but he felt no afterglow of contentment. On the contrary, he felt remorse, and shame – an emotion he had hardly ever experienced in his whole life and with which he was ill-equipped to deal. He stood at the bed-side for a last lingering look at the beautiful young woman asleep there, and his face was still wet with tears.

'Erwin, again . . .' she whispered.

If Erwin had been conscious, Manfred might well have beaten him to death then and there. But there was no satisfaction in revenge on a sleeping rival. Better to leave him where he was, under the bed, so that at least he would not respond to Jenny's whispered invitation.

Manfred rushed out of the apartment, shame-faced and speaking to no one. He wanted to be alone and he wanted to get drunk to wipe out the memory of what he had done. Two hours later he was not only drunk, he was lost. He had walked aimlessly through the streets, stopping at bars as he came to them, downing glass after glass of brandy to stop himself thinking. He found himself at last in a villain-ous-looking back street bar and stood at one of the elbow-high tables, staring morosely into his glass, when an elbow caught him in the ribs. He turned to see a young man of about his own age standing by him, poorly dressed and without a tie, but with a small metal swastika badge in the lapel button-hole of his jacket.

'Do you hear me?' the stranger said loudly. 'We don't want your sort here in your fancy clothes and flash ways. Clear out before I knock your teeth down your throat.'

A fat woman in a plain black frock came to Manfred's rescue.

'Leave him alone,' she said. 'He hasn't done you any harm. He's as much entitled to a drink as you are.'

The young man with the Nazi party badge threw off her restraining hand on his arm and shouted at Manfred.

'You've asked for it! I'll smash your face to a pulp!'

Through the haze of alcohol it dawned on Manfred that this angry stranger intended him some harm. There was no time to ask why, nor any reason either. As the young man squared up to him, his fists weaving, Manfred's torment erupted in boiling rage. He gave an ear-splitting shout, flung his half-glass of brandy into the other's face and, as his hands flew up to protect his eyes, Manfred delivered a punch to the pit of his stomach – a punch fuelled by all his frustrations. The stranger's breath escaped in a wheeze and he doubled over, clutching his stomach, positioning his chin in the right place to receive Manfred's knee hard under it. He went down with a thump and Manfred swayed towards him to trample him into the floor. The fat woman now flung herself between them, this time to restrain Manfred.

'Don't! He's too drunk to know what he's doing. He won't give you any more trouble.'

Much of Manfred's anger had been spent at the moment his fist had connected solidly with the other man's belly. He let the woman drag him to the bar and took the glass she pressed into his hand.

'Have one with me,' she said, 'don't bother about Joachim.'

'Who is he? What does he want with me?' he asked, staring at Joachim, doubled up on the dirty floor among beer-stains and cigarette ends.

'He's nobody. He only picked a fight because he's had a few too many. You look as if you've had a few yourself. What's your name?'

Some time later Manfred found himself in a small and shabby room with her. He sat on a bed, wondering how he had got there, while she took off her clothes. She was on the wrong side of forty and when her breasts appeared they were vast balloons of flabby flesh. Her belly swelled out like a beer-barrel and, below it, whatever hair she sported was lost between her over-sized thighs. Manfred stared at her in a puzzled way, waiting for her to explain why she had brought him there.

'Come on then,' she said, patting herself under the over-hang of her belly, 'this is what you've paid for. I'll help you out of your clothes.'

She had him undressed in no time and on the bed with her. The brandy was making his head buzz but he understood at last why he was with this woman. He handled her great balloons – but in vain. His usually eager stem stayed limp.

'You've had too much booze, dear. Fancy a fine young man like you walking the streets at this hour of the night, blind drunk! Had a row with your girl-friend?'

She had hold of his useless part and massaged it briskly.

'I haven't got a girl-friend.'

'Then you must have lost all your money. I can't think of what else would have got you into a state like this.'

'I've plenty of money,' he muttered as she stroked his limp stem busily.

'What then?'

For no reason at all, except perhaps the drink and his unfamiliar feeling of guilt, Manfred told her what had happened at Ernst's party. Once he started talking he was unable to stop and confessed everything.

'Opium,' said the fat woman, 'I don't hold with that. One of my regulars died only a few weeks ago from cocaine and he was ever such a gentleman. All the same, you shouldn't have jumped on the girl like that.'

'What shall I do?'

'How do I know what you should do?'

'But you know a lot about men – you must do. What do you think I should do for the best?'

'Nothing. You had your fun and now you feel bad about it. By tomorrow it won't seem so bad and inside a week you'll be laughing at yourself. Just stay away from the girl and you'll soon forget about it.'

'You think that's best?'

She grinned at him.

'You can't take her a bunch of flowers and apologise, can you? Don't be stupid. She doesn't know you've had her. She'll wake up thinking her boy-friend gave her a wonderful night. He won't remember, she'll be happy. You're the only one who's suffering.'

'That's true,' he said.

'That's more like it – there's a bit of life in your dangler

166

now. We'll soon have it ready for action and get your little business finished.'

'You're a wonder-worker,' he said, staring down the length of his naked body to where she held his thickening stem in her fist.

'Practice makes perfect. Ready for it now?'

Manfred shook his head.

'After tonight I doubt if I'll ever have the nerve to do it again,' he said mournfully.

She laughed at him.

'You remind me of a man I knew years ago. Time after time he'd come to me, always with the same long face, and he could never get it to stand up. After the third or fourth time, he told me what the trouble was. He was a married man and he was doing it to his daughter while his wife was out at work. He said that the daughter was sixteen, but I never believed him. More like twelve or thirteen, I'd say, from the way he carried on. He was eaten up with guilt about what he was doing, and terrified his wife might find out. He hadn't slept with her for years, from what I could make out.'

'And you helped him?'

That made her laugh again, a full-throated bellow.

'It's not my job to help people! I've got a living to earn. After he'd told me about his problem he managed to get it to stand up. He even got on top of me, but he couldn't do anything. Not that it mattered to me – he paid me regularly once a week just to talk and tell me what a swine he was with his daughter and how he wished he could leave her alone.'

'And did he?'

'Don't be stupid! It was the biggest thing in his life. He was crazy for his daughter. He went on doing it to her day after day and coming to me on Sundays when his wife was at home to tell me what a rotten swine he was. It made him feel better to tell me. He thought I'd understand. My God – if I'd had my way with him I'd have taken a bread-knife

167

and cut his eggs off. That would have solved his problem for him.'

'What happened to him?'

'I don't know. After being a Sunday regular for three or four months he never turned up again. I was glad to see the back of him, even though I started charging him double after he told me about the daughter. Are you ready for the big jump now – you're hard enough.'

'I've had too much to drink.'

'It's too soon after having your sleeping beauty – that's more like it. Well, I'll see that you get your money's worth.'

Her clenched hand slid up and down his stem until Manfred's belly contracted and he spattered himself in nervous spasms.

'You'll feel better after that,' the fat woman soothed him, 'I'll get a towel to wipe you with.'

'Don't go away – I need you here,' and Manfred put his arms round her and rested his head on her swollen breasts.

'I don't know your name,' he said.

'You didn't ask. It's Hanni.'

She stroked his hair clumsily.

'Such a fine young man to get himself into a state over a silly girl who's not good enough to clean his shoes. You'll be all right now.'

'I'd like to stay with you, Hanni.'

'I don't know about that. I've had a hard day and I want to get some sleep. I've got my living to earn, even if you haven't.'

'I'll give you a hundred Marks.'

'You can stay,' she said at once, 'do you want to sleep now?'

'I want to talk.'

'For a hundred Marks you can talk all night.'

She hugged him to her vast bosom and Manfred felt comforted.

'I'm not in love with this girl, you understand,' he said, 'but I am sorry for what she's doing to herself. You see, when I thought she was a lesbian, I didn't worry about her, because she was with women I know – women of good family. But it's not the same now that I see she's letting thugs maul her about. Does that make sense, or am I being a fool?'

'Some women like it rough,' said Hanni, 'they get slapped around a bit and that's part of the fun. There's no sense in getting upset – everybody to their own taste.'

'I suppose you're right, but I don't like to think of this particular girl being like that.'

'Look, don't think I'm a Communist, because I'm not, but I've had a lot of men on top of me in my time and believe me, whether they're rich or poor, high-born or throat-cutters, what goes up me feels the same. It's the same for this girl of yours.'

'No, I don't believe that!'

'Look at it another way, you've been on top of well-born young ladies and you know what that's like. Now don't tell me you haven't had a bit of fun with poor girls as well. They're always ready to drop their knickers for someone like you with money enough to give them a good time. Tell the truth now.'

Manfred thought of Mitzi and Ilse and the romp in his apartment – on the sofa, in the shower and on his bed.

'Yes, but it's different for a man,' he said.

'I knew you'd say that! But tell me, if you can, that it felt any different when you had it up a common working-girl than when you had it up a young lady.'

Manfred found himself picturing the time when Ilse was lying above him, pretending to be a man and making love to him, her weight suspended on her straight arms and her breasts rolling as she thrust her loins at him. How she had made him spurt, while making believe that she was spurting into him!

'Well?' Hanni asked.

'I don't know what to think,' he murmured, his thoughts busy with Ilse.

'Yes, you do – you get the same pleasure from a poor

girl as a rich one. So forget about the one that bothers you and find another one.'

'There's something about that particular girl that attracts me.'

'And it doesn't take much guessing what that is. So you've sampled it and it didn't make you happy afterwards. Was it nice when you stuck this into her?' Hanni asked, her hand sliding up his thigh, 'Good God, it's standing up again already! Do you want me to hold it?'

'Yes,' he said, his eyes closed and his cheek resting on one big pillow of a breast.

As she played with him, Manfred took a nipple into his mouth and sucked at it. While the feelings of pleasure swirled through him, he retreated into a world of warm sensation, as deeply as Jenny had retreated into her opium trance. Before long he forgot that fat Hanni's hand was busy between his thighs – he forgot that she was even present. Something felt nice between his legs and something else felt nice in his mouth – and nothing else existed for him. The feelings got nicer and nicer and spread all the way through his body, so that he tingled from his curled-up toes to his sucking lips. Eventually something went off pop inside him and that was so very nice that he gurgled like a baby and after that he fell asleep, his head on a big fleshy cushion that was very comfortable.

The Film Show

When Wolfgang von Loschingen said that he was asking a few friends to a private film show, Manfred knew what to expect. On the last occasion he had been invited, back in January, there had been four of them watching pornographic films for an hour or two in Wolfgang's drawing-room, drinking his champagne and then, in a state of high exhilaration, they had taken a taxi to a small and illegal brothel in Franzosichestrasse. It specialised in Italian women, or so the proprietor claimed. Wolfgang and his friends took it over completely, told the owner to lock the door, drank a great deal more and got a real party going with the enthusiastic aid of the normally bored women.

A knockabout game of *Cavalry Action* soon established the right mood. Each young man had a naked whore mounted on his shoulders, bare thighs clamped round his neck and feet tucked under his arm-pits. The room was cleared of furniture and the couples took their positions in the corners. Wolfgang, as organiser of the revels that evening, gave the order to begin the action. He used the words of Marshal Blucher at the battle of Waterloo, words familiar to all of them from their schooldays:

'Raise high the black standard, my children! Death to the French!'

Howling the battle-cry 'Death to the French!' Manfred and the others charged towards the middle of the room, spurred on by the jabbing of high-heeled shoes in their ribs. They collided, bumped at each other with their shoulders, the use of hands being forbidden to the horses, while the women shrieked with excitement, swiped at each other's breasts and tried to grab each other by the hair. After only a minute or two of noisy scrummage, Konrad was tripped and went sprawling on the floor, his rider's legs high in the air as she screamed curses in Italian.

Dismounted riders were allowed to save themselves by crawling away, but fallen horses remained on the battle-field. Wolfgang reeled from a dig in the side by an elbow, stumbled over Konrad and went down on his knees to save himself from falling head-long. His rider fell off, yelping in terror, to land upside-down on Konrad, who grabbed her and planted a smacking kiss on her belly before she wriggled free and scrambled away from the field of honour.

Manfred was left facing Hans Dietrich over the bodies of Konrad and Wolfgang. He gave a great bellow and leaped over Konrad, almost unseating his rider by the sudden attack. He strode over Wolfgang's legs and hit Hans with his shoulder, using all his weight. Hans stumbled back, almost off balance, and Manfred had victory in his grasp. But Hans' girl had Manfred's girl by her long dark hair and was tugging furiously. She leaned forward sharply to ease the pain of having her hair torn out and over-balanced Manfred. He landed on his hands and knees, the battle lost. But not quite – for the girl who pitched forward over his head butted Hans by chance in his most vulnerable spot. Hans shouted and bent double, tipping his rider forward, and she brought him down too.

Manfred found himself face-down on the floor, his face on his girl's belly, while the other girl crawled away on her hands and knees, the cheeks of her bottom wobbling comically. Wolfgang resumed command. He rose to his feet, black bow-tie under one ear, to announce with pride:

'Victory! Not a French dog left on his feet!'

A glass or two of brandy restored Hans and the party continued. Manfred proposed another game in which the men were hounds and the girls their quarry, with all parts of the establishment the hunting-ground. It was a good game, with continuous hunting-cries and shrieks of alarm.

When a girl was caught, she was rolled on to her back and dealt with by her captor. The house had six women in all and by midnight they had all been caught, several times over, and the hunters were at a standstill. They divided between them the colossal bill they had run up for drinks and the girls and, at the insistence of the woman in charge, for the loss of business incurred by barring the door to other clients all evening. Altogether it was a most satisfactory evening.

It was therefore with feelings of lively anticipation that Manfred arrived at Wolfgang's apartment for another such evening. The servants had been given the evening off, as usual, and Wolfgang himself opened the door and welcomed him. Konrad was already in the drawing-room, talking to a young man Manfred had not met before – the only one of them not in evening clothes. The projector had been set up on a high stand, a portable screen erected by the wall and bottles stood ready in silver ice-buckets.

The surprise was to be introduced to Frau von Loschingen.

'My beautiful aunt,' Wolfgang explained.

Manfred bowed and kissed her hand, wondering how long she would stay. She was a tall woman of about forty, handsome rather than beautiful, with a slightly beaked nose and a carefully made-up face. Her long evening gown was breath-taking. The colour was burnt orange and it was sleeveless, back-less, and slit in front right down between her breasts. It fitted very closely and displayed a figure that was still good. On the hand she extended graciously to Manfred to be kissed was a diamond ring the size of a walnut. And, he noted, another on her other hand, a matching bracelet on each wrist and diamond studs in her ears. A lady of wealth, fashion and taste, he concluded.

'What a wonderful sun-tan, Madame,' he said, 'have you been on holiday to some exotic part of the world?'

Her long arms and exposed bosom were a golden colour that was most attractive against her gown.

'I live near Lisbon,' she explained.

'Then that is the reason why I have not had the honour of making your acquaintance before, though I have known Wolfgang for years. How long have you lived abroad?'

'I left Berlin at the end of the War. I come back for a week or two each year to see if anything has changed.'

'And has it?'

'Oh yes, Berlin gets worse with every year that passes. My stay will not be a long one this time.'

'I am sorry to hear you say that. In what way are things getting worse, Madame?'

'You must call me Jutta. I suppose I seem an old woman to you but I grew up in the well-ordered Berlin of the Emperor Wilhelm. Such wonderful days they were – the balls, the dinner-parties, the opera – but the War destroyed all that. Nowadays Germany has a government of bolsheviks and anarchists. Some of the old families cling on in the hope that things will improve, but they are deceiving themselves. It will get worse, not better.'

'Do you think so?' Manfred asked.

'You have only to look around you. So-called society in Berlin now is made up of vulgar businessmen and cheap theatre actors – people of no background. I find it intolerable to find myself at the next table to a rich coal-merchant in a good restaurant. Surely you must feel the same.'

'I try not to know people like that.'

'Know them? God forbid! It is enough to see these people from nowhere usurping the places of their betters without having to *know* them.'

Wolfgang brought over the stranger in the brown-striped suit and introduced him as Franz Esschen.

'Franz brought the films we are going to see. Two completely new ones – which he guarantees are positively volcanic.'

Manfred glanced at Jutta von Loschingen and saw that she was smiling wickedly at him.

'I believe that you are shocked,' she said, 'as your friend Konrad was when he arrived and found me here. Do you

174

think that only men are interested in these amusements? Are ladies to be denied their diversions?'

'Few ladies would admit to an interest in amusements of this sort,' said Manfred with a grin.

Franz Esschen said nothing, but he was blushing.

'Hypocrisy is the failing of little people,' Jutta said, 'I heard all about Wolfgang's last film show over dinner the other evening. He claims that you had a wonderful party afterwards with some French women.'

'Italian women,' Manfred corrected her, seeing that she took it all in good humour. 'We had a game of hounds and deer that lasted for hours before we worried the deer to death.'

'If you're ready,' said Wolfgang, 'I'll top up your glasses and we'll make a start.'

'I'm ready,' said Konrad, winking at Manfred.

'Why are you here?' Manfred asked. 'What has come of your rendezvous with a certain married lady we both know well?'

'I haven't seen her all that much since Ulrika's party,' said Konrad. 'It's dangerous, with a husband who can frighten poor Werner away completely. Do you know where he is?'

'He's in Vienna. I wrote him a letter the other day, offering my services to effect a reconciliation.'

'This has the sound of a fascinating story,' said Jutta von Loschingen. 'One of you must tell me later. I smell all the ingredients of a good scandal.'

Wolfgang had refilled the glasses.

'Where will you sit, dear Aunt?'

'Here,' she answered, seating herself gracefully on the silver-brocade sofa. 'Come and sit by me, Manfred.'

The furniture had been arranged in a semi-circle facing the screen. Several possibilities were revolving in Manfred's head as he took his seat as directed. Did this surprising lady propose to accompany them later on to whatever private establishment Wolfgang had made arrangements with? It seemed possible, given her uninhibited personality. Would

175

she join in the revelry and compete with the women of the house? That would be entertaining, but very improbable. She was, Manfred decided a voyeur and she would obtain her gratification from watching the rest of them at play.

Thick curtains over the windows shut out the miserable rainy autumn evening and when Wolfgang switched off the electric lights the drawing-room was in complete darkness. Franz Esschen set the projector going and an oblong of light appeared on the screen. Eventually a lettered title came up: *Tilly Visits the Dentist*, and the film began. The scene opened on a nondescript room with a dentist's chair in the middle and a man in a long white coat facing away and doing something at a glass-fronted cabinet. A woman entered from the right of the picture, wearing a cloche hat and an outdoor coat with a strip of fur round the collar. The dentist turned to greet her, helped her out of her coat and hung it, with her hat, on a peg on the wall. Seen in full-face, he was a villainous-looking man in his forties, short-necked and dark of complexion.

'I wouldn't let him touch my teeth,' said Jutta beside Manfred. 'He looks like a cheap murderer.'

'More like a pimp, I would say,' Manfred suggested.

Tilly was in the chair, her head back against the rest and her short skirt pulled well up over her chubby knees. The best that could be said for her was that she was in her twenties, but she was too heavy-featured to be even passably pretty when seen close-up. Her make-up was plastered on thickly and not very expertly, her eye-brows untrimmed. The dentist peered into her open mouth with his little mirror and words came up on the screen: *'This is more serious than I thought, Fraulein. I must give you gas before I proceed.'* There followed a view of the dentist's hand holding a black rubber mask over Tilly's nose and mouth.

'He has dirty finger-nails!' Jutta exclaimed.

More words were displayed:

'Good, she is asleep. She is so beautiful that I cannot control myself!'

Manfred chuckled at that, feeling that it would require

176

no great effort to control himself in the presence of Fraulein Tilly, conscious or unconscious. The screen showed her from a distance, her eyes closed and seemingly asleep, her knees lolling apart and her skirt up high enough to display her stocking-tops and garters. Standing at her side, the uncontrollable dentist unbuttoned her white blouse from neck to waist to expose a pair of plump breasts. The viewpoint moved in slowly until the screen was filled by Tilly's big melons, over which the short and stubby fingers of the dentist strayed.

'Go on, man -- grab a handful!' Wolfgang called out in the dark.

'Those awful nails!' said Jutta. 'If he touched me I would die!'

For a long time the screen was occupied by the dentist's hand stroking and squeezing Tilly's breasts. Manfred shifted slightly on the sofa to make himself more comfortable as his stem reacted to what he was seeing. But at last the scene faded into a longer view of the sleeping patient, her legs sprawled wider than ever. The evil dentist tugged her skirt higher and under her bottom, until he had it in folds round her waist. She was wearing knickers with short and close-fitting legs with frills round the bottoms.

'I've never seen a girl wearing those,' said Manfred.

'You've never seen a girl wearing knickers of any sort,' Konrad commented from his chair somewhere over to the right.

'I've seen one wearing a scarf round her waist,' Manfred reminded him.

'Yes, and I was the one who had the pleasure of taking it off,' Konrad retorted.

'You were not the only one that night.'

'Shut up, you two,' Wolfgang complained, 'Things are warming up.'

Indeed, the lustful dentist had his hand and much of his fore-arm down the front of Tilly's knickers, as if searching for something. Words appeared on the screen to announce his discovery:

177

'I cannot believe it! I must see it! But how?'

He moved out of the scene, leaving the camera to focus on the join of Tilly's legs, where a dark shadow showed through the white of her knickers. Then he was back, a pair of scissors in his hand.

'My God – he's going to shear her like a sheep!' said Konrad.

The others laughed, but their attention was seized as the dentist wielded his scissors to cut down the front of Tilly's knickers in a ragged line from waist to mound. The cut flaps fell to show her plump belly and the beginning of her curly tuft. He slid one blade under the frill round the leg of her knickers and cut carefully upwards along her fleshy thigh until he met his down-cut, and then up along the other thigh. The ruined knickers fell away to reveal a dark and bushy growth of hair that not only hid her secrets but extended for some little way down the insides of her thighs.

'What a bush!' said Konrad, 'I've never seen one like it.'

'Nor I!' Wolfgang agreed. 'Imagine running your fingers through that!'

'She has an attractive belly-button,' Manfred pointed out, 'deep and round.'

'You find that attractive, do you?' Jutta asked beside him.

In some manner Manfred could not explain, he was holding Jutta's hand on the sofa between them and her fingers were gripping hard.

'It is a special study of mine,' he told her.

Words on the screen proved that the wicked dentist was of the same mind as Konrad and Wolfgang about what he had uncovered:

'BEAUTIFUL! It is like a fur-coat between her legs! There cannot be another like this anywhere – I must have it! But what if she wakes up?'

'Give her more gas, you fool!' Konrad called out.

The same thought occurred to the dentist and he held the mask over Tilly's sleeping face for a second or two.

'More, you blockhead!' Konrad advised.

'He's the expert,' said Manfred, laughing. 'Do you want to kill her?'

The picture flickered and showed Tilly's parted thighs and the anxious dentist's hand between them, his middle finger sunk into her magnificent tuft to the second knuckle.

'This is getting serious,' said Konrad, 'I hope all the arrangements are made for after the film-show, Wolfgang.'

'No problem. Just shut up and watch.'

The evil-minded dentist was down on his knees between Tilly's legs, using both hands to examine her depths. Manfred became aware that Jutta had moved imperceptibly closer to him along the sofa in the dark and her thigh was pressed along his own. Their clasped hands, which had been lying on the seat between them, were now resting in her lap.

This very superior lady may have need of my services before she leaves Berlin, he thought with amusement – and why not? There's many a good tune to be played on an old violin.

The screen showed the dentist and his patient from the side, he still on his knees between her legs. He shrugged off his long white coat to display broad embroidered braces over his shoulders to hold up his trousers.

'Good Lord – what street-market did he buy those in!' Wolfgang exclaimed, but no one was listening to him.

The dentist ripped open his trouser buttons and out sprang a short and thick stem at full stretch.

'It won't be her teeth he's going to drill!' said Konrad.

Jutta was holding Manfred's wrist and rubbing his palm against her belly through the thin silk of her evening gown. He obliged her with a sensual massage, letting his fingers sink into her flesh. Meanwhile the wanton dentist had hoisted Tilly's legs up over his shoulders and, in close-up, the screen showed his stubby stem penetrating her curly tuft.

'Unbelievable!' someone murmured, but whether it was Konrad or Wolfgang was impossible to distinguish. Manfred's slow massage of Jutta's warm belly encouraged

179

her to do the same for him and her hand was pressed close over the stiffness inside his clothes.

Stubby though it may have been in reality, in close-up on the screen the dentist's drill was magnified to the length of a fore-arm and the hairy dependents below it were the size of coconuts. It slid in and out of Tilly like the piston of a railway engine, gathering speed all the time. Jutta's hand was clenched on Manfred's stem so hard as to be almost painful and her legs had parted to let him massage between her legs through the silk of her clothes.

'My God!' she gasped. 'Look!'

And well she might gasp! In the nick of time the rapist-dentist jerked his drill out and directed his outburst of lust on to Tilly's plump belly. The little audience sat speechless as they watched the climactic process to its end. Then the dentist moved away and the screen showed poor sleeping Tilly, her head lolling sideways, her melons uncovered and her bared belly streaked with the dentist's passion.

Jutta's hand left Manfred's lap and she moved silently away from him as *The End* came up on the screen. Manfred tugged his silk handkerchief from his breast-pocket and was dabbing at his perspiring forehead when Wolfgang switched on a floor-lamp in a corner behind them, imparting a soft golden glow to the room.

'More champagne, dear friends,' he suggested, 'I hope you all enjoyed the visit to the dentist.'

'Do you suppose that there are dentists who abuse their patients like that, Wolfgang?' Jutta enquired, her face flushed a delicate pink.

'They all do,' he answered cheerfully. 'Don't they, Manfred?'

'I am going to look for a woman dentist in the hope that she will take advantage of me,' he answered.

'There is a point which bothers me,' said Konrad. 'When Fraulein Tilly wakes up from the gas and stands up to leave, the tatters of her underwear will fall around her ankles. How will the dentist explain that?'

'He has a needle and thread at hand,' said Manfred.

180

'Safety-pins would be simpler,' Wolfgang suggested. 'Have you changed the reel yet, Franz?'

'Nearly ready.'

'This is thirsty work, my dear Aunt,' said Wolfgang with a grin. 'Finish your glass and let me refill it. You're going to need it.'

'I saw a film in Rome last year which would amuse you,' she said, holding out her glass. 'It was made specially for my host and it had two Cardinals doing the most interesting things to a young nun.'

'At the same time?'

'Naturally. What are we going to see next?'

'I don't know. Are you ready yet, Franz?'

'Ready.'

'Good. What's this one about?'

'You will see,' the young man in the brown-striped suit said mysteriously.

. Wolfgang switched off the light and took his seat. The projector whirred and the title appeared on the screen: *The Nudist Club*. Wolfgang groaned loudly in the dark.

'Not another nudist epic! We've seen dozens of them.'

'Not like this one,' said Franz.

The opening scene was of park-land with trees and shrubbery. Half a dozen people lay on the grass, taking the sun. They were too distant to discern more than that some of them were men and some were women. More scenes of the same sort followed, from different angles, all distant, and then a sequence of nudists swimming in a lake.

'What did I say!' Wolfgang exclaimed. 'This is boring! Put something else on, Franz, before we fall asleep.'

'Wait a moment – it gets better.'

After what seemed like a long time filled with harmless nudists splashing about in the water, the scene changed abruptly to show a woman lying on a towel on the grass, her bare back and bottom to the audience. She sat up slowly and turned full-face to sit cross-legged and smiling. She was thin, but her breasts were over-sized and out of proportion to the rest of her body.

181

'Well, at least it's not Tilly again,' Konrad commented.

'How can you be sure?' Wolfgang asked, 'She might have gone on a diet.'

'Tilly had an enormous tuft.'

'She could have clipped it. The dentist might have clipped it for her before she left.'

'This girl does not wear knickers with frills,' said Manfred. 'That proves it is not Tilly.'

'And what about her belly-button?' Jutta asked, 'Is that different?'

'As you can observe, this girl's is round and slightly protruding, not deep-set like Tilly's.'

On the screen the nudist took a comb from somewhere and combed her hair, keeping her elbows well up to give an unimpeded view of her breasts rolling about to her movements.

'A good pair,' said Konrad judiciously, 'if you put your face between those and shook your head you'd knock yourself out.'

The scene faded to one of a man, seen from behind, down on his knees to peer through a big knot-hole in a wooden fence. After a time words came up on the screen to indicate his thoughts:

'What fantastic breasts she has! I wish I had the courage to talk to her.'

'Go on, idiot, she's waiting for you,' said Wolfgang.

The naked man reappeared in side-view, his eye pressed to the fence and his stem standing up boldly. There was a tattoo on his arm of a dagger and a snake.

'Good God! It's Erwin!' Manfred exclaimed.

'You know him?' Jutta asked in disbelief.

'I think it's someone I met at a friend's party. Konrad – you were there at Ernst's – do you recognise him?'

'There were so many down-and-out intellectuals there – how can I be expected to remember them? Are you sure?'

'I'll tell you when I get a better look at his face.'

But the man was gone and the view was of the girl nudist. She was sitting with her knees up and apart and was continuing her grooming by combing the hair between her legs.

'The dentist should have thought of that,' said Wolfgang, 'Tilly really had something to comb! Auntie dear – do you comb between your legs when you are dressing for a party?'

'Naturally – everybody does.'

Words on the screen revealed the girl's state of mind:

'*I wish a nice young man would come and talk to me. It is healthy to sit in the sun, but I am lonely.*'

The words drew hoots of laughter from the audience, which continued even more loudly when the scene changed to show the man behind the fence. His face was not in sight, only his lower half, and his clenched fist was sliding up and down his upright stem.

'Do you recognise him now?' Konrad asked, causing more ribald laughter.

Before Manfred could retort, dramatic developments on the screen gave rise to more laughter. The man rose to his feet and pushed his rigid stem through the knot-hole. His whole body was pressed close to the fence and his face was turned sideways towards the viewers.

'That's him!' said Manfred, 'that's Erwin!'

The scene shifted to the other side of the fence. Erwin's stem stuck through the knot-hole, looking forlorn and ridiculous. But he had evidently done the right thing, for there followed a view of the girl, her face registering surprise as she caught sight of the unexpected projection. She rose from her towel and went to the fence.

'Give it a sharp pull and see if he squeals!' Wolfgang called out.

The girl had other plans. She knelt by the fence and stroked Erwin's projection. She tickled the underside with one finger to make it jump and, satisfied by her examination, moved close to the fence and enclosed Erwin's stem between her big fleshy globes. Her expression changed to one of rapture.

'That's more like it,' said Konrad, 'I wouldn't object to having mine wrapped up warm in those.'

Jutta's hand was back in Manfred's lap and she stroked up and down through his clothes. He put his palm on her thigh and caressed it slowly in a gesture of appreciation.

The viewpoint was from above the girl's right shoulder, looking down on the action. She squeezed her breasts together with her hands, sandwiching Erwin's stem, and rubbed herself up and down against it. The head popped in and out of sight like a tortoise's head out of its shell and Manfred heard Jutta sighing faintly in the dark. The film seemed to be affecting her more than anyone else.

The scene continued until Erwin discharged his passion in a torrent up the girl's chest to her throat.

'What a boring film!' said Wolfgang, 'I knew it would be as soon as I saw the title. You'll have to do better than that, Franz.'

He spoke too soon. Instead of calming Erwin down, the experience cured him of his shyness. The film continued, and Erwin was over the fence and the girl down on her hands and knees on the grass while he mounted her dog-fashion. He pounded away for some time before the scene changed to a close-up of the girl's face. Her eyes were closed and her mouth was moving. Words appeared on the screen for the benefit of those unable to lip-read:

'Yes! Do it to me! Faster! Faster!'

Her face filled the entire screen and it was obvious that she was nearing the critical moments. Her head jerked up and down like the head of a puppet and her lips drew back in a grimace that showed her teeth. For the first time since the film started the little audience was totally silent, caught up in the girl's mounting excitement. They saw raw and naked lust in her face and they felt it themselves. Jutta's hand was so demanding in Manfred's lap that he feared she might bring about an accident in his trousers.

On the screen the girl's face screwed itself up, her eyes blinked open to stare blindly and her mouth gaped wide in a silent scream of orgasmic release. For ten seconds that seemed like an eternity the image of her ecstatic face dominated the audience and then slowly the viewpoint receded to bring her shoulders and arms into sight, and further back still to show her heavy breasts hanging beneath her, and further still, until she was wholly in view, her head drooping in exhaustion and Erwin slumped along her back.

The screen went dark abruptly and Franz switched off the projector. Jutta's hand left Manfred's tormented lap, not a moment too soon in his opinion. He sensed and heard her moving beside him on the sofa and wondered if the incredible close-up of the girl's face had communicated itself so forcefully to her that she had experienced a vicarious release herself.

Some little time passed in silence before Wolfgang roused himself to switch on the single lamp in the corner. Manfred blinked at the sudden illumination, discreet though it was, and then blinked again in astonishment. Jutta was no longer on the sofa beside him. She sat on the floor, her back against an unoccupied arm-chair, where they all could see her. Her beautiful evening gown lay discarded across the sofa near Manfred and she was naked but for flesh-coloured silk stockings and high-heeled shoes.

She sat with one knee up and the other bent and flat on the Persian carpet, showing off her sleek thighs and the tuft of glossy brown hair between them.

She has a good body for a woman of forty, Manfred thought. Her breasts were very well-shaped, small and still firm, with prominent red-brown buds. Her whole body, from forehead to red-painted toe-nails, was sun-tanned a rich golden colour, proof enough that she did not trouble herself with swim-suits.

The four young men stared at her in silence, not wanting to dispell the enchantment. Jutta too said nothing, her expression one of pride as she drank in their wordless admiration. She sat straight-backed and unmoving, like a living statue, one diamond-ringed hand on her upraised knee. Manfred took the initiative. He rose to his feet and stripped off his evening clothes and flung them away from him until he stood naked and his hard stem pointed in the direction of the woman waiting for him. The other men

185

stared in silence, entranced by the drama of the transition from flickering images on the screen to flesh and blood reality. Jutta gazed calmly at Manfred, as if assessing the breadth of his shoulders and his muscular thighs, before letting her look linger on his out-thrust stem.

He squatted on the carpet, close enough to lean forward and kiss her breasts and to stroke the insides of her thighs above her stockings, where the skin felt like fine satin. He forgot that anyone else was present and that his friends were watching in hushed silence. He caressed Jutta between the thighs, running his fingers through the well-groomed tuft of hair and over the protruding folds of flesh. Still she didn't move, nor did her expression change.

Manfred put his hands in her smooth arm-pits and lifted her so that she sat on the edge of the arm-chair and he could move in close on his knees. She uttered a long throaty sigh as he penetrated her and then was silent again. Her dark-brown eyes stared down between their bodies at the fleshy link that joined them and slid to and fro in a stately rhythm. Manfred knew that he would not last very long and he wanted to make the most of this unexpected opportunity. He looked at Jutta's face, trying to read what was in her eyes, but they told him nothing, and soon he was too far gone to focus clearly. His loins bucked furiously to release his passion and Jutta shook in pleasure, but even then she remained silent, though her finger-nails dug deep into the flesh of his shoulders.

'That was charming,' she said eventually, 'you caught my mood exactly.'

Manfred smiled at her and drew away. There was an impatient hand on his shoulder and Konrad's voice telling him to move out of the way. He did so and saw Konrad take Jutta by the hand and pull her off the chair, to take her back to the silver-brocade sofa and spread her on her back.

It was a short, sharp performance once Konrad was on top of her. Her legs twined over his waist, one silk stocking hanging round an ankle, as Konrad pummelled her like a clock-work toy run wild. Jutta seemed to enjoy it well enough and the sound of her panting mingled with Konrad's. Her high-heeled shoes drummed against Konrad's heaving bottom as they reached their climactic moments together.

Konrad was still twitching when Wolfgang dragged him bodily off Jutta and took his place on top of her. In his haste to undress he had forgotten his black silk socks. He sank his long thin stem between Jutta's upraised thighs and groped avidly for her breasts and Manfred found himself wondering if it counted as incest for Wolfgang to make love to his aunt. And did it matter anyway? Both participants gave every sign of enjoying what they were doing, which surely was the only consideration of any importance.

Wolfgang displayed a most vigorous style of love-making. Once embedded in his dear Auntie he twisted and jerked and sighed and moaned. The outcome was not long delayed. Wolfgang's wailing rose to a crescendo and Jutta gave voice herself for the first time, crying out and gasping. Clasped in each other's arms they rolled about on the sofa in spasmodic ecstasy, legs flailing and kicking, their combined outcry thrilling and impressive.

As the bouncing of the interlocked bodies on the sofa slowed down, Manfred glanced round the room for Franz Esschen, whose turn to gratify Jutta had arrived. He was slumped in an arm-chair by the projector, naked as the rest of them, his eyes closed and his legs splayed. It was all too apparent that his passion had overcome his patience. There was a long wet trickle down his belly and his stem hung limply between his thighs.

Wolfgang climbed off Jutta and looked round. He saw Franz's condition and grinned.

'I am sorry to disappoint you,' he said to Jutta, 'Franz couldn't wait.'

Jutta sat up and glared over the back of the sofa at poor disgraced Franz.

'Useless swine!' she said. 'His sort are never any good when you need them.'

187

Manfred got up from the carpet and said that it would be impolite to disappoint a lady of her expectations. Although he had judged Wolfgang's love-making to lack style, the truth was that the moaning and thrashing about had aroused him strongly again. His stem stood hard and glistening in the golden lamp-light and, standing with his shoulders back and his back straight, he knew that he made a good impression. Jutta was off the sofa at once, both stockings now round her ankles. She balanced herself with a hand on Manfred's shoulder while she removed her shoes and stockings, then threw herself into his arms, trapping his upright stem between their bellies.

'Dear Manfred – you have such style!'

'You are in a more vigorous mood now than when we started,' he said, smiling at her.

'These boys have excited me to the point of madness! But they have not satisfied me – will you do that?'

'I shall do my best!'

'You must do more than that! I want to be destroyed!'

Manfred let go of her for a moment and whirled the nearest arm-chair round so that its back was towards them, seized her by the shoulders and flung her roughly against it. She gasped as the padded back caught her across the belly and pitched forward, her head hanging down towards the cushioned seat. Manfred planted himself solidly behind her bottom and kicked her ankles apart with his bare foot to expose the split mound under her belly. The dark-brown hair was plastered wetly to the open fleshy lips. He stabbed a thumb deeply into it and she cried out in shock.

'This could take a regiment of Grenadiers, one after the other,' he said brutally. 'What can three of us hope to achieve? It will swallow us up!'

Jutta shrieked in pleasure as his rigid thumb twisted inside her. She was not a woman to lie on her back, he judged, being far too skilled in the ways of love for so unimaginative an attitude. That she had received Konrad and Wolfgang in that way was due, he believed, to her verdict that they were too young to know better and her

188

desire was too impetuous to delay its gratification by showing them alternatives. She squealed in delight again as he forced both thumbs deep into her wetness.

Manfred glanced up from what he was doing and became vaguely aware that Konrad was sitting on the floor, arms round his knees, and Wolfgang was lying on the abandoned sofa, and both of them were staring intently at what he was doing to Jutta. Even Franz had emerged from his torpor and was gazing glassy-eyed.

Jutta screamed loudly, her head jerked up and her hands clawed at the chair cushions. Before her orgasmic convulsions stopped, Manfred removed his thumbs and plunged his stem into her, so fiercely that his belly smacked against her bare bottom. He ravaged her fast and hard, so over-wrought that he did not hear her continuous shrieks or notice that her body was flopping up and down as if she were a hare shaken and worried in the jaws of a hound. He sank his finger-nails into the flesh of her bottom and pulled the cheeks apart to expose her little knot of muscle. He saw it clench and unclench and he jammed his slippery thumb into it.

His belly contracted, he roared wordlessly in triumph and exploded into Jutta, slamming himself against her bottom as he stabbed and stabbed, almost as if he were trying to kill her. Her screams of pleasure rose to a nerve-wracking peak and stopped abruptly. After that she hung over the chair-back like a rag-doll.

When Manfred regained his senses he glanced at his friends and was puzzled by the expressions on their faces.

'Holy God!' said Wolfgang from the sofa. 'Is she dead?'

'Never better in her life,' said Manfred proudly, it occurring to him that the expression he had seen was that of awe.

He disengaged himself from Jutta, picked her up and carried her to the sofa, where Wolfgang scrambled out of the way and helped to arrange her comfortably with a cushion under her head.

'A glass of brandy would be good,' Manfred suggested.

'She certainly needs it,' Wolfgang agreed, going to the sideboard where the bottles stood.

'Not her, you idiot, me,' said Manfred.

He sat on the carpet and leaned back against the sofa where Jutta lay, pleased with himself. Wolfgang brought the brandy and he swallowed half of it in one gulp.

'And for me,' said Jutta behind him, her voice weak.

Manfred cradled her head in his arm and raised it while she sipped at the glass. Her eyes were languorous as she looked up at him.

'Satisfactory?' he asked with a grin.

'You've destroyed me. It was fantastic.'

'You'd better sleep here tonight,' Wolfgang suggested.

She nodded drowsily. Manfred picked her up again and followed Wolfgang to a bed-room. Jutta was already half-asleep when he settled her in the bed and covered her over. He switched off the light and went back to the drawing-room, to find Konrad and Franz dressing. Wolfgang had put on a long crimson silk dressing-gown with a golden cord round the waist. Manfred put on his underwear and sat down to drink another glass of brandy.

'I must congratulate you,' said Konrad, 'Your performance was heroic – stupendous! I could hear Wagner's music thundering away in the background while you were banging away at her.'

'What a pity we couldn't have filmed it,' Wolfgang said with a broad grin, 'It was better than anything we saw on the screen, wasn't it, Franz?'

'If I'd known what was going to happen, I'd have asked my friend in the film business to be here with his camera,' Franz answered, taking him seriously. 'We had enough actors!'

'Where do they get the actors from for your films?' Konrad asked.

'They're not actors. Everything you see is real and everyone knows how to do that. They pick young whores for the job and pay them a few Marks.'

'And the men?'

'Some of them are students and some are just out of work and want to earn a little money – like the one this gentleman recognised. What did you say his name was?'

'Erwin. I don't know his last name. I think he's some sort of unsuccessful writer, but he may be a criminal.'

'It was a shame that you couldn't oblige my aunt, Franz,' said Wolfgang, 'It was expected of you and you failed her.'

'It was watching the three of you go first – I couldn't hold out. Before I knew what was happening I went off like a water-pistol.'

'It's watching pornographic films all the time that does it,' said Wolfgang, grinning, 'Perhaps you should go into another business before you become incapable with women.'

Manfred waited a couple of days before he made a formal call upon Jutta. In an elegant light grey overcoat and a matching Homburg hat he walked along the avenue of the Unter den Linden under a grey and lowering sky and turned in under the awning of the Adlon Hotel. The doorman saluted him in military style and stood to attention. The dark-suited receptionist bowed when he enquired for Frau von Loschingen, and a uniformed page-boy in white gloves conducted him to Jutta's suite. Her personal maid, in regulation black frock and starched apron took his visiting-card and went to enquire if Madame would receive him. She returned to admit him and take his hat and coat.

Jutta was in the sitting-room of the suite, a large and airy room with arrangements of flowers, even this late in the year, standing on almost every flat surface. She was not alone, he saw with a flicker of annoyance. Franz Esschen, purveyor of unusual films, rose to his feet and bowed in a surprisingly deferential way as Manfred entered the room. Manfred nodded to him and kissed Jutta's hand. She was not wearing her diamonds so early in the day, merely sapphires on each hand. She greeted him in a friendly but reserved manner and instructed the maid to bring more tea with lemon.

191

'It is kind of you to call. I thought of going for a walk in the Tiergarten this afternoon but then Herr Esschen arrived and here I am.'

'Are you engaged for dinner this evening, may I ask?'

She nodded.

'Your visits to Berlin must be busy social occasions, I realise,' he said pleasantly.

'I try to keep up with my friends.'

Franz Esschen, sitting opposite Jutta on an elaborately carved chair, seemed to be uncomfortable, perhaps even embarrassed. He did not have the look of a man who had made any progress in her affections. The maid served tea to Manfred and Jutta told her that Herr Esschen was leaving and to see him out. Franz stood up, pale of face, and took his leave hurriedly.

'That's better,' Jutta said, 'I do not feel at ease with that young man. I am glad that you came, Manfred.'

'I suppose he called to apologise for his failure the other evening.'

'I don't like him,' she said.

Manfred thought it better to change the subject and asked where she bought her wonderful clothes. She was wearing a beautifully-styled costume of jacket and skirt in delicate lime-green.

'In Paris, of course,' she said. 'The women here dress like frumps. Do you like this costume?'

'The colour is perfect with your hair and complexion, even though it conceals your superb sun-tan. To see you golden all over was exquisite. Nothing is less appealing than a woman with tanned shoulders and legs with a white body between. In Lisbon you are able to set aside the petty consideration of wearing a swim-suit.'

'That is true, but what you saw was not acquired in Portugal but in Sicily. I have been there most of the summer and I am on my way back to Lisbon with this diversion to Berlin to see my friends here.'

'Sicily? How interesting. You have friends there too, I'm sure.'

192

'Quite a few – and one in particular, a friend from the old days in Berlin who has lived in Sicily since the end of the War.'

'A connoisseur of antiques, perhaps. I have read that there are very fine Greek ruins in Sicily.'

Jutta chuckled in an exciting throaty way.

'His interest is less in Greek temples than in young Sicilian boys. He lives not far from Taormina, in a house on the high cliffs above the sea, surrounded by groves of olives and lemons and figs – the whole landscape is amazingly beautiful.'

'He perceives some quality in Sicilian boys which is not present in German boys, does he?' Manfred asked dryly. 'It can hardly be a question of availability. Our local variety parade up and down the Kurfurstendamm every evening to look for customers.'

'Exactly! That's why he lives where he does. A vulgar parade of boys offering themselves for sale would be very offensive to him. In Sicily he lives among children of nature, unspoiled by our decadent civilisation. He poses them in the famous Greek ruins and takes photographs – and his pictures are works of art. He recreates the ancient world so well that it is as if you saw the youth of Classical Greece brought back to life.'

'An unusual interest for a man of leisure.'

'You shall judge for yourself.'

Jutta went out of the sitting-room for a moment and came back with a sheaf of large photographic prints. Manfred sat beside her on the sofa and took the first picture she offered him. It showed a boy, leaning against a rock-face in a casual attitude, a reed-flute in his hand. He was curly-haired, naked and bare-foot. His personal flute, not the one in his hand, seemed exceptionally well-grown for a boy of his age and hung heavily between his sturdy thighs.

'There!' said Jutta with enthusiasm, 'The very image of a young shepherd, such as the old Greek poets wrote about! Or he could be a young Pan, resting by the sun-drenched rocks, as self-contained and yet as wary as a young animal.

He listens and watches. He may take fright at the far-off sound of a human voice and skip lightly away into the olive-grove. But if he hears only the sound of bees and the distant bleat of a sheep, he will raise his reed-flute to his lips and play a thrilling melody that hints of gods and goddesses in repose and the deep indescribable tranquillity of nature undisturbed by man.'

Manfred was so struck by her words that he wondered if she was translating from some poet unfamiliar to him.

'Your sensitivity to the secret meaning of this picture is worthy of the highest praise,' he said. 'You have made me realise that it is not just a boy with no clothes on.'

Jutta's dark-brown eyes stared fixedly at him.

'We have allowed our lives to become confused and misdirected, my dear Manfred. The noise and distractions of cities and so-called society have robbed us of our God-given sensibilities towards nature and its truths. Do you not feel this?'

'You put it so clearly.'

She showed him the rest of the photographs, other boys posed in other places – against an antique ruined stone column, under a tree, sprawled on a flight of worn stone steps, on the sea-shore by a wooden boat – all of them naked and displaying their pubescent masculinity boldly. It was to the first picture she returned when she explained further.

'These pretty boys do not understand that they are living an idyllic life. To *understand* is a mental process. But they *feel* it in their hearts. This boy, for example, is wholly natural and wholly himself, because he knows nothing else. And therefore he is happy in a way which you and I cannot share. He eats and sleeps and loves as the mood takes him.'

'He is a little too young to know the delights and torments of love,' Manfred objected.

'Not at all,' said Jutta, her red-painted mouth curving in a slow smile.

'He is well-developed, I agree. Perhaps his flute is not always as docile as when your friend took this photograph.'

'I have seen it far from docile,' she said, and laughed.

It was impossible to mistake the delicate pink flush of her cheeks. Manfred unbuttoned her elegant little jacket and found, as he had expected, that she wore nothing under it. He stroked her small firm breasts with pleasure.

'This is what that fool Esschen came here for,' he said playfully.

'No he didn't – he had something else in mind, though I suppose he would have been pleased if I had let him touch me.'

'What did he come for then?'

'How well do you know him?' she countered.

'Not at all. I met him for the first time at Wolfgang's and I'm sure he was there only because he brought the films.'

'He's a blackmailer,' said Jutta calmly.

'A what?'

Manfred was so amazed that he withdrew his hand from its agreeable task.

'He came here to demand money. If I refused to pay, he threatened to get in touch with my husband and tell him what we did at the film-show – you and I, Konrad and I – and above all, my nephew and I.'

'Good God! What a swine! What did you say?'

'I informed him that he would be wasting his time and postage stamp to write to my husband, except that it might amuse him. He has no illusions about me.'

'And he doesn't mind?'

'He has his own amusements. It was he who first took me to Sicily, years ago. In our collection at Lisbon there are many very diverting photographs of Klaus misbehaving with peasant boys.'

'Esschen must have been greatly disconcerted, to say the least.'

Jutta reached for his hand and drew it back to her breasts.

'It's not the first time I've dealt with blackmailers,' she said as Manfred teased her nipples to firmness, 'I knew that young man was a crook the moment I set eyes on him. I must warn Wolfgang before I leave, otherwise he might pay him in a misguided attempt to protect my honour. Do you have photographs of special moments, Manfred?'

'Not really – only half a dozen pictures of girls I've known.'

'Naked, of course.'

'Of course. But tell me something – even though you distrusted Kessler on sight, you would have let him make love to you if he had been up to it.'

'That's different,' she said, 'trusting and liking have nothing to do with that.'

Her hand was at his trouser-buttons, freeing his stem.

'Will you do something for me?' she murmured, stroking it slowly.

'Anything – you have only to name it.'

'That silly film we saw – you remember the close-up of the girl's face filling the screen at the end?'

'Remember it! I dreamed about it last night and woke up in the state you see me in now.'

'I want a picture of my face like that. I'm sure I looked exactly like her when you had me doubled over the chair and destroyed me. I want you to do that for me again so that a photograph can be taken of my expression. Will you do that for me?'

'But who is to take this photograph?'

'I have made enquiries and I've located a man with a small studio where he does portraits and birthday photographs and that sort of thing. He'll do it.'

'Can he be trusted?'

'He can be bought. Will you do it for me, Manfred?'

'On one condition.'

'And what is that?'

'That you give me a large print of it to remember you by until your next visit to Berlin.'

The Education of Girls

Hildegard Buschendorf was a pleasant enough woman, cheerful, talkative, fair-haired and overweight, with the prominent bosom and backside which Manfred associated with women of his mother's generation. That was a little unfair, for Frau Buschendorf could hardly be forty yet, but her plain way of dressing and her overblown figure placed her quite clearly for him.

He met her at a lunch given by his Aunt Dorothea in her house on Bellevue-strasse. The purpose of the lunch, as he quickly made out, was so that he should make the acquaintance of Fraulein von Ettlinger and her mother. Aunt Dorothea never lost an opportunity to try to marry Manfred off to suitable young ladies and she had invited some of her other friends in order to disguise her motives. Fraulein von Ettlinger was a pretty enough young lady of eighteen, though too subdued for Manfred's taste. He was polite and charming, made a note of her telephone number without committing himself to calling her, and thought no more about her.

It was raining hard that afternoon and Manfred's aunt, aware of his lack of interest in the young lady she was promoting, saddled him with the task of driving Frau Buschendorf home, she living right across the other side of Berlin. On the journey she admired his Mercedes volubly, praised his driving skill and told him a little about herself. She was a widow, her husband being of a military family, and he had met his end in the service of the Fatherland in 1916. All very sad – and very familiar.

As they passed through Alexander Platz they saw a fight in the road – about a dozen men brawling, spilling over the pavement and dangerously near the traffic. Some of them were in the brown uniforms of the Nazi Party, some of them in ordinary workmen's clothes. They were all shouting as they punched and kicked at each other. One man was lying in the gutter in the rain, face-down and evidently unconscious.

'My God, what are they doing!' Frau Buschendorf exclaimed, clutching Manfred's arm in terror. 'Why don't the police stop them?'

'They are settling a political disagreement,' said Manfred thoughtfully.

'They'll kill each other! Look – there's another one on the ground and they're kicking him!'

'Perhaps it would be for the best if they did kill each other, dear lady.'

He drove away as fast as he could. When they arrived at Frau Buschendorf's apartment, she invited him in to meet her children and he, with nothing else to do that afternoon, accepted. The children proved to be two daughters, one about sixteen and the other some years younger. Manfred wondered wryly whether this was the second try that day at getting him interested in a suitable young lady. The two girls were dressed alike, in white blouses, grey pleated skirts and white knee-socks, which he took to be their school uniform. They were both extremely well-mannered and sat quietly with their mother and her guest in the old-fashioned drawing-room, while Frau Buschendorf told Manfred how clever they both were, as mothers do.

He paid little attention as she rambled on, his interest caught by the older girl, Monika. She was cast in the same mould as her mother – the same solid bone-structure and breadth of hip. At her age she presented a slightly heavy attractiveness, but no doubt she would look much like her mother in another twenty years. The little girl, Angelika, resembled her mother in facial features and would develop in the same way as her sister in time, though as yet there was no indication of a bosom under her blouse.

His attention was dragged back to Frau Buschendorf's monologue by the unexpected word *discipline*.

'. . . so important for growing girls,' she was saying. 'Otherwise they run wild these days. I've seen it happen with my friends' girls and it leads to the most dreadful scandal and disgrace. I'm sure you know what I mean.'

Manfred nodded solemnly, without the least idea what she meant.

'My late and dear husband's brother Gunther has been a great help to me. He deals with the girls firmly and they respect him for it.'

'Is he too a military man, Madame?'

'In his youth, just as his brother was. He left the Army after the War and went into business. I never understood the details, of course, but he has done extremely well for himself. He has always been too busy to marry and so, in a sense, we became his family. He has been a great comfort and support to me. He understands what duty means, you see – something which the young people today seem not to care about. We miss him sadly.'

'May I ask what has happened to him?'

'Nothing has happened to him, thank God. His business has taken him to Spain. He imports and exports, you understand. He has been away for nearly three months now and I hope he will be back soon. He is a good influence on my girls.'

'By his example, you mean?' Manfred asked, not at all impressed by this absent paragon of virtue.

'That, of course, and also his method of disciplining them.'

Manfred glanced at Monika and Angelika, sitting demurely side by side on the heavy old sofa. They were looking attentively at their mother and there was nothing to be gleaned from their expressions.

'This method, Madame – what is it?'

'The only method that works with young girls – a strong hand.'

He was almost sure that he caught a flicker of amusement on Monika's pretty face.

'I see that you understand me,' said Frau Buschendorf, 'Gunther's method is a strong hand across their bottoms.'

'He beats these charming children?' Manfred asked, aghast.

'Certainly not! Do you think we are barbarians to beat our children? He has a regular routine of smacking them once a week.'

Manfred could hardly believe what he was hearing. He addressed himself to the older girl.

'What do you think of these weekly smackings, Fraulein Monika?'

'It is for our own good, Herr von Klausenberg. It doesn't hurt much and it is soon over.'

'You are fond of your uncle?'

Both girls nodded at once.

'You see,' said their mother, beaming, 'they miss their Uncle Gunther now he is away. Perhaps I should have remarried years ago to give them a father, but so many fine young men never came back from the War! And with Gunther to stand by me, I felt no need.'

Frau Buschendorf's recital of the problems of a woman alone with children to bring up became dreary and Manfred decided to take his leave. He was not listening to what she was saying, his thoughts set on the idea of sixteen-year-old Monika having her bottom smacked by Uncle Gunther. He nodded and smiled from time to time when Frau Buschendorf looked at him for a response and was surprised when she fell silent and she and her daughters stared at him expectantly.

'I beg your pardon – my thoughts were wandering.'

'So you agree?'

'Oh yes,' he answered vaguely, having no idea of what he had agreed to and thinking it of no consequence anyway, now that he was about to go.

'Then we will proceed at once.'

'I fear I may have misunderstood you, dear lady. What are we to proceed with?'

'To administer the discipline my daughters have missed for three months. I shall be most grateful to you.'

Manfred stared at her in amazement.

'You ask me, a stranger to your home, to punish your daughters? Have they behaved so badly? The idea is unthinkable.'

'I have explained myself badly – there is no question of behaving badly. My girls are very well-behaved. The discipline is a reminder to continue to behave well in future. Isn't that right, children?'

'Yes, Mama,' they said in unison.

Manfred was perplexed as how to escape from this ridiculous situation – and as to how he had got into it. Finally his sense of humour asserted itself and he decided to oblige Frau Buschendorf by giving the girls a quick slap on the backside and make his departure quickly.

'I am at your service, Madame. Please explain what I am to do.'

'Thank you – we are truly grateful, aren't we, girls?'

'Yes, Mama.'

'There is a necessary routine,' Frau Buschendorf explained, 'Monika receives ten smacks because she is nearly grown up. Angelika receives six smacks because she is still only a child.'

'Could you not carry out this domestic routine yourself?' Manfred asked.

'That would be to miss the point. They must be disciplined by a man, not by their mother.'

'Why is that?'

'To remind them of their place.'

Manfred gave up trying to make sense of the proposition.

'I have no experience of domestic routines, but I shall do my best.'

'There, girls! I knew that Herr von Klausenburg was a kind-hearted gentleman as soon as I met him.'

She rose from her chair, Manfred stood up and the girls vacated the sofa.

'It is better if you remove your jacket,' Frau Buschendorf advised, 'Your actions must not be hindered. A strong and steady hand is the main thing.'

Manfred took off his jacket and watched Monika fold it neatly and lay it on a chair.

'We always start with Monika,' said Frau Buschendorf. 'As the eldest it is her right. And it is her duty to show her sister how to conduct herself properly. Correctness is essential.'

'I'm sure it is,' said Manfred, wondering if she were slightly deranged.

'Monika, prepare yourself,' her mother ordered.

What Manfred expected to happen was that the girl would bend over and touch her toes while she was spanked. His expectations proved to be wrong. Monika hoisted her pleated skirt to show her thighs and white knickers, lay on her back on the sofa and raised her knees to her chest. The position exposed her bottom, drawn taut by the raising of her legs. Before he had recovered from this first surprise, another followed. Monika hooked her thumbs in the sides of her knickers and wriggled them down over her bottom and on to her thighs. Manfred stared at the smooth cheeks she had bared.

'The discipline is carried out on the bare flesh,' Frau Buschendorf explained. 'It is more effective like that because it humbles the recipient.'

'Just so,' said Manfred, now convinced that he was dealing with someone not quite sane, 'But the position is awkward. Why must it be so?'

'Surely that is obvious. If she bent over she would not be able to see your face. It is of the utmost importance that the girls see the face of the man and know that he is not angry with them but carrying out his task in a proper spirit of duty. Now, if you are ready, please deliver ten smacks.'

He looked at Monika's face to see how she was taking all this. Her eyes were wide open and she was gazing steadily at him, her expression giving no hint of her feelings. He stepped up to the sofa and smacked one cheek of her bottom, not at all hard.

'One!' Frau Buschendorf counted aloud.

He smacked the other cheek and heard 'Two!' From his vantage point above Monika he had a perfect view, not only of her smooth-skinned bottom but, more interesting, of the pouting split between her thighs and its light fleece of brown hair. He thought it was very pretty and continued to look at it as he continued the smacking, stopping when Frau Buschendorf said loudly 'Ten!'

The younger girl had been standing throughout at the end of the sofa, leaning against it and staring at her sister's bottom, now blushing faintly pink from the smacks.

'Excellently done,' said Frau Buschendorf, 'What do you say now, Monika?'

'Thank you very much, Herr von Klausenberg, for teaching me what I have to learn, I promise that I shall remember this lesson and profit by it,' said Monika, her words evidently a formula used on these occasions.

'Give her your hand,' said Frau Buschendorf.

Manfred held out his hand, thinking to help the girl to rise, and found instead that she kissed it. Altogether, he thought, a very strange family.

Monika got off the sofa, pulled up her knickers and smoothed her grey skirt down.

'Angelika, your turn, my little angel,' said Frau Buschendorf fondly.

The smaller girl placed herself in the same position, knees up and knickers down, to present a taut little bottom. Manfred smacked it very lightly, amused by the hairless little slit between her legs. He was not at all sure at what age girls' tufts started to grow but he guessed that it was at the same time that their breasts started to show and for little Angelika the time was not yet. She went through the same formula of thanking him, word-perfect, and of kissing his hand, before she scrambled off the sofa and stood, skirt

203

held up while she rubbed her bottom as if he had really hurt her.

'I am pleased with the way you have behaved,' Frau Buschendorf told her daughters. 'Off to your room now and read your school-books until dinner-time.'

Manfred smiled and bowed as both girls gave him a little curtsy before leaving the drawing-room.

'My dear brother-in-law says it is necessary for women to be reminded of their place. You see the truth of this in the good manners of my girls.'

'He must be a remarkable man,' said Manfred cautiously.

'He is, in every way. And you have been so understanding and so very helpful that I feel I can confide in you further.'

Manfred inclined his head, not knowing what to say.

'Every week, after the girls have been dealt with and sent to their room, Gunther treats me in exactly the same way.'

'But you are a grown woman – don't you resent being treated like a child?'

'I welcome it,' she answered, pink-cheeked and vehement.

A mental picture of plump Frau Buschendorf on the sofa with her knees up and her bottom being smacked almost made Manfred laugh. He contained himself with an effort, wondering if he could prolong the joke.

'If I can assist in any way . . .' he said.

It was no joke – she seized upon his words instantly.

'You would be doing me a very great favour!'

Before his startled eyes, she was on the sofa, skirt up round her waist and knees on her bosom, displaying a large round bottom encased in dove-grey knickers. She pulled them down and let Manfred see her white cheeks and the prominent fleshy lips between her heavy thighs.

'Ten?' he asked.

'Twenty – it's always twenty for me.'

Manfred took his position by her side and swung his hand hard at the target offered to him.

'One!' she gasped.

204

He continued, landing his smacks on each cheek in turn, trying to make it sting. The massive cheeks wobbled as he struck and their pale skin flushed red after the third or fourth blow. By the time he reached ten Frau Buschendorf was sighing loudly between her counting and her legs were trembling wildly.

Manfred too was breathing faster. Without being aware of it, he had become aroused. What had started as a joke on his part had ceased to be only that and was taking on a very different aspect. By the count of twenty his stem was standing upright in his trousers. Immediately after the final smack, which rang out resoundingly, Frau Buschendorf seized the hand that had disciplined her and pressed her mouth to it.

'Thank you, thank you,' she exclaimed, her face as glowing red as her bare bottom. 'You have a strong hand and a willing heart.'

Manfred wondered whether he had laid it on too hard – the red marks on her bottom were very bright. He laid his hand gently on one of the afflicted spots to see if it felt hot to the touch.

'Is that painful?' he asked, breathing quickly.

'Discipline must hurt, or it has no meaning,' she murmured, her eyes half-closed.

Manfred's finger-tips had somehow found their way between her raised legs. While he was lightly stroking one reddened cheek to ease its pain, his finger-tips were tickling the thinly-haired and pouting lips exposed to him.

'After your brother-in-law has spanked you, what does he do next?'

'He completes the lesson,' she said softly.

'And how is that done?'

'He reminds me in the most forceful way possible that I am a woman and that I must at all times remember my duty. Do you understand what I am saying?'

'I believe that I do. Shall I proceed?'

'If you would be so kind.'

He knelt on the sofa, unbuttoned his trousers and tucked

his bent knees under her bottom to raise it. Frau Buschendorf strained her thighs as far apart as the knickers round them would permit and sighed when he used his fingers to open the thick lips presented to him. His stem slid in easily, the smacking having prepared her for what was to come. He looked at her face and saw so greedy an expression on it that he leaned forward and plunged deeply before going at her with a will. Nothing about this strange woman surprised him any more, not even when she began to count quickly to his jabbing: 'One, two, three, four, five, six, seven, eight, nine . . .'

He was soon so engrossed in what he was doing that he no longer heard her voice. He had been aroused more than he knew by the variety of female charms that had been displayed for him and smacking Frau Buschendorf's bottom while staring at her split peach had wound him up like a spring. He went off like an alarm-clock, rocking the heavy old sofa under them with his impetus. When his spring finally ran down and Frau Buschendorf stopped squirming, he sat back on his heels and grinned. She reached for his hand and kissed it.

'It's months since I was disciplined by a man,' she said. 'Thank you, dear Manfred, if I may call you that.'

To cut short what seemed an excessive show of gratitude for so easy a favour, Manfred asked her how high her counting had gone.

'I lost count at four hundred and something.'

'I suppose you always lose count at some point.'

'Not exactly. With Gunther I always reach six hundred and something before he reaches the culmination of his discipline. After that I relax and experience the deep pleasure that comes from accepting my destiny. But you are younger and stronger than he is and you drove everything out of my head before you were finished. I am sorry, but I cannot tell you the final count. It's wrong of me, I know.'

'Why on earth should I want to know?'

'Gunther insists that it is part of the discipline to make me count for him. He always asks afterwards.'

'He is an unusual man. Personally I am more interested in pleasure for its own sake.'

'That is the failing of many young people nowadays. It was otherwise once.'

'Maybe it was. But you are educating your daughters in the old ways of submission and duty and the world no longer sets the same value on these things.'

'The old ways are best,' she said firmly.

'We must move with the times or we shall be left behind as relics,' said Manfred, as he climbed off the sofa and buttoned his trousers.

'We are passing through a time of moral laxity and rebellion by young people, that's what Gunther says, but they will exhaust themselves by their excesses and the old ways will come back,' she said stubbornly.

She stretched out her legs along the sofa, her frock still up round her waist, showing off the plump article Manfred had just made good use of.

'The pendulum may swing,' he answered, 'but nothing is ever the same again.'

'Only wait. You will see.'

'Suppose that I prove to you that pleasure for its own sake is far to be preferred to the shadowy pleasures of duty and obedience – will that make you change your mind?'

'How can you prove that?'

She got off the sofa to pull up her silk knickers and smooth out the creases in her frock.

Manfred thought for a moment or two.

'Come to my apartment on Thursday afternoon,' he said. 'About three in the afternoon. One of us will be proved right and one wrong '

Thursday was when Manfred's servants were free after lunch for the rest of the day. Not that he had any qualms about them seeing his visitors, married or unmarried. Many was the time that Geiger had brought him his morning coffee and found a young lady cuddled up beside him in bed. His instructions on such occasions were to bring a second cup. There was one memorable morning when he had brought in the coffee just as Nina was perched above Manfred, giving him a special morning greeting, though that was in the days before she married Gottfried.

In the matter of Frau Buschendorf it was different, Manfred considered. She was, after all, twenty years older than himself and much more bound by convention. Delicacy suggested that it would be needlessly embarrassing to her to subject her to the scrutiny of the servants. When she arrived he could not fail to note her smile of approval at his thoughtfulness. He helped her out of her coat and took her straight to his bedroom, there being no reason he could see for elaborate courtesies first. She knew what she had come for, he knew what she had come for – matters might as well proceed without delay.

She was wearing a woollen frock in shades of dark blue and cream and, by the look of her, had come straight from the hair-dresser. Her only make-up was a little powder on her cheeks, but even that was more than she had worn when he met her at Aunt Dorothea's lunch party. As soon as Manfred tried to get her out of her clothes, she blushed and asked him to turn away while she undressed herself. This coquettishness was in such marked contrast to the way in which she had exposed herself to him to be *disciplined* in her own home that it was clear that she felt herself to be on unsure terms with him. He stared out of the window for a few minutes until she said that she was ready, then turned to find her in bed, with only her head showing. He shed his jacket and shoes but, before he could continue, she brought her naked arms out of the bed and asked him to hold her.

This unnatural modesty on the part of a woman who had already allowed him the most intimate access to herself made Manfred slightly impatient. Moreover, this encounter was to be on his terms, not hers – that was the whole point of it. He flicked back the covers and saw her fully naked for the first time. It seemed to him then that Hildegard Buschendorf was the most naked-looking woman he had ever set eyes on and he sought to explain this to himself as he lay beside her and fondled her big soft breasts. After all, he told himself, a naked woman is a naked woman, a head, a body, two arms, two legs, two of these and one of those. Why should Hildegard create this impression of being more naked than a naked woman generally looks? In his mind's eye he compared her with other recent guests in this same bed.

Partly it was to do with her physical size, he decided. Hildegard had so much more flesh to expose than, for example, Vicki Schwabe, who was slender, or even Jutta von Loschingen, who was small-breasted and firm all over. Hildegard was heavy-boned and solidly built, with wonderfully plump thighs, a belly that curved roundly and, of course, her over-sized breasts, each a double handful in itself. But in addition to sheer size, Hildegard's colouring had something to do with the impression of ultra-nakedness. Her hair was chestnut-brown and her skin was extremely pale, a creamy-white with the merest touch of flesh-tone in it. Against this alabaster appearance the pinkness of her nipples was in high contrast. And there was something else — she had little hair between her legs, as he had noticed before when she took up her extraordinary posture on the sofa to be smacked. There was only a sparse covering of brown over the fleshy lips down there and the effect was to make her seem more exposed than, one might say, Helga, who had a fine curly tuft.

All in all, to make love to Hildegard was like gorging oneself on a huge Black Forest gateau — there was so much to enjoy and it was all so rich and creamy! Manfred stroked and felt her all over, thinking as he did that her brother-in-law Gunther must be mad to confine himself to his uncomfortable in-and-out and deny himself the pleasure of all this warm flesh.

For a woman unused to so much handling — or perhaps because of that — Hildegard enjoyed it enormously. She sighed and squirmed, her legs trembled and, when his hand was between them, her belly quivered and heaved. Manfred sat up to get his clothes off and multiply her pleasures by pressing her body to his, but at once she took hold of his arm and pulled him back down beside her.

'Please . . . keep your clothes on.'

'But why? It is so much nicer to be naked together.'

'It couldn't be nicer than it is now. It is right for me to be undressed to submit to you, but you must be strong and demanding.'

'Damnation! That's not the idea at all! Forget this strong man and weak woman nonsense for once. We are two human beings, giving each other pleasure.'

'My way is better. Touch me again and remember how you disciplined me. It was because I was submissive that you were so forceful.'

'What makes you think that?'

'Because you did it so hard and fast! It was wonderful.'

Manfred stroked her belly and then down between her thighs.

'It can be better than that,' he told her.

'What could possibly be better than lying on a submissive woman and exerting your strength? And what could be better for a woman than to feel the weight of a man crushing her as he thrusts into her body and tries to split her open?'

Manfred began to feel baffled by this extraordinary woman – extraordinary to him, that is. He was excited enough from handling her to follow her suggestion, to climb on top of her and do what she wanted. But that would be to admit defeat. He approached the point in another way.

'I understand what you mean, Hildegard. I shall be strong and force you to submit to me. That is what discipline is about, yes?'

'Oh, yes!'

'After I smacked your bottom the other day you thanked me and kissed my hand. Why did you do that?'

'It is correct to kiss the hand that punishes you.'

'But after I had, in your words, split you open, you did

210

not kiss the instrument of punishment. That seems to me to be most incorrect.'

As the import of his words sank in, her eyes opened wide and she stared at him unbelievingly.

'I never thought . . . but Gunther has never suggested . . .'

'Search your conscience,' said Manfred firmly, 'Perhaps he is so shocked by your dereliction of duty that he cannot bring himself to speak of it. Have you considered that?'

'I don't know what to say,' she muttered uneasily.

'I suggest that you begin with an apology.'

That was something she had been taught to understand.

'I ask you most sincerely to forgive me. Believe me, there was no slight intended. It never entered my mind.'

She looked as if she was about to burst into tears. Manfred spoke sharply.

'Your apology is unacceptable until you have put matters right.'

'You mean that you want me to . . .' but she was unable to say the words.

'It is not what I want that is important here, it is what is correct. Your sincerity can only be demonstrated by your actions.'

She looked so confused that Manfred found it hard not to smile. He rolled on to his back beside her and put his hands behind his head.

'I am waiting.'

Hildegard sat up slowly and unbuttoned his trousers with awkward fingers.

'Never in my life . . .' she began, then trailed off.

There was a pause while she gathered her courage to pull up his shirt. She gasped and almost drew away when his hard stem jerked out through the slit in his underwear.

'You flinch from your duty,' Manfred reproached her.

She took a deep breath, bent her neck and leaned down to kiss his twitching stem. Once committed, she did not skimp her duty and he felt her kisses from the head to the root of his stiffness.

She raised her head to look at him.

'Is my apology accepted?' she asked timidly.

'I believe that you are sincere. It would make matters better between us if you proved your submission to this instrument of discipline beyond the mere formality of what you have done so far.'

Hildegard took his meaning. She turned round on the bed to face him, took his stem in her hand and kissed it repeatedly. After a while she said breathlessly:

'This is so strange that you will not believe me. I was married for six years and I have two children. And for the past six or seven years Gunther has been disciplining me weekly. Yet this is the first time I have ever touched this part of a man, or even seen it properly.'

'How is that possible?'

'My husband always came to bed in a long night-shirt and embraced me in the dark. I never once saw him naked.'

'But your brother-in-law – with him you are in your drawing-room and it is not dark – how could you not observe what he uses?'

'When he makes me lie with my knees up to be smacked, I can see little more than his head and shoulders. And afterwards he puts it away before letting me move. At times I catch a glimpse of pink flesh, but no more than that.'

'There is much for you to learn. Now that you see how a man is made, what is your opinion?' Manfred said, amused by her confession and yet sorry for her.

Hildegard stroked her new discovery thoughtfully.

'I've often been to look at the old Greek statues in museums, but they have little things hanging down, not in the least like the big hard things I have felt inside my body. You will laugh at me, but last year I bought a book in one of those dreadful little shops that sell books and pictures about sexual matters. It was so embarrassing to go in – I nearly died of shame.'

'What did you buy?'

'A book of pictures of young men, all aroused. It was a

212

tremendous shock for me to see the different sizes and shapes. But it was very educational.'

'My poor Hildegard, the men you have known have treated you very oddly. They seem to have given you little and asked for little.'

'How can you say that? They gave me all they had and I did the same. What more can any woman give than admittance to her body?'

'I shall try to enlighten you before you leave.'

'But it all comes to the same thing in the end,' she said. 'Whether we are dressed or undressed, in the light or in the dark, whether we touch each other or not, it leads to the same joining together of the man and the woman for a minute or two.'

'That is like saying that all meals are the same because they consist of putting food into your mouth.'

Her hand still held his stem but she had no idea of how to handle it. He showed her how to clasp it and move her hand up and down.

'I do not understand,' she said, 'this must be a poor substitute for putting it where it should really be. Would you not rather have it there than in my hand?'

'This is not a substitute at all,' Manfred sighed, 'the two pleasures are only slightly related. No one has ever told you that in love-making only part of the pleasure is between the legs. The rest is in the mind. The touch of your hand produces another sort of pleasure in the mind from the pleasure I would feel if I were inside you.'

'Surely not,' she said.

Before Manfred could attempt any further explanation, the inevitable happened. His loins jerked upwards from the bed and he poured his stream of passion through Hildegard's busy hand on to his white shirt-front.

'My God!' she exclaimed, her hand moving faster, 'I never guessed!'

He took her wrist to halt her movements.

'What didn't you guess, dear Hildegard?'

'I had no idea of how tremendous a destiny it is to be a

213

man! To see how this wonderful part reared itself up and flung out its torrent! It was awe-inspiring! I never knew!'

Manfred almost despaired. Perhaps she had been too well-trained in her role of submissive female to be rescued now. His well-intentioned attempt to remove the mystery from what a man's stem did when it was inside her had produced the very opposite result. She sat staring at it as it softened as if she had received a divine revelation.

He got off the bed, stripped completely and stood to let her look at him.

'See, Hildegard – I am no marble statue in a museum. I am a living man made of flesh and bones. Now you know what a naked man looks like. Forget your picture book and fix the real thing in your mind.'

She lay propped on one elbow, staring at him.

'You are more like the statues than the picture book, Manfred.'

'Why do you say that?'

'In the pictures the young men are all hard and strong. You are small now like the statues. It was better before, when I held you.'

'A temporary condition,' he said, laughing. 'Soon I shall be like your pictures again.'

She rolled on to her back and smiled. Manfred got back on to the bed, parted her fleshy legs widely and lay between them. He stroked the protruding lips between her thighs.

'There is something I am trying to explain to you, but you have not yet understood me.'

'I know I'm not clever,' she sighed. 'Tell me again and I'll try to understand.'

'I doubt whether words will convey it. What I am trying to get you to grasp is that this warm slot between your legs is every bit as important as anything a man has.'

'That can't possibly be true,' she objected. 'You have a proud and arrogant thing – now that you've let me stroke yours I know how wonderful it is.'

Manfred stopped listening to her nonsense. He opened her widely with his fingers and tickled her exposed pink button. After a little while her legs began to shake and she gasped loudly.

'Ah, no! Not with your fingers – do it the correct way!'

'There is no such thing as a correct way, Hildegard. You must have been played with like this before when your husband took off his night-shirt.'

'Never!'

Manfred worked slowly, determined to make her experience more than she was used to. She moaned softly and rolled her head from side to side on the pillow.

'What did he do to you – at least he took off your night-gown?'

'No,' she moaned, 'no . . . he stroked my breasts through it . . . he never put his hands on my body . . .'

'And then?'

'He had me pull my night-gown up to my waist and he lay on top of me and did what men do . . . this is not possible . . . you must stop!'

Her plump body was shaking all over and Manfred was certain that she had never before felt such wild sensations of pleasure and she was half afraid of them. Her curved belly rose and fell to her panting. Manfred put his hands on her thighs to force them further apart, bent his neck and touched the tip of his tongue to her slippery bud.

'No!' she screamed. 'It's too much!'

She tried to slither away from him. Manfred used his strength to pin her thighs flat to the bed while his tongue flicked over her sensitive button. The conclusion was spectacular – her thighs overcame the pressure of his hands in a spasmodic upwards jerk and clamped round his head. Her body convulsed as if in a seizure and, though his ears were muffled by her legs, he could still hear her staccato screaming. The outburst grew louder and with a final window-rattling 'Uh!' she collapsed as completely as if she had been shot dead.

Manfred sat up and looked at her. For a moment he thought that her climactic release had been so extreme that she had fainted, as Magda had done when she nearly knocked his brains out with her spiked helmet. But Hildegard's pink-tipped breasts were rising and falling regularly to her breathing and her eyes were open. He moved up the bed to cradle her head in his arm.

'What have you done to me?' she asked softly.

'I hope I've shown you what the plump little delight between your legs is capable of.'

'But it can't always be like that . . . it would be too much.'

'The women I know expect pleasure like that two or three times a day and sometimes more. You will soon come to expect the same.'

'I feel so content . . . and so sleepy. Is that dreadful of me? I know you must want your pleasure, but would you mind waiting a little?'

Manfred saw that as real progress. Half an hour ago she would have parted her legs and let him do as he pleased, however she felt. Some of her submissiveness seemed to have evaporated.

'Sleep for a while,' he said, 'I'll wake you later.'

He covered her over and watched as she turned on her side and dozed off. It occurred to him that brother-in-law Gunther was in for a surprise when he returned from Spain. Hildegard was not likely to revert to her former role, legs up on her chest, to give Gunther a quick dip. It would be sensible to show her a few ways in which she could reverse places with Gunther and keep him up to the mark.

So musing, Manfred put on his black and silver dressing-gown and left her to sleep. He was in the kitchen drinking a bottle of beer when he heard the door-bell. He ignored it for a while, but the ringing was persistent. He went down the hall to get rid of the unwelcome caller, flung the door wide and saw, to his astonishment, Jenny Montrose in a long mink coat and a hat to match. She was smiling in a most friendly way, but the smile faded from her face when she saw his dressing-gown and bare feet.

'I'm sorry,' she said, her German tinged with her soft

216

foreign accent, 'I've disturbed you. I saw your car outside and guessed you were home.'

'Please come in,' Manfred said quickly, his heart racing at what this visit might portend, 'I am delighted to see you.'

'Are you sure I'm not disturbing you?' she asked, her finely-drawn eyebrows rising.

'Excuse my appearance. The servants are out today and I was sleeping off the effects of a party last night,' he lied.

He hung her fur coat in the hall and took her into the drawing-room. She looked enchanting in her fur hat and a cream-coloured frock that had a large red rose embroidered over one breast.

'May I offer you something – tea, coffee, a drink? And then I will get dressed and we can talk.'

Plans were evolving in his head. As soon as Jenny was settled he would get Hildegard up and dressed and out by the service door on some pretext or other.

'Nothing, thank you,' said Jenny. 'Are you sure that this is not an inconvenient time?'

'Not in the least. It takes me a little time to collect my wits when I wake up. If you will excuse me, I will dress and be back in a couple of minutes.'

'There's no need for that,' she said, with a smile that sent his heart fluttering. 'That's a beautiful dressing-gown.'

'But I've got bare feet – at least let me go and put my slippers on.'

Jenny kicked off her shiny black crocodile-skin shoes.

'That makes us equal,' she said. 'What else haven't you got on?'

Manfred's dream had come true. Here, sitting in his own drawing-room, was the girl he most desired in the whole world. He had been drawn to her since Ulrika's absurd celebration in the Steam-bath, however ambiguous her actions that night. And this attraction had made it impossible to resist making love to her at Ernst's party, when she was unconscious, though the psychological impact on him of that episode had been so intolerable that he had

217

suppressed his feelings towards her and had deliberately not tried to see her again. Now she had come to him, a warm smile on her beautiful face, and she had not come to drink tea. Fate had ordained this momentous event, he had no doubt of that.

'What else haven't I got on,' he repeated, turning on all his considerable charm. 'A hat, of course – but please keep yours on – it suits you so well. I'm sure I can think of something else for you to take off.'

Her eyes were shining and she looked amused.

'You're asking yourself why I'm here,' she said, 'I'm not sure myself. Who needs reasons, anyway? This may come as a surprise to you but I've been dreaming about you lately – isn't that strange?'

'Flattering, I would rather say. What sort of dreams?'

'Exciting ones. That's what I don't understand. Do you ever dream about me?'

'I never remember my dreams when I wake up, but I'm sure that I have. What do I do in these dreams of yours?'

'You make love to me. But I don't make love to you. I lie there and let you do it, as if I'm paralysed. That's not my style at all – what do you make of it? Do you think I ought to go and talk to one of those Viennese professors who grope about in people's minds?'

'What do they know about it? Are your dreams pleasant or not?'

'They're marvellous. I enjoy them.'

'You don't need an old Viennese charlatan, you need me, Jenny.'

'That's what I thought, so here I am.'

'To tell me about your dreams?'

'To make love with you and find out if it's as good as when I dream about it,' and she hitched up her frock to display a long smooth thigh while she undid her suspender.

'Manfred?' said a nervous voice behind him. 'Are you there?'

It was Hildegard, standing in the door-way, all pink and

218

white and naked. She stared briefly at Jenny with goggling eyes, turned and fled, her big bottom wobbling.

'It was an inconvenient time after all,' said Jenny curtly, refastening her suspender and picking up her shoes.

'Don't go – I can explain.'

'No need,' she said, making for the door.

'If you only knew what that poor lady has suffered at the hands of uncaring men,' he babbled, hurrying after her.

Jenny had her mink coat over her arm and her hand on the door handle.

'I didn't know you made a living as a gigolo, Manfred. You'd better get back to the bed-room and earn your money.'

And she was gone, without even an 'Auf wiedersehen'.

He telephoned her several times that day and the next, but the moment he mentioned his name the servant answering the telephone told him that Fraulein Montrose was out. He wrote her a letter, but it sounded so feeble that he threw it in the waste-paper basket. In the end he decided that it was better to let some time elapse before he tried to repair the damage. He had no intention of seeing Hildegard again, even though he knew it was unjust to be angry with her. All the same, if she had not been with him that afternoon, he might by now be the happiest man in the world.

As things were, Jenny would be forgetting whatever disappointment she had suffered in the arms of another man. Those beautiful pointed breasts Manfred had touched when she lay drugged on Ernst's bed – some other man was kissing them! The warm sanctuary under her fine astrakhan tuft – some other man's hand was on it! Someone like Erwin, perhaps, unwashed, uncultured, some small criminal or pimp perhaps, the dregs of the gutter! Manfred tortured himself with jealous images and got so drunk at home for two nights running that his servants had to put him to bed.

After that he regained control of himself and learned patience. He was at home one afternoon, lying on the zebra-skin sofa with his jacket off and tie loose, reading an illustrated magazine, when Frau Geiger announced that he had a visitor.

'Who?' he asked, starting up hopefully.

'Fraulein Buschendorf.'

He could think of no sensible reason why Hildegard should pretend to be unmarried, but it sounded stupid enough to be in character for her. She had come to apologise, of course, but Manfred had no wish to see her.

'Please tell Frau Buschendorf that I am out.'

'No, Fraulein Buschendorf, Herr Manfred – a young lady.'

'Then show her in. Bring tea and whatever cake we have.'

'There's hazelnut cream layer-cake and coffee cream. I baked them this morning.'

'Then bring them both.'

He had his jacket on and was straightening his tie when Frau Geiger ushered in Monika, the sixteen year old daughter. She was dressed in school-girl style as he had seen her before, plain white blouse and pleated grey skirt.

'Fraulein Monika, how good of you to call! Please sit down and we'll have tea and cake. Is today a holiday?'

'I wanted to talk to you, Herr von Klausenberg,' she said primly.

They sat opposite each other and Frau Geiger served them. Manfred asked politely about Monika's mother and sister and she replied as politely. But no sooner was Frau Geiger out of the room than she broached the subject of her visit.

'Why does Mama let Uncle Gunther smack us?' she asked, coming straight to the point without the least sign of shyness.

'You must ask her that. It would be wrong for me to interfere.'

'You don't have to treat me like a child. Why did you smack me when Mama asked you to?'

'I'm not sure that I know. I was so surprised by the

request that I was prepared to do anything to escape from your home.'

'But you didn't escape. You stayed and smacked Mama's bottom as well.'

Manfred looked at her in alarm.

'If you find that difficult to understand, Monika, so do I. Were you listening at the door?'

'I always do. And look through the key-hole. I saw what you did to her. Uncle Gunther does the same.'

'So your Mama told me. What can I say? This is what happens between grown-ups – and things like it. It may seem odd to you now but in another year or two you'll know much more about it.'

Monika put her cup down and stared at him boldly.

'I know all about it now. I told you I'm not a child. Did you enjoy smacking my bottom?'

'To be truthful, I hardly recall what my emotions were.'

'That's not truthful at all. You had a good look at me, didn't you, when my knickers were down.'

Manfred stopped trying to play the responsible adult and grinned at Monika.

'You're a very pretty girl – I couldn't help myself. I hope you'll forgive me.'

'That's all right,' she said, grinning back at him. 'It was nice when you looked at me. Much nicer than when Uncle Gunther does. Do you want to look at me now?'

'Dear Monika, the suggestion is a tempting one but I don't think it would be a sensible thing to do.'

'Why not – if you want to?'

'Because you're only sixteen and problems could arise which neither of us want.'

'I'm not a virgin,' she told him proudly.

'Uncle Gunther?'

'No, silly! He never touches me. All the girls in my class at school have boyfriends. We all do it, you know.'

'Your Mama would not be pleased if she found out.'

'Who's going to tell her? She's got these old-fashioned ideas about girls knowing their duty, whatever that is. She

221

expects me to be a virgin till my wedding-day, that's how out-of-date she is. She stopped talking to Frau Hammel in the apartment above us when she found out a man friend visits her when Herr Hammel is out. But she lets Uncle Gunther do it to her and pretends it's something to do with her duty. I think she's a hypocrite, even though she's my mother.'

'Children usually judge their parents harshly,' said Manfred. 'But we ought to remember that they grew up in a different sort of world from ours and were taught different values. The main thing is to live and let live.'

'Even hypocrites?'

'Your mother loves you, I'm sure of that. Her ways are not your ways. Why not do what you want and leave her in peace to do what she wants?'

'I suppose you're right. I'm glad I can talk to you. Why do people do such strange things? I mean, like Mama having her bottom smacked before Uncle Gunther does it to her?'

'There is only one true explanation of why men and women do strange things together. It is because they enjoy it.'

'But it doesn't look comfortable, the way they do it. Well, you should know – was it?'

'Comfort is of no great importance in such moments. People do the oddest things when they make love.'

'I don't,' said Monika sturdily.

'You can't have been doing it all that long,' Manfred pointed out. 'You are still at the stage when simple straightforward love-making is new and thrilling. How do you know that in five years from now you won't be experimenting in all sorts of comical ways?'

'Like what?'

'Monika, you did not come here for a lesson in sexual education.'

'But I did!'

'Then I must disappoint you. The only way to find out

is to try things yourself, not hear about them from someone else.'

'Do you do strange things when you make love?'

'To the person involved, nothing seems strange,' he said hastily, suppressing memories of nights with Magda and Vicki and half a dozen others.

'So it didn't seem strange with Mama?'

'I was doing what she wanted rather than expressing any particular wish of my own.'

'Do you always do what women want?' she persisted.

'I try to be as obliging as possible.'

'Will you do what I want if I take my knickers off?'

'What is it that you want?' he asked, grinning at the way she was trying to get him into a corner from which he could not escape.

'I want to be stroked. My boyfriend is so impatient that he doesn't feel me properly.'

Poor girl, Manfred thought, for all her seeming precocity she is going down the same road as her mother. Everything changes and nothing changes!

'And if I do, will you go away and pretend that you were never here?'

'If you ask me to.'

Monika knew that she had won, though not why. She made straight for the sofa, took her white cotton knickers off and lay down full-length with her skirt pulled up to bare the tuft of light brown hair he had seen before. Manfred lay on the sofa with her, his arm under her head, and kissed her lightly while he stroked her belly and thighs.

'That's right,' she said, her eyes staring at him, 'you know how to do it – I knew you would.'

His fingers eased between her thighs to touch the warm lips there.

'What's your boy-friend's name?'

'Heinz. We meet after school and go for a walk in the park. He's very nice really and I like him a lot, but he does it too fast. By now he'd be on top of me and ramming away.'

Manfred warmed to his task. He bent her top knee upwards to part her legs so that he could caress inside her little fleshy folds.

'I hope that proper precautions are taken,' he said, 'otherwise your Mama will find out that you're not a virgin if your little belly starts to swell.'

'No chance of that! I only let him do it when he's wearing one of those rubber things. You're making me feel nice all over.'

'You're moist already – you have a passionate nature, Monika.'

'Do you think so?' she murmured. 'I want to do it all the time, if that's what you mean.'

He felt her hand pressed to his trousers, where his stem stood stiffly.

'I'm nearly there,' she whispered. 'Slow down a bit!'

He teased her tiny bud very slowly and lightly, but the quivering of her body against him increased until she gasped, 'Now!'

Her throes lasted only two or three seconds and then her eyes were open and staring at him again.

'That was fantastic. You really know how to play with girls.'

'I'm glad you enjoyed it.'

'Are you going to do it properly now?' she asked.

Her fingers were unbuttoning his trousers and Manfred gave up resisting and let her pull his hard stem out.

'It's a lot bigger than Heinz's,' she said. 'You won't hurt me, will you?'

Manfred smiled reassuringly at her while he guided his hardness to the right spot and pushed gently. It was a tight fit, but not an uncomfortable one, and at about the half-way mark he stopped.

'Does that hurt?' he asked.

'No, it feels very nice.'

He undid her school blouse, found a slip underneath and pulled it out of the waist-band of her skirt so that he could play with her breasts. Nor were they that small – in fact, at sixteen Monika had breasts as well-developed as those of many a grown woman.

'I love having them felt,' she informed him.

'By the time you're eighteen or nineteen you're going to have wonderful big breasts, Monika,' he said, tickling her nipples to make them firm.

Down below, he was easing himself in and out in a gentle rhythm that gave pleasure without problems.

'Do you like big ones?' she asked.

'I like big ones and little ones and middle-sized ones and fat ones and pointed ones – all of them.'

'I'm nearly there again,' said Monika, 'I love the way you do it. Are you nearly there?'

'Yes,' Manfred sighed.

'Be careful – I don't want you to give me a baby!'

Her words reminded him of Mitzi and the time he had made love to her on this same sofa, her back towards him while he stroked her swollen belly and thrust into her from behind. At once Manfred's belly contracted like a fist and he jerked himself free from Monika in the nick of time and spurted up her bare belly.

'Oh!' she squealed, 'You've done it!'

His fingers found her wet little slit and before his ecstatic spasms ended she was gasping and shaking against him.

When it was over, he kissed her breasts delicately, then her mouth, and got up to button his trousers. He gave her his handkerchief to dry her belly before she scrambled off the sofa and put on her knickers.

He thought it wiser to see her to the door himself so that Frau Geiger would not observe the pink glow on her face and deduce what had been going on.

'Auf wiedersehen, Monika.'

'Can I come back tomorrow afternoon?' she asked.

New Year's Eve

The Bruckners' parties were celebrated far and wide for the lavishness of the hospitality and to be invited was a prize greatly sought after, most particularly their New Year's Eve party, when the wealthy mingled with the fashionable and the dull were lost to sight in the crowd. Socially, of course, Heidi Bruckner was immeasurably superior to her husband, she being a daughter of old General von Dahlenburg, while Bruno Bruckner was from nowhere in particular. But he had the money and she used it to establish the Bruckner family in the society of the new Republic, with the ruthless streak her much-honoured father had displayed as a young Major at the siege of Paris in 1871.

The guests on New Year's Eve would be a carefully selected mixture, Manfred knew, when he received his vast gold-edged card of invitation, and a few telephone calls round his friends told him which of them had been similarly honoured. There would be Bruckner's most important business contacts with their overfed and overdressed wives and daughters. And whichever Government officials were important to his current and future enterprises. There would be people from the theatre and publishing, to give a tinge of culture to the proceedings – a mistake really, since people like that usually passed out drunk after an hour or two of the legendary hospitality. Fortunately there would also be a number of young people of good family to add tone to the event and they would supply the zest which the party would otherwise lack. To keep this throng happy and busy there would be oceans of French champagne to

226

drink, mountains of delicious snacks, music, dancing till dawn, and whatever form of entertainment Frau Bruckner had been told was all the rage just then.

The house was out in Grunewald Forest and the drive up to it was jammed solid on both sides with parked cars, mostly large, dark and sleek. Manfred was forced to leave his rakish tourer some distance away and march briskly up the drive in the freezing night air, thankful for his heavy leather overcoat and gloves. There was a little crowd of uniformed chauffeurs near the house, laughing and smoking, but they fell silent and stood up straight as Manfred passed them.

Those who liked the Bauhaus style found the grand salon of the house impressive. It was vast and high-ceilinged, taking the space of two storeys vertically, and it had a balcony with a silver-grill front across one whole end of the room. The floor was black parquet, some incredibly expensive wood that had been polished to an amazing gloss and the walls almost disappeared behind large geometric-design paintings, of the type Manfred found boring. A grand piano and a hired jazz-band of six men were lost in a corner of this huge zeppelin-hangar of a salon and the thirty or forty men and women dancing the Charleston and the thirty or forty others standing about to talk and drink went only partway to making the room look occupied.

Dieter Bruckner, son of the house, looked slightly drunk already. He wore a most elegant dinner-jacket of midnight blue and had diamond-studs in his starched shirt-front.

'Manfred!' he said, throwing his arms round him in a bear-hug, 'how are you, you dog? I've heard all about what happened at Wolfgang's film-show – why wasn't I there?'

'I expected you to be there. Were you away?'

'It was my own fault – he invited me but I had a dinner-date that evening with a little ballerina and I thought that would be more interesting. But now I've heard about how you all piled on top of Wolfgang's aunt – I could shoot myself!'

'How was the ballerina?'

'So-so. How was the aunt?'

'Fantastic! Where is your Mama, Dieter, I must present my greetings.'

'She's over there somewhere being polite to some of the old man's boring friends. Listen, there are some marvellous girls here tonight – take your pick, but leave one for me.'

Manfred grinned and made his way towards his hostess. Frau Bruckner was a large and handsome blonde woman of fifty or thereabouts. She had been a friend of Manfred's mother during the years she lived in Berlin, when Manfred's father had been alive. He bowed and kissed her hand and said the usual polite things and she smiled appreciatively at him and patted his cheek in a maternal fashion.

'Have you met Herr Grutz and his wife?' she asked. 'And Mr and Mrs Montrose?'

Jenny's father was an imposing man of about sixty, tall, strongly-built and with a well-trimmed mane of curly white hair. His hand-shake was firm and frank and his smile bland. It was his wife who took Manfred by surprise. She was blonde and beautiful, had a gloriously-proportioned figure which her ultra-fashionable frock did little to disguise, and she was no more than two or three years older than Jenny. Manfred kissed her hand with pleasure and was rewarded with a glowing smile.

'I have the honour of knowing your daughter, Madame,' he said. 'Is she here tonight?'

'My step-daughter,' she corrected him, 'She's having dinner with friends and they're all coming on here afterwards.'

Manfred noted that Montrose's genial expression hardened at the mention of his daughter. Perhaps he was not entirely unaware of her unorthodox friendships. The name Grutz struck an echo in Manfred's memory.

'Herr *Albert* Grutz?' he asked, shaking hands.

'That is so. Have we met before?'

'No, but I have heard of you.'

Albert Grutz was not at all what Manfred had expected.

He was a tall and heavy man with stooping shoulders, and he had a humorous expression in his deep-set eyes.

'Who could have been talking about me?' he asked, 'I don't know anyone.'

'Ludwig Kessler has a high opinion of you.'

Grutz eyed him warily for a moment and stood back to let him kiss Frau Grutz's hand, an action which seemed to disconcert her. She wore an expensive black evening frock and a three-strand diamond choker, but whatever her attractions had been thirty years before, they were now sadly faded. A dull hausfrau, Manfred thought – no wonder Grutz seeks amusement elsewhere, even though his style in amusement would appear bizarre to most.

The jazz-band played with lunatic exhilaration, couples danced, Manfred circulated, looking for his friends. He soon came across Max Schroeder, with a very pretty girl on his arm.

'Fritzi von Gerstenberg,' said Max, introducing them, and Manfred wondered, though briefly, what had happened to the great passion for Rosa and the peace of mind Max claimed she had brought him. Fritzi looked no more than nineteen and, whatever her talents, the art of soothing a troubled soul was not likely to be among them.

'I have stumbled across the secret of life, the world and the universe,' said Max, interpreting Manfred's quizzical look at Fritzi.

'That sounds very useful, Max. Are you allowed to tell me or are you sworn to silence?'

'It is too precious to reveal casually to the ignorant mob, but you are my dearest friend and so I shall tell you. But you must promise not to pass it on.'

'I swear! Tell me.'

'Then listen carefully. *Nothing is true or real except what I decide is true and real.*'

'I'm real!' his girl objected. 'Or do you think you were only dreaming this afternoon?'

'Of course you are real – I have decided so. By the way, Manfred, have you seen the lady Werner brought back with

229

him from Vienna? I haven't yet decided whether she is real or not.'

'I had lunch with him the other day and he didn't say a word about a lady from Vienna.'

'Obviously he wouldn't – not to you. You keep on taking his girl-friends away from him. They're dancing over there – come and meet her.'

When the band paused Manfred made the acquaintance of Wolfgang's new friend, Countess Liesl von Lorincz-Androsch, a dark-haired and ivory-complexioned beauty approaching thirty. There was a worried look in Wolfgang's eye when he introduced them and Manfred patted his arm reassuringly.

'Have you spoken to Gottfried?' he asked.

'Not exactly. I nodded to him and to Nina when we arrived, but that's all.'

'There's nothing to worry about now. I've made peace for you. And now if you will excuse me, I want to find Jenny Montrose.'

'I hoped you were going to ask me to dance,' said the Countess, and Werner's expression became glacial.

'I would be honoured – but a little later, if Werner permits.'

Guests were arriving all the time and the enormous salon was beginning to fill up. Somewhere in this mob of laughing, drinking, dancing men and women was Jenny and, with any luck, the disaster of her visit to Manfred's apartment might be forgotten and a new start made. Or so he hoped. But before he found her, Albert Grutz appeared from nowhere, linked arms with him and marched him out into the entrance hall. It was empty but for the man-servant stationed at the door to admit more guests and three or four maid-servants to take coats and hats.

'A few words with you, Herr von Klausenberg. I gathered that you know young Ludwig Kessler. That's your business, of course, not mine. I'm an easy-going sort, anyone will tell you that. I'd rather do someone a good turn than a bad one. I don't lose my temper except under extreme provocation. But . . . if certain little pastimes of mine became public gossip, I would get very annoyed. You understand me? And if any malicious tittle-tattle came to the ears of my wife or business colleagues, I would take steps to make sure that the instigator of vicious lies had reason to be sorry he was ever born. Do I make myself clear?'

'You have no reason to fear anything from me. My interest was in Helga, not Ludwig, and it was fleeting, I can assure you. I haven't seen either of them for months.'

'That may be so, but a closed mouth makes no enemies, if you catch my meaning. See here, young man, I'm not stupid enough or vain enough to think that either of those two stays at home and reads a good book when I'm not around. What they get up to doesn't bother me in the least, but I expect and demand discretion where I'm concerned.'

'With every right,' said Manfred. 'So would I, in your position.'

'A man's amusements are his own business. As long as we understand each other there will be no glass broken.'

'Agreed. But tell me something, if you will, Herr Grutz, unless you think it is not a fit subject for discussion, in view of the circumstances – did you know that Helga and Ludwig are lovers?'

'No! I don't believe it – they're as jealous of each other as two dogs over a bone. What makes you say that – did you see something?'

'I didn't see them making love, if that's what you mean. The last time I saw the twins – back in August I think it was – there were strong indications of an unusual attachment under their rivalry. Enough to convince me, at least.'

'Well I'm damned!' said Grutz, staring thoughtfully at him, 'If that's right, then some fascinating possibilities present themselves. I'm grateful to you. Now you mention it . . . there were signs and I missed them. Well, well!'

'How would you go about settling accounts with someone who harmed your private interests?' Manfred asked, out of idle curiosity.

'No great problem, my boy. Have you any idea of how many political murders there have been in the last few years?'

'No. The newspapers carry small items about people found shot or beaten to death. The Red Front murder National Socialists and the National Socialists return the compliment. I can't recall reading of anyone being arrested.'

'The police know when it is not in their own interests to investigate too thoroughly. And almost any violent death in the streets can be written off as another act of political vengeance.'

'You have useful allies, Herr Grutz, but not with the Communists, I imagine.'

'One hand washes the other, as the saying goes. I'm glad we had this little talk. I like to clear up misunderstandings. And my next visit to the twins may be of remarkable interest now that you have opened my eyes.'

'Perhaps in return you can tell me about something.'

'What do you want to know?' said Grutz, his manner cautious again.

'The American banker, Montrose – no doubt you are acquainted with him.'

'And what is your interest in him?'

'Not in him. I found his young wife charming.'

'Ah yes, of course,' said Grutz with the ghost of a grin, 'You must understand that I have no personal knowledge of any irregularity – and any such suggestion would be scandalous. But it has been whispered that Frau Montrose may perhaps be susceptible to the blandishments of good-looking young dogs like you, though I'm sure the utmost tact and discretion would be called for. If there is any truth in the whisper, that is.'

'Do you find her charming yourself?'

'She's far too old for my taste – she must be at least twenty-five.'

'And the daughter,' Manfred continued, seizing the opportunity.

'I've met her at dinner-parties with her parents. She and her step-mother don't get on together, that's all I know.'

Manfred thanked his informant and made his way back into the salon, just as Gottfried and Nina stopped dancing. They greeted him effusively.

'Dance with Nina,' said Gottfried, 'I need a drink and time to get my breath back. Who was that you were having a private conference with in the hall?'

'A business friend of Bruckner. You wouldn't like him, Gottfried.'

'I'm damned sure I wouldn't. Did he give you anything useful for the Stock Exchange?'

'Nothing. His sort always keep things to themselves.'

Manfred danced with Nina. She was in white, with seed-pearls sewn in whorls on her bodice and skirt, and she was in a very good mood.

'All quiet on the Western Front?' said Manfred cheerfully.

'Peace and marital harmony,' she said, 'even Werner has been forgiven. There's no need to stay away from me – Gottfried knows everything.'

'What do you mean, everything? What is there for him to know?'

'I confessed that you and I have been madly in love for years and have to see each other. Gottfried was very understanding.'

'Good God!' Manfred exclaimed, stumbling and almost falling over. 'Why did you tell him nonsense like that?'

'He was getting suspicious about Konrad – it really was most trying. He kept on pestering me about having a lover and in the end I confessed that it was you.'

'Nina – it's not true!'

'What's that got to do with it? Gottfried likes you. He simply said *That's all right then* and since then there hasn't been a cross word.'

'But this is monstrous! You have an affair with Konrad and I get the blame!'

'As long as he thinks it's you there isn't any blame. That's the whole point.'

'I've never understood Gottfried and now I never shall.'

'There's nothing much to understand. We're happily married and we suit each other. He likes to sleep with me, but there's a little actress he visits that he thinks I don't know about.'

'One of Oskar's troupe?'

'Right – an odd-looking little creature named Magda Nebel. Have you met her?'

'If she was at Oskar's first-night party I suppose I must have seen her,' Manfred answered vaguely, trying to imagine stolid Gottfried strung up on Magda's special device with the thin steel chains, but the effort of imagination was beyond him.

'Speaking of Konrad, he's not here tonight,' he said, 'I wonder why he wasn't invited.'

'If you want my opinion, Gottfried had something to do with that. He doesn't like him.'

'Even though he thinks I'm your lover, not Konrad?'

'Konrad and I parted company weeks ago, darling,' said Nina. 'He was simply too possessive and boring. He started to question me about whether I'd slept with my own husband! Can you imagine?'

'So who is in favour with you at the moment, Nina dear?'

'That's what I've been telling you, if you'd only listen – no one is. You and I can be good friends again, the way we used to be. And since Gottfried thinks we are anyway, there won't be any problems. Isn't that wonderful?'

'Darling Nina, you astonish me. I hardly know what to say.'

'You don't have to say anything. We'll have some marvellous times together, like the old days. How about the day after tomorrow? I'm free all afternoon. We could meet for lunch and then go to your apartment.'

Manfred stared thoughtfully at the beautiful young woman he was dancing with, trying to remember how it had been when he was head-over-heels in love with her –

not so very long ago. The frantic emotions of those days had gone past recall. All that remained was the memory of how very exciting it had been to make love to her, and that was something he could remember about a good many women.

'Nina – before we plunge into another affair I think it only right to tell you that I'm not desperately in love with you and I know that you're not in love with me. We've both changed.'

'Naturally we've changed. We've grown up since then. We don't have to be desperately in love to have a wonderful love affair – you know that as well as I do.'

'Much the same was said of marriage in the days when parents arranged them without consulting their children.'

'I don't see what that's got to do with it, but I do know that you still want me, whether you're in love with me or not. You proved that at Ulrika's party, when you jumped on me the second Konrad's back was turned. Deny that if you can!'

'Speaking of Ulrika – there she is, making a late and dramatic entrance. Come on.'

He led Nina off the dance-floor to where Ulrika stood at the top of the two broad black marble steps which led down into the salon. Her frock was of crimson chiffon, so short that the hem barely reached to her knees, so skimpy of bodice that her arms, shoulders and almost her entire bosom was uncovered, and so flimsy that her nipples were plainly visible through it. She was posing, one knee thrust forwards, one hand on her hip and, in the other, an ivory cigarette-holder almost as long as her forearm.

'Disgraceful!' a woman said loudly as Manfred passed her. 'That woman is no better than a whore!'

'But a magnificent one,' said the man with her.

Manfred halted to turn towards the couple and give them a polite smile.

'Excuse me, but I could not help overhearing what you said, Madame. I must inform you that Fraulein Heuss is my cousin. She is not a whore, she is a lesbian.'

The woman, who was not more than thirty herself, blushed.

'Well, really!' she said. 'Am I to be insulted like this! Heinrich – do something!'

The man stared hard at Manfred for a moment, winked almost imperceptibly, and led his wife away, still complaining. Nina giggled and took hold of Manfred's arm cosily.

'Do you know who that was?' she asked, her tone indicating that the couple had been of great importance.

'No, nor do I care,' he answered, leading her to the steps. 'Ulrika, you look fantastic!'

At close quarters the dark shadow through her flimsy frock made it very obvious that Ulrika's only other items of clothing were her shoes and stockings.

'Thank you, darling,' she said, holding out her hand to be kissed, 'I'm on the prowl tonight.'

'Why is that?'

'I intend to start the New Year with a new lover to bring me luck. Nina, dear, from the way you're hanging onto Manfred I can guess that the two of you have decided to get together again. Old friends are the best – is that it?'

A man-servant approached them with a tray of glasses and stood silent, pretending not to notice Ulrika's near-nakedness. She took a glass of champagne, emptied it in one swallow and gave the man so dazzling a smile that he almost dropped his tray.

'Yes, old friends are the best,' Nina agreed. Don't you find it so?'

'Old friends are like old clothes,' said Ulrika. 'They're comfortable but they don't make you feel beautiful and desirable any more.'

'There are plenty of beautiful women here tonight,' said Manfred, grinning at his outrageous cousin, 'but whether any of them are interested in your advances, who can say?'

'I can say,' Ulrika answered with confidence, 'One look at a woman and I know whether I'm wasting my time or not. Naturally I prefer those who have never made love with another woman before – there's the thrill of seducing them away from their husbands or boy-friends.'

Gottfried joined them on the marble steps, his monocle tightly in his eye and a vaguely drunken expression on his face. He bowed stiffly over Ulrika's hand and, unseen by him, she smiled knowingly at Manfred and Nina.

'I'm planning a special party in a few weeks from now, Gottfried,' she said sweetly, 'I hope you will come – and bring Nina, of course. It will be spectacular.'

Gottfried's genial look vanished at once.

'Thank you,' he said cautiously, 'if we are in Berlin at the time . . . please excuse me, there is someone I want Nina to meet over there.'

He dragged Nina away and Ulrika and Manfred laughed together.

'Who is that marvellous creature over there by the band?' Ulrika asked. 'The young blonde in the white frock – do you know her?'

'That's Wolfgang's sister, Lotti. She's nineteen and she's engaged to be married.'

'You must introduce us. I feel the hand of destiny on me, my dear.'

'It's not the hand of destiny you want between your legs. You shall meet her, but I'd bet a thousand Marks to a Mark that you'll get nowhere with Lotti.'

'It's a bet. You think I'm ugly and charmless, do you?'

'Darling, I think you are sensational, but I'm a man.'

'Raise the stakes then – five thousand Marks to five Marks – how's that?'

'You're so sure of yourself? The odds should be the other way round. Still, a bet is a bet. Tell me something – was it easy to get Jenny Montrose into your bed?'

'She's so eager to try anything and everything that she seduced me. I could hardly believe it was her first time with a woman. There is something touching about Americans in Europe – it's as if they try to catch up on the whole of our history and culture in two weeks.'

'They have so little history or culture of their own. Do you classify an affair with you as history or culture?'

Ulrika smiled grandly.

'To make love with me is a cultural experience of historical significance,' she answered. 'Did you find her the same – eager to the point of frenzy?'

Manfred chose his words carefully, still privately ashamed of what he had done to Jenny at Ernst's party.

'We almost got together once, but it went wrong.'

'What! But you must have been lovers – she always asks about you when I meet her anywhere. Are you telling me the truth?'

'I've no reason to lie. Come and meet Lotti.'

Before that could happen, the entertainment began, with a fanfare from the band and a request to clear the centre of the floor. Frau Bruckner had engaged the services of a troupe of of dancers to perform what was announced as 'The Dance of the Seven Veils'. The music struck up and into the salon tripped half a dozen pretty young women, stark naked and bare-foot, to circle round in modified ballet movements, mainly designed to give the fashionable audience ample opportunity to stare at their breasts and bellies and backsides. In due course the lead dancer appeared, equally naked but trailing panels of transparent chiffon about her as she went through her routine.

Manfred and Ulrika were standing near a wall, in the circle of spectators. Manfred put his arm lightly round his cousin's waist and whispered close to his ear.

'What is the point of bringing a cabaret act into a private party? Especially a mixed party of this sort – if it were a men-only function I could understand it. But here it strikes me as the height of vulgarity.'

'Don't be a prude, darling, I'm enjoying it. You see the girl second from the right – the one with her arms above her head – I'm going to have her. I can never resist plump little breasts like hers.'

'I thought you wanted Lotti?'

'Of course I do, but if her fiancé is here she won't come

238

home with me tonight. Once you've introduced us I shall give her a day to think about me and then invite her to lunch. The little dancer will do for tonight.'

Manfred slid his hand gently from Ulrika's hip up to her breast and stroked it cautiously through the very thin chiffon of her frock. He felt the nipple go firm at his touch.

'You're a beast,' Ulrika whispered. 'But I forgive you – I know I'm irresistible.'

'You owe me something if what you said about playing with me when we were children is true.'

'Young as you were, your little thing stood up stiffly enough even then.'

'And is doing now,' he whispered. 'How about coming home with me tonight?'

'Don't be silly, darling, I've no interest in your stiff little thing now.'

'It's not so little any more.'

'I know – I saw it at my Steam-bath party. Why don't you find Nina and show it to her – she knows what to do with it.'

The dance ended to hearty applause from the spectators and the dancers filed away. Ulrika went after them and Manfred got himself another drink and thought that for him it was a disappointing party. After several glasses of champagne he became more cheerful and towards midnight he was dancing with a girl he had been introduced to – a very pretty fair-haired girl of about twenty named Romy Spengler. Like him she was a little drunk and when the music stopped abruptly, she fell laughing into his arms.

Bruno Bruckner and his wife were on the balcony that ran across one end of the salon. He addressed his guests in a loud and confident voice.

'Ladies and gentlemen – in two minutes it will be midnight!'

A line of servants filed into the salon carrying loaded trays and there was a rush to get another drink. In the scramble at least one glass smashed on the parquet. Manfred forced his way into the crowd.

239

'There!' he said, returning to Romy. 'One for you and one for me – though some of it was spilled when an idiot pushed me.'

The guests were looking up at the Bruckners on their balcony, glasses ready. Herr Bruckner was staring at his gold wrist-watch.

'Happy New Year!' he shouted happily and the salon rang with the cry as the guests shouted back and emptied their glasses.

There followed a positive orgy of kissing, hand-shaking and back-slapping. Manfred kissed Romy on both cheeks and she put her long thin arms round his neck and pulled his mouth to hers. The feel of her body squeezed close to his was very enjoyable and made him realise that the party might not be a complete disappointment after all.

'Ladies and gentlemen – and dear friends and colleagues,' Bruckner called out, 'permit me to say a few words on this important occasion . . .'

The few words proved to be a speech, both long and dull, in which Bruckner went into some detail about the problems which still beset the national economy. This was, no doubt, only a prelude to a proposed explanation of what was to be done in the New Year. But before he had even completed his analysis of the problems, Romy took Manfred's hand and tugged at it. Hand in hand they slid stealthily through the crowd staring up at the balcony until they could dart unnoticed through a side-door of the salon, the entrance through which the servants had been bringing champagne and food all evening.

'What a boring man!' said Romy. 'He asks us to a party and rants at us as if we were his board of directors.'

She was in Manfred's arms again and they kissed hotly.

'Unpardonable,' he agreed.

'Especially when there is something of colossal importance to do,' she added.

'Which is?'

'There is only one way to get the New Year off to a good start. Where can we go?'

They were in a passage that led to the kitchens and no one was in sight, the servants being immobilised in the salon to receive the benefit of their employer's view of the state of the economy, along with the guests. But through a door at the end of the passage there was the sound of singing and merriment, the kitchen-staff having escaped the ordeal. Halfway towards the kitchen Manfred found a door leading on to the back-stairs and led Romy up until they came out in a broad corridor with Persian rugs and doors along each side.

'Bedrooms,' said Romy, 'Just what we're looking for!'

The nearest door took them into a large and sumptuously furnished room, with pearl-grey walls and more of the geometric paintings. More usefully, it had a large and low double bed with a pink satin cover.

'Ghastly!' said Manfred, staring at the pictures. 'He must buy them wholesale.

'Who cares?' Romy chortled and threw herself bodily on to the bed, bounced and giggled uncontrollably.

A moment later Manfred was beside her, hugging and kissing her. She undid something at the side of her strapless frock and pulled the bodice down to show him her pointed little breasts and Manfred kissed them hungrily.

'At last!' she said. 'We've lost ten minutes of 1929 already!'

She rolled away from him on to her back, knees up, and raised herself on her shoulder-blades and high-heeled shoes to pull her copper-coloured frock up round her narrow waist, so revealing her lack of underwear. Manfred slid down the bed and kissed the fleshy little lips below her light-brown tuft.

'Don't keep me waiting at a time like this,' she urged.

Manfred was between her parted knees, his trousers unbuttoned. He lay on her quickly and slid his hard member deep into the warm little recess waiting for it. Romy squealed in pleasure and, at that very moment, a woman's voice cried out in outrage.

'What is going on here!'

241

It was a stupid question, in view of their position on the bed. Manfred scrambled off the girl, tucking his manhood out of sight and doing up his trousers, while she pulled her frock down hurriedly and sat up. There stood Frau Bruckner herself, hand on the door-knob, her face flushed dark red.

'I can't believe my own eyes!' she exclaimed. 'You, Romy! What would your father say if he knew of this! And as for you, Manfred, I am astounded that you should abuse my hospitality so grossly!'

Romy kept sensibly silent, but Manfred felt impelled to offer some sort of excuse. He rose to his feet and bowed slightly to Frau Bruckner.

'Madame, I fear I am guilty of an unpardonable breach of good manners. But I must ask you not to blame Fraulein Spengler, since it was I who brought her here. She is a little drunk from your excellent champagne and was unaware of my intentions. The blame rests entirely on me, I assure you.'

'Very well,' said Frau Bruckner grimly, 'I will take your word for that. Romy, you may go and no more will be said. But I must ask you to conduct yourself more decently while you are in my house.'

'Yes, Frau Bruckner,' said Romy demurely, jumping off the bed.

'You will remain here, Manfred,' Frau Bruckner continued unrelentingly, 'Romy may be young enough to act foolishly after a glass or two of champagne, but that is hardly true of you. I have more to say to you on this matter.'

She moved away from the door to let Romy scuttle out, still fastening the bodice of her frock. Then, to Manfred's slight alarm, she crossed the room to the dressing-table by the far wall and sat down to examine her make-up in the mirror.

'This is *your* room?' he asked, his heart sinking, 'I had no idea – what must you think of me!'

'Think of you? I think that you are a young man of

unusual courtesy. I wish my son Dieter had manners half as good as yours. I don't know how I prevented myself bursting out laughing when you told me that little slut didn't know what you brought her here for. But the lie did you credit. Do you know her well?'

Frau Bruckner was patting her hair in the mirror and her manner had changed remarkably for the better.

'I don't know her at all,' said Manfred, 'someone introduced us tonight. The time seemed appropriate to make her closer acquaintance.'

'Closer acquaintance! What a polite way you have of putting things. You had her sprawled across my bed and you were on top of her – that's really what I call closer acquaintance!'

Manfred sat down on the bed, much relieved by Frau Bruckner's attitude, and lit a cigarette from his gold case.

'Perhaps I am old-fashioned, Madame, but I find coarseness of expression unpleasing.'

She turned on her pink satin-topped bench to face him.

'Always?' she asked. 'Surely not.'

'I am not sure that I understand you.'

'And I'm sure that you do, my dear. There are some situations in which the use of coarse expressions can be very exciting.'

'So I understand. But is this a suitable topic of conversation between us, dear lady, especially in your bed-room?'

'What better place? And my name is Heidi, as I'm sure you know.'

'If your husband were to surprise us here, as you surprised me, I do not know what I would say to him. I could hardly claim that I had dragged you to your own bedroom, unaware of my intentions.'

'I locked the door when Romy left. No one will surprise us.'

She stood up, undid the fastening of her long gown and crossed her arms to pull it over her head. Manfred's feelings were extremely complicated at that moment. The brief episode with Romy had stirred his blood and some urgent relief was necessary – but it had never entered his head that the woman offering the relief might be his friend Dieter's mother.

Frau Bruckner wore no brassiere and had no need of one, her breasts being surprisingly small and flat. She stepped out of her lace-trimmed black silk knickers and stood for his judgment in her stockings and suspender-belt. She was a big woman, broad of hip and solid of belly, but neither flabby nor sagging. Her remarkably healthy-looking pink flesh looked everywhere firm and appealing.

Her most unusual feature lay between her thighs. Her mound was shaved – or plucked – completely smooth so that her long vertical slit was totally exposed. Manfred stared in fascination – he had never before seen a hairless woman. Frau Bruckner walked slowly towards him.

'You like the look of my Fotze,' she said softly.

From a lady of her age and position, the common word startled Manfred and made his stem twitch in his trousers. When she halted immediately in front of where he sat on the bed he reached out to run his fingers over the smooth flesh between her legs.

'Why do you have no hair?'

'For a simple and shameful reason. My husband can't keep his hands off little girls. The only way I can get him into bed with me at all is to be like one.'

'Is it important to get him into your bed?' Manfred asked, delighted by the feel of her soft flesh under his hand. 'You must have friends to make you happy, Heidi.'

'Several, but I don't want Bruno to escape from me completely. I have to keep some hold on him by offering him something he can't get elsewhere. He can't do much more than play about with his little girls, but with me he can let himself go with no fear of the consequences.'

She came a step nearer, straddled his knees and sat down on his lap. While she was busy with his trouser buttons Manfred stroked her breasts. Small and flat as they were, they were pleasant to the touch and her large nipples quickly lost their softness under his fingers.

244

'So you brought that little whore Romy Spengler up here to celebrate the New Year,' she said, smiling at him. 'And now you're celebrating it with me instead. What do you think of that?'

Her fingers played very expertly with his stem and at that moment Manfred felt no particular regret about the change of partners. He could catch up with Romy later after he had finished with Heidi.

'The New Year is starting with a surprise,' he answered. 'That must be a good sign.'

'Do *you* like little girls?' she asked, not listening to him.

'Only grown-up girls.'

'How about boys?' she murmured, obviously excited by the sight of his stiffness.

Manfred smiled and teased her nipples.

'What a question! You have the proof in your hand of what I like.'

'What do you want to do with it?'

'I want to put it in your Fotze, Heidi.'

Her breath hissed between her teeth in excitement at the word. She pushed him down on to his back and heaved herself forward to get his stem into the soft bare lips between her legs and sink down on it.

'You've got what you wanted,' she gasped. 'Now you're going to give me my New Year present!'

She rode up and down on him, very agile for a woman of her size. Manfred took her engorged nipples between thumbs and forefingers to squeeze them and encourage her efforts.

'Tell me what we're doing,' Heidi panted.

He told her, using the most brutal and coarse expression for the act in which they were engaged.

'Ah!' she moaned, 'say it again!'

He said it again, over and over, as she slammed against him and brought on her climactic convulsions so fiercely that Manfred's back arched off the bed as his crisis swept through him.

Afterwards Heidi scrambled off him quickly and he sat

up to rearrange his clothes decently. He would have kissed her and caressed her pink flesh for a moment or two as a mark of gratitude and respect, but she had retreated to the bench before her dressing-table and was sitting there facing him with her knees pressed tightly together.

'You must go downstairs and back to the party before you are missed,' she said, 'I shall be some little time.'

'Is anything wrong?' he asked curiously.

'I don't know what came over me. It must have been the sight of you with that little slut Romy. My God, you're young enough to be my son!'

'Don't you like young men, Heidi. I mean, what about your special friends, the ones who make you happy while Herr Bruckner is off pursuing his own amusements – are none of them young?'

'They're a good deal older than you and I can trust them. What have I done! This will be gossipped all over Berlin by tomorrow.'

Manfred knelt by her feet and put his hands on her bare shoulders.

'No one but you and I will ever know how we celebrated the New Year together, I give you my word.'

'Thank you,' she said, 'I know I can trust you.'

Manfred leaned forward to kiss her mouth gently, then her flat breasts. She stroked his hair and he parted her knees reassuringly to kiss her belly and the smooth lips between her thighs.

'A happy New Year,' he said, getting to his feet.

'And to you, Manfred. May it bring you everything you wish for yourself.'

Which was all very well, he thought as he made his way down the broad main staircase towards the sound of music and noisy hilarity, but what had taken place in Heidi's bedroom was not what he had wanted for himself in the New Year. The quick act of love with her was by no means as agreeable as it would have been with Romy. With Romy underneath him they would have giggled together like naughty children while their loins thrust at each other and

246

it would have been innocent and natural – a game. But with Heidi Bruckner it was not like that at all. She had used him to bolster her own waning confidence in herself and had suffered pangs of ridiculous remorse afterwards. In retrospect Manfred was irritated by what he had allowed to happen.

The salon was like a beer-garden. Everyone was dancing to the frantic music of the jazz group, laughing and shouting as if they were totally drunk. As they probably were. The heat was over-powering and the smell of cigar-smoke, perfume and perspiring bodies nauseating. Manfred felt that he had had enough – it had been a disappointing party after all. The servants seemed nearly as drunk as the guests and in the room near the entrance hall where the hats and coats had been taken, he found a footman on top of a maidservant, the two of them hard at it on top of a pile of very expensive fur-coats. Without disturbing them Manfred found his black leather overcoat and left the house.

Outside it was freezing cold, with the threat of snow in the air. The sky was over-clouded but there was enough light from the windows of the house to illuminate the drive between the double row of parked cars. He was thirty or forty paces from the front door when he heard scuffling ahead of him and low voices. At first he thought it might be the chauffeurs, but commonsense told him that they were in the kitchens, getting drunk and making advances to the female staff. His curiosity was aroused and he moved forward silently and slowly towards the sound and stopped behind a huge limousine to peer over its top. He saw two figures ahead of him and their position admitted no ambiguity as to what they were doing. One of them was sprawled face-down over the bonnet of the next parked car in the line, feet apart on the ground, trousers down, to show a pale gleam of flesh. The other stood close up between his companion's legs and leaned forward to make thrusting movements with his loins. Manfred heard him say 'Fantastic!' and recognised the voice of Dieter Bruckner.

Astounded is too mild a word for Manfred's state of mind

247

at that moment. He had known Dieter for years and was well acquainted with at least half a dozen women Dieter had been with. There had never been the slightest hint that he was interested in young men. Yet here he was, battering away at the rear end of one! And to judge from the vigour of his onslaught and his exclamations of pleasure, he was thoroughly enjoying the experience.

This is unbelievable, Manfred said to himself – either I am drunker than I thought or Dieter is blind drunk and doesn't know what he's doing. But neither hypothesis fitted the facts. However drunk Dieter might be, he could hardly mistake a man for a woman at such close quarters. What on earth could it be like, this imitation love-making, Manfred wondered – this exchange of the curved and tender body of a woman for whatever paltry substitute another man could offer? He remembered Ludwig dressed up as a girl and his own violent reaction at the moment of discovery.

Dieter gasped loudly as his crisis arrived. His partner writhed on the shiny car bonnet and cried out and at once Manfred knew the truth. It was Jenny Montrose in men's evening clothes lying face-down on the car with her trousers round her knees! Black rage exploded in Manfred's heart and he ran round the limousine which had concealed him, seized Dieter by the hair and spun him round, away from Jenny. In the faint light Dieter's expression was one of shock, as well it might be, his mouth hung open and his eyes bulged from his face. His trousers were open to let his hard stem stick out, still dribbling feebly.

'You swine!' Manfred bellowed and punched Dieter in the face, sending him staggering backwards.

'Manfred! Have you gone mad?' he yelped. 'What's the matter with you?'

'Get out of my sight before I murder you!' Manfred shouted.

There was a dark trickle of blood from Dieter's nose. He brought his fists up to defend himself and threw a punch at Manfred's head. Manfred blocked it and punched him hard over the heart and, as he staggered, followed it with a punch to the chin that knocked Dieter over backwards.

'Out of my sight!' he shouted again, waiting for Dieter to get up so that he could knock him down again. But Dieter wanted no more. He got up slowly, backed away a few steps, then turned and lurched away into the dark. Manfred swung round to confront Jenny, who was off the car bonnet and fastening her trouser buttons.

'What the hell is going on?' she demanded, surprise causing her to lapse into English. Manfred took her by the throat, pulled open the car door and hurled her inside. He heard her cursing as he scrambled in after her and slammed the door behind him. She had fallen half across the back seat of the car and half on the floor.

'What the hell do you think you're doing?' she said furiously, still speaking in English.

'Bitch!' Manfred shouted, dragging her upright. 'Dirty whore of a bitch!'

She recognised him at last.

'Ah, it's Herr von Gigolo,' she said in German. 'Drunk as usual! You've got the wrong woman. I don't pay for it.'

Manfred slapped her face, left and right, growling in his throat, like a dog on the attack. Without hesitation she slapped his face, hard enough to hurt. Manfred grabbed her arms and they wrestled on the car seat, she trying to knee him between the legs, until he found himself kissing her. For a while she struggled furiously but then she relaxed and returned the kiss.

'Why didn't you say that's what you wanted?' she asked, easing herself from his clutch, 'I thought you were trying to hurt me.'

She tugged at the gold studs in her starched shirt-front until she had it open from bow-tie to waist. Manfred pulled the shirt wide open to kiss her bare breasts voraciously.

'That's better,' she said. 'All that flitting about and kissing the hand and mealy-mouthed politeness – why didn't you push me on my back months ago and do this?'

'I didn't want it like this,' he growled against her flesh.

He hooked his fingers in the waist-band of her trousers and ripped the buttons open.

'Are you always this wild?' she gasped.

His hand clenched tightly over her furry mound and two fingers were deep into the warm wetness of her earlier love-making.

'My God!' she moaned as his fingers ravished her. 'Not so fast . . . wait!'

But he didn't wait and soon she gave a long throaty wail and shook hard against him. Even before her crisis was over he dragged her trousers down her long legs with impatient hands until he had them off completely and could push her on her back and heave himself on top of her, one leg along the car-seat and one on the floor. He tore his own trousers open as roughly as he had treated hers and, two seconds later, penetrated her with a lunge that made her cry out.

'It's like being raped!' she gasped while he slammed into her, his mind a red haze, 'slow down!'

Her complaints trailed off as she was caught up in the fierceness of his passion and she jerked and squirmed beneath his thrashing body, her hands clutching at his hair to pull his mouth down to hers. A thunderous stroke seemed to rip through Manfred and he screamed in ecstasy, his rage draining away with his passion.

When he came to himself again he asked Jenny if she was all right, some recollection of her wailing making him anxious that she might not be.

'I'm dead and in Heaven,' she said faintly.

She put her arms round his neck and kissed him again and again.

'I think I must confess that I may be in love with you, Jenny, boring though that may be for both of us.'

'I don't care whether you are or not – you're not going to escape from me after that. What don't you take me home – or is there another fat old hausfrau waiting in your bedroom for you?'

'Come and see for yourself.'

He rolled off her awkwardly in the confined space and they got out of the car. Jenny had her trousers draped over her arm and presented a slightly comical appearance in her black tail-coat and crumpled shirt.

'No point in putting them on again,' she said, 'it's not a long drive. Come to think of it, the owner of this handsome vehicle deserves to have them as a souvenir of what took place here tonight.'

She threw her trousers into the back of the car and slammed the door. Manfred picked up the long leather coat he had dropped when he attacked Dieter and put it round her shoulders to keep the cold wind off her while they walked down the long line of parked cars to his tourer. Jenny looked at it approvingly and asked him to put the top down.

'And if we die of cold?' he asked.

'Then we'll die happy – what more do you want?'

With the hood down and an icy wind over the top of the wind-screen they drove away from the Bruckners' house and towards the city centre. The Kurfurstendamm was jammed with people, arms linked, singing and laughing and idiotically happy that a New Year had begun. Jenny shrugged the overcoat off her shoulders and stood up, clinging to the windscreen with one hand, to wave and shout greetings at the people on the pavement, while the wind pulled her undone shirt open to expose her shapely breasts.

'You are the most beautiful woman in the world!' Manfred shouted to her, 'and I am crazy about you!'

She sat down to take his face in her hands and kiss him, so distracting him that the car wobbled halfway across the road and brought a blare of car-horns from traffic going in the other direction.

'Don't kill us!' she said, 'We've too much to say to each other.'

Then she was up again, perching on the back of the seat while she struggled out of her tail-coat.

'What are you doing?' Manfred shrieked.

'I can't stand these silly clothes! I want you to know I'm a woman.'

She bundled the tail-coat up and hurled it at two policemen standing on the pavement. One of them waved and the other shouted and Manfred put his foot down hard to get away from them. He looked up at Jenny and saw that she was pulling her shirt over her head. She sat there, her black hair tousled by the wind, her face glowing, naked except for a tiny suspender-belt and silk stockings, the shirt trailing out behind her like a banner as she held it high. On the pavement people pointed and cheered.

'Don't freeze to death now!' Manfred called to her, 'I need you!'

'I'm on fire for the first time in my life!' she called back 'Happy New Year, Manfred!'

BLUE ANGEL SECRETS

Foreword by the Translator

Margarete von Falkensee was born in Potsdam in 1896 and was the daughter of a civil servant. After some experience in the Berlin theatre she worked, after 1924, in the flourishing German film industry. Her remarkable first novel, available in English as *Blue Angel Nights*, was published in Berlin in 1931, though it was written some years earlier.

Like many other writers and performers she emigrated to America after the Nazi Party took office in Germany in 1933. Her efforts to establish herself as a screen-writer in Hollywood met with only limited success, perhaps because, as this novel shows decisively, she was unable to take her new environment seriously. In her view Hollywood had become as corrupt in the twenty-five years of its existence as the centuries-old society she had left behind, and she set out to satirise it viciously. As in her earlier novels about Berlin, she utilised the theme of sexual corruption as an image of the collapse of social values.

It is interesting to note that at a time when she was earning her living by writing film-scripts in English, she chose to write this novel in German. A reasonable conclusion is that she felt her grasp of English inadequate for anything more important to her than a few lines of film dialogue. There is another reason, which will be touched upon later.

Blue Angel Secrets is linked to Margarete von Falkensee's earlier work by more than her continuing theme of degen-

5

eracy. Two of the characters of *Blue Angel Nights* are here transposed to Hollywood, as the author herself had been. They are Oskar Brandenstein, a Berlin theatrical producer, and Hugo Klostermann, a young actor who starred in Brandenstein's most successful comedy, *Three in a Bed*. When the story opens, Brandenstein has already established himself as a film director and Klostermann has just arrived from Berlin to launch himself on a film career.

The central event of *Blue Angel Secrets* is a shooting and for this the author has combined two infamous Hollywood deaths – the murder of William Desmond Taylor in 1922 and the suicide of Paul Bern in 1932, the year in which the novel is set. Taylor was a middle-aged film director at Famous Players-Lasky and was found shot in the living-room of his house on Alvarado Street. The circumstances of his death were so complicated that no arrest was ever made, though it became widely known in the film community who was responsible.

Bern was another middle-aged film director. He became an MGM executive, married twenty-one year old *platinum blonde* Jean Harlow and shot himself in the bathroom of their mansion in Benedict Canyon two months later. He was found in front of a mirror, naked and drenched with his wife's perfume.

Though the plot of *Blue Angel Secrets* is based on a murder, it is not in any sense a detective story. The novel's main character, Hugo Klostermann, asks questions of everyone he encounters who knew the dead man, but he is not a detective and does not try to be one. His view is that it is the business of the police to track down murderers and his own questions spring from curiosity about the relations between men and women – none of which turn out to be what they seem.

This is the key to the author's attitude – nothing is ever what it seems. Klostermann's questions are not answered, the facts he is given can almost never be verified. To his confusion he is presented with a series of elaborately fabricated deceptions, all of them disgraceful and some more plausible than others. The conclusion he reaches is

6

that there is no such thing as truth in any absolute sense, merely a series of differing versions, based on the interests and convenience of the person concerned.

By the time Klostermann learns who committed the murder and why, it is no more real to him than any of the other stories he has been told. By then he has been thoroughly indoctrinated with the ethic of those he has associated with in Hollywood. Moral considerations have vanished and his principal concern has become self-interest. He assesses the murder in terms of how it will affect his career.

In this way Margarete von Falkensee makes her point – that men and women are capable of infinite self-deception and self-corruption in the pursuit of sexual pleasure and money. While it is the same point as she made in her two earlier novels set in Berlin, the Hollywood setting gives her greater scope for wilder and more comic indecencies.

There was never any possibility that *Blue Angel Secrets* could be published in America when it was written. This was not only because of its open attitude to sexuality, which would have been viewed as obscene until recently, but for an equally dangerous reason. The novel would have been regarded as highly defamatory by a number of important film personalities, who appear here under different names but whose antics make them readily identifiable. The author knew this very well and was writing for her own amusement, hence her use of her mother-tongue instead of her adopted language, English. Fifty years later, when the persons she satirised so acidly are dead, we too can share in that amusement.

Egon Haas
Munich, 1988

7

Chapter 1

New friends

Pretty though nineteen-year-old Patsy was, Hugo found her boring in bed. Whether this was the result of her small-town upbringing or a natural lack of interest, he was not sure. Her range went no further than a few kisses and yielding glances before she rolled on to her back and spread her legs, and though she was compliant, this to a man used to more enthusiastic partners, was less than inspiring. Hugo did his best to extend her experience, but achieved little and so, with a shrug of his shoulders, he slid into her soft little pouch. She sighed and wriggled her bottom on the bed while he was satisfying himself, but he doubted that she ever experienced a true climax.

Like himself, Patsy was in Hollywood to seek fame and fortune in movies. The difference was that he had travelled from Berlin at the invitation of an important film director, while she had run away from home. She was a fair-haired, healthy-looking girl with blue eyes and a broad mouth, average in height and build, with nicely-shaped, average-sized breasts. For a young woman with ambitions to be a film-star she was, in Hugo's eyes, too ordinary altogether. But she was soft and warm beneath him and he enjoyed what he was doing to her, whether she did or not. He was easing himself off her belly when the bedside telephone rang.

It was Oskar Brandenstein, booming at him in German

9

and sounding more than half drunk, inviting him to a party.

'Now?' said Hugo. 'I've been trying to reach you for three days, ever since I arrived from Germany and you phone at eleven at night! I'll be with you in half an hour – where are you?'

Hugo saw that Patsy was propped on an elbow, staring at him.

'Was that Oskar Brandenstein the big movie director – the friend you told me about?' she asked, her voiced hushed reverently.

'He wants me to go to his party now. I'll get a taxi to take you to your boarding-house.'

'You're going to be a star, I know it,' she said.

To his surprise she slid down on to her back again and opened her slender legs wide. For the first time since he had known her she took hold of his stiff part and pulled him towards her.

'Do it to me again!' she sighed.

Hugo needed no urging for that. He slid on to her trembling belly and she steered him into her wet little entrance.

'I want you to do it to me, Hugo,' she gasped, kissing his face frantically and more aroused than he had ever seen her.

'Don't forget me when you make it big!' she pleaded.

'I won't forget you, Patsy,' he assured her, feeling the tide of his passion rising strongly as he stabbed between her splayed legs, 'I'll do what I can for you.'

'Give me some of your luck!' she moaned. 'You can spare some of it for me!'

'Oh, yes!' Hugo groaned as his golden moments arrived and he gave her all the luck he had available just then. As it flooded into her she wailed and shook under him in the first climactic release she had ever enjoyed with him.

Her unexpected response put him in such a good mood that he took her with him to the party. Oskar's house in Beverly Hills would have made a useful set for a film about Old Mexico, being vast and white, with arches half-hidden

10

behind scarlet wistaria and bougainvillaea. The entrance hall was the size of a ballroom, floored with pink marble and adorned with life-size replicas of classical statues, mostly nude goddesses.

Hugo asked for Oskar and was directed towards the back of the house and, with Patsy clinging to his hand, he emerged on to a flood-lit terrace giving on to an acre of close-cropped lawn and an oval swimming-pool. A hundred or so guests in evening dress stood talking and drinking, while white-jacketed waiters flitted about with trays of drinks and snacks. A naked young woman with breasts like melons bounced up and down on a springboard and dived perfectly into the pool. And there at last was Oskar, surrounded by pretty girls and applauding the diver as she surfaced.

The moment he caught sight of his old friend, Hugo understood much about Hollywood. There stood *big-time* movie director Oskar Brandenstein among his elegantly dressed guests, solid and corpulent in shiny black riding-boots and cavalry twill breeches. A short-sleeved white shirt with buttoned pockets enclosed his ample chest and it was open at the top over a polka-dot foulard silk scarf tied round his thick neck. When Hugo had known him in Berlin, Oskar's sandy-coloured hair was already receding fast, and this sign of unacceptable ageing had been banished by the simple expedient of shaving his head completely, so that it looked like a huge pink cannon-ball. But the best touch of all, in Hugo's view, was the intimidating monocle screwed fiercely in Oskar's left eye.

Contemplating this comical figure, Hugo saw that there was a role to be played and, as Berlin's best young actor, he knew how to play it, even if he must improvise his own lines.

'Oskar!' he sang out, loudly enough to attract the attention of everyone on the terrace. The girl in the water heaved herself up by her elbows on the pool edge until her white globes were fully displayed above the tiling, but no one paid any attention to her.

Oskar knew to perfection how to play his own role. He

11

flung his arms round Hugo, thumped his back, shouted and hooted in such delight that they could have been brothers reunited after a distressing absence.

'Listen, all of you – this is my good friend Hugo!' Oskar bellowed in heavily-accented English. 'He is the finest actor in Berlin and the best-equipped Casanova in Europe!'

There was laughter and cheers, glasses raised towards Hugo and looks of interest from several women. The girl in the pool blew kisses towards him and Hugo waved back. When opportunity served he introduced Patsy to Oskar.

'Enjoy yourself,' Oskar told her, 'go and meet some of these nice people while I talk to Hugo.'

He waved her away and led Hugo back through the house to a large room decorated as a study. It had a reproduction Louis XVI desk as large as a double-bed and five or six thousand leather-bound books on shelves round the walls. Oskar gave him a glass of brandy and stretched his bulk full-length on a Madame Recamier style chaise-longue upholstered in dark green velvet.

'I would have phoned you before this,' he said, 'but I have been working twenty-four hours a day to complete my latest movie. Have you enjoyed your few days in Hollywood – it never takes you long to find a girl, does it?'

'Nor you, as I recall,' said Hugo with a grin. 'When will you start work on your next movie – the one you want me for?'

'I need a week or two's rest,' Oskar answered vaguely, 'and there are arrangements to be made.'

'What sort of arrangements?'

'You're an actor,' said Oskar, 'don't worry about production arrangements – leave that to me.'

'What sort of film will it be?'

'I can't discuss that yet,' Oskar replied, rubbing a hand over his shiny bald head.

'But there is a part for me?' Hugo asked, alarmed by the elusive nature of the answers.

'My dear man, of course there is! That's why I asked you to leave Berlin and come here. I want you under contract the moment that the production arrangements are agreed.'

'Why not now?'

Oskar dangled his monocle in his brandy and licked it thoughtfully. 'I am thinking of your best interests, believe me,' he said. 'If I get them to sign you on now, with nothing specific agreed, they will pay you the smallest possible salary. But when I say that I must have you for a leading man in a particular movie, that will be very different. You will be able to insist on much more money.'

'So how long am I to wait?' Hugo persisted.

'Two weeks, maybe, three perhaps,' Oskar said after a pause.

'Very well, I regard myself as on vacation in the Californian sunshine for the next three weeks. But tell me one thing – why me? Why do you not employ one of the many well-known stars here? Why should you do this for me, Oskar?'

'Because you are a good actor,' said Oskar. 'You were first-rate in my production of *Three in a Bed* – it was the most profitable play I ever staged in Berlin. I'll tell you a little secret, as between professional colleagues – American actors are cowboys at heart, all of them, even if they have never ridden on a horse! They walk like cowboys and speak their lines as if they are chewing on straws. I cannot work with them seriously, particularly not on what I have in mind to do next.'

He emptied his brandy-glass and lumbered to his feet.

'I must get back to my party, Hugo, and see what wonderfully wicked things are being said and done. Enjoy yourself – the women are here to be used, especially the married ones.'

'I suppose I'd better find Patsy,' said Hugo.

'Forget her – she's nobody. Does she like film-stars? By now she's been rampaged by one of them out there. I will introduce you to someone more useful to you.'

Good as his word, he led the way through the ground-floor rooms of his house until he sighted a woman Hugo recognised instantly from his visits to the cinema.

'Thelma, darling!' said Oskar. 'This is my dear friend

13

Hugo who has arrived from Berlin and knows nobody. Look after him for me.'

Thelma Baxter was too big to be elegant, being tall and well-built, with prominent breasts and well-defined hips. Her straw-yellow hair was cut stylishly short and swept back from a central parting. Her eyes were bright blue and her cheeks a trifle too chubby for glamour – yet for all that she exuded an air of comfortable sexuality that had made her a star. She was never the leading lady, Hugo thought, always the second lead in romantic comedies – the heroine's friend or room-mate who spoke the funny lines when the director wanted to change the mood. She was about his own age – twenty-seven.

'Is that Berlin, Wisconsin?' she asked.

'Berlin, Germany!' Hugo exclaimed, shocked that there could be any other, and then he saw that she was joking.

'I have seen you in the cinema and have admired your talent greatly,' he told her.

'My talent? Is that all?'

Hugo glanced approvingly at the two plump breasts pushing out her peacock-blue frock and turned his head a little to give her a view of his classic profile.

'That was to be polite,' he said, subjecting her to the full force of his charming smile. 'Naturally, I find you irresistibly attractive, Miss Baxter.'

'Call me Thelma. There's someone over there I know wants to talk to you.'

'Who? No one knows me but Oskar.'

'Over by the bar talking to Chickenhawk Chester – see him?'

Chester Chataway's international reputation as the screen's Great Lover had been won in the days of silent movies and he was still playing the same part now he was over forty and had to speak to his leading ladies as well as flashing his dark eyes at them. Thelma tucked her arm under Hugo's and led him towards the bar.

'Why do you call Mr Chataway a chickenhawk? I do not understand this, Thelma.'

'That's his girl-friend in the pink satin,' she answered.

14

The girl she meant was very slender and had a mop of blonde curls and a face as blank as a china doll. Hugo put her age at about thirteen, but commonsense insisted that she must be older.

'This is Hugo,' said Thelma, 'Oskar's brought him over from Europe for his next movie.'

Close up, Chester looked his age. He was discreetly made up, but the lines showed round his eyes and mouth and his jowl was slack. He was drunk and swaying slightly.

'I'm Ambrose Howard,' said the man Chester had been talking to.

The name registered at once with Hugo. Howard was a director of very considerable reputation and, like Oskar, he worked with Ignaz International studios. He was a strongly-built man in his mid-forties, with a thin black moustache and hair sleeked back without a parting.

'Hey, Norma's arrived!' Chester exclaimed, waving his arms above his head.

Norma Gilbert waved back daintily from across the room and stayed where she was. As a child-star her appealing innocence had achieved such renown that the studio had publicised her as *All the World's Sweetheart* and it had stuck, inapt though it was now she was grown up and trying to make the transition to adult roles.

'Look at that sweet little ass!' said Chester, grasping at Hugo's arm to steady himself, 'I could die happy diddling Norma.'

'Who is the man with her?' Hugo asked.

'A goddamn phoney, that's what he is!' Chester snarled. 'He calls himself Prince something or other and he's got Norma mesmerised! When I think of his dirty hands feeling up that sweet girl I could go right over there and flatten him!'

'Easy, Chester,' said Thelma, 'Norma's too grown up for you. She's an old lady of twenty-one now. You stick with your Lily.'

Lily in the pink satin was paying no attention. She emptied her glass and took another full one from a passing waiter.

15

'You and I must get together and talk,' Ambrose said to Hugo. 'Ring me at the studio on Monday and we'll fix something.'

'How about talking to me?' Chester demanded. 'Am I going to get the part?'

'I've told you,' said Ambrose, 'nothing's been decided yet.'

'The hell with you,' said Chester in a surly tone and walked away. Hugo noted his shoulder-rolling gait and thought he understood what Oskar meant by *cowboys*.

'You should see the rest of this house,' Ambrose told Hugo. 'It was built for Vanda Lodz, one of the great silent movie stars. It stood empty for some time before Oskar rented it to accommodate his gigantic ego.'

'I remember Vanda Lodz in movies when I was a schoolboy – what happened to her?'

'Her career nose-dived when talkies came in four years ago,' said Thelma, slipping her arm into his again. 'The first time they recorded her she sounded like a parrot. So she retired to live abroad.'

'That's right,' Ambrose agreed. 'Thelma will show you round Vanda's house. Especially the master-bedroom. Our local historians claim that Vanda gave her best performances there.'

From the grandiose entrance-hall a pink marble staircase swept up in a wide quarter-circle to the upper floor of Oskar's house. Thelma pushed open a door with white satin quilting and stood aside for Hugo to go in. He found himself on the threshold of a setting for an epic of Borgia decadence – a very large room with ceiling-to-floor drapes of ivory watered-silk hung between long crystal mirrors. In the centre of the room stood the tallest and broadest bed he had ever seen – a four-poster with crimson velvet curtains and thick gold cords with giant tassels.

The frolic taking place at that moment needed no such generous space. A dark-haired woman was sprawled face-down, naked but for a black silk stocking on her right leg. Her arms were stretched above her head, bound at the wrist with her other stocking, and tied to the corner bed-

16

post. Silk pillows were pushed under her loins to raise her round bare bottom. A fully dressed man knelt beside her on the bed and slowly spanked her rump with his open hand, so deeply engrossed in his entertainment that he failed to hear the door opening.

'Bad girl!' Hugo heard him gasp. 'Bad, bad girl!'

His trousers were open, revealing his thick and angry-looking prong which stood out stiffly. It nodded up and down with the raising of his arm to slap the woman's bottom again. Hugo stood still in the open doorway and Thelma pressed herself against his back to look over his shoulder. She tittered slightly and Hugo caught his breath as her hand slid into his trouser-pocket.

'Stop, please . . . please, Ted!' the woman on the bed moaned theatrically.

She squealed as the hand landed again, her thighs parted wider on the silk pillows that supported them and Hugo glimpsed her dark-fuzzed peach. So too did the man spanking her and his free hand was thrust between her thighs to grasp her while the other hand rose and fell.

The revelry on the bed and Thelma's hand rubbing warmly through his trouser-pocket had brought Hugo's adjunct to an upright position.

'What are you – some sort of pervert?' she whispered in his ear. 'You get your kicks just watching, or what?'

He backed out of the room and pulled the door shut silently before turning to run his hands over Thelma's plump breasts. Her hand was still deep in his pocket to grip him while she led him into an adjacent bedroom – empty but with signs that it had been used very recently, the covers hanging half off the bed and the pillows rumpled. In this room everything in sight was quilted in rose-pink satin – walls, bed, dressing-table, chairs, sofa – even the ceiling. Not that Hugo paid much attention to the decorations, for he had one arm around Thelma to press her to him and his other hand up her blue frock to squeeze the fleshy cheeks of her bottom and then round between their bodies until he could get it into her loose knickers and touch her furry mound. She moved her feet apart and let him feel her until his fingers found their way into her warm alcove.

'That's more like it,' she said, grinning as she disengaged herself from him to reach under her frock and slide down her legs a fragile little creation of pale blue silk and lace.

Hugo murmured in pleasure as she stuffed her warm knickers down the front of his trousers. She sat on the side of the bed, grinning up at him, then lay back and flipped her frock up to her waist. Hugo stared delightedly at her broad belly and thick fleece while she put her diamond-ringed hands on her parted thighs above her stocking tops. Still grinning up at him, she pulled herself slowly open. Unable to wait another moment, Hugo crashed to his knees between her legs and ripped his trousers open.

'Not bad!' Thelma exclaimed, staring at his long and very hard spike. He pushed it instantly into the pink socket waiting for it and see-sawed to and fro vigorously.

'First time today,' Thelma murmured, a happy smile on her plump-cheeked face.

Her hands were up under his starched evening-shirt to pinch his flat nipples between her finger-nails, and Hugo was squeezing her big bouncers through her frock. It was not Hugo's first time that day, but that was no obstacle to his rapid arousal. He rode hard between her legs and cried out as he fountained his offering into her belly. Thelma gasped and jerked furiously under him a dozen times before she lay still and slack.

'Nice,' she said lazily, 'you're very handy at it, Hugo.'

He sat on the side of the bed to tuck away his softening equipment and do up his trousers. Thelma flipped her frock down carelessly over her thighs and asked him for a cigarette. While they were smoking he asked her who was the woman they had seen playing on the four-poster.

'That was Peg Foster.'

'Is she a film star? I couldn't see her face because of the way she was lying.'

'She's no film star, but she's a good little actress,' said Thelma, 'she puts on a great act for her customers.'

'You mean that she does it for money?'

'Doesn't everybody in this town, one way or another?'

He stared at her to see if she was joking but her grin told him nothing.

'They call her Perversity Peg,' she said. 'She'll let you slap her, whip her, punch her around, tie her up sixteen different ways and scream her head off for you while you shove your dong into any opening you fancy. She's very popular with the over-forties round here.'

'That sounds very dangerous,' Hugo objected. 'How can she tell if a client will get carried away and hurt her badly?'

'That's what she hopes for – they have to pay her off to keep her quiet then. I can name a studio head and a has-been cowboy star who've paid her a hundred thousand dollars each after they put her in the hospital.'

'But why is she here at this party?'

'Oskar asks her to all his parties. Some say he takes a cut, but I think they're buddies and she makes mischief for people he wants to get a hold over.'

'You have strange customs in Hollywood, Thelma.'

'Don't tell me you haven't got girls like her in your home town and men like Ted Moran who can't get it up any other way.'

'Now I think of it, Oskar had a girl in Berlin who liked whips and ropes,' said Hugo, 'Magda, her name was. She lived with him for a while. Who was the man we saw doing the spanking?'

'Ted Moran. He's General Manager at Ignaz International – Mr Fix-it for Stefan Ignaz. How come you're dressed so fast – are you a one-shot man?'

'No, I carry a revolver,' he said, grinning at her.

'A six-shooter?' she asked, her fingers hooking into the front of his trousers and ripping the buttons wide open so that she could reach in and take hold of his stiffening part.

'Wait while I lock the door,' said Hugo, 'I want you naked.'

In the short time it took him to lock the rose-pink quilted door and walk back to the bed Thelma had all her clothes off and was lying flat on her back, her knees up and widely parted. Hugo shrugged mentally as he undressed, begin-

19

ning to think that this basic approach was an American characteristic. He leaned over her to play with her roly-poly breasts and found that their reddish-brown buds were already firm.

'Put it in me!' she urged him, and so he mounted her at once and saw her happy smile as she felt him push deeply into her slippery entrance.

'My God, I love it!' she sighed. 'It doesn't matter how often I have it, it's fantastic every time!'

In spite of the pounding of his heart Hugo heard the door-handle being rattled and was glad he'd locked the door.

'Oh yes!' Thelma gasped loudly. 'Oh, *yes!*'

Her finger-nails clawed down his back from his shoulder-blades to the cheeks of his bottom and then sank into the flesh as she tried to pull him deeper into her. Hugo shortened his stroke and almost at once exploded wetly into her heaving belly.

Thelma's rhapsodic convulsions were brief but intense. When they were finished, her legs slid down the bed on either side of Hugo and he could feel how limp her body was beneath him, as if her short climax had wrung her out like a wet towel. Her face was shiny with perspiration and her blue eyes were almost closed. Hugo kissed the tip of her nose and she smiled up at him. He rolled off her broad belly and she got up and went to the mirror over the dressing-table.

'I look like a train-wreck!' she exclaimed, running a hand through her dishevelled straw-coloured hair. Naked as she was, she sat down and began to repair her make-up.

Hugo stood behind her and used the mirror to straighten out his tie and comb his hair. Thelma stared at her reflection and cupped her soft bundles in her palms to hoist them up a little.

'Good for another year,' she said critically, 'then I'll get a tuck taken in to pull them up. Do you know where I live?'

'Tell me so that I can visit you, Thelma.'

When she let go of her heavy breasts Hugo reached over her shoulders and cradled them in his own hands.

'I am sure that the most important film stars in Hollywood have played with these,' he said.

'Only the men,' she answered with a grin, 'I've never joined the girl's sewing-circle with Natasha and the rest of them.'

'Then all the important male stars,' Hugo corrected himself.

'Not just the important ones,' she chuckled, 'I like men more than that. Every star you can name has felt them – except Mickey Mouse. I live on Glendale Boulevard and I hope you'll call me. Now go on back to the party while I get myself together.'

On his way past the main bedroom Hugo could not resist peeping round the door, but the four-poster was deserted. At the top of the marble staircase he stood politely aside for Chester Chataway's very young girl-friend to pass him. She reached the top step and stood swaying so dangerously that he grabbed at her arm to save her from falling backwards down the stairs.

'Too much champagne,' she said, her eyes out of focus as she peered at him, 'got to lie down.'

Drunk as she was, Lily was still extremely pretty. Her frock was a knee-length creation in pink satin, with large crystal buttons down the bodice to a tight waist-line and it reinforced the impression of a life-size doll – not a person but a plaything. Even while Hugo pondered the preferences of famous screen lover Chester Chataway, Lily's eyes closed and she sagged against him. Hugo got an arm round her tiny waist as her knees buckled and picked her up. She needed to sleep it off, and there was an empty bedroom behind him. He carried her into the master bedroom and set her down on the crimson four-poster. He was smoothing her frock down her legs when her blue eyes opened and she smiled up at him.

'I like you,' she whispered, 'do you like me?'

'I think you're very pretty.'

Her thin-fingered hands were at her bodice, undoing the big crystal buttons. She held it open to show him little round breasts the size of pomegranates.

21

'I'm wearing lace panties,' she murmured, 'you can see them if you want to.'

'I'm sure they're very elegant,' he answered, 'close your eyes now and sleep.'

But her doll-like allure was more than he could resist and, to his astonishment, he found himself pulling her pink frock up her long legs to look at her ivory lace underwear. He put his hand between her legs to touch the satin skin of her thighs above her stocking-tops.

'Take them off,' she whispered very faintly, her eyes closed.

Hugo eased her lace knickers down over her narrow hips to uncover her flat little belly and the light fuzz of blonde hair between her very slender legs. Her hands had fallen away from her bodice and only the pink tip of one smooth pomegranate peeped out. She had slid into unconsciousness at last, Hugo realised. For fear of waking her he left her knickers round her thighs and her bodice undone, but he locked the bed-room door and took the key with him.

He found Oskar on the flood-lit terrace, stretched out on a sun-lounger, his shiny-booted ankles crossed comfortably and a large glass in his hand. He was surrounded by a group of young men and women who laughed flatteringly at his jokes, and one of them was Patsy, perched on the end of the sun-lounger. She had been persuaded to take off her frock and stockings and sit at Oskar's feet in only her small pink knickers and high-heeled shoes. She blushed when she saw Hugo.

'What nice round bobbles your girl-friend has, Hugo!' Oskar bellowed cheerfully, 'you didn't tell me she is in movies!'

'I'm sure she has told you herself,' said Hugo.

'Go away, children!' Oskar exclaimed suddenly, waving his arms as if to shoo away birds, 'I must speak in private to Hugo.'

They scattered obediently at once. Patsy ran to the swimming-pool, kicked off her shoes and dived in.

'When she comes out her little wet panties will cling like a second skin,' Oskar sighed, 'I shall make her lie here

22

while I sit at *her* feet and stare between her legs until the force of my thoughts makes her so excited that she will have a climax right here in front of everyone. You have no objection?'

'You can have her,' said Hugo, feeling generous now he had established friendly and enjoyable relations with Thelma, 'I'll leave her here for you when I go.'

'She's a very ordinary girl with two bumps and a slit,' said Oskar, 'but she wants to get into films and she'll do anything to please a tired old director like me. What wonderfully perverse things I shall have her do to me! Thank you, Hugo, one favour deserves another. Did Ambrose Howard say anything about his next film when you talked to him?'

'No, he suggested that we should meet.'

'The swine!' Oskar exclaimed loudly, his monocle dropping from his eye, 'we must protect your interests! Talk to him and see what he has to say, but do not commit yourself. Whatever offer comes to you through him, I'll see it doubled.'

'Thank you, Oskar. What is going on between you?'

'We are rivals,' said Oskar with a ferocious grin, 'we compete against each other for the studio's budget and stars. We are friends too, naturally.'

Hugo remembered the key in his pocket and took it out.

'On your big red bed you will find Mr Chickenhawk Chester Chataway's little girl-friend, drunk and asleep. Her knickers are down round her knees to show the prettiest little mink coat you ever saw.'

Oskar's grin stretched from one ear to the other and his bald head seemed to glow pinkly.

'You've desecrated Chester's little Lily?' he guffawed. 'He'll go mad if he finds out – your life will be in danger!'

'I'd only just made love to Thelma Baxter,' said Hugo with pride, 'so I did nothing to Miss Lily except to take her knickers down and look at her a little. Do you want to play with her?'

Oskar took the key with a hand trembling with emotion.

'Little Lily, by God!' he breathed, 'I can't resist! I'll have

23

her clothes up round her bobbles and ruttle her forwards and backwards as she lies dreaming. Thank you, Hugo, thank you!'

'You won't want Patsy, then?'

'Leave her here – after Chester takes Lily home I can start to teach Patsy things she never imagined possible.'

With the key clutched in his hand, he levered himself off the sun-lounger and made for the house. Patsy came back from the swimming-pool, her fair hair plastered to her head and her knickers, as Oskar had predicted, clinging wetly. Hugo let her lie on the sun-lounger and sat by her bare feet, smiling to see how right Oskar had been – her plump little mound was clearly outlined through the thin wet material and the shadow of her curls showed through plainly.

'Are you enjoying yourself, Patsy?' he asked, fascinated by the drops of water trickling down her bare breasts.

'Oh yes – I'm having the most marvellous time!'

'Oskar Brandenstein has invited you to stay on after the party and be his guest for a while. He'll be back soon to ask you himself.'

'I've been discovered!' she gasped, 'I knew I would be one day! Oh, Hugo – you really have shared your luck with me!'

She took his hand and held it against a wet and cool breast.

'Do you want to make love to me?' she whispered, her eyes shining. 'We can go upstairs and find an empty bedroom.'

From the way she spoke Hugo was certain that she had been upstairs with someone already.

'We must think of your career,' he said, 'I've done what I can to help you get started – you mustn't waste your time on me now. Seize this opportunity, Patsy, it may be the best you'll ever get.'

And that's no lie, he thought.

'You're so right,' she breathed, 'I must go and dry my hair and make myself look attractive before Mr Brandenstein comes back.'

Off she went in her pursuit of stardom, leaving Hugo to sit and grin.

24

Chapter 2

Dinner with Ambrose

On Tuesday evening Hugo presented himself at La Belle France restaurant as requested by Ambrose Howard's secretary on the telephone. Naturally, it was greatly fashionable with the highly-paid sector of the movie business and Hugo wore his elegant fawn gaberdine summer suit for the occasion. A formidable maitre d'hotel led him to Ambrose's table and in passing Hugo recognised a star or two in the same line of work as himself – Douglas Fairbanks and John Barrymore in particular – and noted with pleasure that they were past forty and for that reason fading as Great Lovers. Even if Valentino had still been alive Hugo would have had no qualms about taking him on in a flaring nostril and burning glance contest before any jury of women.

Ambrose stood up smiling behind his table to hold out his hand. He was wearing a most beautiful dove grey suit and Hugo decided he must at a convenient moment find out who the tailor was. They shook hands and Hugo glowed with pleasure at the sight of the two women Ambrose had brought with him. One was Thelma Baxter, smiling up at him, her generous wobblers half out of her low-cut copper-brown frock. He kissed her hand and then her cheek while her hand slid briefly and unseen up the inside of his thigh.

The other woman was as well-known a star as Thelma – Connie Young, very slim and elegant in jade-green chiffon and pearls, her beautiful face framed by bangs of dark hair.

25

She held out a small hand and gave Hugo a smile of devastating charm when Ambrose introduced them. He returned it with his own, hoping to have the same effect on her, and kissed her hand delicately.

Over dinner Ambrose and the two stars set out to make Hugo feel welcome. He blossomed when they asked about his stage career in Berlin and told them about Oskar's celebrated production of *Three in a Bed* with himself in the lead and soon had them laughing. When he thought that he had sufficiently established himself with them as an actor of talent, apart from his good looks, he praised Thelma and Connie in turn, mentioning the movies they had been in that he had seen, and then Ambrose's work as a director and asked him how long he had been making movies, knowing well that every successful man likes to reminisce about his own career.

'I directed my first picture in 1915, when you were still at school and these ladies were hardly out of the cradle — what an old man that makes me!' said Ambrose, taking the opportunity that had been offered.

He was exaggerating, to appear gallant. Hugo, Thelma and Connie were all much of an age and Ambrose was only about fifteen years older.

'That was before Hollywood,' he went on, 'I started with the Vitagraph studios back East in Flatbush. I hadn't been in the United States long — I'm British and I only came here in 1914 when I saw how unpleasant things were going to be in Europe.'

'You came to America to escape from the War?' Hugo asked, surprised that anyone would admit openly to such a dereliction of his patriotic duty.

'That's right,' said Ambrose cheerfully, 'I had no burning ambition to fight your countrymen. I wanted to make films, that's all — and I must be the only director who has never made a war movie.'

'Your first, then — what was it?'

'This will make you chuckle — it was called *Ambush at Deadman's Gulch*! Can you imagine shooting a Western in New Jersey? I made that film in three days — it was a two

26

reeler and the studio liked it and let me make more. I made seventy-eight movies in three years and then came out to the Coast in 1919 to work at Tom Ince's new studios in Culver City. After he was shot I got together with Stefan Ignaz, who'd just bought up the Ziegler lot to start Ignaz International.'

'Who shot the man you worked with?' Hugo asked.

'That was never decided,' said Ambrose. 'He was a guest on a tycoon's yacht with a bunch of movie stars and he wound up with a bullet in his head. Some say he was caught in bed with the tycoon's girl-friend and some say it wasn't like that.'

As dinner progressed, Hugo's mood became progressively elevated – and so too did something else when Thelma put her hand on his thigh under the table and stroked it slowly. The sensations were extremely pleasant, and became doubly so when, to his amazement, another hand touched the rock-hard bulge in his trousers. He glanced at Connie sitting on his left at the round table and she gave him a brief smile. *I'm dreaming*, he thought, *not one but two beautiful film stars are feeling my tail*!

'You goddamn foreign pervert!' a man's voice roared behind him and a heavy hand grabbed him by the shoulder and dragged him half out of his chair. It was Chester Chataway, drunk, red-faced and furiously angry.

'Chester!' said Ambrose sharply. 'Calm down!'

'This slimy foreign pimp molested an innocent girl!' Chester rasped. 'Is that right, Lily?'

Doll-faced Lily was shrinking away from her protector, tears shining in her pretty blue eyes.

Chester swung a fist at Hugo's face, cursing all the while, which Hugo blocked with his forearm while he kicked himself free of his chair. Chester's fist went back in best bar-room brawl style for another punch, so slow that Hugo grinned and jabbed a hard left and right into Chester's belly. Chester doubled over as the breath fled from him and Hugo uppercut him neatly and dropped him to the floor. By then waiters swarmed round Hugo and seized his arms in a belated attempt to protect so important a client

27

as Chester. The maitre d'hotel's face was set in an expression of stony outrage.

'No problem, Marcel,' Ambrose said to him, 'Mr Chataway has had a little too much to drink and is tired. He should go home and rest.'

'Of course, Mr Howard,' and he instructed two waiters to pick up Chester. They carried him from the restaurant, Lily trotting after them wearing an expression of anguish.

'How did you manage to sample his little girl-friend?' Ambrose asked. 'He hardly ever lets her out of his sight. It had to be at Oskar's party.'

'He is mistaken,' Hugo answered with no great regard for the exact truth. 'If anyone made love to his girl it was not me.'

'Poor Chester – he's really on the skids,' said Connie. 'When I was a kid back home I went to every one of his movies and I was more in love with him than any other fourteen-year-old in the country. Now look at him – even Lily only hangs on for what she can get out of him.'

'He is a fool to try to play the young lover when he is middle-aged,' said Hugo scornfully. 'Why doesn't he move on to more serious roles?'

'He's type-cast,' said Thelma, 'because he was tops as a young lover the studio kept on giving him the same part. And he kept taking them because the money was good. Now he's scared they're not going to want him any more so he diddles Lily to prove he's still under twenty-one.'

'At Oskar's party he was asking you to put him in your next film,' Hugo said to Ambrose, 'do you intend to?'

He was relaxed again after the surprise attack, but not entirely calm with Connie's hand and Thelma's hand back in his lap under the table. And since both sets of fingers were playing over his long bulge, each woman knew what the other one was doing to him and did not object. The possibilities of that were so enthralling that his pommel jumped eagerly in his trousers and Connie giggled.

'Nothing's been settled yet,' said Ambrose, grinning so broadly across the table that Hugo realised he knew that the women were fondling him. Hugo was as vain as any

28

other actor and vainer than many because of his looks, but it entered his mind that the evening had been arranged to serve Ambrose's ends and that the attentions of Thelma and Connie were part of the arrangement. It was interesting, if puzzling, to know that Ambrose could command the obedience of two such well-established stars.

'What sort of film will it be?'

'That's what I want to talk to you about, Hugo,' Ambrose said in tones of the utmost sincerity. 'If we turn in a good job it will be the biggest thing Ignaz International have ever done. It will make reputations and fortunes! And I think you could be a part of it. Let's go to my place where we can talk undisturbed.'

'Let's do that,' said Thelma, her round face as flushed with emotion as Hugo's.

'Great idea,' Connie agreed, pinching the soft inside of Hugo's thigh with her long finger-nails before taking her hand away from him.

Ambrose's limousine was a maroon Cadillac of impressive dimensions and was driven by a young chauffeur in a high-necked grey livery and riding-boots. He held the door open for Thelma and Connie before reaching in to pull down the jump-seats facing them.

'Don't bother with that,' said Ambrose, 'you get behind the steering-wheel and we'll make our own arrangements back here.'

'Si, senor.'

'Home.'

Ambrose climbed in and soon had the seating to his liking, he and Hugo occupying the broad and well-cushioned rear seat, with Thelma on his lap and Connie on Hugo's.

'That's cosier than staring at each other,' he said. 'Home, Luis.'

Connie put an arm about Hugo's neck and pressed close to him. On leaving the restaurant she had thrown a silver fox wrap round her bare shoulders, though the June evening was very warm. In the darkness of the limousine, Hugo uncrossed the ends of the wrap so that he could kiss her throat and cup a chiffon-covered breast in his hand.

The warmth of her skin and the fragrance of her expensive perfume excited him quickly and he put his hand between her knees and up under her frock. The silk of her stockings gave way to the bare skin of her thighs and then the lace edge of her underwear.

He paused for a moment, then she kissed his cheek as if to encourage him, and he slid his fingers into her loose knickers and sighed in pleasure as he touched tight little curls. Connie sighed too and moved her legs apart on his lap. He stroked the soft lips under the curls until he heard her sigh again, then parted them and pressed his middle finger inside. She pushed the tip of her wet tongue into his ear while he played with her secret bud and the limousine rolled smoothly eastwards with the traffic on Wilshire Boulevard. She and Thelma had positioned themselves back to back and though Hugo had been aware of movements and whispers from the other couple, he could not have seen what they were doing even if he had wanted to.

Not that he had any interest just then in anything but his little game with Connie – the limousine had stopped at a red traffic light and she was shaking like a leaf on his lap. As the light turned green she whimpered softly as her critical moments arrived and flung her into ecstasy. To Hugo every little twitch and gasp of her climax was a personal triumph – he had made it happen to a woman who set alight the fantasies of millions of men when she appeared on the cinema screen. And what was more, before long he proposed to have his exciting film star on her back and make love to her with such tremendous passion that she would want him again and again.

She recovered her calm and kissed his mouth while her hand burrowed down between them, down inside the waistband of his trousers until she had hold of his hard stem.

'That was sensational,' she whispered in his ear, 'I'm going to do things to you tonight you've only dreamed about.'

Maybe, thought Hugo, hoping that she was more adept at love-making than either Patsy or Thelma, though there was no gainsaying Thelma's enthusiasm. But however enjoyable it proved to be, if it had been truly a matter of getting what he dreamed of, then it would have been Greta Garbo's breasts he would have been kissing that night, not Connie's. But as Miss Garbo was not available to him, Connie Young would do very well instead.

Before Connie's nimble fingers threatened his self-control, the limousine came to a smooth stop at the kerbside. The chauffeur was well-trained and did not open a door and so switch on an interior light to reveal what the passengers on the rear seat were doing to each other. He sat still, facing forward, and announced in a voice devoid of expression that they were home.

'What's that?' Ambrose gasped breathlessly.

'We're home,' Thelma told him with a chuckle. 'Do you want to go inside or shall we ride around the block until I've finished with you?'

'Unhand me, wench!' Ambrose intoned. 'Out, I say, out!'

Before the chauffeur could get out and open the kerbside door, Connie had it open and was off Hugo's lap and out of the limousine. Hugo followed her, determined not to look back, but his curiosity was too strong for him. He cast a quick glance over his shoulder into the lighted interior of the Cadillac and saw that Thelma was astride Ambrose's lap, her copper-coloured frock up round her hips to show her plump thighs. Ambrose's trousers were wide open and there was a vanishing glimpse of pink as Thelma tucked his plunger into his underwear and pulled his shirt down.

Connie slipped her arm into Hugo's and led him across the broad pavement and through an arch in a long wall. Inside, half a dozen white-walled houses faced each other round three sides of a square.

'This is where Ambrose and Thelma live,' said Connie.

'They live together!' Hugo exclaimed in surprise. 'Are they married?'

'Of course not! They each have a house.'

'But how strange!'

'Why? Everybody has to live somewhere, and they've been the best of friends for years. It was Ambrose who got Thelma's career started and she still does nothing without his advice. I guess she found it sensible to live close to him.'

31

The house was more spacious than it seemed from outside. Even so, when Hugo was settled with a glass of French cognac on one of the white leather sofas in the sitting-room, he could not resist asking the question in his mind.

'You must excuse my ignorance,' he said, smiling to remove any possible offence, 'I had the impression that film directors live in palaces with chandeliers and marble staircases – but I find you in bourgeois comfort.'

'Only the top stars make enough money to live like that,' said Ambrose, laughing. 'You're comparing me with your friend Oskar hamming it up in Beverly Hills with Vanda's sunken bath and onyx bidet. But that's all front to get himself noticed. He's interviewed non-stop for the newspapers and he plays up to reporters by swishing his riding-crop and saying outrageous things for them to quote.'

'In Berlin he did outrageous things, but he kept them private,' said Hugo.

'You have to understand that he spends everything he makes and borrows the rest. He's making a very expensive investment in his own future. His movies make money but he's never directed a smash hit yet, so he fools around with an eye-glass and riding-boots to keep his name in people's minds.'

Thelma and Connie were sitting side by side on the white sofa facing the men. Hugo looked across at them and wondered which he would have first, if he were given the choice – big, blonde Thelma with her breasts half out of her low-cut frock or slim dark-haired Connie who was laughing at something Thelma was whispering into her ear.

'The dear creatures!' said Ambrose, as if he had read Hugo's thoughts, 'a man hardly knows where to begin.'

Thelma pulled her copper-brown frock up to expose her thighs. Hugo gazed happily at the long expanse of bare flesh between her stocking-tops and her knickers. Connie gave a whoop of laughter and hoisted up her own frock to show her thighs.

'Hussies!' Ambrose exclaimed. 'Come here, Thelma, and we'll take up where we left off in the car.'

'And about time too!' she said and in three seconds she

was across the carpet between them and astride his lap again. Hugo grinned at her and moved across to the sofa where Connie was still showing off her green silk knickers. When he sat down she swung her legs up to lie full-length on the sofa, facing him, her head on a big striped cushion. Hugo lay down and took her in his arms to kiss her, feeling her fingers tugging impatiently at his trouser buttons. He shook with delight as her hand went inside, under his shirt, and stroked his hot shaft.

'Let's go upstairs, Connie,' he suggested.

'Let's stay here,' she said.

'But I want to undress you and kiss and feel you all over.'

'So undress me – you're not shy, are you?'

The fact is, thought Hugo, we are dancing to Ambrose's tune here. Is he a *voyeur* or has he another motive? Then the thought left him as Connie sat up and he helped her out of her short evening frock and her underwear. Her long string of pearls hung between breasts that were fuller than he had expected.

'Play with me,' she sighed.

'Wait until I get my clothes off,' he murmured.

'Keep them on – it reminds me of when I was a high-school girl being felt in the back of a beat-up old Ford.'

Hugo smoothed his palm down her belly until he touched her curls. In another moment his fingers retraced the route they had travelled in Ambrose's car and played gently inside her slippery warmth. She raised her top knee to separate her thighs and pulled at him to squeeze closer to her until she could guide him into her as they lay face to face on their sides. Hugo held her by the cheeks of her bottom for his long and steady thrusts.

'You are so beautiful, Connie,' he murmured close to the ear hidden under her long straight hair, 'so beautiful!'

Connie swung her hips and belly against him to drive him deeper if she could, then pushed at his shoulders and rolled him over on to his back and was on top of him before he could miss a stroke, her legs outside his.

33

'Yes, I'm beautiful!' she gasped. 'You thought you were going to have me, didn't you? But I'm having you!'

She beat her belly against his in a fast and jerky rhythm. Her fingers worked feverishly at his shirt until she ripped the buttons off and could get her hand inside to use her red-painted fingernails on his chest.

'I want it!' she said, 'I want it now!'

Hugo's bottom bounced up and down on the sofa as he stabbed frantically upwards and gushed his submission into her belly. She cried out shrilly and slammed herself down hard on him to force him in further and together they writhed in paroxysms of release.

Afterwards she subsided limply on his body, her face flushed and breathing through her mouth. But in her eyes Hugo caught a glint of some other emotion besides gratification and he turned his head to see what she was looking at. Thelma had taken off her frock and was on her knees between Ambrose's sprawled legs. He had removed the jacket of his beautiful grey suit, his trousers were gaping wide and Thelma's smooth blonde head was down between his thighs, her round and fleshy bottom in white satin knickers thrust towards Hugo and Connie.

Ambrose's head jerked sharply upwards from the sofa-back his face contorted as he wailed *Ah, ah, ah*! and although Hugo's stilt inside Connie was softening, it twitched at the sound. She turned her head to look down at him.

'Get your breath back first,' she said with a slow smile.

Thelma got up from her knees to sit close to Ambrose on the sofa, an arm round his neck and her big bare bobbins squeezed against his shoulder.

'There's nothing like it for clearing the mind,' he said to Hugo. 'Have you finished with Connie for now? Is your mind clear? Time for our little talk – and for a drink, girls.'

Connie scrambled off Hugo in nothing but her silk stockings, and he sat up to fasten his trousers, as Thelma performed this office for Ambrose. Connie took the cognac bottle across to Ambrose and filled his glass, her bare and pretty round bottom bobbing up and down as she walked. She came back to fill Hugo's glass and then curled up in a

34

corner of the sofa where he sat, her knees up and ankles crossed, so presenting him with a view of her dark fleece and the moist lips they decorated.

'To you and your success,' said Ambrose, raising his glass to Hugo. 'Though you may not think it, I believe that your success and mine are connected.'

'How is that possible?' Hugo asked.

For the sake of politeness he looked at Ambrose while they were talking, rather than at the more interesting sight Connie was displaying, though he thought it reasonable enough to rest his hand on her little fur coat.

'I'll tell you,' said Ambrose, smoothing down his thin black moustache with a finger-tip. 'Ninety days from now I start work on the biggest and most expensive picture in the history of Ignaz International. And while Stefan Ignaz has the final say-so, I am also casting it.'

'I see,' Hugo said cautiously, sure now what was coming, 'What kind of film is it?'

'A Bible epic that will make Cecil De Mille look small-time. Did you ever see his *King of Kings* – four, five years ago?'

Hugo shook his head, thinking the question absurd.

'It was good – you have to hand it to the miserable old bastard, he knows how to get a riot and an orgy going on the screen. But when he sees my epic he'll break down and cry, believe me!'

'He'll go right out and shoot himself,' said Thelma, snuggling close to Ambrose while he fondled a breast as an aid to conversation.

'It's the story of Mary Magdalene,' said Ambrose. 'The whore who is converted by Jesus and becomes a saint. Just think of the possibilities of that story! I'll put her in the fanciest whore-house you've ever seen, all pillars and sunken baths and black slave-girls with fans made of ostrich-feathers. Mary and the other bimbos will lie around on big cushions in transparent robes – well, damn nearly transparent – with jewellery all over them, including the biggest diamond in the world in Mary's belly-button. Have you got the general idea?'

35

'I think so,' said Hugo. 'You're going to use her profession as an excuse to put more sexual provocation on the screen than anyone has before. But can you get away with it?'

'Naturally. Half way through Mary hears Jesus preaching and sees the light. She tries to persuade the other girls to give up their jobs. They laugh at her, the customers humiliate her by ripping off the heavy robes she's put on, and the owner of the cat-house has her tied to a marble pillar and lashed by a black slave. But all this suffering turns her into a saint and right at the end she stands by the cross with the Virgin Mary and is blessed by Jesus before he dies. How do you like that?'

'It has great possibilities,' said Hugo, seeing no role for himself in it, 'Who will play Mary Magdalene?'

'I haven't made a final decision. Stefan Ignaz is half-convinced that Norma Gilbert should get it.'

'And you?'

'Let's say I'm half-convinced too. With that innocent face of hers Norma would be cast against type, which makes for high tension and gripping results.'

'Ambrose!' Connie exclaimed, 'you know what you said to me!'

'I haven't forgotten,' he said, grinning at her, 'I'm half-convinced you could do it too.'

'You know I can do it!'

She flicked Hugo's hand away from its warm resting-place between her thighs and hurled herself across the room, arms flailing. Thelma jumped out of harm's way as Connie landed bodily on Ambrose, screeching like an angry cat and thumping at his head and chest with her fists. He roared aloud at the onslaught, but whether in amusement or distress, Hugo could not decide. A moment later Thelma moved further away from the fight by coming to sit on Hugo's lap.

'Don't worry about them,' she said, seeing his puzzled look, 'they love to fight like that.'

She took his hand and rubbed it against her bare breasts. Ambrose was rolling so wildly to avoid the blows rained on

36

him that he fell sideways off the white leather sofa and he and Connie grappled on the carpet. He managed to heave her off him and rolled her on to her back. She was still screeching in rage as he got his hand under her hips, her legs up over his shoulders and plunged his face down between her naked thighs.

'I'll tame you, you wild-cat!' he exclaimed, his voice muffled.

'Don't you dare! I hate you!' Connie squalled.

'She loves him really,' said Thelma, undoing Hugo's trousers to grasp his stiffness, 'we both do.'

'Will he give her the part, do you think?'

'She's going to get his best part in about thirty seconds from now. The movie part will take longer, but I'll lay odds she'll get it.'

Hugo used both hands to roll Thelma's well-filled white knickers down until he could finger the soft folds of flesh between her legs. He took the swollen tip of her nearest breast between his lips and used his tongue on it and, very soon, Thelma stood up from his lap to take her knickers off completely. Before he could make any other arrangement, she sat down astride his thighs and held his quivering spindle at the right angle to impale herself upon.

Hugo sighed loudly as he felt himself driven into her wetness. Her inner muscles seemed to grip him tightly while she wrestled him out of his jacket and shirt and he remembered how prompt for love-making she was at Oskar's party. He massaged her plump breasts firmly as she rocked backwards and forwards on his lap to send waves of pleasure through his body.

'This is the biggest chance you'll ever have, you know that,' she breathed, her strong fingers kneading his belly.

'But I shall make love to you many more times,' he gasped, misunderstanding her.

'Many, many, many . . .' she sighed, 'I meant Ambrose's offer.'

'He has made me no offer,' Hugo panted, hardly able to speak and in no mood to discuss business as his crisis came rushing towards him.

'Oh!' Thelma exclaimed, her eyes round and dilated.

'But I love *your* offer,' Hugo managed to gasp out, 'and here is my acceptance!'

He suited the action to the word by gushing his passion into her, his hands clutching cruelly at her heavy breasts. Her back was arched and her eyes were rolled back in her head, showing only the whites below her half-open eye-lids. Her whole body was rigidly upright on Hugo's lap and she had stopped breathing. For five seconds she held this strained position, unmindful of the leaping of his hilt inside her, before falling limply against his chest. She slid off his spike and would have slid off his lap altogether and to the floor if he had not quickly taken her by the hips and held her fast. Her pent-up breath escaped in a long rush and she lay against him gasping.

'Thelma – are you all right?' he asked, alarmed by so overwhelming a response, and when he heard her very faint *Yes* he lifted her with some difficulty off his lap and laid her on the sofa full-length. He stood up, his open trousers falling round his ankles and arranged Thelma more comfortably on her side, her back to the room. He patted her bare bottom affectionately, pulled up his trousers and went to get himself another drink.

The bottles stood on a blackwood sideboard under the window. Hugo treated himself to a good measure of cognac and sipped it while he surveyed the scene. Thelma appeared to be sound asleep, the smooth skin of her back and plump bottom pearly in the lamp-light. The cat-fight on the carpet had ended – Ambrose and Connie lay in each other's arms, whispering and kissing. Her string of pearls had broken in the tussle and the pearls were scattered around them. Ambrose's shirt had been torn and was half off his back, his trousers were round his knees and Connie held his soft tassel in her hand. After a while Ambrose got up and helped Connie to her feet, then picked up one of the pearls and grinned broadly as he pressed it into her perfect belly-button.

'I'm taking Connie to bed,' he told Hugo. 'You can stay here all night with Thelma on the sofa or you can take her home and make love to her there. I'm glad you've accepted my offer – I'll get a contract typed out for you to sign in the next day or two.'

'What am I supposed to have agreed?' Hugo asked.

'The part I offered you in my *Mary Magdalene*, of course.'

'You've offered me nothing – unless you want me to play Jesus Christ, which is ridiculous!'

Ambrose stared at him in slight confusion. He was a comical sight with his dark hair ruffled and his trousers round his ankles. Connie beside him had one arm round his waist and her other hand up under his shirt.

'Ah, this hussy distracted me,' he said with a self-satisfied smile. 'How can I be expected to conduct business properly when she was rubbing her fig against my face!'

'Perhaps we can meet and discuss things tomorrow,' Hugo suggested.

'It's tomorrow now. We must get this settled before I ravage Connie again. Come along.'

He kicked his trousers off and turned his back towards Connie and bent over. She put her hands on his shoulders and jumped up to get her legs round his waist and cling on tightly. His grey trousers were left on the carpet as he made his way across the room, Connie giggling as his supporting hands under her bare bottom found her moist niche and tickled it. Hugo followed their unsteady progress up the stairs and into Ambrose's bedroom.

In contrast to the uncomplicated leather and polished wood of the sitting-room, the bedroom displayed a distinct though unsubtle attempt to achieve a note of decadence. The broad bed was turned down to show black satin sheets and over it on the wall hung a large reproduction of what Hugo recognised as a picture by Aubrey Beardsley – Salome naked at her toilet table. She was stroking herself between the legs while a masked pierrot dressed her hair. Beside her stood a naked boy serving coffee and at the side of the toilet table sat another naked boy staring at Salome's pointed breasts and playing with his peg.

Most surprisingly – and like everyone else Hugo had heard of such a thing and never seen it – the entire ceiling was covered in mirror glass. He stood in the open doorway, arms folded, watching Connie help Ambrose out of his shirt and pondered what the room revealed about his host.

'You're perfect for my movie,' said Ambrose, sitting down to let Connie remove his socks, 'I know Oskar brought you here to play in his next one, but all's fair in love and war, my old beauty, and I know you haven't signed anything yet.'

'I don't even know what his next movie will be – he was very secretive about it.'

'He's going to direct one I refused to do – a war movie about the German navy. Most of it's set in an officers' brothel with Mata Hari-type girl spies in their underwear, but there are some sea-battle sequences. It ends with your ship being sunk and you going down with it for Kaiser and Fatherland.'

'It sounds like a good heroic weepie,' said Hugo, 'I think I would look good in uniform.'

'Almost any fool looks good in uniform!' said Ambrose. 'To be honest with you, Oskar will direct it well. Not as well as I could, but I have this aversion to war movies. It will do well at the box office and give you a good start as a film star. But I'm offering you more than that.'

'Are you, Ambrose? I'm listening.'

Connie pulled back the black satin sheets for Ambrose to get into bed, and slid in with him, still wearing her silk stockings and nothing else. He sat up, his back propped by large square black pillows, and under the thin satin sheet Hugo could see Connie's hand stroking his belly.

'You haven't grasped it yet, Hugo. My *Mary Magdalene* is going to be the biggest smash in the history of movies. All of us associated with it will be made for life – me, you, Connie – if she gets the part!'

'I'll kill you if I don't!' she threatened and Ambrose winced as she did something painful to him under the satin sheet.

'You sound very confident,' said Hugo.

'I know about movie-making – it's been my job for the

40

last fifteen years. I'm offering you a thousand a week, which is more money than you've ever earned in your life.'

A thousand dollars a week sounded very attractive indeed to Hugo.

'You still haven't told me what part I am to play,' he said.

'What part? The male lead, of course – Marcus, a young Roman aristocrat who falls in love with Mary Magdalene and wants to take her away from all that. The story develops as a struggle for her soul – will she go away with Marcus as his mistress to the rich and degenerate life of Rome or will she renounce her sinful ways and follow Jesus?'

'Who will play Jesus?'

'Who cares? It's only a bit-part – he never speaks in the movie, just passes through a couple of times looking holy. We finish on Mary Magdalene down on her knees at the foot of the cross and Marcus riding away on his horse from this final defeat for him. It's a hell of a part to play, Hugo. We're getting all the dewy-eyed reverence we need from Jesus – I want raw, throbbing emotion from Marcus – I want women all over the States to wet their knickers when they see Marcus on the screen. Think you can do it?'

'Naturally, but I would like to see the script before I make my mind up.'

'You shall,' Ambrose promised, 'and you'll be astounded by its brilliance. Ignaz has had five writers on it for nearly a year, including one Nobel Literature Prizewinner, two Pulitzer Prizewinners, a best-selling novelist and a Professor of History from Yale.'

'I am impressed.'

'So you should be. I'll send you a copy of the script to read. Connie wants to rehearse the brothel scene with me now to show me how good she'd be as Mary Magdalene, so I'll bid you goodnight.'

Hugo also said goodnight and went downstairs to see if Thelma was still asleep on the white leather sofa.

Chapter 3

News of a shooting

Hugo had heard nothing from Ambrose by Thursday when he went on a shopping-spree. He sauntered in the hot sunshine, pleased by the sight of palm-trees growing along the boulevard and stopped to look into a window displaying silk shirts and pyjamas. He turned away and caught sight of a newspaper-seller on the corner with the early afternoon editions – and the front-page proclaimed in very large letters MOVIE DIRECTOR SLAIN. Below the headline was a picture of Ambrose Howard.

Hugo bought a paper and stood trying to make sense of the report. It said very little of substance, other than that famous film-director Ambrose Howard had been found shot dead in his home on Glendale. Captain Bastaple of the Los Angeles Police Department was quoted as saying that it was too soon to say what had happened until the autopsy report was in. There was a brief tribute from Mr Stefan Ignaz, head of Ignaz International, with which Ambrose had been associated, to the effect that the death of so talented a director was a tragic blow to the whole motion picture industry. Finally, there was a brief list of Ambrose's better-known movies, very obviously contributed by the studio publicity department.

'Excuse me,' Hugo said to the newspaper seller, 'I do not speak English perfectly and I may not have understood what it says here.'

'Try the public library – I've got papers to sell,' he retorted, 'what do you want to know?'

'It says here a man was *found shot*. Does it mean he shot himself to death or someone else shot him?'

The newspaper seller skimmed through the account and handed the paper back to Hugo.

'It don't say,' he told him, 'you'll have to ask the cops.'

Hugo found a telephone booth and called the studio to see if Oskar knew more about the shooting, but all he got was an operator telling him that Mr Brandenstein was in conference. After a moment or two's thought he took a taxi to Thelma's – she lived next door to Ambrose and ought to know what had happened.

A uniformed policeman stationed under the porch of Ambrose's house glared suspiciously at Hugo when he rang Thelma's bell. After a while the door was opened by a maid whose broad face and raven-black hair suggested that she was Mexican, and her accent confirmed it when she announced that Senorita Baxter could not see anyone.

'I'm a friend – she'll want to see me. Tell her that Hugo Klostermann is here.'

'You sure you're not a reporter?' the maid demanded.

'Do I look like one? Please tell her I'm here.'

'You wait,' said the maid, closing the door firmly on him.

So I've made love to her, but this is when I find out if I'm a friend or just a useful prong, Hugo thought. He was pleased when the maid opened the door again and invited him in. Thelma was in the sitting-room, pale and red-eyed with grief, and dressed very simply in a long-sleeved pullover and grey slacks. Hugo took her in his arms and held her close to comfort her.

'I am so very sorry, Thelma. I came as soon as I heard the terrible news.'

'I'm glad you came. The police have been here all morning, and the people from the studio – and the newspapers keep trying to get to me.'

Hugo led her to the sofa and sat beside her, holding both her hands.

'What happened?' he asked. 'The newspaper was not clear.'

'Ambrose was shot late last night.'

'Yes, I read that. But did he shoot himself or was he killed by someone else?'

'Ambrose would never kill himself!' she exclaimed in high indignation. 'He enjoyed life too much for that!'

'Has anyone been arrested yet?'

'This is Hollywood,' she said. 'People don't get arrested for little crimes like murder – not important people. Let a taxi-driver strangle his girl-friend and they'll send him to the chair – *he's* not important.'

'But what are you saying?' Hugo asked, astonished by the implications of her words.

'Nobody's going to be arrested,' she said. 'The studio has clamped down tight.'

'I find it impossible to believe that the police authorities can be prevented from investigating a murder.'

'You've got a lot to learn,' Thelma said sadly, patting his cheek in a patronising way. 'Didn't you understand what Ambrose told you himself about the shooting of Tom Ince? The studio moguls like Ignaz have got this town sewn up tight and what happens is only what they want to happen.'

'What gives them such extraordinary power?' Hugo persisted.

'Good old money, that's what,' she said bitterly.

Hugo stroked her face gently to soothe her.

'I loved Ambrose,' she said. 'Maybe that's hard for you to believe after the foursome we had, but I was never jealous when he wanted Connie or somebody else – I like to play around with other men myself. But he always came back to *me* when he'd had enough of the others, just like yesterday morning after you and Connie had gone.'

'He was still interested after having Connie all night?' Hugo asked with respect in his voice.

'Well, he couldn't do much then – it took a long time to get him hard, and I had to climb on him, but that didn't matter. He wanted *me*, that's what was important.'

44

Her bitterness seemed to have gone, and Hugo concluded that his gentle stroking of her face and neck was having a good effect. He thought it reasonable to soothe her even more by stroking her plump breasts through the soft wool of her baby-blue pullover.

'I don't expect anyone else to understand how it was between us,' she said. 'If you were in love with me and saw another man on top of me you'd go crazy with jealousy. But Ambrose wasn't like that. He watched you and me make love and he was happy for me, because that's the way he loved me. And that's the way I loved him.'

It seemed to Hugo that he was hearing more than he wanted to hear, but he knew that love was a topic women found difficult to leave alone for long, though what they meant by the word could be very mysterious at times. He put his hand up inside Thelma's jumper and found she was wearing nothing under it. He ran his hand over her big bobbles with pleasure and she leaned heavily against him.

'I'm so glad you're here, Hugo,' she sighed, 'I was going crazy on my own and I daren't leave the house – there are two reporters across the road waiting to pounce on me.'

Under his finger-tips her buds were warm and prominent. Her head was on his shoulder and he guessed that the sensations he was giving her had allayed her sorrowing for a while. He found the side-fastening of her slacks, undid it and put his hand down the top of her knickers to stroke her broad belly.

'Will the maid come in?' he asked.

'What if she does? She's not the Virgin Mary,' Thelma replied, pulling impatiently at his trousers.

His fingers probed the fleshy petals of her moist flower, and Thelma had his long peg out and was jerking it up and down fiercely. Hugo eased her down onto the carpet on her knees, her head and breasts resting on the sofa cushions, while he got behind her and dragged her slacks and underwear down her legs. He fondled the soft flesh of her bottom and ran a finger-tip up and down the lips that pouted at him from between her thighs.

'Give it to me, Hugo!' she groaned. 'I need it!'

45

He put the head of his blunt instrument into her recess, took her by the hips and pushed slowly, staring down to enjoy the sight of it sliding into her. Halfway in he stopped, almost dizzy with excitement, until Thelma moaned and squirmed and begged for more. He sank in all the way and pressed his belly against her bare bottom, leaned forward over her back to reach under the pullover and grasp her dangling breasts while he rode her.

'Hard and fast!' she gasped. 'I want it hard and fast.'

She panted and sighed and shuddered under him, she babbled *Yes* and *More* and *Harder* while his belly pounded against her rump and she clutched at the soft cushions of the sofa in her frenzy. Her climax of pleasure was like an earthquake in her belly – she heralded its arrival with a long and loud squeal and her slippery tunnel contracted to grip Hugo like a hand and milk him instantly in ecstatic jolts. The violence with which she drained him added to Hugo's excitement and he rammed into her uncontrollably, making her squeal again and again.

It was a long time before they were calm enough to separate and sit on the sofa again. Thelma had been like a clockwork spring wound up tight and now suddenly released. The strained look was gone from her plump face and her blue eyes had lost the dull expression they had when Hugo first arrived.

'That was exactly what I needed to shake me out of it,' she said. 'It was the shock of finding him that really got to me.'

'*You* found him?' Hugo asked, very much surprised.

His surprise deepened when she related the events of the previous night. She had just gone to bed and was dozing off when she heard a shot, she said. That was about midnight, or not long afterwards. There was no doubt in her mind that the sound had come from Ambrose's house next door and she jumped out of bed and at once ran to investigate, just as she was – which was naked, that being the way she always slept. She guessed his front door would be locked and so went by the back way, by the patio. The

46

back door was neither locked nor bolted and in she went, afraid of what she might find.

Ambrose was nowhere downstairs, though all the lights were on, nor was he in his bedroom, where the black satin bed was rumpled suggestively. She found him in his bathroom, sitting on the floor with his back propped against the side of the bath, his legs sprawled out flat in front of him. He was naked and he had been shot through the heart, a long red line down his chest and belly where the blood had trickled. A revolver lay beside him on the black and white tiles.

Thelma was not the sort of woman to scream and collapse, shocked as she was. So little time had elapsed since the shot that she thought the killer could only just have left the house and, with revenge in her heart, she picked up the revolver and ran down to the front door. Seeing nobody outside, she ran stark naked, brandishing the gun, to the archway into Glendale Boulevard and looked both ways. A passing car or two sounded its horn at her and she ran back to the house to search it again in case the killer was still hiding there. But there was nobody, upstairs or down.

'Would you have fired the gun?' Hugo asked, fascinated.

'I'd have blasted anybody in the house,' she said without hesitation. 'Five shots in the belly, whoever it was, man or woman.'

'Where was your maid while you were running about naked?'

'She goes home at night and comes back in the morning. I was alone.'

Whatever her own feelings, Thelma was a film star first and foremost and understood the Hollywood system. Her telephone call for help was not to the Police Department but to Ted Moran, General Manager of Ignaz International. He told her to stay where she was and do nothing until he arrived. She was not to get drunk – he was very forceful about that. So Thelma went into her own house and got dressed and made coffee while she waited. Only in one small particular did she disobey Moran – she telephoned Connie and told her what had happened.

'Why?' Hugo asked. 'Why Connie?'

'We're good friends and she loved Ambrose too. I thought she ought to know.'

'What happened when Moran arrived? He checked to see you had told him the truth and then telephoned the police?'

'He brought Mr Ignaz with him,' she answered. 'That's how big a cover-up it is.'

Stefan Ignaz, his burly frame wrapped in thousands of dollars of astrakhan coat against the night air, said not a word as he stood in Thelma's sitting-room, hands thrust deep in his pockets and a look of concern on his face that an employee should be so inconsiderate to die violently in the middle of the night. Thelma explained in detail what she had seen and what she had done and showed him and Moran how to get into Ambrose's house by the back door.

That was about one o'clock. Connie arrived soon afterwards, flustered and distressed. She wept in Thelma's arms when she heard the detailed account, dabbed at her eyes with a wisp of lace handkerchief and went after Ignaz and Moran into the house next door. Thelma forced herself to sit down in her kitchen and drink more coffee, but after half an hour the wait was too much for her and she went to see what was happening. She found Ignaz in Ambrose's sitting-room, where he had lit the log fire laid in the ornamental hearth. He was holding a bundle of papers as big as his head, glancing at each in turn before throwing it into the leaping flames.

Ted Moran, looking badly in need of a shave and wearing a golf jacket and cap, was in the kitchen, washing powders, tablets, pills and bootleg booze down the sink, evidently put off using the bathroom for this purpose by the presence there of the deceased. Connie was in the main bedroom, down on her hands and knees peering under the black sheeted bed. She had left her home hurriedly, pulling on the first dark-coloured frock to hand, and was bare-legged and in flat shoes.

'Found what you want?' Thelma asked her.

Connie got to her feet and showed her a packet of letters tied round with pink ribbon.

'I knew they'd be in the top drawer by the bed,' she answered, 'they were his favourite bed-time reading. I was checking round to see if I'd missed anything.'

Having no pockets or hand-bag, she lifted the front of her navy and white frock and slid the bundle of letters down the front of her knickers.

'What letters was Connie looking for?' Hugo asked Thelma. 'I do not understand this.'

Ambrose had discovered, she explained, that Connie had a talent for writing and let her change her scripts extensively. For his own amusement he also encouraged her to write letters to him giving explicit accounts of what she and he would do when they were next in bed together.

'She would not want the police to find letters of that sort,' said Hugo, 'I envy Ambrose his success with beautiful women!'

'You've no need to,' said Thelma. 'Whatever it was he had, you've got plenty of it – you've only been here a week and you've had me and Connie. You can ask women for anything you want and they'll give it to you.'

Hugo was flattered and delighted by her words. An endless orgy of pleasure lay ahead of him, he considered, there being so many beautiful film stars he wanted to make love to. Clara Bow was high on the list – there was an indelible image stamped on his mind from a film he'd seen five years ago – beautiful tempestuous Clara in white silk camiknickers and high-heeled shoes. He also wanted Mary Pickford, of course, forty now and past her prime, but a powerfully erotic figure in Hugo's adolescent cinema-going, perhaps because of the contrast between her innocent face and her well-developed bosom.

Also on Hugo's list of the women he most wanted to make love to were suavely sophisticated Constance Bennett, elegant Norma Shearer, Gloria Swanson, Joan Crawford – in fact the list in his mind was a very long one and included the ultimate for him, Greta Garbo. He told himself that the stars who aroused his fantasies were no longer shadows on a silver screen – they were flesh and blood women who lived and worked within a few minutes drive of where he now was. And if dear Thelma was right about the irresistibility of his charm, they were within his reach. He let his mind run freely on the incredible delight of putting his hand up Clara Bow's silk camiknickers, of kissing Norma Shearer's smooth belly, or parting Gloria Swanson's legs to fondle her . . .

When Ignaz had thrown everything he considered embarrassing into the fireplace to burn, he told Connie to go home and forget she had ever been at Ambrose's house that night. He told Moran to wipe all door-knobs and handles and remove all signs that the house had been ransacked, then went next door to Thelma's and sat on the sofa in her sitting-room, still wearing his astrakhan coat, and sipped a large glass of Scotch whisky while he instructed her what she was to tell the police and what she was to leave out. Thelma was certain that she would be arrested because her finger-prints were on the gun, but Ignaz told her she need not worry as he would explain why she had picked it up. He waited until Moran joined them and then telephoned the police.

'Unbelievable!' Hugo exclaimed at the end of Thelma's story, but before he could say more, the Mexican maid came in to say that Mrs Gilbert was at the door.

'Norma Gilbert, you mean?' Thelma asked sharply.

'No, Senorita, the mother.'

'Mildred Gilbert wanting to see me? That old harpy! Why on earth should I . . . never mind, show her in, Conchita.'

It was unfair to describe Norma Gilbert's mother as an old harpy, Hugo decided when he saw her. She was in her forties, a tall, thin woman who had never been a beauty, but she was most elegantly dressed in a black and white hound's-tooth suit, with a stylish white hat pulled down over short brown hair that tended towards ginger. She and Thelma pretended to kiss each other on both cheeks, Hugo was introduced and she sat down and crossed her legs carefully as she peeled off her grey suede gloves.

'I've heard so much about you, Mr Klostermann,' she said. 'May I call you Hugo? They say you're going to be Hollywood's next Great Lover.'

'You must not believe all you hear, dear lady,' he answered, delighted that he was being talked about already.

'We'll have tea, Conchita,' Thelma said to her maid. 'Unless you'd like something stronger, Mildred?'

'Me, dear? You know I hardly ever touch strong drink. But don't let me stop you if you feel you must,' Mildred returned.

'I saw your beautiful daughter at Oskar Brandenstein's party,' Hugo put in, to lower the temperature.

'Really?' said Mildred Gilbert, staring at him as if to warn him off. 'Her fiancé, Prince Dmytryk escorted her. I never go to that sort of function – I believe there were some very disreputable people present.'

'Just the usual bunch,' said Thelma. 'You've known most of them for years, Mildred.'

'I'm sure I haven't,' she answered primly.

'Chester was there,' said Thelma brightly. 'He and Norma have been special friends since the first movie they made together when she was about twelve.'

Mildred's face flushed dark red at the implication.

'Norma was seventeen when she starred in *Nell of Drury Lane* with Chester Chataway,' she snapped, 'and I chaperoned her right through the shooting of that film!'

'Right!' Thelma agreed. 'There was even a rumour that Chester took such a shine to you that he shared a bottle of booze with you most days and you slept it off together in his dressing-room. Not that I ever believed it, but you know what the gossiping tongues are like in this town.'

Mildred's face darkened from crimson to purple and she twisted her beautiful gloves together ferociously. Conchita brought in the tea and the pause in the conversation gave Mildred time to get herself under control.

'Has anyone been arrested yet for the murder?' she asked.

'Not that I know of,' Thelma answered. 'The police are still in there searching and finger-printing.'

'I've heard a whisper that you were first on the scene, not that you're mentioned in the newspapers. I suppose you asked them not to use your name.'

'What are you after, Mildred?'

'Nothing, dear – it's my curiosity. I had a lot of respect for Ambrose. He directed Norma in some of her best pictures. He was a very talented person. It is monstrous that a man like that can be blotted out in a second by a common burglar.'

'What makes you think there was a break-in?' Thelma asked.

'Ambrose was too kind-hearted and easy-going a man to have enemies,' Mildred answered. 'Did you see anyone running away?'

'I thought I saw a shadow disappearing out on to Glendale,' said Thelma, 'I ran after it but I was too late.'

'You saw the killer running away!' Mildred breathed, her brown eyes staring unblinking at Thelma. 'Was he young or old, black or white – could you see?'

'There was something not right about what I saw,' Thelma said slowly. 'It might have been a woman.'

'No!' Mildred gasped. 'Whoever heard of a woman burglar? You must be mistaken.'

'Who said anything about a burglar? When Mr Ignaz and I identified Ambrose's body for the police his big diamond ring was still on his finger.'

'Oh! But what made you think it might have been a woman you saw running away?'

'I don't exactly know. Whoever it was wore trousers and a cap,' said Thelma. 'But women run differently from men and there was something about the movement that made me suspicious.'

'This is incredible!' said Mildred. 'Was she tall or short, slim or heavily-built?'

'I only caught a glimpse from the back. Slim-hipped, as far as I could make out. Medium height. And definitely young.'

'How can you be sure of that if it was so dark?'

'The way she ran – it was fast and neat, not a middle-aged shuffle.'

'My Lord – is that the time!' Mildred exclaimed, staring at her tiny gold wrist-watch, 'I must fly!'

'Drop in any time,' said Thelma, her tone not in the least welcoming. 'By the way, when's Norma marrying the Prince? The engagement party was months ago – we're all waiting for the big event.'

'Next spring,' said Mildred. 'We haven't fixed an exact date yet. A marriage alliance with a member of a European royal family needs a lot of planning.'

'That's right,' said Thelma. 'For one thing you need time to inspect his diploma.'

'What do you mean?'

'Don't Princes have some sort of diploma to prove they're royalty? Otherwise any used car salesman could put on a phoney accent and call himself Prince Dingaling. Baby Norma must have a big stack of cash saved up over the years and that makes her a better mark for con-artists than even her virginal little body.'

Mildred was on her feet, scowling as she pulled on her gloves.

'You needn't concern yourself with my daughter's welfare,' she said in freezing tones. 'I can take care of her.'

'So I've heard,' Thelma retorted. 'It's good for a girl to have a loving mother to take care of her. You'll insist on being there when the police question her, of course.'

'Why should they want to do any such ridiculous thing?'

'They'll question all of Ambrose's friends and ask where they were last night. Not that Norma's got anything to worry about – I'm sure she was tucked up safely in bed. Alone, of course.'

'You are being offensive,' said Mildred, and walked out.

'What was that about?' Hugo asked. 'Did you really see someone running away? You didn't tell me that.'

'Maybe I did and maybe I didn't,' said Thelma, with a grin of pure malice, 'just so that old alley-cat Mildred gets shaken up. It was pretty obvious why she was here.'

'She is afraid that her daughter shot Ambrose,' said Hugo. 'But I don't understand why.'

'The reason she's scared that Norma shot Ambrose is because it's true,' Thelma said with total conviction. 'She knows it and I know it, but nobody's ever going to prove it. Norma will get away with it!'

'What reason could she possibly have for doing such a terrible thing?' Hugo asked her, amazed by what she said.

'The little bitch has got her mind set on marrying Prince Dingaling – not because he's anything special and she sure as hell doesn't love him. She wants to be a real Princess and go touring in Europe to stay in castles and have aristocrats kiss her hand and stuff like that!'

'Many a rich American girl has done the same,' said Hugo. 'What of it?'

'You don't get it, do you? Norma Gilbert's not the little goody-goody she plays in her movies. She's been on her back for half the stars in Hollywood, starting with Chester Chataway when she was only a kid. Ambrose had her whenever he felt like it. He got a laugh out of how hot she was to get her pants off for him.'

Hugo added Norma's name to the list of beautiful film stars he intended to enjoy. From what Thelma said, it ought not to be difficult.

'So Miss Gilbert is not as untouchable as her screen image,' he said, 'I still see no motive for murder.'

'Do you believe this blue-blooded Prince will marry her if he finds out she's opened her legs for more men than he's had hot dinners? His own people would laugh themselves sick if it got out that their new Princess was a little tramp.'

'I have not had the honour of obliging any Princesses,' said Hugo, 'only a Countess or two and a Baroness – and they were all, as you say, tramps. No one thinks any the worse of them for that, so long as they are discreet.'

'You just don't understand Hollywood,' said Thelma, sounding exasperated by his failure to grasp what was important. 'What makes you think that Ignaz will let a major box-office star sail for Europe and waste her time being a Princess and having her ass kissed when she could

54

be right here making money for him? He knows everything about his stars – it's his business to! He knows who did her the first time and who she's doing it with now besides her fiancé. He knows Ambrose had her front, back and sideways and he told him to talk her out of this marriage. Or else.'

For a moment Hugo was taken by surprise at the depths of deviousness being revealed to him.

'You think that she shot Ambrose to shut his mouth?' he suggested.

'I know she did, but it won't do her any good. She thinks she can go ahead with her wedding now Ambrose isn't here to spread the dirt, but she doesn't know that Ignaz was behind it. He'll find some other way of stopping her.'

'I can see how she might get away with it,' said Hugo. 'Her finger-prints on the gun would have been overlaid by yours. And her mother will swear that Norma was home all night.'

'Not so easy now they don't live together.'

'Really? I took Mildred to be the type of overbearing mother who would live with her daughter even after she was married.'

'Yes, but under her girlie charm Norma's as tough as Mildred. The day after she turned twenty-one she moved out of Mildred's apartment into a house of her own. If she needs an alibi for last night she'll have to get the Prince to say he was there with her all night – and she wouldn't want to see that in the newspapers!'

'So you managed to send Mildred away more worried than when she arrived. Your story about a girl disguised as a man was a brilliant invention. Is it from a movie you were in?'

'Me disguised as a man – with these?' Thelma asked, sliding her hands up her baby-blue pullover to make her balloons wobble about enticingly.

'No one would ever mistake you for a man, even on the darkest night,' Hugo agreed.

'Norma was disguised as a boy in a movie Ambrose directed – that's why Mildred looked so sick when I

55

mentioned men's clothes. It made him so bone-hard to see her like that he had to pack up shooting for the day and rush her home to have her dressed like that.'

The jiggling of Thelma's breasts under the soft wool of her pullover drew Hugo to her side as surely as a magnet attracts iron. He pulled the jumper up to her arm-pits and handled her in delight.

'He certainly liked to experiment,' he murmured, kissing her warm flesh.

'There'll never be another like him,' Thelma sighed. 'He tried everything you've ever imagined – and some things you haven't.'

Her hand stroked the front of his trousers, where his hard shaft was making itself apparent.

'Mildred was staring at *this* all the time she was here,' she said. 'Did you know your buttons weren't properly done up? Your pecker's been practically hanging out the whole time.'

'Oh!' Hugo exclaimed in dismay.

'Poor Mildred,' Thelma said with an evil chuckle. 'She's gone home all steamed up over you – she'll have to see to herself!'

Hugo stripped off her pullover and slacks, her stockings and knickers, and arranged her naked so that she lay back on the sofa, her legs hooked over his shoulders as he knelt on the floor. He stroked her belly with his palms, making her tremble and sigh, and reached forward to roll and fondle her plump breasts. He pushed his trousers down round his thighs, tucked up his shirt, flicked the end of his silk tie over his shoulder and leaned forward to penetrate Thelma's pink flower with his stiff stem.

'Oh my God!' she gasped. 'This is it!'

And for her very quickly it was – Hugo's strong see-sawing soon had her bare bottom writhing on the cushions and her legs drumming on his shoulders. Through it all he plucked at her breasts, urging her to ever greater heights of delight, while forcing himself to remain as unaffected as possible by the ecstatic turmoil of her belly. Half an hour ago the strength of her climactic release had siphoned his passion from him – this time he intended to master her.

When her throes subsided she grinned up at him in satisfaction.

'Was I too quick for you that time?' she asked.

'No, I wanted to watch your face,' he said, grinning back as he continued his to and fro motion.

'So now I'll watch your face.'

Hugo had other ideas on that. He rolled the slack tips of her breasts firmly between his fingers and pinched them to make her gasp at the sensation. When they were hard again he forced his thumb into her wet furrow, just above his sliding piston, and rubbed her secret bud.

'No, no . . .' she exclaimed, shuddering violently.

His other thumb found the knot of muscle between the soft cheeks of her bottom and pressed until it gained admittance. Thelma stared up at him incredulously, spasms shaking her belly.

'It's too much . . .' she gasped, 'I can't bear it . . .'

Hugo paid no attention to her words, her little cries, her gasps and moans – he maintained a strong and steady stroke, feeling his shaft growing ever harder and thicker. Thelma passed totally beyond words and made gurgling sounds as she rolled and bounced beneath him, frantic for release from the overbearing stimulation.

Hugo was loving every second of it. *This is Thelma Baxter, the world-famous film star, begging me to finish her off!* was the exultant thought in his whirling mind, *At this moment she is my slave!*

He felt the first throb of his own climax and said sharply *Now, Thelma!* while he stabbed hard into her quivering belly. Her climactic squeal was so piercing that the Mexican maid ran into the room, thinking something was amiss, just in time to see Thelma's legs kicking in the air above the sofa and Hugo's bare bottom driving to and fro between her spread thighs. Conchita stood with her hand to her mouth for a moment before she backed out of the room and closed the door quietly. On the sofa, Hugo and Thelma were too deeply engrossed in ecstasy to even notice.

Chapter 4

Connie is distressed

The telephone woke Hugo at one-thirty in the morning and the hotel switchboard insisted that the call was for him. To his surprise it was Connie Young, and she sounded drunk.

'You got a girl there with you?' she asked, her voice a little slurred.

'I'm alone and I was asleep,' he answered, yawning.

'I'm alone too, and I can't sleep. I need you here.'

Hugo said nothing, not in the least flattered to be awoken in this way.

'You still there?' Connie asked. 'What's wrong – you got the droops, lover, This is me, Connie Young, offering you something every red-blooded American boy bangs himself off dreaming about.'

'I'm not a red-blooded American boy. Perhaps you've got the wrong number.'

'Don't turn your back on me,' she pleaded, her voice losing its drunken arrogance instantly, 'I'm counting on you, Hugo!'

'What's troubling you, Connie?' he asked, rolling over to reach for a cigarette.

'The stupid, empty futility of it all, that's what's troubling me. When a sweet and talented man like Ambrose can be switched off just like a light-bulb, what the hell's the use of anything?'

Fortunately for Hugo he was not required to attempt an

58

answer to the most fundamental question of philosophy and religion, for Connie burst into noisy sobbing.

'Connie!' he said. 'Calm down! I'll come over to see you right away – where do you live?'

Through her sobs she gave him an address in Beverly Hills that meant nothing to him. He pulled on a soft cashmere roll-top sweater and dark trousers and took the lift down to the lobby to get a taxi. Connie's house was, he saw twenty minutes later, a real film star's abode, big and impressively vulgar, in the style of a French chateau. Every window was brightly lit on both floors. A maid with an exasperated expression let him in.

'First right at the top of the stairs,' she said. 'Maybe you can do something. I've called her doctor but he's out on an emergency and won't be here for a while.'

'Isn't this an emergency?' Hugo asked, making for the broad and polished redwood staircase.

'I guess this is a grade two emergency and he's on a grade one,' said the maid, keeping pace alongside him up the curving staircase. 'Maybe you can keep her talking till the doctor gets here. She's locked herself in and she's got enough sleeping pills and booze in there to kill an elephant.'

'Connie!' Hugo called, rapping loudly at her bedroom door. 'It's Hugo. Let me in – I want to talk to you!'

'Hugo? What a lovely surprise!' and the key turned in the lock.

He went in quickly, closed the door and leaned against it. Connie had taken a step or two backwards and stood swaying, a broad smile on her flushed face. She was wearing a myrtle-green negligee, wide open over a knee-length nightdress of the same colour. She lurched towards him and pressed her hot body against his, her fingers entwining themselves feverishly in his hair to pull his mouth down to hers. Her kiss tasted and smelled strongly of whisky.

'I'm glad you've dropped in for a drink,' she said blurrily when she released him. 'There's something I want to ask you . . . what was it . . . I can't just recall, but it's sure to come back to me.'

Connie's bedroom was not quite as large as a tennis

court, but more than ample. The bed itself was a broad divan, wide enough for several people to lie on, and it was raised up on two steps above the floor. The sheets and pillows were a delicate oyster-grey, and indeed that was the predominant colour throughout the room, even to the upholstery of the chaise-longue and elegantly thin-legged chairs grouped round a glass-topped low table on which stood bottles and glasses.

Hugo led Connie away from the bed to spread herself on the chaise-longue, while he took a seat facing her on a chair. She insisted he poured a drink for himself and another for her. The whisky had made her movements clumsy and she sprawled along the chaise-longue with her negligee hanging half off. Hugo could not help but look at her breasts, hardly covered at all by the lace-trimmed and deeply scooped-out top of her nightdress. He glanced down to the slight swell of her belly and lower still, where the shadow of her dark thatch showed faintly through the thin silk.

'Will you help me get even with that stupid bitch for Ambrose?' she asked, waving her glass at him and slopping whisky down her breasts.

'Norma Gilbert? It won't be easy – the studio will protect her,' he answered diplomatically.

'Norma Gilbert? Why her?' Connie asked in a surprised tone. 'She had nothing to do with it.'

'Thelma thinks she did. And so does Mildred Gilbert.'

Connie shook her head slowly and seriously.

'Thelma would love it to be Norma,' she said. 'But she's kidding herself if she believes Norma shot Ambrose – never in a million years would that little whore do anything to risk her career.'

'But if her engagement to Prince Dmytryk was threatened – wouldn't that inspire her to violence?'

'The kind of money Norma's made over the last ten years she can buy herself a prince any time she wants one. Dmytryk's just a title from some one-horse European country, he's nothing special.'

'Suppose that she is in love with Dmytryk – it has been

known for girls to be in love with their fiancés. That would be a powerful motive to silence anyone who might tell tales that would put her engagement at risk.'

'You don't know Norma. What makes her tick is money, not men.'

'Why do you and Thelma dislike her so much?'

Connie held out her glass to be refilled. She leaned so far forward while Hugo poured the whisky that her dumplings fell out of the low-cut top of her nightdress. She lay back again to sip at her glass, completely oblivious of what she was showing.

'It's not just Thelma and me,' she said. 'You won't find a woman in Hollywood with a good word to say for her.'

'Except her mother,' Hugo corrected her.

'Mildred hates her as much as the rest of us, only she never says so out loud because Norma's her meal-ticket.'

'Then why does *everyone* dislike Norma?'

Connie shrugged and her breasts swayed enticingly. Hugo moved from his chair to sit with her on the chaise-longue and fondle her.

'That's friendly,' she said, giving him a bemused smile. 'What took you so long?'

Hugo's stilt was upright in his underwear as he played with Connie's pretty breasts. But her eye-lids were heavy, he saw, and it might not be long before she passed out.

'So Norma was not the one?' he prompted her.

'What one? Ambrose had her a few times, but she was nothing to him. I was the one he loved – you saw that the other night.'

'I meant Norma was not the one who killed him.'

'Nobody killed him,' she said, uttering a long and heartfelt sigh. 'It was a stupid accident.'

'What?' Hugo exclaimed. 'But that's impossible!'

'You know he loved to play games with girls . . . he was fooling around with Peg Foster. Have you heard about our great little local turn, Perversity Peg? All tastes catered for – you want to wear her silk stockings while you whip her white ass and stick your pecker in her ear, step right up, Peg's your girl.'

61

'I saw her by chance at Oskar's party, tied face-down on a bed.'

'That's our Peg!' said Connie bitterly. 'Ambrose used to get her round to his place sometimes. He showed me a picture once of how he'd trussed her up bent double and dangled her from the ceiling while he stuck it in her. She was with him last night and they played games with a pistol. Maybe he tied her up and threatened her with it, maybe he had her tie him up. Anyway, in the excitement the pistol went off by mistake and Ambrose took it in the heart.'

'Ridiculous!' said Hugo, forgetting to fondle her breasts for a moment, 'I don't believe a word of it – you're making it up!'

'I was right there less than an hour after he died. Thelma called me.'

'I know that. And she saw more than you saw and she says it was Norma who fired the shot. What makes you think otherwise?'

Connie's eyes were so heavy and her voice so unsteady that Hugo pinched the soft tips of her breasts with his nails to keep her awake. 'He was in the bathroom, stark naked,' she mumbled, 'he had a black velvet ribbon tied in a bow round his pecker. I took it off so the cops wouldn't get the wrong idea about him. I'll show it to you if you like.'

'Is that all?'

'There were cords hanging over the side of the bath – the sort they use to tie each other up. I asked Ted Moran to take them away with him. And that's not all – Ambrose stank of the perfume Peg Foster uses. Norma's is different. You could tell who'd been all over him.'

'Thelma didn't mention any of this,' said Hugo doubtfully.

'She was in shock when she found him . . . she didn't go back into the bathroom after that. Nor did Ignaz, but Ted and I were in there. Did she say it was Ambrose's own pistol?'

'Was it?'

'He kept it in the bedside cabinet. The hand-grip is

62

mother of pearl and his initials are engraved on the barrel. He liked to show it off and play about with it.'

'And you think Peg Foster killed him with it?'

'I'm as certain of it as if I was there and saw her do it,' Connie muttered almost inaudibly, her head nodding forward. 'You can bet the autopsy will find that Ambrose was coked up to the eyeballs and full of booze . . . I want to sleep now . . . help me to bed . . .'

'Do you know what you're saying?' Hugo demanded, pinching the soft flesh of her breasts hard to get a response.

'She encourages men that so they get carried away and hurt her . . . just enough for her to put the squeeze on them afterwards . . . only this time it went wrong . . . Ambrose was the one who got hurt . . .'

There was a prolonged rapping at the door and the maid's voice made itself heard with *'Miss Young – the doctor's here!'*

Connie was breathing noisily through her open mouth, her eyes closed. He tucked her soft breasts back into her nightdress and wrapped the negligee decently round her before he opened the door.

'Come in,' he said. 'She's fallen asleep.'

The maid stood aside to let the newcomer in. He was a slightly-built man in his forties, pale-faced and with a fluffy moustache. He wore an expensive charcoal-grey suit and carried a black leather bag in one hand and a grey homburg hat in the other.

'I am Doctor Theodor Prosz,' he said. 'Who are you?'

As soon as he had an answer he went to the chaise-longue, took Connie's wrist and stared at his watch.

'How much has she had to drink?' he asked when he had completed his counting.

'Not much while I've been here,' said Hugo, 'but the bottle is almost empty.'

'She finished another before that,' said the maid. 'She threw it over the banisters and it broke on the hall floor. I swept the glass away.'

'How long ago was that?'

'Soon after midnight. She started drinking as soon as she

63

came in, and I guess she'd had pretty much a skinfull before she got home.'

'I don't think we're dealing with anything more serious than excessive drinking,' said Theodor Prosz. 'But I'll observe her for a while to be sure she's just sleeping and not slipping into a coma. Perhaps you'll fill in the details for me before you go, Mr Klostermann.'

He sent the maid to make coffee for him and then looked appraisingly at Hugo.

'You're a strong-looking young fellow. Would you be so kind as to move Miss Young onto the bed, please? She's more than I can lift.'

With an arm under her shoulders and one under her thighs Hugo lifted Connie with no great effort, limp as she was, and put her on the oyster-satin bed.

'Did she fall down?' asked Dr Prosz.

'No, why?'

'Drunks often do. They sometimes injure themselves quite severely. I like to make sure.'

He opened Connie's green negligee and drew her short nightdress up to her arm-pits to expose the entire front of her body. Hugo stared as Prosz felt her slowly from her ankles upwards, her knees, the insides of her thighs, over her belly and rib-cage and up to her round breasts, which he handled gently for some time.

'There's no bruising that I can detect,' he announced.

The two men stood on opposite sides of the broad bed, gazing down at Connie's beautiful body.

'Her breathing is steady,' said the doctor, though without enthusiasm, 'I've been called out to her before and found her like this. No worse harm will befall her than an excruciating hangover tomorrow. Are you in films too, Mr Klostermann?'

'I'm here from Berlin to make a movie at Ignaz International.'

They both heard the rattle of cups outside the door Theodor Prosz drew the satin sheet up to cover Connie to the chin.

'I've brought coffee for you both,' said the maid. 'How is she?' She poured two cups of coffee from a silver pot.

'She will be all right,' Prosz answered, his smile melancholy, 'I'll sit with her for a while. My office knows where I am if they need me. But you look exhausted, Ena – go to bed and I'll let myself out.'

'Thank you, doctor,' said the maid gratefully.

When she was gone Theodor Prosz perched himself on the side of Connie's bed with a cup of black coffee in his hand.

'Miss Young is an extremely beautiful woman,' he observed. 'That is one of the advantages of practising medicine in Beverly Hills – the female patients are marvellously attractive. To set against that is the disadvantage that a large proportion of these emergencies take place in the middle of the night, being caused by over-indulgence in alcohol, drugs or unusual sexual practices.'

He put his cup down and bent over Connie to pull the sheet down to her waist and clasp her left breast in his hand. After a few moments he looked across at Hugo, his face without expression.

'Her heart-beat is strong and regular,' he said.

'That is good news,' said Hugo, observing that the doctor's hand stayed on Connie's pointed breast.

'I will conclude my examination before we leave her to sleep. I was interrupted before I could look at her back. Perhaps you will be good enough to help me turn her over.'

Hugo set a knee on the soft bed and took Connie by the shoulder and hip to pull her over towards him until she was face-down, her head turned sideways on the satin pillow. Dr Prosz raised her nightdress to reveal her back and felt his way slowly from the nape of her neck to her well-shaped calves, paying particular attention to the chubby round cheeks of her bottom.

'Fine,' he said eventually, 'roll her back, if you please.'

Hugo slid his hands under Connie's breasts and belly and enjoyed the feel of her warm flesh as he turned her carefully on to her back again. She was totally limp and unresisting, so deeply asleep was she.

65

Her legs had fallen apart while she was being moved. Dr Prosz put his hand between her thighs and felt her plump mound.

'What are you examining her for now?' Hugo enquired, his eyebrows rising.

'Was she already unconscious when you had sexual congress with her?' the doctor asked casually.

'She was too drunk when I got here,' Hugo answered, slightly indignant, 'all I've done is talk to her.'

'There's no point whatsoever in lying,' said Prosz, his fingers inside Connie's pink-lipped niche, 'I don't care what you do.'

'But it is the truth,' Hugo insisted.

'Then some other man did it to her before you arrived. The signs are unmistakable,' said the doctor, his tone one of total disbelief. 'If you will rearrange Miss Young's night clothes while I wash my hands, I think we might treat ourselves to a tot of her whisky before we leave.'

While Prosz went into the adjoining bath-room Hugo pulled Connie's thin silk nightdress down over her breasts and belly. And though he told himself it was no business of his, he could not refrain from putting his fingers where the doctor's had been and found that Connie's brown-thatched entrance had a most familiar wet and slippery feel. He put her legs together and covered her with the oyster-grey sheet.

He and Prosz sat by the glass-topped table and enjoyed a glass of Scotch whisky and another cup of coffee.

'You will find me listed in the telephone book when you have need of my services,' said the doctor, raising his glass to Hugo.

'It is not probable – I am a very healthy person.'

'That has little to do with it. The major pastime of film stars is sexual relations with each other in endless permutations. This leads to complications, as you can imagine – unwanted pregnancies, for example, cases of social diseases when someone experiments outside the charmed circle, incapacity from over-exuberant activity, paternity suits and the threat of them, the need for aphrodisiacs, and so on.'

'All this is within your duties as a physician?'

'And much more. The problems rising from excessive consumption of alcohol are obvious enough – fist-fights in public and in private, sometimes causing serious injury and legal action, automobile accidents and potential manslaughter charges, nervous breakdowns, coma, woman-beating to the point of hospitalisation and beyond, murder and suicide.'

'You paint a dismal picture, Dr Prosz.'

'Dismal enough – and I am speaking only of the outcome of the most obvious pleasures. Do you take drugs? Many of my patients do, and that gives rise to another set of problems.'

'Are none of your patients normal?'

'This is Hollywood, Mr Klostermann, where everyone has too much of everything and chokes on it. Do not hesitate to call on my services when the need arises, night or day. My fees are high and my discretion is guaranteed.'

'My present problem is not one you can help me with,' said Hugo, chuckling.

'How do you know until you tell me what it is?'

Hugo laughed and emptied his glass.

'I need a woman and it is three o'clock in the morning.'

'No doubt the sight of Miss Young naked when I examined her aroused you. Let me urge you most sincerely not to pick up a hooker on the Strip. Only the dregs will still be there at this time – old, ugly, diseased.'

'I'm sure you know this town better than I do, doctor.'

'It is for that reason I can recommend a place where you will be accommodated in congenial surroundings by a pleasant young woman of your choice.'

'A brothel!' Hugo exclaimed, surprised yet again by the doctor.

'A most unfortunate word – it is never used here.'

'And it's safe to go there – no spies under the beds in the pay of the gossip columnists?'

'You have my word that it is perfectly safe and discreet. I will introduce you there myself.'

'I see that examining a beautiful naked patient has heated the good doctor's blood,' said Hugo, with a chuckle.

'Your conclusion is mistaken. The past few hours have been most trying for me. Since nine last evening I have made five house-calls to deal with emergencies, two of them since midnight. Not all were as uneventful as attending Miss Young.'

'My apologies, Dr Prosz. I am sure you are trained in complete professional detachment when you touch beautiful and naked women. But you were correct in thinking that the sight of Miss Young's body excited me. I swear that if you left me alone with her now. I'd climb on top of her, fast asleep though she is.'

'There is no need for such paltry pleasures,' said Prosz, the ghost of a smile on his face, 'I need to unwind and sleep for a few hours before morning consultations start in my office. If you care to join me you will enjoy the services of an attractive, healthy and responsive young woman, rather than a furtive release with a deeply unconscious person.'

'You are a man after my own heart,' said Hugo cheerfully. 'In the theatre I have always needed to relax myself with a woman before going on stage.'

The house Dr Prosz drove him to was large, anonymous and dark, with closely-drawn blinds at every window, upstairs and down. A large black woman in theatrical French maid costume of shiny black frock and frilly apron opened the door and greeted Prosz as an old friend. She led the way into a large sitting-room which, to Hugo's eye and nose had the look of a room where a long and noisy party has just ended. The ash-trays were full to overflowing, used glasses stood everywhere. The air was thick and stale as if it had been breathed by dozens of people. A heavy-set man dressed only in grey socks and blue-striped under-pants lay asleep on one of the battered sofas, his ginger-haired head resting on a girl's lap.

She was eighteen or nineteen, and wholly undistinguished of appearance. She wore a creased pink petticoat and black high-heeled shoes and she was chatting to another girl sitting astride the sofa-arm, her charms displayed in a white brassiere and loose white knickers. Both girls were drinking orange-juice in big glasses.

By one wall stood a black upright piano, over which slumped a man in a starched white evening shirt, his bow-tie swivelled round under one ear. He lay heavily on the key-board and seemed as unconscious as the man on the sofa. From a deep arm-chair a woman of at least fifty got to her feet and threw her muscular arms around Dr Prosz.

'Never thought to see you so late!' she said. 'Mabel – get off your fat ass and pour a drink for the doctor and his friend!'

The girl on the sofa-arm got up slowly, letting a brassiere strap slip from her shoulder until the russet tip of a breast was exposed while she yawned and stretched. Hugo was introduced to Ida. She had a hard and lined face under permanent-waved hair tinted crow-black. She at least was fully-clothed, though not pleasingly, in a black and white striped evening frock that did nothing to flatter her lumpy figure.

Hugo and Theodor Prosz sat down and took the drinks Mabel brought them. A quick sniff warned Hugo that his contained cheap whisky that had its origin somewhere other than Scotland.

'You're new in town,' Ida said to him. 'You're an actor – I can always tell. Got anything going yet?'

'I expect to sign an important contract in the next few days,' he answered proudly.

Ida nodded in disbelief, having heard aspirations of that sort all her life.

'Busy night?' Theodor asked, waving his hand at the debris.

'It's been like Thanksgiving, the Fourth of July and Lincoln's Birthday all in one,' she answered. 'Most of the girls are upstairs for the night. I was just about to throw these two gentlemen out on the street and call it a day. But you're welcome any time.'

Mabel in the white knickers sat on Theodor's lap and put an arm round his neck. Her shoulder-strap had slipped right off, so that a big bare breast dangled a hand's-breadth from his face.

'You must look after Mr Klostermann very well,' he said to Ida. 'He has all the right connections to become a very important film star.'

'Is that so?' said Ida, her interest instantly aroused.

There was a crashing discord from the piano as the man slumped on it put an elbow on the keys to lever himself up and turn to face the room.

'Good morning, Prince,' Theodor said, bowing politely, so far as Mabel's bottom on his lap permitted, 'I trust you have had an enjoyable night.'

'I can't remember,' said Dmytryk, 'have I enjoyed myself, Ida?'

'You surely have,' she answered warmly, 'you've had four bottles of champagne and taken three of my girls upstairs.'

'Excellent,' he said, his eyes focusing on Hugo, 'I know you – you're the one they sent to Berlin for. We met at Brandenstein's party the other day. I've forgotten your name.'

Prince Dmytryk looked to be in his mid-thirties, broad-faced and heavily-built, with black hair in long waves and a superior expression. It occurred to Hugo that slender little Norma Gilbert would be severely crushed if she allowed her burly fiancé to mount her.

'I've always liked Berlin,' Dmytryk went on, 'a man can enjoy himself there without the necessity for concealment and hypocrisy that rules here. Don't you find it so?'

'I haven't been here long enough to judge,' said Hugo.

If they had been speaking German together he would have addressed Dmytryk as *Prince* automatically. But in English, and in America, it seemed to him excessive.

'Another bottle of champagne, Ida,' said Dmytryk. 'Join me in a glass, Mr Klostermann – I detest drinking alone. And you, doctor.'

Hugo grinned when he heard his name – Dmytryk remembered it very well after all, it seemed. Mabel had taken her white brassiere off and was making her melons

70

bob up and down against Theodor Prosz' face, giggling as his fluffy dark moustache tickled her buds.

'I must be up early in the morning,' he said to Dmytryk. 'If you will excuse me, I shall retire with this charming young lady.'

'In your place, so would I,' said Dmytryk.

'You already have,' Mabel told him, 'twice – don't you remember?'

'How could I possibly forget, my dear? You were perfectly delightful.'

Ida returned with the champagne, popped the cork and poured it.

'Brandenstein told me that you played the leading part in a comedy of his I saw in Berlin a year or two ago,' said the Prince, raising his glass to Hugo.

'You saw *Three in a Bed*?' Hugo asked gleefully.

'It was very funny. It made me laugh. And it had wit – that is something one does not find in this terrible country.'

'You do not like the United States?'

'How could any person of distinction possibly like a country where the proletariat has triumphed far more completely than the Bolsheviks ever will in Russia? Everything here has been reduced to proletarian tastes and standards – I find it most depressing!'

'But you are going to marry an American girl,' said Hugo, astounded by Dmytryk's words.

'Amy, dear,' Ida said to the fair-headed girl on the sofa, 'come and get acquainted with our new gentleman caller.'

Amy lifted the ginger-haired man's head from her lap and drifted across the room, smoothing her rose-pink petticoat over her belly and hips. She sat herself on Hugo's lap and kissed his cheek wetly.

'You'll enjoy her,' said Dmytryk, 'she's a friendly little thing.'

'You speak from personal knowledge?'

'Oh, I'm sure I've had her – haven't I, my dear?'

'Not tonight,' Amy answered with a smile.

'You're a friend of Thelma Baxter?' Dmytryk asked Hugo, 'I saw you with her at Brandenstein's party. To be

71

frank, I saw you doing it to her – not an impressive performance, if I may say so.'

'You couldn't have seen us,' Hugo retorted, irritated by the Prince's off-hand verdict, 'the door was locked.'

'I watched you through the spy-hole. Not only you, of course, all the others upstairs as well.'

'Spy-hole? What do you mean?'

Amy's hand found its way under Hugo's roll-top sweater to stroke his chest, 'Let's go upstairs,' she suggested.

'Shut up!' Ida snapped at her. 'Let the gentlemen talk. You'll be on your back soon enough, my girl.'

'Brandenstein's house was built years ago by Vanda Lodz,' said Dmytryk. 'Did you know she came from my country? She was a whore at fourteen, but when she came to America she did very well as a film star. She came back home for a triumphal visit at the height of her fame -- that would be about 1925 or 1926. An uncle of mine, the Grand Duke Kasimir, took her to his hunting-lodge and kept her in bed for six days without a break.'

'What a man!' Ida exclaimed. 'Pity he never came to the USA.'

'But he did – he was here the very next year to stay with Miss Lodz. He told me about the secret gallery she had built in her house to spy on the bedrooms. I found it easily – the way in is through a cupboard at one end of the upper floor. Help me finish this bottle now and I will leave you to your pleasures – it has been a fatiguing day.'

'So I imagine,' said Hugo.

'Not the girls – I could have every one of them in this house and still not be tired,' Dmytryk boasted. 'My fatigue comes from being interviewed at length by an uncouth detective who smokes cheap cigars. As if I had anything to do with the squalid crime he is investigating! And if that were not enough for one day, my future mother-in-law descended on me full of alarm and apprehension. Only then was I permitted to hurry to my fiancée's side to comfort her for the sad loss of a valued colleague.'

'I met Mrs Gilbert myself yesterday,' said Hugo. 'She

72

seemed worried that the murder might somehow cast a shadow on her daughter.'

'Ridiculous! I was able to calm her fears. It is obvious enough that Ignaz was responsible for the crime.'

That disappointed Hugo, who was hoping the Prince suspected his fiancée. He put his champagne glass down and stroked Amy's belly through her thin petticoat, his interest in Dmytryk at an end.

'It's not safe to talk like that,' Ida said, pursing her lips. 'Mr Ignaz is very big in this town.'

'I shall say what I like!' Dmytryk exploded angrily. 'I will not be intimidated by a jumped-up peasant. Everyone in Hollywood knows Ignaz did it and no one has the courage to say so.'

'Let the cops worry about it,' Ida advised him. 'It's no skin off your ass if a studio bigwig gets gunned down, whoever did it.'

'But it is! Don't you understand that Ignaz controls the lives of those who work for him? Nothing escapes his attention, not the smallest detail!'

'Does that include Miss Gilbert?' Hugo enquired, feeling Amy's loose breasts through her pink petticoat.

'He has enmeshed her in a vicious contract that gives him complete control of her life! She must have his permission to travel outside America. She is forbidden to travel by airplane. She cannot take part in sports or games with an element of risk, which means on our honeymoon I cannot take her either skiing or boar-hunting!'

'I never knew honeymooners went shooting wild animals,' said Amy, 'I thought they stayed in bed all day.'

'And there is more!' Dmytryk said furiously. 'She must give Ignaz six months notice of her intention to marry. She must not become pregnant without his consent in writing – I tell you, this damned fellow wants to control my relations with my own wife!'

'You mean you won't be able to bang her when you feel like it?' Amy asked, open-mouthed, but the Prince ignored her.

'Ignaz certainly protects his investments,' said Hugo.

'But how would it further his interests to shoot his top director?'

'This man Howard was notorious,' Dmytryk grated, his broad face an unpleasant shade of mottled red. 'He was some kind of low-life Don Juan, out to slake his lusts on every woman he met.'

'Most of us do the same,' said Hugo, amused by Dmytryk's rage and guessing it had to do with Norma.

'Not in the way this degenerate fellow went about it! You have no idea of the depths to which he would stoop! When Miss Gilbert was hardly more than a child he lured her to his house on the pretext of going through a script with her. Her mother was unaware of the man's nature and did not chaperone her, as she should.'

'Great God!' Hugo exclaimed. struggling to hold back his laughter.

'To ask you to guess what Howard did would insult you by suggesting you could imagine the depths of his depravity! To be brutally frank, he exposed himself to her in this way!' and the Prince parted his legs and jerked his clenched fist up and down between his thighs to make clear what Ambrose had done.

'I am astounded!' Hugo gasped, his belly hurting from suppressed laughter.

The girl on his lap giggled at the sight of Dmytryk's empty fist jerking up and down.

'You'd be amazed how many men pay me to watch them doing that to themselves,' she said, grinding her soft bottom into Hugo's lap to attract his attention. He slipped a hand under her petticoat and she opened her legs obligingly to let him feel her crinkly fleece.

'Naturally, Miss Gilbert turned and fled,' Dmytryk gasped, beads of sweat on his forehead. 'Otherwise he might have achieved his beastly purpose and soiled her clothing!'

'However distressing the scene,' said Hugo, 'what has it to so with Ignaz?'

'But don't you see? Howard had forced every one of Ignaz's stars to have sexual relations with him – except

Miss Gilbert, of course. And he had proof of it – letters, photographs, diaries. If this proof fell into the hands of a newspaper reporter so many reputations would be ruined that Ignaz International would be out of business – you know how prudish the Americans are! Films would be boycotted, cinemas picketed, petitions presented, stars dismissed! Howard was an enormous threat to Ignaz.'

'How do you know all this?' Hugo asked, his fingers exploring the thick and warm lips between Amy's thighs and his thoughts turning towards what else he might slip between them.

'I have my sources. Few know this, but Ignaz spent some hours in Howard's house burning incriminating papers after he shot him.'

'But Ignaz was summoned to the house by a neighbour who heard the shot and found Ambrose Howard dead,' Hugo countered.

'For that fairy-tale you have the word of the neighbour herself – Miss Thelma Baxter – on whose naked body I observed you entertaining yourself last week-end,' said Dmytryk. 'And where do her interests lie? Ill-natured people say that her career in films has passed its peak and that she will be finished by the time she is thirty. But not if Ignaz decides otherwise – he can have parts written to suit her modest talents for as long as he chooses.'

'That seems sufficient reason for her to be loyal to him,' said Hugo, acutely aware that Thelma had told him two versions.

'What undoubtedly took place was that she heard the shot and went to investigate,' Dmytryk said, tapping the fingers of his right hand on the palm of his left, to tick off the points of his argument. 'She found Howard dead – and she also found Ignaz calmly burning the evidence which would destroy his business. They talked. He made her certain promises about her future, and she rearranged the sequence of events to his advantage.'

'Mr Howard was never one of my gentlemen callers,' Ida said unexpectedly, 'but you can't help hearing things in this business. There was a fight between him and Mr Ignaz

75

a day or two before the shooting – I heard that from one of my regulars when he'd had too much whisky. It seems Mr Howard was balling someone Mr Ignaz didn't want him to.'

'Not Miss Gilbert -- I can assure you of that!' Dmytryk snarled.

'No, course not – maybe Gale Paget. Yes, I remember now – it was Gale Paget he was fooling around with.'

'Ignaz is out of reach of the police,' Dmytryk growled, his face suffused with rage again. 'They are hunting for Howard's chauffeur instead. If they catch him he will be executed for the crime and the case will be closed.'

'I didn't know the chauffeur was missing,' said Hugo, trying to remember the young Mexican he had seen briefly the evening he dined with Ambrose.

'It was in the evening newspaper – his name is Luis Hernandez. He has been paid to vanish, of course.'

'By Ignaz, I suppose,' said Hugo, trying not to sound sarcastic.

'Naturally. Hernandez has been given a lot of money and told to disappear to Mexico or South America. He will not be caught, mark my words!'

'I must congratulate you on exposing this conspiracy,' said Hugo. 'Now, if you will excuse me, the bottle is empty and I shall take this young lady upstairs.'

'It has been interesting to talk to you, Mr Klostermann,' said the Prince, his voice spiteful. 'Please tell Miss Baxter that I for one know her to be a murderer's accomplice.'

'Take the gentleman upstairs, Amy,' said Ida quickly.

In her sparsely-furnished room, Amy helped Hugo undress, made him lie on his back on the bed and spiked herself on him with the ease of long practise. She bounced up and down in a businesslike way, holding her pink petticoat up under her chin with both hands to show him her pale, slack breasts. Hugo closed his eyes and imagined that it was Connie Young sitting astride him and his response was as rapid as Amy desired. His fingers sank into the soft flesh of her thighs and his loins bucked sharply upwards to squirt his passion into her.

Afterwards, when they were lying side by side, Amy yawned and asked if the Prince was *for real.*

'Is he a real Prince?' said Hugo. 'Probably. Does he come here often?'

'Often enough – Ida's tickled pink when he visits. She'd get down on her knees and lick his ass if he asked her to. Me, I never understand the half of what he says.'

'I'm sure you understood what he was saying about Ignaz shooting Ambrose Howard.'

'Oh, sure, but he hates Mr Ignaz because he thinks sweet Norma's been putting out for him.'

'He suspects him as well as Ambrose Howard?'

'From what they say, she started doing it for Mr Howard when she was a kid. Only lately they say she's been playing Mamas and Papas with Mr Ignaz as well.'

'Hollywood is flooded with rumours,' Hugo protested, 'you can't believe a word anyone says.'

'It's no rumour – it's the truth. You heard what Ida said.'

'But she said something completely different!'

'She twisted something I told *her.* The gentleman caller who got drunk and talked out of turn was flat on this bed with me at the time.'

'And he is reliable?' Hugo asked sceptically.

'He's got a direct line into Mr Ignaz's private office on account of he's balling his secretary a couple of times a week. The guy who got shot was slipping it to Mrs Ignaz and that's what the fight was about, not Norma Gilbert. The secretary heard every word and told it to my gentleman caller after he popped her.'

'Then why did Ida tell it differently?'

'How do I know? She's nuts over the Prince and she'd do anything for him. She'd die of pure pleasure if he ever let her hold his peter. The joke is, he thinks she's dirt under his feet.'

'If he needed an alibi for the night of the shooting, would Ida give him one?' Hugo asked.

'She'd swear it on the Bible itself if he asked her,' Amy answered, yawning again.

77

Chapter 5

Names on a list

Hugo had a good look at the secretary in Stefan Ignaz's outer office when Oskar conducted him into the mogul's presence. She was a pleasant-faced woman in her thirties, dark-haired and dressed in a businesslike manner in a black skirt and jacket over a plain cream blouse. No doubt she would have been flabbergasted to learn that her intimate moments with an anonymous colleague were talked about in Big Ida's sporting house. But, thought Hugo, there appeared to be very little inside the crisp white blouse and it was probable that her lover pleasured her for the sake of her information rather than for her own sake.

Stefan Ignaz proved to be a large man in his fifties, bulky, florid, with a high complexion and liquid brown eyes. His hair had once been jet-black and was now streaked with silver so very symmetrically that doubtless nature's own endeavours had been improved upon by a studio hairdresser. His suit was worthy of respect, being manifestly cut by a master hand, and the effect was only slightly spoiled by the quantity of gold on display – a heavy gold watch on Ignaz's left wrist, a thick-linked gold bracelet on his right, numerous broad gold rings on his fingers, a diamond-topped gold pin holding his tie to his shirt, and even a gold tooth that gleamed in his smile.

He came round his desk to take Hugo's hand in a firm grip.

'I'm very, very pleased to meet you at last, Mr Klostermann,' he said warmly, 'I've heard good things about you from Oskar.'

The walnut desk was about the size of a double-bed. The gold-blocked burgundy-red leather top held no letters or files or other trappings of office-work. Instead, there stood on it a dozen or so silver-framed photographic portraits of women – Connie Young, Norma Gilbert, Gale Paget, Thelma Baxter and other stars Hugo recognised at once – and one strikingly beautiful woman he did not.

'My beauties,' said Ignaz expansively, observing Hugo's sideways glance at the portraits, 'they are like my daughters – beautiful, talented, wonderful daughters of whom I am madly proud. Sometimes they do not know what is best for them and need a firm hand to guide them.'

'They are all your stars?'

'Except that one – she is my wife.'

He indicated the one Hugo had not recognised. It was a head and shoulders portrait of a breathtakingly beautiful woman in her mid-twenties.

'My compliments,' said Hugo, 'Mrs Ignaz is more beautiful than your stars. Was she also in films before your marriage?'

Ignaz stared at him as if he had taken leave of his senses to suggest that a sensible man would contemplate marrying a film star.

He waved Hugo and Oskar to chairs and went back to his own side of the desk. He talked without interruption for some time, mainly about the size and importance of Ignaz International and how very fortunate were those selected by him to be associated with so eminent an organisation.

'We have ten directors and twenty-six writers on the payroll,' he said proudly, 'and over a hundred players on contract, including some of the top stars in the business! You'd have to go to Paramount or MGM to find a bigger set-up than that!'

What it amounted to eventually was that he wanted to sign Hugo as a contract player for five years at a salary of two thousand dollars a week. That was twice what Ambrose had proposed, and in line with Oskar's promise of double,

Hugo noted – and he concluded that if Ignaz was so forthright with the offer, then there was more to be had. Consequently, he argued that he was alone in a new country, unused to its ways and values, without the advice of agent or lawyer. Only the prospect of five thousand dollars a week would reconcile himself to committing even two years of his future to Ignaz.

Stefan Ignaz professed to be deeply shocked by a demand of that size from an actor unknown outside his own distant and unimportant country. Oskar supported his chief loyally by telling Hugo of the hundreds of talented young actors who lined up outside the studio gates each morning in the hope of being taken on as extras at five dollars a day. Hugo reminded them both that he was in Hollywood at Oskar's invitation and in this office at Ignaz's.

By now Hugo guessed that he'd won and was bored. He had an oblique view of the picture of Mrs Ignaz on the desk and he was wondering if she found pleasure in having her slender body crushed under the heavy bulk of a man thirty years older than herself. Women were perverse creatures in Hugo's experience, and it was possible that she enjoyed being squashed under him and having her tender thighs forced apart for his penetration. On the other hand, perhaps it was his wealth that was alluring.

Ignaz offered a compromise – a three year contract at three thousand dollars a week. Hugo pretended to think it over and accepted. He intended to be so famous and sought-after in three years that he would be able to dictate his own terms, which would be half a million a year to start. And if Stefan Ignaz demurred at that, he would go round to Paramount or MGM and sign on with them.

Ignaz came round the desk again to take Hugo's hand in both of his own.

'Welcome to the team,' he said grandly. 'This is the most important day of your life. Together we shall do great things. I want you to think of me as a personal friend, a counsellor, a father even – someone you can bring your problems to.'

'Thank you,' Hugo responded, trying to sound sincere.

Behind his walnut desk again, Ignaz showed what he meant by being a father – he expressed his dissatisfaction.

'Your name,' he said, the corners of his mouth turning down, 'it doesn't sound right.'

'What do you mean – doesn't sound right? If it were Knoblauch or Pfangelstein I might agree. But what's wrong with Klostermann?'

'Why do you think Douglas Ullman changed his name to Fairbanks?' Oskar asked rhetorically. 'Why did Jakob Krantz become Ricardo Cortez? A man who plays romantic roles needs a name with glamour.'

'Besides,' said Ignaz to clinch the matter, 'there's a delicatessen downtown run by a family named Klostermann.'

'What am I to call myself then?' Hugo asked, 'Ricardo Fairbanks?'

'Hugo is fine,' said Ignaz, 'we like Hugo – it's got class. Tell him what we thought about his other name, Oskar.'

Oskar was wearing another version of his film director's outfit that day – a brown-checked shirt buttoned tightly at the neck and wrists, jodhpurs and glossy brown riding-boots. He opened a breast-pocket of his shirt and pulled out a folded sheet of paper.

'I have in my hand three suggestions from Publicity,' he said. 'They are all very good.'

'Three? Is that all they could think of?' Hugo exclaimed.

'They came up with scores of names,' Oskar assured him. 'They worked non-stop on this project for twenty-four hours. These three names were selected by me from the lists they sent me. The final choice is yours.'

'So what are they?' Hugo asked, resigning himself to losing the name his father had bequeathed him and which had served him well enough through the twenty-six years of his life in Berlin. Berlin, Germany, he corrected himself wryly.

Oskar read them out slowly, 'Carson, Castlemaine, Cornford.'

'These are very English names,' Hugo objected at once.

'We are making movies for an English-speaking country,'

said Oskar. 'The good people who pay to go to the cinema across the United States have names like Brown and Robinson.'

'And Brandenstein and Ignaz,' said Hugo, not convinced.

'Do not judge the whole of America by Los Angeles,' said Oskar. 'Choose one.'

'I've forgotten them already. What were they?'

Oskar repeated them.

'Castlemaine,' said Hugo, 'I'll have that one.'

'Hugo Castlemaine,' said Ignaz, rolling the name over his tongue as if he were tasting fine wine. 'Yes, that's a good choice. From now on you're Hugo Castlemaine. Start using it right away to get used to it.'

'Tell the people I have met here that my name has been changed?' Hugo asked. 'They'll think me very strange.'

'This is Hollywood – nobody will even notice,' Ignaz told him. 'Now, another thing – that crystal chandelier accent of yours! You have to do something about it before shooting starts. Oskar will fix you with lessons from a language coach.'

'Anything else?' Hugo asked, far from pleased.

'Just one thing – I heard that you beat up Chester Chataway in a restaurant a day or two ago. I won't stand for brawling in public from my stars – it lowers the tone of the studio.'

'I did no more than defend myself!' said Hugo, outraged. 'The man was drunk and abusive and attacked me without provocation.'

'The way I heard it, you played games with his girl-friend,' said Ignaz, frowning across his desk at Hugo.

'I did no such thing! She's only a child and Chataway should be ashamed of himself!'

'Chester is very touchy about his little girl-friend,' said Oskar, his face the picture of innocence. 'We all take care not to give him grounds for suspicion.'

'Thank you, Oskar,' Hugo retorted, his voice heavy with irony. To Ignaz he said, 'You are well informed.'

'I have to be – stars are like children at times. They grab

82

for new toys without a thought and sometimes they have to be spoken to for their own good. Was anything said over dinner which made you think that Ambrose was disturbed in his mind?'

'I'm sure you've asked Miss Baxter and Miss Young the same question. He was in an excellent frame of mind and enjoyed himself all evening.'

'With Connie and Thelma there I'm sure you both enjoyed yourselves,' said Oskar, beaming innocently.

'It's sad your arrival in Hollywood is overshadowed by the death of one of my most talented directors,' said Ignaz. 'But people here have short memories and he'll be forgotten by the week after next.'

'I have read that the police are looking for his chauffeur,' said Hugo quickly, seizing the chance to explore and see if he found anything to confirm Dmytryk's assertion that Ignaz had murdered Ambrose, 'Do you think Hernandez did it?'

'Did what?' Ignaz asked, his face puzzled.

'Shot Ambrose Howard, of course.'

'But Ambrose took his own life,' said Ignaz. 'Didn't you know?'

'What?' Hugo exclaimed, staggered by the statement.

'He shot himself with his own gun. If the police are looking for his chauffeur then it's only because he's missing. Maybe he stole something and ran away. Maybe he's dead drunk in a whorehouse in Long Beach and doesn't know Ambrose is dead. Maybe the police have a few questions for him, but they don't want him for murder.'

'But if Ambrose shot himself, where's the suicide note?' Hugo demanded, astonished by this version of events.

'With the police department, where else?'

Hugo stared across the desk at his new employer, reminding himself that he was talking to the man who had rushed to Ambrose's house to burn documents. And now he had the effrontery to propose suicide! At this moment Hugo became sure that Ignaz was the killer, though the motive was far from clear to him.

'You must excuse me now,' said Ignaz, 'my next appointment is due. Goodbye for now, Hugo – don't forget what I told you. I'm here whenever you have a problem. Most problems in Hollywood come from sex and booze and as it's no use advising a young fellow like you to avoid both, all I can say is – be careful who you get drunk with and who you get into bed with.'

From Stefan Ignaz's office Oskar took Hugo to see what had been cut and edited so far of his film about Frederick Barbarossa. They sat in a miniature cinema with six rows of seats and watched a sequence showing hundreds of men in helmets swarming up ladders set against a stone city wall.

'No sound track yet,' Oskar explained, 'that comes later when I know what level of shouting and screaming I want over the background music.'

The scene changed abruptly to a view of the city gate, beaten down in splintered wreckage, to let Barbarossa's men charge in.

'The traditional cast of thousands!' said Hugo, laughing.

'Just over four hundred,' said Oskar. 'They look more because they turn left inside the gate and come round again from behind the camera – the usual stage army trick.'

The camera moved into the city with the victorious army, and a city square was shown, with a church at the end, a colonnade down one side and a row of market-stalls down the other. Dead defenders were strewn everywhere and the rape of the city's women was in full swing. Under the colonnade, on the market-stalls and up the steps of the church Barbarossa's men pinned struggling women of all ages down and thumped their loins against them. Hugo watched closely as bodices were ripped open and skirts torn off to see how much Oskar dare put on the screen. A girl with long hair broke away from a soldier and ran into the church, her peasant frock torn off one bare shoulder. She was on her knees before the altar, her hands raised in supplication, when the soldier caught her by the hair.

'Oskar – you cannot show a rape in a church! Your movie will be banned in every city in the United States!'

84

'I know,' said Oskar sadly. 'The first time we shot this scene I had her raped on the altar itself – you saw the girl's legs kicking in the air and the back view of the soldier crouched over her. But Ignaz said what you've just said, so I shot it again.'

On the screen, the brutal soldier was smitten by his conscience at the sight of the crucifix on the altar. He let go of the girl's hair and knelt beside her to pray for forgiveness, tears streaming down his face.

'What do you think of that, my boy – wonderful, yes? The churchgoers will call down blessings on me when they see that tender little scene.'

'I am sure your movie will be a great success, Oskar. Ignaz will bless you too when the money pours in.'

The office assigned to Oskar in the directors' building was comfortable and well-furnished, in an anonymous sort of way. There was a desk, half a dozen arm-chairs, a cocktail cabinet in light polished maple and what Hugo could only think of as a casting-couch of tan leather under the window.

'We will celebrate your contract,' said Oskar, his monocle catching the light as he beamed at Hugo. 'What will you have -- Scotch whisky, Canadian whisky, bourbon, rye whisky, French cognac, gin, Jamaica rum, Cuban rum, Russian vodka, Polish vodka, marc, grappa, schnaps or moonshine?'

'My God, what is moonshine?'

'A liquor made by American peasants secretly up in the hills away from law officers. It tastes like gasoline and has the same effect on your brain.'

'All this is too heavy at eleven in the morning,' Hugo complained, wrinkling his nose.

'Good boy,' said Oskar, 'here is a bottle of best French champagne I put to chill before we went to see Ignaz. You will not refuse that, I'm sure.'

Hugo accepted a glass and thanked Oskar for his good wishes, but with a certain lack of enthusiasm.

'I want you to be frank with me,' he said, 'Ignaz has never seen me on the stage or on the screen. He dislikes my name and the way I speak English. From his manner I suspect that he despises all actors. So why has he hired me at a huge salary?'

'For your looks, of course,' Oskar answered in surprise.

'And that's all?'

'He saw you have the actor's trick of projecting your personality, even when you are silent. What more is there?'

'I came ten thousand kilometres to be insulted?'

'You came ten thousand kilometres for the money,' said Oskar. 'There is nothing else in Hollywood – no culture, no art, no true talent, no warmth of heart, no genuine feeling, no sincerity, no conscience, no loyalty, and above all, no love. But there is all the money you want.'

'Is that how you see Hollywood – a city to plunder?'

'Why do you think I showed you part of my movie? You have the same choices as the soldier – you can get down on your knees and pray for your soul, or you can pitch the girl on to the altar and give her a good tousling. And the way you haggled with Ignaz to get three thousand a week shows that your choice is made. You did well – his top price for you was three and a half.'

'What – I've been cheated out of five hundred a week!'

'Spoken like a true Hollywood star!' said Oskar, grinning.

'Mrs Ignaz – what is her first name?'

'You should wait until your contract is signed before you try to get your hand up her skirt. Her name is Virginia. They have been married for less than two years and Ignaz is very possessive.'

'Possessive enough to kill Ambrose for her?'

Oskar laughed and said that Ambrose had killed himself.

'I think that Ignaz was making a joke about that,' said Hugo. 'Your friend Prince Dmytryk is absolutely convinced that Ignaz did it.'

'That idiot is as wrong about this as he is about everything else,' said Oskar, leaning back in his swivel-chair so that he could put his glossy boots up on the desk. 'What happened was this – Ambrose had dinner alone while he was working on the shooting-script of the *Mary Magdalene* epic . . .'

'How do you know that?'

'The police found the script on his desk next to a tray with the left-overs of a meal. Like everyone else who knew Ambrose well, I have been grilled by the police and made to produce an alibi. But I learned as much from them as they did from me. Do you want to hear the rest?'

'Most certainly!'

'Very well – Ambrose was working in his study. The door-bell rang and he had an unexpected visitor.'

'Who – Stefan Ignaz?' Hugo asked eagerly.

'Norma Gilbert. Why do you think her mother jumped to the conclusion that Norma shot Ambrose? Because she knew her sweet daughter had gone to see him that evening.'

'Then Thelma was right – it *was* Norma she saw running away.'

'No, she made that up. Norma was long gone before the shot was fired that woke Thelma.'

'Why did Norma want to see Ambrose that evening?'

'She wanted the lead part in *Mary Magdalene.*'

'But that's absurd! She may be twenty-one but she looks like a seventeen-year-old virgin!'

'Her ambition may seem laughable to you and to me, but to her it is very real. She went to persuade Ambrose she could play the part. When discussion failed, she took her clothes off and used her pretty body instead. They went up to his bedroom – and horror! Ambrose's tail refused to stand up! He could do nothing, however hard Norma tried with hands and mouth to arouse him! After a while he told her to get dressed and go.'

'Even if it were true, Norma would never have told any of that to the police,' said Hugo. 'And even if she had been mad enough to tell them, they wouldn't have told you.'

'You're right – they didn't. Norma told me herself when she came to ask my advice on whether to tell the police that she was with Ambrose that evening. I advised her to say nothing, as it was bound to be misinterpreted.'

87

'Why did she ask you instead of going to Ignaz? He claims to be Father-Confessor to his stars.'

'Dear Hugo, you have not yet understood the ways of Hollywood. Norma came to me because she guessed that Ignaz would ask me to take over the *Mary Magdalene* movie and she still wants to play the lead. Her little confession that she took off her clothes for Ambrose was accompanied by charming blushes and downcast eyes and was intended to stir my protective instincts — and for the first time I saw that she has some ability as an actress. In no time at all she was naked on my lap with her tongue in my mouth. What could I do — I ask you?'

'You did what I would have done,' said Hugo, a grin on his face. 'Where did this tender scene take place?'

'Here in my office. I laid her on her back on this desk with her legs straight up in the air and stood right here while I rumpled her. But I digress. We left poor Ambrose sitting naked and disconsolate on the side of his bed. He did the obvious thing — he got drunk. Moran removed an empty bottle from the bedside cabinet.'

'So that the police would not became confused,' said Hugo, with heavy sarcasm.

'Naturally. Norma left about ten o'clock. By midnight Ambrose was blind drunk and grieving for his lost virility. He drenched his body in perfume and tied a black mourning bow round his useless appendage. He decided to hang himself in the bathroom — he knew the old tale about the hanged man's last emission as he dies, and that seemed appropriate. But with the cord in his hand, he was unable to do it. He fetched his revolver from the bedroom and sat down before the full-length mirror to admire himself one last time. When he was ready he put the gun to where he could feel his heart beating and pulled the trigger.'

'Pure conjecture,' said Hugo instantly. 'Everything after Norma left him sitting on the bed is your imagination. You have only her word that she left before ten — maybe she stayed until midnight, lost her temper when he refused her the film role and shot him with his own gun.'

'You speak without knowing the facts,' Oskar said smugly, 'Ambrose wrote a note to explain his intentions.'

'But nothing appeared in the newspapers about the police finding a note!'

'The police didn't find it when they searched the house at first,' said Oskar. 'He had scribbled it on a blank page at the back of the script of *Mary Magdalene* and it came to light when Ted Moran went through Ambrose's possessions two days later on behalf of the studio.'

'Now I am absolutely certain that Ignaz killed Ambrose. He made the story up and had someone imitate Ambrose's handwriting.'

'You are very free with your accusations,' Oskar commented mildly. 'Why do you refuse to accept the simple truth that the man killed himself? After all, how well did you know him – you spent one evening with him and two women. Does that make you an expert on his state of mind?'

'Thelma knew him better than anyone – she believes he was murdered.'

'Because you enjoy rolling about on top of her is not a good reason to attribute intelligence to her,' Oskar answered abruptly. 'Thelma's brains are between her legs. She'd say anything to get at Norma Gilbert.'

'You're claiming that Ambrose shot himself because he couldn't do it anymore – but I was with him and saw him do it to Thelma and Connie. That demolishes your theory completely.'

'But did you see him do it? Think! What exactly did you see?'

Hugo cast his mind back.

'In the back of the car he and Thelma played about – that was nothing,' he said, 'but then she was down on her knees between his legs, using her mouth on him. I heard him moaning.'

'Anyone can moan – but did you see whether his tail was stiff or soft?'

'To be truthful, no. I was on the sofa with Connie and she was occupying my attention.'

'So you changed partners – what happened then?'

'Ambrose and Connie were rolling about on the floor. When I'd finished with Thelma I got up to pour myself a drink and they were side by side on the carpet, whispering and kissing. Connie was holding his tail and it was limp – because he'd just done it to her.'

'But he hadn't,' said Oskar, removing his monocle and shaking his big head solemnly. 'He hadn't been able to do it for months.'

'Then why should Thelma and Connie pretend he could?'

'Old friends trying to be helpful,' said Oskar, rubbing his bald-shaven head thoughtfully. 'And for the sake of their careers – he was top producer at Ignaz International.'

'Did Norma tell you that he couldn't do it?'

'She hinted at it. The trouble with her is that she keeps up her innocent girlie pose all the time. Even when she has a climax she manages to look surprised, as if this was something entirely new and shocking to her. There is no way to persuade her to speak openly about whether Ambrose stuck it in her or not.'

'Then your theory is without foundation.'

Oskar took his feet off the desk, unlocked the middle drawer and took out a sheet of paper.

'It's more than a theory, and it doesn't depend on Norma,' he said. 'You know that the house was searched before the police arrived? But the searchers were in a hurry and missed one or two things. The police took a whole day and were very thorough. In a cupboard they found a wooden box containing over thirty pairs of women's knickers. Each had a small tag attached, on which was written a set of initials and a date.'

He slid the paper across the desk to Hugo.

'This is a copy of the list made by the police from the tags.'

'The studio has an arrangement with the police department – of that I'm sure. But how did *you* get this list, Oskar?'

'I told you that I got more out of the detective who

90

questioned me than he got from me. I got this from him – for a consideration.'

Hugo ran his eye down the typed list of initials and dates.

'TB stands for Thelma Baxter, presumably,' he said, 'NG is Norma Gilbert, perhaps. GP might be Gale Paget. CY is Connie Young, no doubt. But as for the others . . .'

'Yes, the others,' said Oskar, grinning mischievously, 'it is fascinating to guess who they might be. Could CB stand for Clara Bow – or Constance Bennet – or Cissy Ballard – or Claudette Brenner? All important names, you'll agree. And there is JH on the list. An evil-minded person might say that stands for Jean Harlow. Or could it be Juanita Hansen? Or even Jilly Holloway, though I doubt that as it is generally known that Jilly's bed-time preference is for other women, not for men.'

'MD, LL, MP, TT, GS, CW,' Hugo read out. 'I could put the names of famous stars to all those initials, but it would be no more than guessing.'

'We can be sure they are the initials of ladies who left their knickers with Ambrose as a souvenir. There is no mystery about TB or CY or NG, as you said yourself, and so we can reasonably conclude that the rest of the ladies are also film stars. Ambrose was not likely to pick up waitresses when he could have the most beautiful women in Hollywood. But look at the dates – what do you observe there?'

'They cover a period of nearly six years. The most recent is last January. From that I conclude that Ambrose made no new conquests after that and contented himself with his established girl-friends.'

'He made no new conquests because he couldn't do it for the last six months of his life,' said Oskar. 'There is no similar gap in the previous five years. The break with routine is too complete for any other explanation. Poor Ambrose had run out of steam.'

'You said that Mrs Ignaz's name is Virginia,' Hugo observed. 'There is no VI on this list and so presumably none of her underwear in Ambrose's trophy box. Yet I have

91

heard a rumour that he and Ignaz quarrelled over the lady. On the other hand, there is no MG on the list either, and you told me that Ambrose had romped with Mother Gilbert as well as Norma Gilbert.'

'I didn't tell you that,' said Oskar, his eyes widening with interest.

'Someone told me.'

'I can well believe it, though. Mildred has managed Norma's career with an iron hand and Ambrose may have found it necessary to ravage her from time to time to keep her happy while he was directing Norma. But it would be fairly casual – Mildred hires young chauffeurs to drive her about and they never last more than six months.'

'She wears them out fast!' said Hugo, impressed by such exertion by a middle-aged woman.

'Where do you suppose her daughter inherited her hot nature from? I've heard it said that the father was a Baptist preacher in Fort Worth twenty years older than Mildred and he died when Norma was three.'

'Oskar, you are an old gossip!'

'You have to be here, to survive. They tell lurid stories about me, of course – mainly that I'm a depraved old beast who vents his lusts on helpless young girls. Can you imagine!'

'Very easily – you were very keen to get at little Lily.'

'You can talk!' said Oskar, grinning at him, 'I'm sure you did more to her than take her knickers down when she was drunk. And what about Connie and Thelma – not to mention Patsy! You've not been here two weeks yet and you've cut quite a swathe. Keep that up and your future is assured!'

'How so? Men like Ignaz decide what is to happen, not actors.'

'Ignaz decides what to do when he knows what will make most money. If you can make women here open their legs for you that easily, then you can make women across America swoon over you on the screen. As soon as Ignaz is sure of that, your fortune is made.'

'You didn't say whether you promised the Mary Magdalene part to Norma Gilbert.'

'I didn't promise and I didn't refuse,' Oskar answered with a glint in the eye behind the monocle, 'I said there's a lot to think about. She's coming to my house tomorrow to talk about it again. I imagine our discussions will go on for hours and leave me deliciously exhausted.'

'I think that Ambrose more or less promised the part to Connie.'

'Connie could play it well. She's on my short list for consideration, though I do not enjoy the same intimate friendship with her that Ambrose did.'

'I'm sure you could change that,' said Hugo, suddenly far from pleased by the thought of beautiful Connie stripped naked for Oskar's casual entertainment.

'No doubt,' Oskar agreed, 'but my taste at present is for sweet young girls like Lily and Norma and Patsy – I am in your debt for two of them.'

'A debt easily paid – if you've taken over the big Bible movie, put me in it.'

'That's already decided – you are to play Marcus.'

'The handsome young Roman aristocrat who falls in love with Mary Magdalene? The real star of the picture – the one Ambrose said must make women in the cinema wet their knickers!'

'Exactly so – play this role right and you'll be bigger than Chester Chataway was in his hey-day – bigger than Valentino even! But no announcements yet – Ignaz wants to announce the stars and the start of shooting himself when the role of Mary is cast. This film is very important to him – it will be the most expensive he's ever produced and he is looking for a gigantic profit from it.'

'If I'd known this I would have demanded more than three thousand dollars a week,' Hugo said mournfully.

'The ingratitude of actors!' Oskar exclaimed, 'but never mind, I have arranged a special welcome to Ignaz International for you,' and he lifted the telephone and spoke briefly into it.

93

Almost at once the door opened and two girls came into the office.

'Patsy!' Hugo exclaimed. 'How are you?'

'I'm fine,' she answered cheerfully. 'This is my friend Sylvie.'

Patsy seated herself on Oskar's lap behind the desk and kissed his shaven head. Sylvie held her hand out to Hugo and, when he took it, led him to the casting-couch under the window. She was nineteen or twenty, he guessed, with short dark hair and thick black eyebrows, and she wore a white roll-neck pullover that clung to her full breasts. She sat beside Hugo on the leather couch and without saying a word took his hand and pushed it under her pullover.

'Where have you been since I saw you last, Patsy,' Hugo asked across the office as he felt Sylvie's mangoes.

'Oskar's been looking after me,' she replied, 'I'm going to be in his next movie – you really did give me some of your luck, Hugo!'

'Little Patsy is going to be a movie star,' Oskar said with a chuckle, 'because she's young and very pretty and she's very nice to Oskar. Oh, the naughty girl isn't wearing her panties today!'

Handling Sylvie had aroused Hugo quickly. He had been surprised at first that Oskar had brought the girls to his office instead of arranging the encounter in a private place, but he realised that, as with Norma Gilbert on his desk, he was deliberately flouting common decency to prove that he was above convention.

Oskar's voice trailed away as Patsy slipped off his lap and knelt between his legs. She was hidden from Hugo by the desk but he knew well enough what she was doing – she had unbuckled Oskar's heavy belt and opened his jodhpurs to pull out his stem.

'I'm going to give you a good feel,' Sylvie whispered in Hugo's ear, and she was off his lap and down on the floor, doing for him what Patsy was doing for Oskar. She smiled up at him when she had his stiff shaft out of his trousers and he recognised her face.

'You were in Oskar's film' he murmured, 'you were the

94

girl in the church – I didn't recognise you without the long wig.'

'That's right,' she said, grinning up at him as she stroked his stilt firmly. 'The soldier threw me on the altar and jumped on top of me. Oskar kept the camera running so long we got hot pants for each other from jerking up and down. Only the scene got changed afterwards.'

When she lowered her dark head and took his spindle into her mouth it reminded him of when he saw Thelma do the same for Ambrose in his living-room. She had had her frock off and her round bottom in white satin knickers was towards Hugo on the sofa with Connie.

'I'm certain Ambrose could still do it,' he gasped through the tremors of pleasure that shook his belly, 'he didn't shoot himself . . . Connie thinks it was an accident with Peg Foster – her perfume was all over him!'

'Not now!' Oskar moaned. 'He drenched himself with perfume – Moran found an empty Chanel bottle and took it away so that evil-minded policemen wouldn't become confused – oh yes, Patsy, don't stop!'

'Moran does what Ignaz tells him to do,' Hugo said, hardly able to speak for the pleasure that was about to engulf him, 'Ignaz shot Ambrose and is trying to set it up to look as if he shot himself . . . ah, ah!'

Sensation blotted out all conscious thought and he cried out again and again as Sylvie sucked his passion from him. When he regained his wits she was wiping him dry with his shirt. She looked up at him as she fastened his trousers and grinned.

'You're crazy,' she said, 'I never met anybody before who talks right through it – who the hell cares who shot who so long as you're having a good time?'

Behind the desk Oskar was huffing and puffing like a steam-engine. His swivel-chair creaked to the convulsions of his heavy body and, forgetting his English, he groaned *Ja, ja, ja!*

Chapter 6

Mildred pays a call

Now that he knew he had come to stay in Hollywood, Hugo looked for an apartment and with Thelma's assistance found one he liked on Beverly Boulevard. It was the penthouse of a new building, furnished in the most modern of styles – and it had a roof-garden with orange trees growing in wooden tubs. He moved in immediately, glad to leave the hotel on Wilshire, with all that he had brought from Berlin packed into two large suitcases. He had been in the apartment less than an hour when the doorman rang from the lobby to tell him that Mrs Mildred Gilbert was on her way up.

What on earth she wanted with him was beyond conjecture. Hugo abandoned his unpacking and put his jacket on to receive her formally. She was dressed very stylishly in dark grey silk with white polka dots and a black straw hat with a long feather.

'Dear Mrs Gilbert, come in,' said Hugo, taking her hand, 'you are my first visitor. Please sit down – I wish I could offer you something but I have only just moved in and have as yet nothing to drink or eat.'

'The thought is what counts,' Mildred answered easily and sat herself on one of the facing steel-grey velvet sofas. 'This is a pleasant room, though it lacks the personal touch yet.'

They chatted for a while of nothing much, Hugo waiting for her to declare the purpose of her call. The resemblance between her and her daughter was not great, he thought. Her features were larger than Norma's, making her long face somewhat plain, where Norma's was delicately appealing. There was a difference in the way they spoke, even to Hugo's foreign ear, though he did not know enough about it to recognise Mildred's distinctly Texan accent.

'I hope you don't mind me calling on you,' she said at last. 'We have been introduced, but you may think it strange for a lady to visit a gentleman's apartment unaccompanied. But I'm so worried for my daughter – somebody is spreading disgraceful lies about her.'

Hugo assured her that he found nothing improper in her visit and asked her what sort of lies were being put about.

'I can hardly bring myself to repeat them! They're saying that my Norma was at Mr Howard's house the night he died! Can you imagine what Prince Dmytryk would think if he heard it said that his fiancée had been visiting another man after dark! You're a European gentleman yourself, Mr Klostermann – what would you think?'

'I have changed my name to Castlemaine,' said Hugo, 'but please call me Hugo. I do not think I can answer your question with any certainty, as I have never been engaged to be married. But I might be tempted to think that she was there for a very private purpose.'

'You see! That's what everyone will think – that Norma has been unchaste and unfaithful to the Prince!'

Hugo looked at Mildred Gilbert carefully, wondering why she thought this pretence necessary. She could hardly be unaware that Ambrose had been making love to Norma for years. He had forgotten the exact date on Oskar's list for NG, but it was long ago, when she was fifteen or sixteen.

'I know who's responsible for these lies!' Mildred burst out, 'Thelma Baxter – she's always hated my girl!'

Hugo thought it best to say nothing to that. It was not only a matter of what Thelma saw or imagined, not now that Oskar had it from Norma herself that she was at Ambrose's house on the fatal evening.

'Why are you telling me this?' he asked.

97

'You're a close friend of Thelma's – you can persuade her to stop spreading these terrible lies.'

'But I have no influence at all over what she says!'

'Yes, you do. I could see what you'd been doing with her before I called to see her the other afternoon. If you're that close, she'll listen to you.'

'What are you suggesting?' Hugo asked, his smile charming.

'You'd been fooling around with each other – you hadn't done your trousers up properly.'

At last Hugo understood the main purpose of Mildred's visit. Why she thought he would bother with her when so many younger and prettier women were available was obscure and her presumption surprised him. He decided to amuse himself a little at her expense and slowly unbuckled his new snake-skin belt. Mildred's pale blue eyes bulged as he opened his trousers, pulled up his shirt and flicked out his pink peg through the slit in his underpants.

'What are you doing?' she gasped, her cheeks flushing bright red. 'Cover yourself at once – I've never been so insulted in my life!'

'On the contrary,' he said, 'I am paying you a compliment, my dear Mildred, by showing you something I treasure highly. See how long and hard it is growing!'

'You're going too far!' she exclaimed, struggling to preserve her facade of modesty. 'You are no gentleman – put it away!'

Mildred's cheeks were scarlet as she stared at the stiff plaything Hugo was stroking while he directed his most charming smile towards her.

'You didn't come here to meet a gentleman,' he answered softly, 'you came to make the acquaintance of the fifteen centimetres of hard flesh that is the delight of more than one beautiful film star.'

'If you won't put it away, then I will!' she declared and crossed the floor swiftly to sit beside him on his grey velvet sofa. She took hold of his hilt with firm fingers and pushed it back into his trousers, saying, 'Leave it alone – I have to talk to you.'

All the same, her outraged modesty did not compel her to let go of what she had tucked into his trousers. Perhaps she was afraid he would expose it again if she released it, and so while she gripped it tightly, Hugo undid the small black buttons down the front of her frock.

'What do you think you're doing!' she exclaimed, blushing again.

'Feeling your melons,' he answered, his hand in her frock to explore the heavily elasticated brassiere she wore. There being no obvious way to unfasten it, he hoisted her slack breasts out of the cups that supported them and let them hang outside her frock.

'Is this the way to treat a lady who only wants to discuss important family business?' Mildred sighed.

The formality of her black hat with the feather was much at odds with the excited expression on her face as Hugo rolled the red-brown buds of her breasts between his fingers.

'We are discussing important personal business,' he said. 'The rest must wait. Let me see you play with your bundles, Mildred.'

She let go of his hidden stiffness to raise both hands to the fleshy balloons hanging out of her bodice and squeezed them, the sound of her breathing very audible. Hugo pulled out his spindle again and massaged it while he watched her.

'Can you kiss them?' he asked.

She bent her neck, lifted one loose bundle and licked its bud with the tip of her tongue.

'Yes!' Hugo murmured, highly aroused by the sight. 'Don't stop, Mildred!'

She raised the other bud to her tongue, her eyes shifting from his sliding hand to his flushed face. She saw the effect she was having on him and her pink tongue flickered quickly.

'Oh my God, yes . . .' Hugo whispered, the little throbs that ran through him warning him that his critical moment was almost upon him. Mildred recognised the warning too and was off the sofa at once and down between his legs to

99

wrap the warm flesh of her slack breasts round his stalk. Hugo fell back against the sofa, his hands on her shoulders, his passion spurting up her long cleavage to her chin.

'More, more, more!' Mildred demanded, the clasp of her breasts pumping him dry in ecstatic jolts.

When it was all over she used his fine linen handkerchief to wipe herself. Hugo lay slumped against the back of the sofa, surprised by how quickly it had happened. He grinned to see Mildred lever her big flaps back inside her frock and sit upright beside him.

'That's all that it was about – your deliberate rudeness to me?' she asked, displeasure very evident in her voice, 'You have no respect – you think you can insult decent people for the sake of your silly little satisfactions.'

'Dear Mildred, you wouldn't say that if you knew me better,' he returned, smiling at her.

'All I know about you is that you insult me by exposing your private parts and relieve yourself without a thought for my feelings.'

She was staring at the parts by which she claimed she had been insulted, watching with an expression of dismay Hugo's tall mast collapsing until it lay small and limp on his belly.

'Take your clothes off,' said Hugo.

'What's the point?' she asked, gesturing at his drooping limb.

'You have been too many years a widow,' Hugo answered her, putting authority into his voice, 'you have an irritating habit of questioning and doubting. While you are in my home you will do what I say – take your clothes off, all of them, and be quick about it!'

Without another word she stood up and did as he said. Off came her hat, making Hugo grin at the memory of it on her head while she had been down on her knees pleasuring him with her fleshy bundles, off came her polka-dotted frock, her large satin brassiere, her loose-legged white knickers and her stockings.

'Is this what you want to see?' she asked.

Her breasts hung heavily, her belly was plump and its

100

button set deeply in its curve. The broad thatch between her thighs was a darker shade than the gingery brown of her head.

'Yes,' Hugo answered, 'come and sit on my lap.'

The press of her bare bottom on his exposed tail felt very pleasant. He played with her loose bundles until she was breathing rapidly and put his hand between her thighs to probe her moist petals. Mildred sighed and shivered, her eyes closed.

'You are concerned that Dmytryk may believe your daughter was with Ambrose when he was shot,' he said, wondering how much he could get her to tell him, 'but there is no reason for your concern – Dmytryk is sure that Ignaz killed him – he told me so himself.'

'When was that?' Mildred murmured, her eyes opening.

'A day or two ago – we ran into each other by chance,' Hugo answered evasively, thinking it improper to reveal that he had met Norma's fiancé in a brothel.

'Good, very good,' she sighed, and he was undecided whether she meant that his information was satisfactory or his touch on her secret button.

'You're trembling like a girl, Mildred,' he whispered. 'you are so excited that your whole body is shaking.'

'It's too much!' she moaned, 'I'm dying of pleasure!'

Hugo's fingers fluttered inside her open pocket until her eyes snapped wide open again and she squealed. He put his head down to her drooping breasts and worried a hard bud between his teeth while his fingers sustained her shuddering climax to its limit.

While she was recovering, he turned her to lie along the grey velvet of the sofa, her head pillowed on his lap. His pink shaft stood upright from his open trousers, close to Mildred's cheek.

'Do you think Ignaz shot Ambrose?' he asked, taking advantage of her contented frame of mind.

'That's foolish,' she said, 'Mr Ignaz would never risk his whole life and fortune by shooting a man. If he wanted to get rid of Ambrose Howard he'd find some other way to do it.'

'I agree,' Hugo said, stroking her bare belly lightly, 'but Dmytryk was so insistent that I assumed that he was hiding something. He knows that your daughter and Ambrose have been lovers and, to be honest with you, Mildred, it crossed my mind that perhaps Dmytryk killed him out of jealousy.'

'Such nonsense!' Mildred answered, a wariness in her voice. 'You've been taken in by Thelma Baxter's lies. Norma is a pure young woman who will go to her marriage-bed unblemished.'

'That may be,' said Hugo, not wishing to get into a discussion of Norma Gilbert's hypothetical virginity, 'but you can't blame Thelma for all the rumours. Even Dmytryk has heard of the occasion when Ambrose exposed himself to Norma.'

'That was years ago,' Mildred insisted, 'she was a child – it meant nothing to her innocent mind. I ought to have had him put in jail then, but I tried to protect my little girl from scandal and in my foolishness I only warned him of what I would do if he tried it again.'

And Ambrose stripped you and made love to you until your eyes popped out, Hugo thought suddenly – *that was how he kept you sweet, Mildred, while he went on playing with Norma. He had her knickers for his collection but not yours, because you're not a star.*

His hand moved up from her belly to her melons and she trembled when he fingered their red-brown tips.

'Yes, but Dmytryk wouldn't let it go at that,' he said. 'He's from the Balkans – he'd want blood revenge for an insult to his fiancée.'

'The Prince didn't shoot Ambrose,' she sighed, 'even though he knows that he abused my little girl.'

Hugo used both hands to tease her buds, aware that she would tell him all she knew if he kept her highly enough aroused to overcome her caution.

'If you're so certain he didn't do it, then I think maybe you did. Your daughter was with Ambrose that night – you found her there naked and you chased him into the bathroom and shot him with his own revolver.'

'No, no,' Mildred whimpered, her body squirming in

102

delight under his hands. 'It wasn't me, any more than it was the Prince.'

Hugo understood what she meant.

'Dmytryk was in your bed that night,' he said softly. 'You have given each other an alibi to the police.'

'Oh, oh, oh, oh, oh . . .' she gasped, her belly swelling with excitement as he rolled the tips of her breasts sadistically between his fingers. He crushed handfuls of warm and slack flesh in his hands, aroused himself by what he was doing to her.

'Doesn't Norma let him have her enough?' he demanded, his voice shaking, 'does he need her mother on her back to satisfy himself? How many times did he do it to you that night, Mildred?'

His stilt was quivering and Mildred turned her head to peer at it. A long moan began somewhere down in her heaving belly, rose up past the breasts Hugo was cruelly misusing and reached her throat. With an awkward twist of her body she got her mouth to Hugo's upright part and engulfed it so deeply that he thought she was swallowing it. He jammed a wedge of three stiff fingers into her juicy opening as the long moan of ecstasy escaped her and then squealed himself as her teeth bit into the flesh of his shaft down towards its root.

Hugo's hot passion burst from him in spasms that made him cry out again and again, so that together he and she gave voice and shook and clung to each other in climactic frenzy. On it went, Mildred's gingery-brown head jerking up and down, her teeth sunk into his hard flesh and his joined fingers jammed ever harder into her wet depths. When at last their nervous systems could tolerate no more, they collapsed against each other and lay twitching.

Though neither was conscious of time, a good five minutes passed before Mildred sat up from Hugo's lap and he opened his eyes. She put her hands under her long breasts and hefted them slowly and ruefully.

'I declare you nearly twisted them off,' she announced, smiling at him, 'but it was terrific!'

'For me too,' said Hugo, 'I thought you had bitten my tail right off – look at those teeth-marks!'

'Poor little thing!' she said, and indeed it was small and soft again, 'I think I have some cold cream in my hand-bag – that will soothe it for you.'

While she was rummaging through her hand-bag Hugo took off all his clothes and lay full-length on the sofa. Mildred couldn't find what she was looking for and instead fetched a few ice-cubes from the kitchen and applied them to his wounded part.

'That's very uncomfortable,' Hugo complained.

'It will go numb in a minute and you won't feel a thing,' she reassured him. 'Now, if you're so all-fired keen to know who shot Ambrose Howard, I'll tell you. It was Chester Chataway and he won't be arrested because the studio is protecting him.'

'Why him?'

'Because he's every bit as degenerate as Ambrose Howard was,' Mildred answered primly. 'He's got a six-teen-year-old girl up at his house and he's turned that poor child into a pervert already. She wants to get into films – and who better to help her than a director who likes to molest girl-children.'

'How can you say that when Thelma Baxter and Connie Young were Ambrose's girl-friends? And heaven knows how many more!'

'That was a cover-up,' said Mildred. 'Since he exposed himself to Norma I've kept my eye on him. He was crazy about young girls and when he used Lily Haden for his degenerate pleasures he came up against a man as evil as himself and paid with his life.'

'Well, well!' said Hugo, chuckling, 'I'd never have guessed it! So Chester Chataway the cinema's Great Lover shot Ambrose for the favours of a sixteen-year-old girl!'

'You think I don't know the ways of men?' Mildred asked. 'My husband was a preacher and as old as my Daddy when I was married to him at fifteen. I know more than you ever will about the desires of middle-aged men for young girls.'

'And you were determined to protect Norma?'

'It wasn't just fooling around in the ordinary way,' said Mildred, her voice suddenly blurred with emotion, 'Ambrose did things to girls which are not decent to be spoken of. That's why I called him a degenerate and a pervert.'

'There's no feeling in my tail at all!' Hugo exclaimed in alarm. 'You've given me frost-bite!'

Mildred removed the handkerchief that held the melting ice-cubes to his shrunk and wizened little spur. She knelt beside the sofa, still naked, and took it into her warm mouth.

'Thank you, Mildred,' Hugo said fervently, looking down with true gratitude at the rather plain and middle-aged woman performing this office of mercy for him.

'Mm, mm,' she replied, her tongue assisting his frozen tail to assume its normal size and temperature by slow stages. Soon it occurred to him that it would be sensible, when it reached full stretch, to lay Mildred on her back on the floor and plunge it into her wet warmth, to make sure no lasting damage had been sustained.

The next morning he awoke about nine o'clock with an ache where he had never had one before. He threw aside the sheet and took off his pyjama trousers to examine the seat of his pain and was dismayed to see that Mildred's teeth-marks were an angry red-purple. He made coffee for himself and while he was drinking it leafed through the Los Angeles telephone directory for the name Prosz – the only doctor he knew – and at ten he was at the doctor's place of business on Cahuenga Boulevard.

Theodor Prosz looked as pale and withdrawn as the night Hugo had met him in Connie's bed-room, though today he wore a handsome brown suit and a tiny white carnation in his button-hole. He shook hands with Hugo, waved him to a comfortable chair and sat down again at his desk, his fingers pressed together to form a steeple with its point at the level of his fluffy moustache.

105

'I see that you remember me, Mr Klostermann – perhaps because we met in exceptional circumstances.'

'Castlemaine, please – I have changed my name. I am now a film star on contract with Ignaz International.'

'My sincere congratulations, Mr Castlemaine! Let me wish you every success. What brings you here?'

Hugo explained the reason for his visit. Prosz took him into the adjoining room, which was set out as a treatment area, and introduced the white-uniformed woman there as Nurse Bell. She helped Hugo remove his jacket, trousers and underwear and lie on the examination couch for the doctor to inspect his damaged tassel through a large magnifying-glass.

'Yes, the skin is broken in several places,' Prosz observed, 'and there is extensive bruising.'

He did not ask how Hugo had acquired so unusual an injury. When his inspection was completed he gave instructions to his nurse and went back to his office, leaving Hugo on his back with his shirt up round his waist. Nurse Bell washed her hands and dried them meticulously without even a glance at Hugo or his bruised equipment. She took a large jar from a glass-fronted cabinet and brought it to the couch.

'What's that?' Hugo enquired.

'It will clear up the bruising,' she said, 'legs apart, please.'

She took hold of his dangler between finger and thumb and stretched it upwards while she rubbed white cream from the jar over the teeth-marks round its base.

'That's pleasantly cool,' said Hugo, trying to catch her eye and failing, her gaze being fixed on the seat of operations.

'I expect Dr Prosz will prescribe this for you three times a day,' she said. 'It's important to work it well into the skin, not just smear it on top.'

'I understand,' said Hugo, a little breathlessly.

No young man in the world, and certainly not Hugo, could remain unaffected by the treatment Nurse Bell was administering to his prize possession. The emollient cream she was rubbing in was cool, but his dip-stick was not – it thickened and lengthened under her touch, so that the purple marks of Mildred's passion stood out vividly, like a collar round a neck.

Hugo lay at his ease and watched the little miracle that never failed to win his admiration as his stalk reached its full girth. He glanced up at Nurse Bell's face and saw only an expression of concentration – if his little miracle impressed her, she certainly gave no sign of it. She was in her mid-twenties, he guessed, with dark brown hair under her white-starched cap and a thin body inside her uniform.

'Are you a film star, Mr Castlemaine?' she asked. 'Most of our patients are.'

'Yes, I am,' he answered proudly, 'I've come from Berlin to star in the big new Ignaz International movie.'

'I love the movies,' she said, looking him in the face at last, 'I go two or three times a week. Your injury looks angry – it must have been very painful at the time.'

'At the time,' said Hugo, smiling at her in the way no woman had ever yet been able to resist, 'I didn't even notice it. It was another strong sensation on top of those I was already experiencing.'

'Do you like strong sensations, Mr Castlemaine?'

'Oh yes,' he said softly, feeling his stem twitch in her grip.

She scooped more of the cream from the jar and spread it the length of his stilt. This time she did not rub it in with her finger-tips – she clasped him full-handed and massaged it in with firm up and down strokes. A faint pink glow had appeared on her cheeks.

'The doctor will tell you to rest it for a week,' she said, and gave him a little grin, 'otherwise you will chafe the skin and slow down the healing.'

'A week – impossible!' Hugo exclaimed. 'If I go for a day without making love I get headaches and feel terrible. What on earth shall I do?'

'Don't let on that I said so,' she whispered, her cheeks a brighter pink now, 'but you can make love to yourself with

107

your hand as long as you're careful not to cause any more damage.'

Hugo was certain that the treatment was long since complete and she was deliberately stimulating him for her own reasons. Perhaps she wanted to be in films, perhaps she wanted money, perhaps she liked to play with men's pommels, perhaps she had fallen in love with him at first sight – what did it matter so long as she finished what she had started?

In the event, she took him all the way, her clasped hand sliding up and down his throbbing stalk, until his loins lifted off the couch and she put her free hand quickly over his mouth to stifle any cry that might reach the adjoining room. Hugo's shaking hand found its way between her knees and up her white uniform, but she clamped her thighs together to stop him reaching her plum. Almost before he had expelled his last drop, she wiped him with cotton-wool, pulled his shirt down over his swollen part and helped him to sit up on the side of the examination couch.

'Get dressed, please, Mr Castlemaine. Dr Prosz is waiting for you in his office.'

'Dear pretty, clever, kind-hearted Nurse Bell – do you give private treatments?' Hugo asked, fairly sure of the answer.

'The doctor sends me out to special patients who need treatment at home,' she answered, confirming his conclusions.

Theodor Prosz was at his desk, making notes in a black-bound book. He took off his tortoise-shell reading-glasses and waved Hugo to a chair with them.

'I hope you are a little more comfortable now,' he said, 'I have written you a prescription for the cream.'

'I am afraid of blood-poisoning unless the treatment is right,' said Hugo. 'Is it possible that Nurse Bell could visit me to make sure – for a few days at least?'

'You are wise to take the matter seriously,' Prosz replied, rubbing the bridge of his nose, 'I once had a patient who suffered much the same injury. He was too ashamed to seek proper treatment in time and eventually it became necessary to amputate.'

'My God – what women do to men!' Hugo exclaimed.

'To be accurate, it was his boy-friend who did it to him, Mr Castlemaine. His girl-friend left him and his wife sued for divorce.'

'You've put a thought into my head, doctor – perhaps Ambrose Howard was shot by a boy-friend and not by a woman, as everyone assumes.'

Dr Prosz shook his head solemnly.

'Ambrose Howard was my patient for years,' he said, 'he was a fine man, a gentleman of the old school. Normally I would not talk about him, of course, but his private life has been thrust into the public domain by his tragic death. He was interested in women – exclusively and excessively. His problem was satyriasis.'

'What's that?' Hugo asked in alarm.

'A condition of overpowering and obsessive sexual desire. In women it is called nymphomania and in men satyriasis.'

'I think I suffer from the same thing, doctor. Is it dangerous?'

'In my experience most film stars suffer from this condition. We might almost call it an occupational hazard. Usually it is of no significance, but for poor Ambrose it proved fatal.'

'You mean that he was shot by a certain important person whose wife he had made love to?'

'Nothing of the sort. He ended his own life. I will be frank with you – the most important thing in his life was his potency and when that failed him, his self-esteem was destroyed and he thought life no longer worth living.'

'Most people believe that he was murdered,' Hugo pointed out.

'What nonsense! I was present at the autopsy. There were powder-burns on his skin which showed that the muzzle of the gun had been pressed to his chest when it was fired. Murderers fire from a safe distance away, suicides hold the gun tightly to themselves. And, of course, he left a note.'

'I've heard of this so-called note in the back of a film-script,' said Hugo, smiling derisively. 'Forgive my asking, but have you attended many suicides?'

'Far too many!' Prosz answered sadly. 'Film stars are very prone to self-destruction. Eleven of my patients have put an end to their lives in the past four years, including Ambrose.'

'By shooting?'

'No, that is very rare. Mainly it is by an over-dose of sleeping-pills. One of them crashed his automobile deliberately, two sat in their closed vehicles with a hose-pipe to the exhaust. But for the fact that the person who found Ambrose picked up the revolver, the case would be closed by now.'

'Yes, what problems Thelma caused when she picked up that gun,' said Hugo.

'You know it was Miss Baxter? She told you herself, I suppose. You will also know then that he died naked in front of a full-length mirror – the classic Narcissistic suicide setting.'

'Did he consult you about his so-called problem?' Hugo asked, wondering how far the limits of medical confidentiality could be stretched and why Dr Prosz was prepared to stretch them at all.

'For some months before his death. And this may surprise you, but he came to see me on the morning of the day he died and he was in a depressed frame of mind. He told me he'd been at a party with two women friends and another man a day or two before and he had been completely incapable.'

Hugo maintained a look of interest, though he did not believe a word of what Prosz was saying and he put out a morsel of bait to see if he caught anything.

'Something else happened after he saw you which you should know,' he told the doctor. 'The evening it happened he was visited by a very pretty young woman whose name it would be discourteous to mention. She claims he tried to make love to her and failed. She left him getting drunk.'

'Yes, the autopsy revealed large quantities of alcohol.

110

Thank you for the information you have given me – another failure would have given him the final push over the edge.'

'I suppose you mentioned the problem of his wilting stem to the police?' Hugo enquired, certain what the answer was.

'Oh, yes indeed! It is, after all, the motive for his suicide. They are trying to keep it out of the newspapers, out of respect for his memory.'

'Naturally,' said Hugo, trying hard not to let his disbelief show. 'Well, thank you for your assistance, doctor. I am sure I shall make a complete recovery in your care.'

'I will arrange for Nurse Bell to call at your home at nine in the morning and nine in the evening to continue your treatment,' said Prosz, scribbling on his note-pad. 'You will be safe in her capable hands and you may trust her absolutely to do her best for you.'

'I'm sure of it,' Hugo said, grinning as he stood up and held out his hand.

'Call on me any time, night or day,' said Theodor Prosz, shaking his hand. 'Incidentally, I bill monthly.'

Chapter 7

Mourners at a funeral

The night before Ambrose's funeral Hugo took Thelma to dinner at La Belle France. He would rather have taken Connie, but he had been unable to reach her since the night she had got drunk and Dr Prosz had been sent for. Telephone calls to her house were answered by the maid, whose message was that Miss Young was staying with friends at the beach. This, he found on enquiry, meant Santa Monica, but there the information ended.

Thelma was calm and in control of herself, from which Hugo concluded that whatever had originally been between her and Ambrose had changed long before his death into friendship and an almost family affection. For dinner she wore a strapless evening frock of poppy-red satin moire, as if to emphasise that she was no longer in mourning. It made her full breasts look very prominent and bare, and the green emerald pendant hanging between them drew attention by jiggling and sparkling to her movements.

'Connie's staying with Jake and Audrey Callan at their beach house,' she explained in answer to his question. 'You can call her there if you want to.'

'Why has she gone there?'

'Ambrose's death hit her very hard. She wants to get away from everyone for a while.'

'I did not know that she was so devoted to him. I thought you were, but not Connie.'

112

'Ambrose and I were like brother and sister,' Thelma surprised him by saying, 'with Connie it went a lot deeper.'

'Brother and sister! After what you and he did together?'

'We liked to fool around together, and we both fooled around with other people as well. He was my dearest friend and I miss him. For Connie he was more than that – I guess she needed somebody older to love and admire, never having known her own father.'

'Just like Norma Gilbert, you mean? Her father died when she was a small child, I have been told.'

'All that little bitch ever wanted from Ambrose was a boost for her career,' Thelma snapped back at him. 'For that she'd open her legs anytime. And when he turned her down for his new movie, she shot him!'

'Not so loud, please! I know what you think of her. But there is something I want to ask you – I've been told by two people that Ambrose couldn't do it with women any more.'

'That's crazy!' she exclaimed, her blue eyes round with amazement. 'Who told you that?'

'Dr Theodor Prosz claims he was treating Ambrose for it and Oskar Brandenstein says he has some sort of evidence he bribed out of a policeman on the case.'

'Two of the biggest phonies in Hollywood!' Thelma exclaimed angrily, 'Theodor is as much on the studio payroll as Oskar and they're both backing up Ignaz's cover-up for Norma Gilbert.'

'Mr Castlemaine,' said a waiter's voice at Hugo's elbow, 'there's a message for you – Mr Chataway is at that table by the wall and would like to join you for a few moments. He asked me to say that he's not looking for trouble.'

Hugo nodded to the waiter, grinned at Thelma, and stood up and pushed his chair back as Chester approached, just in case. But Chester was sober, or nearly so, and Lily looked like a big blonde doll in pink, with a sash round her tiny waist.

'I'm man enough to apologise when I'm in the wrong,' said Chester, holding out his hand to Hugo. 'Shake hands and let's wipe the slate clean.'

113

Hugo shook hands and invited Chester and Lily to sit down.

'I made a fool of myself,' said Chester, planting his elbows on the table, 'some louse took advantage of Lily at Oskar's party and I thought it was you and took a swing at you.'

'I hope I didn't hurt you too much when I swung back,' said Hugo. 'What made you think I did anything to Miss Lily?'

'I found her passed out in a bedroom with her clothes round her neck and her panties ripped off. Somebody told me he saw you carrying her in – what else could I think? She couldn't remember much of anything at first, but it's pretty well come back to her now. She was wandering about upstairs drunk and she remembers you helping her into a room to lie down. It was after you'd left her to sleep it off that she was interfered with.'

'Does she remember who it was?' Hugo asked, not daring to look Lily in the face.

'She remembers all right – it was one of the waiters!'

'That's right,' Lily confirmed. 'It was a waiter.'

'She thinks he only gave her a good feeling up,' said Chester, 'but I don't know . . . she was so drunk he could have got it up her while she was passed out. I've chewed out the head man at the catering company, but the trouble is they hire casual staff for parties and so I didn't get anywhere.'

'Maybe it's just as well,' said Thelma tartly, 'with your temper there'd be another death, and one's enough.'

'It's Lily's birthday next week,' said Chester, ignoring her remark. 'You're both invited. Saturday, starting about midday.'

After dinner Hugo took Thelma back to his new apartment and while they were resting between bouts of lovemaking, she said something that made him laugh.

'The jail-bait kid was trying to feel you under the table. I guess it's true after all that you diddled her.'

'Not I,' said Hugo, 'but you're right about her hand

114

under the table. How old do you suppose she'll be on this coming birthday?'

'Seventeen, maybe. Chester's been kicking up such a rumpus that everybody wants to know who slipped it to Lily while she was out cold. Tyler Carson's running a book on who did it – you're favourite at five to two on.'

'I don't understand that,' said Hugo, and Thelma explained the odds to him.

'Did you bet on me?' he asked, rolling towards her to nuzzle her pumpkins.

'No, I didn't think you'd be up to it so soon after fooling around with me. I've got a hundred dollars riding on Ted Moran – he's got a nasty streak. The second favourite after you was Ambrose.'

The next morning at eleven Hugo made his way to the Rosedale Funeral Home, not knowing what to expect. Long-faced attendants in black ushered him into a large and softly-lit room with fake oak panelling and equally fake stained glass windows. Organ music half-covered the conversation of the assembled mourners. Ambrose Howard was on show in a handsome open coffin. The undertakers had dressed him in a black swallow-tail, a dove-grey stock and striped grey trousers, as if he were attending a wedding rather than the more solemn occasion in hand. His hair was sleeked back, his thin moustache neatly trimmed, and his face so well made up that he could almost have been asleep in his white satin padded box.

There were at least a hundred people in the room, all in deepest black, and Stefan Ignaz stood near the head of the coffin, very much in charge of the proceedings. He welcomed Hugo with a nod and a brief hand-shake and introduced him to his breathtakingly beautiful young wife Virginia. Hugo gazed into her violet eyes and when she smiled her acknowledgment of his delicate kiss on her hand, he almost forgot that he was secretly half in love with Connie Young.

He went to find Thelma and squeezed her black-gloved hand in comfort and affection. The famous Baxter bosom he had enjoyed to the full only a few hours before was now

115

chastely covered, though not concealed, by a high-necked and long-sleeved black frock with spiral patterns of jet beads sewn on the bodice.

He exchanged no more than a few words with Thelma before Connie arrived, supported by a man Hugo did not know and followed by a woman whose black coat-frock was a perfect setting for her diamond bracelets and choker. Ignaz greeted Connie with an avuncular kiss and stood beside her with a protective arm round her shoulders while she stared down at Ambrose's composed features. She put a single long-stemmed rose into the coffin, crossed herself and moved away, dabbing her eyes with a tiny lace-edged handkerchief.

'Is that Jake Callan?' Hugo asked. 'What does he do?'

'His old man owns half the oil wells in California and Jake helps him spend the money. Audrey is his third or fourth wife, I forget which.'

'Are he and Connie lovers?'

Thelma looked at him oddly and, before she could answer him, Connie saw her and came across the room, followed by the Callans. She and Thelma kissed and then, to Hugo's delight, she put her small black-gloved hands on his shoulders and kissed his cheek too. There was no time to say anything before she was introducing her friends and almost immediately Oskar arrived and captured all attention by his bizarre appearance. For so melancholy an occasion he had given up his riding-breeches and boots in favour of a frock-coat of a kind Hugo thought had vanished for ever. The effect of his tightly-buttoned black coat and his shining bald head was to make him look like a comical vulture and Hugo was not the only one who suppressed a giggle.

Norma Gilbert was leaning on Oskar's arm and he led her by slow steps towards the coffin. She wore a dramatic knee-length frock of finest black silk and a long rope of pearls hanging down over her small but perfectly-shaped bosom. Her hat had a little veil that did not hide her face from the newspaper photographers waiting outside, and she carried a bouquet of white lilies. Even before Stefan

116

Ignaz could take her hand, she uttered a heart-broken sob loud enough to attract the attention of everyone in the room and sank gracefully to her knees by the coffin, her hands together in prayer and her tear-filled eyes raised towards the Almighty – or at least towards the ceiling.

'Look at that little bitch!' Thelma exclaimed, 'I've a good mind to go over there and kick her ass!'

'Me too!' said Connie. 'Who does she think she is – his fiancée?'

She and Thelma looked at each other and smiled wanly. Hugo drew their attention to the fact that Norma's mourning frock was so closely fitted that it outlined her body more revealingly than even a swim-suit would.

'I'll be damned if she isn't trying to get Stefan hot for her!' said Connie, her eyebrows arching up her forehead. 'Look at the way he's staring at her!'

'And look at the way Virginia is staring at him,' said Thelma. 'Maybe she'll kick that female rattle-snake for us.'

Ignaz stooped to put his hand under Norma's arm and raise her to her feet, whispering to her.

'Is he feeling her lollops? I can't see from here,' Thelma said in a voice loud enough to be heard by half the room.

'I think so,' Connie answered at once. 'You can see the bulge in his trousers – his indicator's rising.'

'Are there any of Ambrose's family here?' Hugo asked to divert the two women from their pet hate.

'Nobody could find any,' said Thelma, 'I guess there must be some in England, but nobody knows where to look. The studio's taking care of the arrangements.'

Oskar in his antique frock-coat came over to kiss the ladies' hands.

'What an actress Norma is!' he said heartily. 'I swear I saw real tears running down her cheeks!'

Connie and Thelma stared at him with hostility and turned away to talk to each other.

'Hugo, my boy – I have acquired something outrageous – come to lunch with me when this circus is over.'

'I'm riding with Thelma and I've promised to take her

117

to lunch afterwards. She may be able to persuade Connie to come with us.'

'Forget about Connie – she is not for you. And what I have to show you is not for Thelma's eyes.'

In the event, the arrangements were changed. Thelma decided to ride with Connie in the Callan's limousine and was going back to Santa Monica with her after the funeral. Hugo was free to accept Oskar's invitation and go with him and the Gilberts. About eleven thirty the Funeral Home attendants marshalled the assembly out to the limousines lining the street outside so that they could screw down the lid of Ambrose's coffin and wheel it out to the waiting hearse. Hugo had never before seen so many flowers – somewhere among the mountain of wreathes, crosses, hearts, pillows, sprays and other floral tributes was the one he had sent, but it would have taken a diligent label-reader several hours to pick it out.

There were a great many uniformed policemen holding back the crowds of onlookers who had come not to pay their last respects to Ambrose, of whom they had never heard, but to catch a glimpse of the many film stars attending his funeral. Eventually the long procession started on its way to the Memorial Park Cemetery, Hugo alongside Oskar on the jump-seats of a limousine, facing rearwards to where Norma sat in almost regal dignity beside her mother and tremulously raised a black-gloved little hand from time to time to acknowledge her waving fans on the pavement.

For most of the journey Mildred Gilbert tried to catch Hugo's eye and exchange meaningful glances with him. After one brief look and his standard charming smile in her direction Hugo looked elsewhere and it fell to Oskar to keep the conversation going. The injuries Mildred had inflicted on Hugo's most tender part were barely healed after five days of Nurse Bell's attentions and the memory made him determined to have no more to do with so sharp-toothed a woman. Instead he gave himself up to admiration of her daughter. Whether the stories he had heard of her affairs were true or not, Norma Gilbert had not gained the ridiculous title of *All the World's Sweetheart* without being marvellously attractive.

Her mourning frock had very obviously been designed and made specially for this occasion and was a masterpiece of understated sexuality. It was made of layers of flimsy black silk that clung so closely to her body that her apple-sized breasts and their tiny tips were clearly outlined. It moulded her flat belly and slender thighs so well that Hugo decided to observe her closely when she got out of the limousine, being almost sure that the clinging silk would show the outline of the mound between her legs, and the cheeks of her bottom.

No one knew what religion Ambrose professed, if any, since no one could remember that he had ever said a word on the subject. The studio's decision was that he should have an Episcopalian funeral, on no better grounds than that he had been born in England and the undertaker had confirmed what his women friends knew, that he had not been Jewish. The cemetery was crowded with sightseers, again held back by policemen, so that the hundred or two official guests could stand in the warm sunshine round the flower-covered coffin and listen to the reading of the burial service.

In the second row, screened by those about her, Mildred Gilbert flicked her hand across the front of Hugo's trousers to get his attention and startled him so much that he gasped. When the nearest mourners looked back from him to the coffin, she took hold of his wrist and rubbed his hand against her frock where her thighs joined, to encourage him, while she whispered that she would be at his apartment at eight that evening. He whispered back in great alarm that he had been invited out to dinner and that he would telephone her. After that he held his black Homburg hat over his vital parts like a shield to ward off any further assault by her.

Back at Oskar's mansion in Beverly Hills Hugo stripped off his black jacket and tie and sat on the patio behind the house with a cold drink while Oskar went to change his clothes.

'Amuse yourself with these till I get back,' he said, handing Hugo a thick white envelope.

It contained eight large glossy photographs. Hugo flicked through them in amazement, before he studied each one slowly and in detail, chuckling incredulously at what he saw. The photographs were of Ambrose enjoying intimate moments with various women-friends and they were no mere snapshots, being well-posed, carefully-lit and expertly taken.

The topmost picture showed him in a pullover and checkered trousers, sitting on a sofa with his legs apart so that there was room for Connie to sit cross-legged on the floor between his feet. She was naked and had her back to him and Ambrose was reaching down over her shoulders to clasp an elegant breast in each hand. Hugo looked closely at the neatly-trimmed tuft of curls between her open legs and then at her smiling face – and he sighed. He slipped the picture to the bottom of the pack and smiled to see Thelma in the next one.

She and Ambrose lay naked together on grass, which Hugo took to be the lawn behind Ambrose's house – or maybe Thelma's house next to it. The picture was taken from behind the couple's heads and showed the long perspective down their bodies to where Ambrose's hand lay between Thelma's thighs, two fingers conspicuously inserted in her. She was holding his pointer bolt upright and had exposed its whole head. Hugo guessed that seconds after the picture was taken Ambrose would have rolled onto Thelma's plump belly, well on the way towards his golden moments.

'Dear Thelma,' Hugo said aloud to himself, 'so well-fleshed, so wholesome, so uncomplicated, so enthusiastic, so cooperative – I am very pleased that we have become friends.'

He recognised the celebrated Gale Paget in the next picture, the dark-haired temptress of three or four movies he had seen. She was as naked as Connie and Thelma had been and she was on all fours, her face turned to look over her perfect shoulder at the camera. Ambrose was behind

120

her on his knees, incongruously dressed in full evening attire, white tie, black tails, even a shiny top hat perched above his broadly smiling face.

Ambrose's trousers were undone to let his hard shaft stand out like a broom-handle, its end just touching Gale, as if at the very moment of sinking it into her. It was an indoor scene by artificial lighting and Hugo did not recognise the room from what he could see of it. The carpet on which the smouldering beauty that was Gale Paget (as the publicists usually described her) knelt, looked a good quality Persian and was not what he had seen in Ambrose's sitting-room or bedroom.

There was no such difficulty in placing the setting of the next picture. There was a wall and in the top left of the photograph a corner of the large Beardsley picture which hung in Ambrose's bedroom. A young and sensual-faced platinum blonde had her back to the wall and was holding her frock up round her waist. She wore no knickers and her legs were apart. Ambrose knelt before her, totally naked, his mouth pressed to the light-coloured curls between her thighs. The picture was taken from the side, so that he was in profile and the blonde had turned her head to stick her tongue out at the camera. What gripped Hugo's attention was that Ambrose's upright pole had a ribbon tied round it in a bow.

The ribbon was too light to be black – perhaps it was pink, Hugo thought – and perhaps Ambrose had a penchant for decorating himself with ribbons in this way when he was in a light-hearted mood, for assuredly these photographs had been taken as comical souvenirs. Perhaps the ribbon Connie had removed from his fallen mast in the bath-room had no special meaning at all – black velvet might look very stylish round a pink tail.

It was easy enough to put a name to the platinum blonde with her back pressed to the wall. The same was true of the next picture, in which a very pretty woman, famous for her sentimental roles in movies, was entertaining Ambrose on a leather sofa – probably the very one on which Hugo had himself enjoyed Connie and Thelma that memorable night.

In the picture Ambrose lay on his back and the famous star squatted above him. Once more he had chosen to be inappropriately dressed for what was taking place, confirming Hugo's views that the pictures were intended to be comical rather than erotic. He wore a Fair Isle pullover and what looked like grey flannel trousers, while his partner was naked except for her wrist-watch.

The photograph had been taken from behind and above Ambrose's head and showed his friend's enticingly rounded breasts to good advantage – and Ambrose's stiff prong disappearing up between her splayed thighs. The look on her beautiful face made Hugo catch his breath – her red-painted mouth was open and her eyes were rolling up in her head, as if the cameraman had caught her in the very moment of ecstatic release. Ambrose's face was too near the camera to be in clear focus and his expression was indecipherable. But if that were me embedded in that beautiful body, thought Hugo with a grin, the look on my face would be one of pure bliss.

There were three more photographs. One was of Ambrose washing Norma Gilbert in a bath. She wore a frilly bath-cap and a pert smile, and Ambrose was rubbing creamy soap-suds over her pointed little breasts with the palm of his hand. He was on his knees at the side of the bath, wearing a maid's white apron and nothing else. He was sideways on to the camera, the thin apron sticking out like a tent over his unseen but obviously stiff part. His mouth was open and it looked as if he had been caught at the moment of saying something to Norma. Hugo looked long and hard at Norma's girlish pomegranates and decided that he must have her soon.

The next picture was taken in the same bathroom and was the only ambiguous one so far. It showed Ambrose without his apron, stark naked, and a slightly-built friend in a dark blazer, white trousers and a yachting cap. There was no way Hugo could see to identify the friend or even determine the sex, for he or she was two-thirds turned away from the camera and bent over, with both hands resting on the side of the empty bath, white trousers sagging down

122

round the knees. Ambrose stood close up behind, his spigot well sunk between the cheeks of his friend's bare bottom. The look on his face this time was clear enough – the photographer had caught him at the instant when he delivered his little message of love.

Surely it could only be Norma with him, Hugo told himself, studying the bent-over figure. But if it was, then her hair was well tucked up inside the yachting-cap and her face was away from the camera. Oh, but it must be Norma, he told himself again, Norma disguised as a boy to amuse Ambrose. But there was no way to be sure – because it was taken in the same bathroom the obvious assumption was that it made a set of two with the one of Norma sitting in the bath. And an assumption was all that it was. The picture was ambiguous about which aperture Ambrose was making use of. And if it was Norma, then she was the only girl-friend of whom there were two photographs in the collection.

The final picture was staged in Ambrose's sitting-room – Hugo was certain of that because it showed Ambrose perched on a corner of the blackwood sideboard he had noticed there. He was wearing a light-coloured suit and had a glass in his hand. A round-faced woman in her thirties sat on a leather pouffe in front of him, stripped down to lace-trimmed and almost transparent camiknickers. Ambrose's trousers were unbuttoned and his friend held his long stalk between her fingers, her head bowed over it so that she could touch it with the tip of her out-thrust tongue.

Yes, it's her! Hugo thought, *her initials were on Oskar's list!* And indeed it was the familiar face and body that had thrilled him when he was fifteen and took a girl named Ursula to the cinema in Berlin to play with her bobbins in the dark. And there was the never-to-be-forgotten time when Ursula had put her hand in his trousers and played with him for so long that he had squirted in his underwear while staring transfixed at the face of this famous film star on the screen. Here was photographic proof that she had no inhibitions about entertaining Ambrose, and that gave

123

Hugo strong hope that he could make her acquaintance and persuade her to allow him to transform his adolescent fantasies into adult pleasures.

It seemed that Oskar had found the heat oppressive in his black frock-coat and cravat, for he reappeared in Mexican sandals and a pair of baggy green shorts. He stretched himself out on one of the lounger-chairs on the patio and let the sun shine on his barrel of a chest, where the hair was greying.

'Did you find my pictures amusing?' he asked jovially.

Before Hugo could reply, a manservant in a white jacket brought a tray of sandwiches and a bottle of chilled wine. It seemed sensible to wait until he had poured the wine and gone before saying anything.

'Who had these?' Hugo asked. 'How did you get hold of them?'

'The police found them locked in Ambrose's desk – Ignaz missed them when he searched. My detective friend offered me a set of prints for a small fortune. Sentimental old fool that I am, I couldn't resist snapshots of friends in happy moments.'

'Who do you think took them? It must have been someone Ambrose trusted completely – not to mention the ladies.'

'I thought that was obvious,' said Oskar, munching a sandwich, 'the chauffeur, Hernandez. That's why he ran away – he was afraid he'd be arrested on suspicion of blackmail and murder when his handiwork came to light.'

'These pictures destroy your theory, Oskar. Ambrose performed with some highly celebrated film stars and was proud enough to want photographs of what he could do.'

'We do not know when these pictures were taken,' Oskar pointed out. 'They prove nothing about Ambrose's abilities a week ago.'

'You're hedging,' said Hugo. 'Could he still do it or not?'

Oskar shrugged his bare and heavy shoulders carelessly.

'I never believed the studio line that he shot himself,' he admitted, 'but I do not bite the hand that feeds me lavishly. The suicide note in the script is a forgery and Theodor

124

Prosz has falsified his records to prove that Ambrose was consulting him for a bad case of the droops.'

'And who is the one man powerful enough to order a cover-up on that scale?' Hugo asked rhetorically, but Oskar only shrugged his shoulders again and refilled their glasses with wine.

'Norma Gilbert was here yesterday to resume our discussions on her suitability for the part of Mary Magdalene,' he said, letting his monocle drop from his eye and dangle against his hairy chest.

'She looked so fresh and virginal this morning at the funeral,' said Hugo, 'you would swear that no man has ever laid a finger on her, much less anything else.'

'She has that professional quality to enable her to appear what she is not,' Oskar said. 'We did wonderfully degenerate things together all yesterday afternoon. Between her auditions we even talked a little about the film and about Ambrose, and her account of her final visit to his house differed from the one she told me in my office.'

'Namely?'

'It was nothing she said in words – she's altogether too evasive for that. But in my office I gathered the distinct impression that Ambrose had not been able to make love to her when she offered. Yesterday – maybe because she had forgotten or was relaxed and a little careless after I'd pleasured her – she hinted that he banged her a couple of times and they quarrelled after that when he wouldn't promise her the lead in the new film.'

'In other words, you're coming round to Thelma's view – that Norma shot him.'

'No, I don't believe that. She'd never do anything to risk her career. They quarrelled and she stormed out – I'd bet money on that. Ambrose was shot later that night by someone whose name I will not mention because he pays my wages.'

'Ignaz? You've been talking to Prince Dmytryk, I see.'

'Talk to that idiot? I'd get more sense out of Rin Tin Tin. There's a photograph I haven't shown you yet – come into the house.'

In his study Oskar opened a wall-safe concealed behind an oil painting of nothing much and took out another envelope.

'We both know who that is,' he said, handing Hugo a photograph from the envelope.

It was Virginia Ignaz, kissing Ambrose. They were both naked and lay on the black satin sheets of his bed. Virginia was on her back and had one knee up a little, parting her slender thighs. Hugo noted with rising interest that she was smooth-shaven and bare between them. Ambrose lay on his side and leaned over to press his mouth to hers, his pointer beginning to droop down towards her superb belly.

'And we can guess what they had been doing just before the picture was taken,' Hugo added, 'but her initials were not on the list you showed me. What do you make of that?'

'Perhaps Mrs Ignaz never wears panties and was unable to leave him a souvenir for his collection – but I think it more likely that it was a collection of film stars only. I can think of at least two women with whom Ambrose amused himself – a script-writer and a language coach – whose initials were not on the list either.'

He took the photograph back from Hugo and locked it in the safe.

'Now you know something very dangerous, my boy,' he said affably. 'It would be most unwise to mention what you know about Virginia Ignaz to anyone – that is if you want to stay in Hollywood and be a big movie star.'

'I wish you hadn't shown me that picture,' Hugo complained, 'I don't like other people's secrets.'

'But I do,' said Oskar, 'especially if they are secrets about people so highly placed. From the beginning I had strong suspicions of Stefan Ignaz but I could see no evidence apart from the fact that he destroyed some of Ambrose's papers. So I offered cash to the detective who questioned me and he gave me a copy of the list of initials. As a testimony to Ambrose's drawing-power it was impressive, but it did not implicate Ignaz. So I offered more cash for any further information and obtained the photographs you have seen.'

'But why? The police can draw the same conclusions as you have but they haven't arrested Ignaz.'

'I hope they won't! He's no use to me – or to you – if he's in jail. We want him free and running Ignaz International so that we can make a lot of money and live like Sultans.'

'Then why are you so interested in whether he shot Ambrose or not?'

'Knowledge is power, they say. Who knows what concessions I may be able to extract from him or from Virginia when the investigation is over?'

'Oskar – you are a rogue!' Hugo exclaimed with a laugh. 'What you are suggesting is almost blackmail!'

'The laws of evolution operate in a particularly brutal way in Hollywood,' said Oskar. 'Here the survival of the fittest means exactly that. And I intend to survive and make large amounts of money and enjoy as many pretty girls as my constitution will permit. Let's go into the garden and drink another bottle of wine in the sunshine. Patsy will be back about three and I asked her to bring Sylvie with her. A little nude swimming in the pool would be invigorating and drive all these unhealthy speculations about murder out of our minds.'

'What a sensible man you are, Oskar. Patsy is still staying here with you, then? I'm surprised that you find her so interesting – I never did.'

'That may be, but she is much improved now that I have educated her. It needs a devoted pervert like me to bring out the best in a girl. Have her yourself and see, and I'll ransack Sylvie for a change.'

On the way back to the patio Hugo asked Oskar mockingly for his expert opinion as a *practising pervert* on whether it was Norma Gilbert dressed as a boy in the ambiguous photograph.

'Ah! At last a mystery worthy of a sensible man's attention!' said Oskar, chuckling heartily. 'Do you know, I have examined that picture under the largest magnifying-glass I can find and I am still not sure whether it is a girl or a boy. Or if it is a girl, whether it is our dear Norma.

And if it is Norma, which of her girlish crevices Ambrose is making use of.'

'I incline to the view that it is Norma,' said Hugo, 'Thelma told me that Ambrose once directed Norma in a movie where she was disguised as a boy.'

'Oh yes, but I've seen that movie and you obviously haven't. It's about a pair of sixteen-year-old twins, one a girl and the other a boy. Norma played both twins – but which of the two did Ambrose fall upon and rampage with most gusto, tell me that if you can!'

Chapter 8

Norma offers an explanation

Towards seven in the evening Hugo got back to his fine new apartment after the funeral, agreeably indolent from the attentions of Patsy Sharp by the side of Oskar's swimming pool. Acquainted though he was with the lengths to which budding actors and actresses would go to promote their careers, he was still surprised at the extent to which Patsy had become so submissively attached to Oskar for the sake of a bit-part in *The Soul of Mary Magdalene* as the script he had been sent informed him that the movie was now called.

Naturally the title could change a dozen times before the movie was made, if the Ignaz International publicity department thought of anything considered an improvement. Not that the title mattered much, in Hugo's opinion – big and garish posters of half-naked women outside the cinemas and some slightly shocked comment in newspapers would pull in the audiences and make Ignaz a richer and happier man, and consolidate Hugo's career in Hollywood.

His plan for the evening was to change his black suit for something more casual, eat and see Ignaz International's newly released film starring Chester Chataway and Gale Paget. It would be mildly entertaining to watch whisky-raddled Chester, under a thick layer of make-up, cavorting like a twenty-year-old and struggling to make his love scenes with the delectable Gale convincing. More to the point, Hugo wanted to see Gale Paget's acting technique, there being in his reasoning a good chance that she might be cast as Mary Magdalene. He was pretty sure that Oskar was only playing with Norma Gilbert, and after her the studio's next top stars were Connie Young and Gale Paget.

Naturally, he hoped that Connie would get the part so that they could be together right through the shooting. Ambrose had more or less promised it to her, but that was no guarantee that Oskar would see things the same way. Indeed, he might drop her for no better reason than that his predecessor as director had wanted her. If he did, then in Hugo's view, Gale Paget was the next logical choice. He had seen her on the screen and in person that morning at the funeral, where she had looked extremely beautiful in black lace. He had also seen the private photograph of her down on her hands and knees naked for Ambrose. Evidently she was not averse to a frolic and, given an opportunity, Hugo would be delighted to frolic with her.

His plans for the evening changed when the doorman gave him a letter that had been delivered by special messenger that afternoon. The envelope was large and square in shape, made of thick lilac-tinted paper, and scented accordingly. In the lift up to his penthouse Hugo unfolded the thick sheet of paper inside. At the top there was an elaborate monogram made up of the letters N and G interlaced.

'Dear Mr Castlemaine,' he read, 'though I hesitate to address you as *Dear Hugo* on so slight an acquaintance, yet I have the strangest feeling that I can trust you – perhaps you will sneer at my trusting nature, but at poor Mr Howard's funeral today you made such an impression on me as a man of decent feelings and of moral strength – not another of the cynical pack of curs who infest the motion picture business – someone to whom a young girl can turn in her bewilderment of spirit and her deep and tragic sense of loss for one of the finest men who ever drew breath, and so I trust that you will not think it presumptuous of me or forward if I pour out my heart to you so soon after meeting and in circumstances which were heart-breaking for me, whatever others thought – but there are so few I can have any confidence in not to betray and cheat me for their own selfish purposes, as I have come to know all too well and to my bitter cost – but I know that I can appeal to you in the surety that you will not fail me.'

It was signed, with a flourish, 'Norma Gilbert' and she had scrawled a Beverly Hills telephone number in brackets.

In his apartment Hugo shed his jacket, drank a cold beer and read through Norma's letter again, wondering what she wanted, before telephoning the number. A maid answered and put him through when she knew who he was.

'Oh, Mr Castlemaine,' Norma said in the slightly breathless voice that had endeared her to millions of movie fans, 'is it really you?'

'Yes, it's Hugo,' he replied, making his voice manly and confident, 'I've only just received your note or I would have called you before.'

'I hope you aren't offended,' she said tremulously. 'It's so very hard for a girl on her own to know what to do for best.'

'I was touched by what you wrote,' Hugo said untruthfully. 'If there is anything I can do to be of service, please ask.'

'You can't imagine how comforting it is to hear you say that, Hugo,' she said, making his name sound like a chaste caress.

'Let me take you to dinner so that we can talk things over,' he suggested, only to hear her utter a little gasp of horror.

'I can't be seen in public on the day of Mr Howard's funeral,' she told him, clearly wounded by his lack of sensitivity in suggesting dinner. 'And yet life must go on – Mr Howard would be the first to say that if he were still with us – I must pick up the threads of my life, even though my heart is aching.'

She's remembering lines from some terrible movie, thought Hugo. He added to the bathos by telling Norma she must be brave, though it meant smiling through her tears.

'What was that?' she asked sharply, and he knew he had laid it on too thick. But after a pause she spoke softly again.

'You could come over here,' she said, 'my house-keeper can fix something for us to eat. Would you like that?'

'I'll be with you in forty-five minutes,' he promised and ran for the shower, shedding his clothes on the way.

Norma's house was much as he expected it to be – a flamboyant architectural imposture that was grotesquely large for one person. When Oskar rented this sort of house it was as a sardonic gibe at Hollywood values, but in Norma's scheme of things this was the proper way for a film-star to live. The statutory Mexican maid met him at the door and conducted him into Norma's presence in a drawing-room large enough to house an airplane and containing enough expensive furniture to stock a department store.

Hugo had chosen a cream silk shirt and a new olive-green jacket in nubbly tweed as suitably romantic and dashing for an informal meal that might lead on to something more exciting. He was therefore dismayed to see that Norma was still in the black frock and pearls she had worn at the funeral that morning. She stood up and offered her hand, her brown eyes filled with gentle reproach at his lapse of good taste. Hugo carried the moment off by bowing gracefully over her hand and kissing it.

'Oh, Hugo,' she breathed, forgiveness in her tone.

She drew him down to sit by her on a pink and grey sofa in front of a marble fire-place big enough to roast an ox in and told her maid to bring him a drink and a glass of iced tea for herself, explaining to Hugo that she had never in her life touched alcohol.

'When I saw your tears at the Funeral Home I realised how devoted you were to Ambrose,' said Hugo, trying to move things forward.

'I have dedicated this day entirely to him, as a tribute to his greatness of spirit and his genius,' she murmured.

Not to mention his appetite for women, thought Hugo, and his ingenuity in amusing them.

'I loved Mr Howard deeply,' Norma continued, 'I loved

him with all the admiration a young girl naturally feels for a man of his talent and position. From the very first movie he directed me in, he was like a father to me.'

Hugo thought of Oskar's photographs and reflected that while many fathers bath their daughters when they are small, very few did so after they were grown up. And when Norma stepped from the bath and Ambrose removed his apron, he had most surely done very unpaternal things to her clean little body.

'What has happened has been a sad loss for you,' Hugo said, secretly astonished by Norma's capacity for deception, even though she had been a star since she was ten years old.

'That's why these vicious rumours hurt me so much, Hugo – how can people be so evil-minded?'

'What rumours do you mean?'

'You must have heard them. You are trying to shield me from further hurt and I respect you for that. But the damage is done and I will not flinch from these disgusting slanders.'

'You mean . . .' he prompted, not at all sure what he was supposed to be protecting her from.

'Wicked and depraved people are spreading the lie that Mr Howard had a collection of ladies' garments,' she said, and blushed furiously.

Hugo shook his head in pretended sadness that anyone could be so depraved as to invent so preposterous a tale. He told Norma that he had heard the rumour but refused to believe it.

'I knew you were clean and decent!' she exclaimed, her eyes shining and her small hand laid trustingly on his sleeve. 'The vulgar lie that there was something belonging to me in Mr Howard's so-called collection is absolutely beyond belief.'

'Absolutely,' Hugo agreed, thinking what a polite young lady she was to continue to call Ambrose *Mr Howard* after all the times he had slipped it to her – maybe even by the backdoor if that was her disguised as a boy in Oskar's photograph. He wondered why she wanted to talk to him about Ambrose's box of knickers.

'I can guess how this nasty lie started,' she told him, her voice desolate with the misery of being misunderstood and slandered by wrongdoers.

'Can you?' Hugo asked, most anxious to hear how she would explain away the presence of her underwear in Ambrose's house.

'We were at the premiere of *Orphans and Strangers* and I was so overcome by the beauty of the sentiments that I had to wipe away a tear,' and she pulled from her close-fitting sleeve a tiny handkerchief edged with black lace to demonstrate what she meant. 'Mr Howard in his gentle way took it from me and gave me his own big white hankie to dry my eyes.'

'That was very kind of him,' said Hugo, straight-faced.

'After the premiere we all went on to Mr Ignaz's party. I forgot to give Mr Howard's hankie back to him and he must have forgotten to return mine. It had my initials embroidered on it. That's what started this evil slander — my poor little hankie in Mr Howard's house.'

Hugo had been right about Norma's black frock at the funeral. Now he was sitting closer to her than in the limousine to the cemetery, he was more sure than ever that she was wearing nothing at all under it apart from her black silk stockings. The buds of her little dumplings showed through the fine material and, down between her uncrossed legs, a darker shadow was visible through the flimsy silk.

'How disgraceful that innocent events can be seized upon and distorted by ill-natured gossip,' he said, deciding to liven up the conversation. 'Your handkerchief has been changed into a pair of silk knickers in the story that is being circulated.'

Norma gasped in embarrassment and blushed at his words, her hand clutching his sleeve for support.

'Vile as that rumour is,' he went on, enjoying her silent-screen reactions, 'there is an even viler one going around.'

'Oh, no!' she moaned, her chin trembling and her eyes

134

filling with tears. She took a deep breath, faced him bravely and asked him to spare her nothing.

'It is being said that the police found photographs,' he said, 'photographs of Ambrose with some of the stars who were his special friends. It is said that they are very private and personal pictures, not the sort that should ever be seen by strangers.'

A spot of bright colour had appeared in the centre of Norma's otherwise pale cheeks.

'Who told you this monstrous lie?' she asked faintly.

'It's all round the studio, Norma,' he said untruthfully.

'Does anyone know the names of the women who are supposed to be in these photographs?'

'A lot of names are being mentioned – all of them stars, and not all at Ignaz International. Three that keep coming up are Thelma Baxter, Connie Young and you.'

'But those two have terrible reputations!' Norma exclaimed in outrage. 'How can anybody link my name with theirs!'

'How indeed?' said Hugo, enchanted by the extent of her hypocrisy. 'I would never have believed such a thing myself – except that I have seen the picture of you, dear Norma.'

She gave a long sigh, redolent of martyrdom.

'Betrayed yet again!' she said. 'When will I learn not to trust people? I was given a firm assurance that any photographs of me that were found would never be mentioned – very firm assurances from a person in a very responsible job.'

'Alas, someone paid another policeman more to give him copies of the pictures than you paid to have them suppressed. I imagine you were questioned very thoroughly when the photographs came to light – and your *hankie* with the initials.'

'The police are satisfied that I did not shoot him.'

'You were at his house earlier that evening, I know that. But you have an alibi for later on, which means you spent the night with someone else. I wonder who it was?'

'It's none of your business,' she retorted, losing her

135

demure tone, 'but if you must know, I was with Prince Dmytryk.'

Hugo smiled at her in his friendliest manner and told her he knew for certain that the Prince was with another woman that night.

'You know a lot that doesn't concern you,' Norma answered. 'Well then, I was with someone else and I had no choice but to tell the police to avoid being arrested for murder. Did you see all the photographs?'

'How many were there?'

'About a dozen altogether,' she answered.

Hugo wondered whether Oskar had more than he had shown him or whether the member of the Police Department he bought them from had kept the rest back to sell him later on.

'There was a charming picture of you being bathed by Ambrose,' he said, 'and another of you dressed up as a boy.'

He waited to see if she confirmed his guess. She blushed deeply.

'It was wrong and foolish of me to let Mr Howard talk me into having photographs taken. But I was so fond of him and he was so persuasive.'

Hugo grinned and put an arm round Norma's waist to pull her close to him while he kissed her blushing cheek and caressed her little breasts through the black silk of her frock.

'You look delicious sitting in the bath,' he said. 'Was it the chauffeur who took them?'

'Yes, Luis Hernandez,' she said a little breathlessly, doing nothing to prevent his advances. 'He had to run away because he thought he'd be blamed.'

'But how did he know that Ambrose had been shot? Was he at the house when you were there?'

'No, Ambrose was working at home on the script and he'd given Luis the evening off. Mr Moran sent for him when he got to the house and saw what had happened – after Thelma called him for help, I mean.'

'Moran gave him money to disappear?'

136

'I don't know, but I guess so.'

Norma's little dumplings were extremely pleasant to play with, Hugo considered. That she was letting him do as he wished indicated that she wasn't ready yet to tell him what she wanted – and it was nothing to do with making love, he was sure.

'Come with me, Hugo,' she said, and slipped from his hold.

She stood up and tugged him to his feet, to lead him by the hand out of the immense drawing-room, across the Spanish-tiled hall and into a smaller room. In a man's house it would have been called the study and be furnished with an ornate desk. Norma's had no such thing, just a burgundy-red leather chesterfield and half a dozen matching chairs, grouped round an elaborately-carved mahogany chimney-piece in which a sweet-smelling log-fire blazed cheerfully.

The focus of attention of the room was not the fire-place but a big black bear-skin lying in front of it on the polished wood floor. The head was attached, glass eyes reflecting the fire in golden glints, and awesome fangs showed between the open jaws. Norma took her shoes off and smiled shyly at Hugo while she undid her frock above the hip and pulled it slowly up and over her head.

She was not as naked as Hugo had thought. The plaything between her girlishly slim thighs was modestly concealed in a black silk *cache-sexe* held in place by a thin elastic string curving up over her narrow hips. She had left her rope of pearls on and it hung between bare little breasts, almost to her tiny dimple of a belly-button.

'You are even more enchanting than your fans can imagine,' said Hugo, knowing it pleased stars as much to hear their fans mentioned as their personal beauty.

Norma smiled at him very graciously for that and lay down on her side on the thick black bear-skin, her back to the fire.

'I call this my den,' she said, 'do you like it?'

Without giving the room a second glance Hugo told her that he thought it very distinguished. A look of dismay

137

flitted across her face when she saw that he was undressing himself, then she blushed again and averted her eyes. Hugo lay down naked, facing her, and put a hand lightly on her shoulder.

'Why have you taken off your clothes?' she asked, a tiny frown on her face. 'Surely you don't think I would encourage any familiarity between us? I am engaged to be married to Prince Dmytryk,' and she waved before his eyes a hand on which was a ring set with diamonds the size of larks' eggs.

Like mother, like daughter, thought Hugo, almost laughing. They say *No, no*! while they're opening their legs for you! He hoped that Norma would be less strenuous than her mother had been — for one thing he wanted no more painful bites on his extension and, for another, he had used up much of his stamina on Patsy that afternoon.

'You must not leap to conclusions,' he said, caressing the delicate pink bud of Norma's right breast with a finger-tip, 'I have taken off my clothes as a symbolic gesture — to show you that I have no secrets from you. I am sure the same motive was in your mind when you undressed.'

'I did it to show you that I trust you, Hugo,' she murmured, staring down at his belly where his stiff pointer was nudging at her, 'I regard you as a true friend — that's the only reason I have for letting you see me like this.'

'I am honoured,' he said, moving closer to her on the bear-skin to reach over her hip and fondle the bare cheeks of her little bottom. 'Very honoured to be allowed the same privilege as Ambrose.'

'But can you ever be as good and true a friend to me as he was?' she sighed wistfully. 'Oh, if only I thought so!'

'He was *very* privileged,' said Hugo. 'You sat in his bath while he rubbed scented soap over your beautiful little bundles and down between your legs. You could see how excited that made him in the photograph.'

Norma laid a soft hand against his face and touched her lips to his in a warm little kiss.

'Would you like to bath me, Hugo?' she whispered. 'I've

138

got a much bigger bath here than his – there's easily room for both of us in it together while you wash me all over.'

Hugo's stilt jerked against her warm belly at the thought. She glanced down to see what was pressing against her and took it loosely in the hand with the engagement ring, and he saw that she was left-handed – something he had not noticed before. He eased a hand between her thighs and she didn't resist – nor did she make it easy for him by parting her legs.

'Yes, I'd like to bath you, Norma,' he said.

His hand slid along the smooth skin above her stocking-top until his thumb lay against the fragment of black silk that covered her soft little purse.

'Would you wear boy's clothes for me too?' he asked, pushing his questions as far as he could while the mood was right.

'To prove that I trust you, yes,' she whispered, her hand squeezing his hard spout, 'but you would have to promise not to get any wrong ideas.'

'I wouldn't, I promise you,' he said, 'you must have been terribly shocked when Ambrose let himself· get carried away.'

'I was so dumbfounded I couldn't even scream,' she breathed, her face crimson, 'I thought he wanted a photograph as a sort of keep-sake to remind him of a movie he directed me in where I acted a boy's part.'

Hugo's thumb stroked her fleshy petals through the thin silk that modestly concealed them from sight while he murmured with a voice full of sympathy *My poor darling Norma*!

'It was so unexpected,' Norma gasped, her blue eyes closed, 'Luis was grinning at me over the camera and without a word of warning Mr Howard made me bend over and yanked my trousers down.'

Hugo grinned broadly as Norma hid her pink face against his bare shoulder.

'But you forgave him?' he asked, his thumb under the edge of her little *cache-sexe* at last to stroke the pouting lips he found there. He could feel very little in the way of curls

139

between Norma's legs – only a light fluff under the ball of his thumb.

'I forgave him because I was so very fond of him. He fascinated me, though at times he shocked me.'

'The first time being when you were only a girl and he undid his trousers and showed you his tail,' said Hugo, determined to establish the truth or falsity of as many as possible of the stories he had been told about Ambrose.

'Who told you that?' she gasped, her face still pressed to his shoulder.

'Two people mentioned it separately. There seems to be no privacy in Hollywood.'

'Well, they were both wrong, whoever they were,' said Norma, and she raised her head to stare Hugo boldly in the face, 'I wasn't in the least shocked the first time Mr Howard did that – it was my mother who pretended to be shocked when some busybody told her.'

'She had reason to be shocked, surely. How old were you at the time?'

'Thirteen – and Mr Howard wasn't the first to show me his lollipop. I was a very pretty girl.'

'And you've grown into a marvellously beautiful woman.' said Hugo, his mind busy with this new information, 'I suppose that Chester must have been the first?'

'Yes, in his dressing-room on the Ignaz International lot. He was in front of a big make-up mirror and when he saw me come in he turned his chair round and got it out. Mother had brought me up so strictly that I thought boys and girls were the same down there. I didn't know what it was he was showing me and he grinned when he saw how interested I was and jerked it up and down in his hand.'

'And you ran away.'

'No,' she whispered, her fingers gliding gently along Hugo's spindle, 'I stood there and watched him. And after a while he went red in the face and started saying *Oh, oh, oh*, very fast. He . . . well, I guess you know what happened then.'

'I don't believe it!' Hugo exclaimed with a chuckle, his

140

thumb pressing gently between the warm lips under her silken *cache-sexe*.

'After he was through he winked at me and said come back tomorrow.'

'And did you?' Hugo asked, fascinated by what she was telling him while her fingers massaged his shaft firmly enough to make it quiver pleasurably.

'I couldn't help myself,' she murmured, no longer hiding her face but looking at him with an expression of innocent trust, 'I had to go back and watch him do it again the next day. I didn't understand what he was doing, so I asked Mr Howard about it because I knew he would explain.'

'If you were so completely innocent, why didn't you ask your mother?'

'She was always telling me I mustn't let boys touch me on the chest or between the legs because it was sinful, so I guessed she wouldn't approve of what Chester was doing.'

'But you could trust Ambrose?'

'Always! When I told him about Chester he laughed and got his own lollipop out and let me hold it while he explained the difference between girls and boys. And then he took my panties down and felt me up till I went off pop. After that he was my idol and I'd do anything for him.'

'Chester must have been disappointed to lose your interest.'

'But he didn't!' Norma exclaimed, surprised by his failure to understand, 'I went to his dressing-room every day while we were shooting that movie, as well as to Mr Howard's.'

'What a remarkable girl you were,' said Hugo. 'No doubt Chester had your panties down too.'

'Because I trust you I'll tell you a big secret, and you have to promise never to repeat it.'

'I promise.'

'Chester was the man I gave my virginity to. I fell madly in love with him the first time I saw him on the screen and to surrender my maidenhood to him was the proudest moment of my life. Mother thinks it was Mr Howard, but she's wrong.'

'He was the second, though,' Hugo murmured lazily as pleasant sensations ran through him from Norma's stroking of his tail.

'That's right – a couple of days after Chester.'

'So there have been two great loves in your life so far,' said Hugo. 'I can think of no way that I can measure up to what either of them did for you and so become the third.'

Her hand slowed on his stem and stopped, stretching his nerves tight with anticipation.

'There is something very important you can do for me,' she whispered, her eyes on his and shining with sincerity. 'You'd be my best and dearest friend forever if you did.'

'Oh, Norma – what is it?' Hugo sighed, his stalk twitching impatiently in her hand.

'Before Mr Howard was shot he promised me the lead in *Mary Magdalene.*'

'Did he? I was told he'd offered it to Connie Young.'

'Oh, no – she's far too *worldly* to play a sacred part like that.'

'But I've read the script,' said Hugo, 'Mary Magdalene is a whore.'

'I've seen the script too,' said Norma. 'She repents of her sinful ways and becomes a saint. The part could have been written for me. But now Mr Howard is gone, Oskar is under no obligation to honour the promise he made to me.'

'Have you spoken to him about it?' Hugo asked, knowing that by way of inducement she had let Oskar enjoy two sessions of rumpling her, so far.

'Yes, he's giving his serious consideration to it, but he hasn't given me a firm promise yet.'

'I wish I could help you, Norma, but I don't see how.'

'He thinks the world of you – he brought you from Berlin to be a star. He'll listen to you.'

Norma was consistent, Hugo had to admit to himself. To get the coveted part she had forced her charms on Ambrose, made them available to Oskar, and was now offering them to him. Like the other two, he decided that he owed it to himself to enjoy the situation to the full. He rolled Norma on to her back on the bear-skin rug, got both thumbs under the elastic string about her waist and slid the tiny black *cache-sexe* down her slender legs and out of the way.

'Promise me you'll speak to Oskar!' she stipulated as he separated her legs to look at what lay between.

As his sense of touch had informed him earlier, Norma had only a thin covering of blondish floss over the well-developed and protruding lips of delicately pink flesh. Hugo lay on his belly and kissed her between the thighs, regretting that he had dealt so generously with Patsy that afternoon, for he suspected that after making love only once to Norma, his soldier would slump and refuse to stand to attention again for hours.

'You're so sweet,' she murmured inanely as the tip of his tongue fluttered against her secret nub. 'Oh, Hugo darling!'

He was lying between her parted legs, his hands under her bottom to squeeze the tender cheeks while he kissed her rosebud. His shaft pressed into the thick fur of the rug and he was excited and happy at what he was about to do to *All the World's Sweetheart*. Norma was sighing in modest arousal and shuddering deliciously as she waited for him to mount her.

They were so entranced by what they were doing that neither heard voices in the hall or footsteps on the Spanish tiles. Only the sudden opening of the den door and an angry shout brought them to their senses. Hugo looked up from Norma's blonde-flossed peach to see Prince Dmytryk looming over him, his face crimson with fury.

'Dimmy – what are you doing here?' Norma gasped in dismay.

She sat up quickly, reached out for the black frock that lay on the floor beside the bear-skin and clutched it to her breasts and belly. Hugo moved backwards to let her close her legs and fumbled for his trousers. If there was going to be a fight, he would feel better with his precious part covered.

'You can go, Maria,' Norma told the open-mouthed maid standing in the doorway.

'You low German swine!' Dmytryk hissed at Hugo. 'This

143

lady is my fiancée – how dare you force your dirty attentions on her – you shall answer to me for this!'

If Norma's betrothed had been an American, Hugo thought, he would have behaved like a cowboy and we would be punching each other now. But being an outlandish Balkan mixture, he would probably want to fight with guns or knives.

'There is really very little I can say,' Hugo said, pulling on his socks.

'Swine!' the Prince shouted again, waving his fist at him.

'Stop that, Dimmy!' Norma said sharply.

She slipped her mourning frock over her head and stood up to confront her intended while Hugo hastily finished dressing.

'Mr Castlemaine and I are professional colleagues and we have strong feelings of respect and friendship for each other,' she said. 'We were rehearsing a scene from the movie of *Mary Magdalene* in which we are to be the stars.'

'Am I a fool?' Dmytryk demanded. 'I know what I saw! You were naked with a man and his mouth was on your body! My God, if I'd come in half a minute later I would have caught you in the act itself!'

'You would have seen no such thing,' Norma said firmly, 'I am disgusted that you could think me capable of such a thing.'

'I saw with my own eyes!'

'You saw nothing except two co-stars rehearsing a most important scene. If you choose to believe that you saw something improper, then I cannot continue to be engaged to a man who thinks me capable of betraying his trust.'

She pulled the diamond ring from her finger and held it out to him. For a moment or two Hugo thought that Dmytryk was going to take it and storm out, but after an internal struggle that darkened his crimson face to purple, he breathed out noisily and let his fists drop.

'Dearest Norma,' he said, almost choking on the words, 'I beg your forgiveness – I did not intend to insult you or your guest. When a man is as deeply in love as I am with you, his jealousy may lead him into misinterpreting things.'

144

'Very true,' Hugo said helpfully. 'Do you know Shakespeare? In one play a black man strangles his wife because he believes she has been unfaithful, but she is the soul of innocence, just like Norma.'

Dmtryk glowered at him murderously.

'You'd better run along, Hugo,' Norma said quickly. 'Call me when you've spoke to Oskar. Dimmy – come and sit beside me while I explain the scene you misunderstood so grossly.'

Hugo picked up his shoes and left with an unceremonious wave of farewell to them both. As he closed the door he glanced back to see Norma and the Prince holding hands on the chesterfield.

The Mexican maid was waiting in the hall – Hugo guessed that she had been listening at the key-hole and grinned comically at her.

'I am sorry, Senor Castlemaine,' she said. 'He pushed past me and I couldn't stop him.'

'That's all right, Maria – it wasn't your fault. Fortunately Miss Gilbert knows how to handle him.'

The maid took his shoes from his hand and went down on one knee to put them on for him.

'The Senorita is very rich and beautiful,' she said with a shrug, 'the Prince is poor. They say he makes big debts to live like a Prince. Naturally she can handle him.'

'I understand why he will put up with almost anything to marry her, but not why she wants him.'

The maid smiled up at him and got to her feet to tug the knot of his tie into place.

'It is no small thing to be a Princess, even if your husband is stupid and mean.'

The hint was not lost on Hugo. He gave Maria a ten dollar bill and patted her cheek before she showed him out.

145

Chapter 9

Gale speaks her mind

Hugo's pleasure was unbounded when Connie telephoned him two days after the funeral to say that she was back from the beach and would like to see him. As part of his status as the cinema's next Great Lover he had bought an open white Buick tourer and it was highly gratifying to drive it along Wilshire to Beverly Hills to meet the woman with whom he was half in love.

The maid who opened the door for him was in a better mood than the night he arrived to find Connie drunk. She gave him a smile of recognition and said that Miss Young was out back by the pool. She showed him the way but did not go with him to announce him, excusing herself by saying that she had a mountain of packing to do. Hugo thought her behaviour odd, but only until he emerged from the house to find Connie lying on a sun-bed near the swimming-pool. She was wearing dark glasses and nothing else. Hardly able to believe his luck, Hugo stared across the lawn at the bangs of dark hair that framed her face, then down at the elegant breasts he wanted to touch and the tuft of dark-brown curls that marked the entrance to bliss for him.

As he approached her across the grass, Connie sat up and pulled her knees up to her breasts, wrapping her arms around her legs. Even so, Hugo looked at her with so much admiration that she responded with a smile and suggested he sat down. He threw his jacket on the grass and perched on the end of her sun-bed, close to her feet. Her toe-nails were painted the same shade of pink as her finger-nails, he noticed, though her face was completely clean of make-up.

'Are you feeling better, Connie?' he asked.

She showed no sign of letting go of her legs to extend a hand to him and so he reached out to touch the back of her hand lightly. At that, she cocked her head sideways a little, presenting a cheek to be kissed. Hugo touched his lips to it gently and enjoyed one quick glance down the cleft of her bare breasts before resuming his seat.

'I've been bad company lately,' she said, 'I fell apart.'

'It was a severe shock,' Hugo agreed sympathetically.

'It didn't hit me right away. When Thelma rang me and I rushed over to Ambrose's house that night to find my letters I was so numb inside that I didn't take in what had happened, even though I saw him sitting dead on the floor. But afterwards – that's when it got to me. I stayed drunk for three or four days.'

'I was there,' Hugo reminded her.

'Were you?' she asked, frowning slightly as she tried to remember. 'Yes, I think you were. Did I ask you to come over?'

'I should have stayed with you, Connie, but Dr Prosz insisted it was better to leave you to sleep.'

'Maybe you should, but it's water under the bridge now. Jake came over and took me to stay with him and Audrey. They're helping me put my life back together.'

'I wish I could,' said Hugo, but she only smiled at him and rested her cheek on her knees so that her bangs fell forward and almost hid her face.

'Your maid said she was packing – does that mean you're going away again, Connie?'

'I'm going to Europe,' she answered, 'I can't work and I have to get away. I talked to Stefan Ignaz and he's given me six month's leave of absence.'

'Then you won't be playing Mary Magdalene.'

'I don't want to play anything right now – I just want to go away from here.'

'Are you going alone?' he asked miserably.

147

'Jake and Audrey are going with me.'

'Especially Jake,' he said, and Connie raised her head from her knees to look at him.

'Jake's a good friend,' she said, 'I'd have died without him this past week. Audrey understands and she doesn't mind.'

'I wanted you to play that part, Connie, so that I could work with you and be with you. I'm a little crazy about you, I think.'

'Maybe we could have given each other something if Ambrose hadn't died,' she answered, 'but things didn't work out that way.'

'When are you leaving?'

'I'm taking the train to New York tomorrow and sailing five days from now. I asked you over this afternoon to say goodbye.'

'And you wait for me naked,' said Hugo, trying to smile and not succeeding at all well, 'an extravagant gesture — genuine Hollywood!'

'I thought it would please you. Would you prefer me dressed, Hugo?'

'Every man who has ever seen you on the screen would like to see you naked, Connie. They all want to make love to you.'

'And you don't?'

'Desperately — but there is a difference. I want more from you than just that.'

'There isn't any more,' she answered, 'the rest died with Ambrose. Making love is all that's left. If that's what you want, you're welcome to it.'

Hugo took hold of her wrists gently and unwound her arms from her shins. She offered no resistance and her face was without expression. He put his hands on her ankles and drew her legs slowly along the flower-patterned sunbed, to reveal her round and pretty breasts.

'Is it enough for Jake?' he asked, an edge in his voice.

'That's for him to say.'

Hugo touched her lightly between the breasts and then ran his finger-tips down her satin skin and the softness of

148

her belly. Her eyes were on his the whole time and gave no hint of either pleasure or annoyance, though her legs parted a little in submission when he cupped her dark-curled mound in his palm.

'I could have made love to you that night you were drunk,' he said slowly. 'You were flat on your back on the bed and so far gone that you would have slept right through it and never known.'

'Then you should have had me when you could,' she said. 'This is Hollywood – everybody grabs what they can. There are no prizes for being noble.'

'Was Ambrose noble?'

She was warm in his hand and in his trousers his shaft was so stiff that it was uncomfortable. She had made it clear enough that he could do what he liked with her – and that to her it was a matter of indifference, a consideration that held him back from the realisation of his desire.

'Ambrose was the best,' she answered softly, 'and look what they did to him!'

'Who was the man who made love to you that night before you called me and begged me to come here?'

'Who said there was a man?' she replied nonchalantly.

'There was – Theodor Prosz told me that when he examined you.'

'You let that creeping Jesus feel me? I'm glad I was dead drunk! Why did you let him – don't you know he's a pervert?'

'I'd never seen him before and your maid said he was your regular doctor. He seemed to think I'd beaten you up and he insisted on examining you for bruises.'

'He's full of excuses to give his patients a good feel!'

'He felt you well enough to know you'd been with a man. Was it this Jake Callan?'

'Does it matter?'

'You went to Jake and he made love to you. But it wasn't enough to chase away your misery, so when you got back here you telephoned me because you thought I might be able to help you more than he did.'

'Maybe I just wanted you to make love to me till I

passed out. I can't even remember what I wanted. Not that you did anything – or so you say now.'

Hugo squeezed the warm flesh of her mound hard in his hand. She blinked but said nothing.

'I'm sorry now that I passed up the opportunity,' he said, quietly angry.

'You wouldn't have been the first man to have me when I was out cold,' said Connie with a fleeting grin, 'I passed out once in Ambrose's study and he got Luis to carry me upstairs. He did it to me three times in a row before he went to sleep – at least, that's what he told me the next day.'

'Did he take any photographs?' Hugo asked, his interest caught.

'Plenty – me on my back with my legs open and Ambrose feeling me and stuff like that.'

That was not the picture Oskar had shown Hugo. His suspicion was confirmed that someone had another and larger collection of Ambrose's photographs somewhere – either a member of the Police Department or Oskar himself.'

'What stuff like that?' he asked.

'He liked to play around – you know that. While I was out cold he lugged me around in different positions and had Luis take snaps.'

'You saw them?'

Connie looked at him in surprise.

'He gave me a set,' she said, 'they're a laugh!'

'Did you know that his collection of pictures was found by the police when they searched the house?'

'They found some that he kept separately, but Ignaz burned most of them – I saw him do it. I know what the Police Department got because they showed me when I was questioned.'

A sudden thought occurred to Hugo.

'You said *look what they did to him*! Who did it to him, Connie – you told me before that it was an accident, but you don't believe that any more, do you? What's happened to make you change your mind?'

150

'I was wrong about Peg Foster,' she said. 'It was the black ribbon that fooled me – it was meant to fool everybody, only I took it off him.'

'But who put it on?'

'What do you care?'

'I liked Ambrose. I want to see whoever shot him caught and punished.'

'You think it's as easy as that? The police grab the killer and lock him up, the DA convinces a jury and it's Death Row for the murderer? Is that what you think happens here? Maybe if a small-time crook holds up a bank and shoots a teller – but not when the big names are involved.'

'You know something!' Hugo exclaimed. 'What?'

'I don't know anything,' she said at once. 'They'll soon close the investigation down because there's too much at stake for too many people. At least I won't be here when they tell the newspapers what lies they want printing.'

'The police raised no objection when you told them you were going to Europe for six months?'

'Stefan Ignaz told them for me.'

'You're not the first to elect him the killer,' Hugo told her. 'At least two people have suggested it to me and they offered different motives. One is that Ambrose was trying to pressure him with compromising photographs of his stars and the other is that Ambrose dabbled with Mrs Ignaz. Which do you think it was?'

'I haven't mentioned any names,' said Connie and she shook her head so vigorously that her bare breasts shook and brought Hugo's mind back to where it had been before he started asking questions, 'not Ignaz and not anybody else.'

'No, indeed,' said Hugo, his hand still cupping her brown tuft affectionately. 'Why did you ask me here, Connie?'

'To say goodbye.'

'I am more flattered than I can tell you by the charming manner in which you decided to receive me. But I hope that I am not a complete fool. I am a little off-balance over you, but your emotions are not engaged as mine are. You could have said goodbye on the telephone. You didn't have

to invite me over and sit here naked to greet me –
enchanting though I find the situation, of course.'

Connie wriggled her perfect hips a little to rub her fleshy
mound against his palm. She lifted her arms and used both
hands to take off her sun-glasses.

'I felt I owed you something when Thelma told me how
you feel about me,' she said. 'I'm sorry I can't return your
feelings, because I think you're a very nice person, but I
can't and there's no point in pretending. What you see is
all I have to offer you,' and she raised a hand to gesture
along her body from breasts to thighs.

Hugo considered the proposition and found it not entirely
convincing. It seemed to him more probable that Connie
was offering the delights of her body as payment for
something – but what? What did she want him to do?

While he was asking himself that unanswerable question,
her fingers trailed lightly along his thigh and his stem
jerked in his trousers.

'You want it like the first time we did it?' she asked in a
soft voice. 'You on your back on the sofa and me on top
humping away at you – is that how you like it, Hugo, the
girl on top?'

She smiled and started to sit up, as if to oblige him, but
he put a hand on her bare shoulder and pressed her down
again.

'Remember what I did to you in the back of the limousine
when we left the restaurant to go to Ambrose's house,' he
said. 'You sat on my lap and I had my hand up your frock.'

She smiled more broadly at him and moved her legs
further apart to let him ease his middle finger between her
soft petals and feel for her hidden bud.

'You were twiddling me,' she said, her eyes half-closed
in contentment as his touch sent tremors through her belly,
'and you got me at a traffic-light. It was red and you turned
it to green and I took off at a hundred miles an hour.'

Hugo turned round on the sun-bed to lie alongside
Connie while he played with her. He kissed her cheek and
she turned her face to him and he kissed her mouth. She
did not respond with any great enthusiasm, but she did

nothing to discourage him. This was to be, he guessed, the last time he would ever have the chance of making love to her and the bitter-sweet thought impelled him to make of it a memory he could delight and agonise over when she was gone.

In the back of the limousine, the first time he had played with her, she had responded easily and quickly to his touch, but that was when she was exhilarated and full of French champàgne. Today in her garden it was not the same at all – she lay loose-limbed and with her eyes closed, uttering little sighs now and then as her excitement grew by very slow stages, but her climactic moments were long delayed. Her arm lay down between their bodies, hers naked, his clothed, and the back of her hand pressed against Hugo's pommel through his trousers. She made no effort to do more than that and so he jerked his buttons open and pushed her hand inside. She grasped his shaft and held it in a loose clasp.

Reluctant though her body was to respond, Hugo persevered, flicking his tongue at the nubs of her breasts and dabbling his fingers skilfully in her slippery furrow. It took a long time, but at last she gave a long moan and her legs kicked on the sun-bed. At once, Hugo rolled between her spread thighs, set the end of his spar to her moist entry and pushed in hard and fast. Her brown eyes opened and she stared up into his face as he rocked to and fro with determination.

'Hugo,' she whispered. 'I wish things had worked out your way.'

'Then stay with me,' he murmured, 'stay with me, Connie.'

'Love me hard!' she gasped, putting her arms round him for the first time since he'd arrived, her body rocking to his thrusts

Hugo pressed his mouth to her open mouth in a long kiss and shuddered violently as he gushed his passion into her beautiful body.

'Connie, Connie,' he was gasping, 'I adore you!'

153

'Yes!' she cried. 'Yes, Hugo!' and she shook in the throes of her climactic release.

Long after they were calm again Hugo lay on her belly, kissing her and stroking her face. Eventually she sighed and pushed at him gently. He eased himself away from her and sat looking down at her face.

'You have to leave now, Hugo,' she said, 'I've a lot to do before train-time tomorrow.'

'But . . . I thought . . .' he stammered.

'What did you think? That you would change my mind by making love to me?'

'But I can't get away just now, you know that,' he protested. 'The shooting starts on the big movie in a few weeks – I'm tied up with wardrobe and make-up and publicity and rehearsals and the rest of it.'

'I know you can't go with me,' said Connie, sitting up and clasping her arms round her legs again as if to show him that the time for tenderness was over. 'You have to stay here and be a big star and I have to get away from here. Jake is going with me and maybe we'll be married by the time we get back. That's all there is to it.'

'You said that his wife was also going along!' Hugo exclaimed, aghast at this new information.

'Only for a month or so, then if things go the way Jake thinks, she'll come back to the States to arrange a divorce.'

'There's nothing I can say then. Goodbye, Connie.'

'Goodbye, Hugo. I wish you luck.'

He stood up and fastened his trousers and walked away without kissing her. Jacket over his shoulder he made for the house and was halfway there when Connie called after him.

'Yes?' he said, turning to look at her again. She was lying down on the sun-bed, an arm under her head and one knee propped up and she looked so delicious that Hugo wanted to go back and make love to her again, even though he knew it was without significance.

'Take one word of advice, Hugo,' she said, 'stop asking questions about who shot Ambrose. Otherwise your career will never get off the ground, believe me.'

'I'm not afraid of Ignaz,' he answered.

'You haven't been around long enough to know how the movie business works. You should ask your friend Oskar – he knows a lot more than he's saying.'

'He's told me what he knows.'

'I'm sure he's told you what he thinks it safe for you to know. But he won't tell you everything.'

She waved at him briefly and put on her sun-glasses, as if in dismissal. Hugo stared for a few moments at her beautiful golden-skinned body and turned away.

He saw no sign of the maid as he went through the house. His Buick was parked in the driveway and a woman in a white shirt was sitting in it smoking a cigarette. She turned to look at him when she heard his foot-steps and he saw that it was Gale Paget, the beautiful black-haired star of many an Ignaz International melodrama.

'I've been waiting for you,' she murmured, flicking her half-smoked cigarette away.

She looked very much at her ease, one bare arm along the back of the seat and her red-skirted legs crossed comfortably. Hugo threw his jacket in the rear seat, got behind the wheel and held out his hand.

'We haven't been introduced,' he said with a smile, 'but we last saw each other at Ambrose's funeral.'

'I'm Gale and you're Hugo,' she said, holding his hand for a moment. 'That's all the introduction you'll ever get in this town. I want to talk to you, Hugo – have you got time?'

'Of course. Shall I drive you home?'

'Let's go to your place,' she suggested, 'I wouldn't want my husband to turn up and interrupt our talk.'

Hugo started the Buick and drove impetuously out of Connie's driveway.

'It didn't occur to me that you're married, Gale.'

'I'm always married,' she said, 'Tommy's my fourth.'

Looking at her flawless complexion and figure, Hugo guessed that she was in her late twenties, within a year or two of Connie and Thelma and himself. To have had four husbands already seemed to him excessive, even by American standards.

155

'How did you find me at Connie's?' he asked.

'I didn't – I dropped in to say goodbye before she goes to Europe, only the maid told me she couldn't be disturbed. We all know what that means, so I sneaked round to the back way into the garden and saw how busy she was. So as I wanted to talk to you anyway, I sent my driver away and waited for you.

Hugo grinned at her and asked if she and Connie were good friends.

'The best,' she said, 'Tommy was her steady boy-friend before I married him – she wanted to get him off her hands. She said he wasn't up to much in bed, but I've found him all right so far. At least he's not out chasing little trollops like my last one.'

'How could a man married to someone as beautiful as you even think about making love to other women?' Hugo asked, not entirely sincerely.

'Save that for the fans!' said Gale. 'This town's jam-packed with beautiful women and rats like my third chase them just like you do.

'But I'm not married, Gale.'

'It wouldn't make any difference if you were married to Miss America in person. When you'd banged her a dozen times you'd hanker for something else – men are like that.'

'And women?'

'When I see a man who really gets me going I make sure I have him,' she answered, 'I won't look this good forever. so I have to make the most of it.'

She had uncrossed her legs and stretched them out under the dashboard, her ruby-red linen skirt hitched up a little to show her smooth knees in fine silk stockings. Her arm still lay along the top of the seat-back and her jewelled fingers just reached Hugo's shoulder. When he glanced at her she half-turned towards him, her skirt sliding a fraction higher and her breasts thrust into prominence under her close-fitting white shirt.

'That sounds a lot like Connie's version of Hollywood ethics – grab it when you can.'

156

'Right – and she grabbed you!' said Gale with a cheerful laugh.

'Maybe you're right. Are *you* going to grab me?'

By way of answer she dropped her hand from his shoulder to his lap and gripped his dangler through his trousers, open car or not.

'Yes, I can see you were serious about wanting to talk,' Hugo commented.

'Oh, I've things to talk to you about, Hugo. But there's time for a little fooling around first.'

She kept her hand in his lap until the moment he parked outside his apartment building. The doorman gaped in admiration to see the celebrated Gale Paget and rushed to summon the lift. Hugo was in acute discomfort as he strolled through the lobby arm-in-arm with Gale, his jacket held nonchalantly in front of him to conceal the hard bulge in his trousers. Riding up in the lift to the penthouse, Gale had his trousers open and his twitching stem out in an instant.

'You don't have to grab so fast,' said Hugo, surprised by her urgency.

'Can't wait!' she gasped, pulling her skirt up at the front with one hand while the other jammed his stock between her legs.

He caught a glimpse of fragile lace and silk wrenched aside by her frantic fingers as she impaled herself and gripped the cheeks of his bottom to hold him close. Her face was turned up to his and she was panting as she jerked her loins very fast against him. Her beautiful eyes, so dark as to appear black, stared sightlessly at his face while she strained to relieve the tension she had created in herself by feeling him on the way from Connie's. Hugo had his arms round her waist, waiting for her paroxysm of desire to run its course.

The lift stopped at the top floor with a little jerk that drove him deeper into Gale's wet burrow, making her wail climactically and shake against him very hard. Neither noticed that the lift doors opened and closed automatically before it started downwards again, Gale's throes diminishing as the floors slid past. At the ground floor the doors opened again and the uniformed doorman stood looking at them across the lobby. Hugo caught the look on his face and grinned briefly over Gale's shoulder at him.

'That was just great!' she said as the lift started upwards again, 'I've made love in some crazy places, but that was a first.'

In the secure haven of his bedroom Hugo removed her pleated red skirt and white shirt and stretched her out on the bed to play with her round and velvet-skinned breasts. She was wearing a thick necklace of pink and white coral and this he left on, thinking that her flesh-tones set off its colours admirably. Finding her russet-brown buds firm under his fingers, he slid her triangular little knickers down her legs and pressed a finger along the thin lips under her patch of brown curls. They opened easily to show him her wet pink folds.

'Your finger's no good,' she murmured, her almost-black eyes gleaming and her long legs parting wide, 'I want something thicker than that!'

There was no time for Hugo to strip. He jerked his trousers open, pulled his shirt up over his belly and stretched himself on top of her. Neither his hand nor hers was needed – the instant that his staff touched her wetness he found himself sliding in deeply. The sensation was so strong that Hugo at once began to pound her belly with his own in a fast, smacking rhythm, and Gale signified her approval with loud gasps of delight. The pace was too hot for either of them to sustain for long – Hugo's fingers dug into her soft bottom and he cried out hoarsely as his passion erupted in her belly. She bucked hard underneath him, her cries of delight louder and longer.

'You're very good, Hugo,' she said, kissing his cheek, 'I guessed you were when I saw you popping Connie. Though I knew I had to have you when I saw you with Thelma at the funeral. I tried to think of some way to get you to ride back from the cemetery with me, but you went off with Norma and Oskar. Did you have her, afterwards?'

'I had lunch with Oskar to talk about the new movie.'

'That's why I wanted to talk to you,' she said, easing him off her body to lie beside her as his stalk drooped. 'They say Ambrose promised the lead to Connie, but she doesn't want it now she's going to Europe.'

'Norma wants it – did you know that?'

'I heard she's been taking her panties down for Oskar, but he's too good a director to ruin a movie for a bang or two. He's taking a hell of a chance – sticking it up Norma Gilbert is the kiss of death for movie careers. Look at Chester – a drunk and finished. And Arnold Wigram – no studio will touch him since his run-in with the law, even though a jury found him not guilty. And darling Ambrose got shot. If you want my advice, you'll give her a miss – she's Little Miss Bad Luck in person.'

'Do you see yourself starring as Mary Magdalene?' Hugo asked, smiling at this latest manifestation of dislike for *All the World's Sweetheart*.

He lay with his hands behind his head, the profile that had thrilled Berlin audiences well displayed.

'You and I would be great together,' she said. 'You'll be a sensation with your looks – and as for *this*,' and she took hold of his limp tail, 'every woman in Hollywood will be after you when the word gets round.'

'I hope they're all as beautiful and desirable as you, Gale. Now we've got together at last, there is something you can tell me – were you with Ambrose the night he was shot?'

'You think I shot him?' she asked incredulously, 'you're crazy!'

'No, I don't think you did. But Theodor Prosz's nurse let slip something that made me wonder.'

He saw no reason to tell Gale that after she had ministered to his injured tail in the privacy of his own home Nurse Bell had confided to him the doctor's movements on the fatal night.

'Theodor Prosz!' said Gale scornfully. 'That little crook.'

'Connie says he's a pervert,' said Hugo, hoping to provoke further disclosures.

'What's a pervert in this town?' she said, eyebrows

159

raised. 'Some like boys and some like girls, some like one end and some like the other. Who cares a cuss? The night Ambrose was shot I was throwing a party at my place and I hit the cokey too hard. I woke up in a clinic next day with Theodor's hands all over me.'

'I saw him do that to Connie when she was unconscious. He claimed he was examining her.'

'I didn't latch on that he was giving me a good feel,' said Gale, 'I was pretty groggy, because he'd got his other hand in his trouser pocket to finger himself. I'm sure he squibbed off in his pants before he stopped examining me! The nerve of the man – pulling a stunt like that right after shooting Ambrose!'

'No, he didn't do it. He was in his office playing games with his nurse right up to the time he was called out to take care of you. She told me so herself.'

'Little nursie says the doctor was diddling her in the office, so it must be true!' Gale said derisively.

'You have a point. But why would he want Ambrose dead?'

'Because of Norma Gilbert. Theodor had her a few times when she was pregnant and needed his help without her mother finding out.'

'Who made her pregnant – is it known?'

'You can take your pick from half a dozen,' said Gale, taking hold of his soft tail and giving it a tug, 'maybe she was pregnant and maybe she wasn't. If she was, Theodor fixed it and had his fun with her and fell for her. He even asked her to marry him – can you imagine that! He shot Ambrose because he thought he was the one who knocked Norma up.'

'So the motive was unrequited love, in a sense? I find that hard to accept.'

'You haven't been here long enough to get to know Theodor. He's at the end of his rope and only keeps going on cokey. Nursie will find him dead of an overdose one morning in his office – and he'll make a big production number of it!'

'How do you mean, Gale?' Hugo asked, his stem pleasantly stiff again, so that he sat up on the bed to take all his clothes off.

'I don't know what his sick mind will dream up, but you can bet he'll be naked when they find him, or maybe wearing little nursie's panties with a wet stain down the front.'

'That's madness! I don't believe a word of it!'

'He's been more than half mad for years. Ask anybody you like.'

'Ambrose was found dead, naked with a black ribbon tied round his tail – did you know that?' Hugo asked.

'See what I mean!' she exclaimed. 'That proves Theodor killed him!'

Hugo lay naked beside her and she pushed his hands up to her full breasts.

'I've seen a photograph of you, Gale,' he said, fondling her fleshy bundles with zest, 'on your hands and knees – do you know the one I mean?'

'Ambrose's favourite picture of me,' she answered with a grin, 'top-hat, white tie and tails – and me bare-assed! That the one you mean?'

'You looked absolutely adorable!'

'That was after the Academy Awards,' Gale said, 'when we got back Ambrose gave me the Oscar he said I should have won for *Shanghai Rains*.'

'A fair-sized Oscar, as I recall the photograph.'

'Big and hard,' she agreed, her mouth close to his ear and her hands busy with his stilt, 'but yours feels even bigger – do you want to present me with it the same way?'

Without waiting for an answer, she was up on her hands and knees, her beautifully rounded bottom towards Hugo. He ran his fingers along her luscious split peach and shuffled close on his knees, Oscar in hand, to present it where it would be most appreciated.

161

Chapter 10

Chester has cause for concern

At Chester's party for Lily's birthday Hugo came to realise that all Hollywood parties were continuations of the same party. The same two hundred film stars and studio executives, give or take a few more or less, the same music, drink and food. The guests did the same things – drank too much, talked too much and too loudly. About the same number paired off part-way through the party and disappeared upstairs. Whether they paired off in the same couples at every party was unclear to a newcomer.

Hugo decided that the only difference between functions was the time (this party began at noon) and the location – and after a few drinks the interiors of Beverly Hills mansions started to look the same anyway. The outsides might be Spanish Colonial, Early American, French Chateau, German Hunting Lodge, Belgian Gothic, Italian Renaissance, English Tudor, but the interior decoration and furnishings were all much of an expensive muchness.

These thoughts passed through his head not when he was chatting to other guests in the house but while he was fondling Lily in Chester's garage. More precisely, on the back seat of Chester's silver Rolls-Royce inside the garage, his hand up Lily's frock to play with the cuddly little toy between her legs. Now that Chester believed him innocent of the ransacking of Lily at Oskar's party, it seemed not unreasonable to Hugo to enjoy her charms on her birthday.

Lily was more than eager to permit him. In a corner of the crowded living-room she stood on tip-toe to whisper in Hugo's ear that she must tell him a secret. He suggested they went upstairs, but she said that was the first place Chester would look if he missed her. Her suggestion was the garage, where Chester's five gleaming motor-cars stood in a row. Hugo chose the Rolls, not out of regard for the make but because it had the broadest and most comfortable-looking rear seat.

As proof of her desire to tell him her secret, Lily removed her knickers before she got into the Rolls. She covered his face with hot little kisses and asked him if he had missed her. The question meant nothing, nor did his answer.

'Of course I have,' he said, feeling her delicately between the legs. 'What was that ridiculous story about a waiter at Oskar's?'

'You saw how Chester was when he suspected you, darling,' Lily sighed, 'I had to tell him something before he got furious enough to shoot you. He would, you know – he's crazy about me. Do you know he's got four hand-guns and two shot-guns? Oh, Hugo, that does feel good!'

She snuggled against him on the car seat and undid his trousers to put her little hand in and stroke his upright part.

'You're getting me terrifically wound up,' she murmured, 'I think I'd better lie down for you before it's too late.'

She arranged herself along the seat, her white lace frock up round her belly. Hugo kissed the blonde-fluffed peach between her thighs and split it with his hard stem. The seat was not really long enough and he had to lie half on Lily and half across her, his legs over the side of the seat. But as the saying has it, there is always a way if the will is present and the awkwardness of his posture did not hinder Hugo from riding merrily in and out of Lily's warm little pouch until, with great satisfaction, he flooded it.

'That was lovely!' Lily announced, when she was able to speak again.

By unspoken agreement they sat up from their uncomfortable position and put their arms round each other.

163

'All those guns,' said Hugo, 'did Chester shoot Ambrose? Mildred Gilbert says he did.'

'She would!' Lily declared. 'She hates Chester for making love to Norma when they were in a movie together. She's always trying to make trouble for him. But she can't pin this on him – I've already told the police he was home that night.'

'And was he?' Hugo asked, his hand still up her lace frock to stroke her narrow belly.

'He was out getting drunk somewhere. A taxi brought him home helpless the next morning.'

'So he could have done it, Lily.'

'Why should he?'

'You know why – because he suspected that you had been with Ambrose.'

'He's only got himself to blame,' said Lily defensively. 'He keeps on promising to get me into films and never does because he's jealous if another man as much as looks at me. Why does he think I moved in with him and let him love me all he wants? I keep my side of the bargain, but he doesn't, so he can't blame me for talking to Mr Howard to see if he'll put me in a movie.'

'But Chester would be very angry if he found out.'

'It didn't mean anything, making love to Mr Howard. Not like doing it with you, Hugo – that really means something,' she assured him. 'With Mr Howard it was only a game to please him so he'd give me a start in films. Besides, Chester never found out.'

'How can you be sure of that?' Hugo asked, continuing to fondle her.

'If he had, he would have punished me like he does when he thinks I've been too friendly with anybody. He says I encourage them and he goes insane with jealousy.'

'Punishes you? My God, does he beat you?' Hugo asked in genuine anxiety for her, his hand at rest between her thighs.

'No, he's too crazy about me to hurt me. If he catches me laughing and joking with the boy who comes to clean the swimming-pool, he drags me upstairs and rips my clothes off like a wild beast! He makes me get down on my knees while he says terrible things about what I'd let the pool-boy do to me if I had the chance. And all the time his face gets redder and redder!'

'My poor Lily – you must be terrified when this happens,' said Hugo, appalled by what a girl of her age was subjected to.

'I was the first time,' she answered, kissing his cheek, 'but not now I know he won't hurt me.'

'How long do these lunatic scenes go on for?'

'Hours,' she said. 'You see, when he's worked himself right up, he makes me lie on the bed with my legs apart and ask his pardon while he tongues me. I like that part of it – he goes on so long, you see.'

Hugo was fascinated by this insight into the private life of Hollywood's Great Lover and urged Lily to tell him more.

'He pops me off five or six times with his tongue,' she continued, 'and I have to keep on asking his pardon right through it. And when he's wrung me right out, he gets on top and does his business.'

'Unbelievable!' Hugo murmured, his handle sticking up again from his open trousers. 'You must get away from him – have you no family to go to?'

'Mom and Pop and two brothers and a sister in Pasadena,' she replied. 'Why would I go back home? They want me to be a movie star too, that's why they let me stay with Chester. They love me – you don't think Pop would let me go off with just any man, do you? All my family thought Chester would help me get started, but so far he's been a big disappointment.'

'Did Ambrose promise to help you?'

'He said he would, but I don't know if he meant it. Not that it matters now he's been shot.'

'You're not lucky in your choice of sponsors, Lily. I wish there was something I could do to help you, but I'm so new here that I have no influence with anyone of importance.'

It was a mistake to tell Lily that – she decided at once that she'd been away from the party long enough and

165

Chester was sure to be looking for her. She pulled Hugo's hand from between her legs and got out of the Rolls-Royce to put on her knickers. A brief wave of her hand through the window and she was gone, leaving Hugo to button his trousers over his stiff spindle.

Out by the swimming-pool he ran into Chester, full of drunken bonhomie.

'Hi, Hugo! Having a good time?'

'I'm enjoying your party,' Hugo answered truthfully.

'Great! You know something – now we've got that little misunderstanding all cleared up, I like you. You're too decent a guy to do the dirty on me with my sweet and innocent Lily.'

After Lily's confidences about Chester's bedroom activities when in his jealous mood, it struck Hugo as both comical and irritating to hear him speaking like that and he cast around in his mind for some way of getting back at the outworn *Great Lover*.

'Chester,' he said, smiling in as friendly a manner as he could manage, 'I like you too and I'm worried for you. Have the police questioned you about Ambrose?'

'Me and everybody else,' Chester said gloomily. 'Somebody's putting the word round that I shot him because of Lily.'

'Between ourselves, this story is being spread by someone who may be listened to by Stefan Ignaz. If he believes it, the outcome could be worse than if the police do – is that so?'

'Damned right!' said Chester. 'He had me in his office the other day and acted very strange – I think he wants to fire me and is looking for a get-out from my contract. Who's spreading the poison – do you know?'

'Mildred Gilbert – she seems to know something,' said Hugo, watching with deep pleasure as Chester turned pale. 'Not that I think you shot Ambrose – I'm sure you're in the clear.'

'I was home that night,' Chester blustered, 'Lily told the detectives when they were here.'

'She's a loyal friend,' said Hugo, shaking his head sadly,

166

'but in a court-room that would count against you. They'd say she was lying for you.'

Chester was beginning to look sick. He walked Hugo to the long bar by the pool and downed a half-tumbler of neat Scotch whisky in three swallows.

'See here, Hugo – I'll come clean with you because I trust you. I wasn't home that night – Lily lied to get me off the hook. The truth is I don't know where the hell I was. I had a few drinks somewhere and the next thing I remember is sicking up in a taxi the next morning.'

'Do you often have lapses of memory?'

'Every now and then when I'm loaded. I thought I might have been at Big Ida's that night, but I've checked and she says I wasn't. What in hell am I going to do about Mildred?'

'I'm sorry you should be in so dreadful a predicament,' said Hugo, piling on the agony. 'There are two things you must do at once – consult your lawyer about your dangerous position, and see your doctor about your very serious medical condition.'

'I can't tell Theodor Prosz I'm having black-outs. He may be my doctor but he's on the studio pay-roll and Ignaz would know right away.'

'Then at least get your lawyer's advice.'

'There's no way a lawyer could shut that damned old witch's mouth,' Chester said, rapidly draining another glass of whisky, 'Mildred's had it in for me since she got it into her head that I'd diddled her little girl when we were making *Nell of Drury Lane* together. Did you see that movie? I think it was one of my best. Anyway, Mildred made a big commotion when somebody told her Norma had been to my dressing-room for a little dialogue coaching.'

'Naturally, with your experience you knew that you could improve Norma'a performance,' Hugo suggested.

Chester raised a sickly grin and held out his glass to a waiter for more.

'You'll never guess what I had to do to shut Mildred up so she didn't go straight to Ignaz and get me kicked off the set,' he said.

167

'You gave her money, I suppose,' said Hugo, knowing full well what the true answer was.

'No, she had plenty of that – Norma was making big money. I had to bang that old bitch every day for seven weeks till the movie was finished. She didn't even give me a weekend off – Saturdays she'd be ringing my door-bell right after lunch and Sundays she'd come round straight from church! I've never hated anyone so much in my life as I did Mildred!'

'But you saved your career,' Hugo pointed out.

'Right! I'm still America's number one heart-throb,' Chester said with drunken pride, 'And where's Mildred now? Norma's grown up and moved out and Mildred's nobody. All she's got is an allowance from Norma and the best she can do is hire chauffeurs to bang her. So she's trying to destroy me again out of spite.'

The chauffeur is not exactly the best Mildred can do, Hugo thought ruefully, remembering how she had deceived him into believing he could amuse himself at her expense, only to find that she was capable of using him for her own pleasure. Not to mention the injury she had inflicted on his most cherished possession – an injury that had required Nurse Bell's devoted attention on five consecutive days.

'You can save your career the same way again, Chester – you must be able to see that.'

'You're not suggesting I should bang her again!' Chester exclaimed indignantly, his face mottling a very ugly shade of purple.

'From what you've told me, it is obvious that Mildred is extremely susceptible to you,' said Hugo. 'She's in love with you even – women are, all over America.'

'Right round the world,' Chester corrected him at once, 'I get fan mail from as far away as Singapore, wherever that is.'

'Then you'll have no trouble in silencing Mildred.'

'By God!' said Chester, stunned by the thought of climbing aboard the woman he most disliked in the world. 'You're right – but I don't know if I can bring myself to do it to her, and that's the truth.'

'Consider the alternative,' said Hugo, his voice melancholy. 'The best is that Ignaz fires you. The worst is that you're arrested for murder. And the very worst of all is a grotesque end in the electric chair for a crime you did not commit.'

Chester's hand trembled so much that he spilled whisky down his shirt-front.

'I guess you're right,' he said, looking as if he'd already received a sentence of death. 'What's a few rattles with Mildred compared with that? I'll bang her twice a day for the rest of her life rather than get fired from the studio. I'm the tops and I'll teach her to respect me.'

'Oh, she'll respect you, Chester, when she feels your tail inside her.'

'Damned right she will – and the sooner the better,' Chester said thickly, 'I'll drive over and slip it to the old bag right now.'

He lurched away, empty glass in hand, towards the garage. Hugo was pleased by what he had achieved – he felt that he'd wreaked a fitting revenge on Chickenhawk Chester for his treatment of Lily. And not more than ten minutes later, Lily herself came across the lawn towards him, looking incredibly young and pretty in her white lace frock and fresh make-up.

'I've lost one of my diamond ear-rings,' she said. 'They were Chester's present for my birthday. It must have fallen off while we were fooling around in the garage.

'I'll go and look for it,' Hugo offered.

'I've just looked, but the Rolls-Royce has gone. Have you seen Chester?'

'I was talking to him a few minutes ago. He's very worried that he's suspected of shooting Ambrose. He said he had to see Mildred Gilbert about it.'

'Was he very drunk?'

'He was unsteady on his feet.'

'That's good – he won't be back for hours. Do you still love me, Hugo?' and her doll-like face shone with girlish enthusiasm as she asked the question.

169

'You know I adore you, Lily,' he answered, wondering what devious plan was forming in her blonde-curled head.

'Then you want to help me get started in movies,' she said, 'and I've thought of a way. Do you want to hear it?'

'Of course,' he said, smiling at her, 'tell me.'

'It's too secret to tell you here. My room's the third on the right upstairs,' she said, smiling back with such innocence that Hugo was astonished.

'I'll be waiting for you in ten minutes from now,' she went on, the tip of her little pink tongue appearing for a moment, 'we can talk there without being disturbed.'

'But what if Chester comes back while you're explaining how I can help you? He'd be very angry and I'd have to knock him down again.'

'He won't be back for a long time,' Lily assured him, 'Mrs Gilbert's crazy about him – she'll drag him into bed and wear him to a frazzle. If half what they say about her is true, she'll open her legs and swallow him.'

Seeing that Hugo still hesitated, she told him that he could take all her clothes off in her room. Hugo's tassel stirred at the suggestion and he nodded quickly. He glanced round to make sure no one was looking at them and smoothed his hand gently over Lily's lace-covered thigh. She smiled and turned to go, thought of something and came back, her blue eyes shining.

'Hugo – we'll meet in Chester's room, not mine. It's the first on the right at the top of the stairs. You can see the bed he makes me lie on when he punishes me.'

'Ten minutes,' Hugo promised, his pointer vertical in his trousers. 'I'll be there.'

Such was his impatience to strip Lily naked and spread-eagle her girlish blonde charms over Chester's bed, that Hugo was upstairs only five minutes after she left him. His hand was on the gold-plated door-knob when a scream of terror from further along the landing diverted his attention. The thought flashed through his mind that Chester had returned to find Lily naked and was beating her. As he ran to the next door along the passage he heard the scream again, somewhat muffled, but with real pain in it. He flung

170

the door open and hurtled in, ready to thrash Chester to a pulp, and stood dumbfounded at the scene which confronted him.

There was a four-poster bed and from the top of one of its sturdy posts a naked woman hung upside-down by a thick golden cord tied round her ankles. An equally naked Prince Dmytryk, heavy-bottomed and slightly pot-bellied, stood near her with a black leather belt in one hand and a bottle of champagne in the other. To judge by the red marks on the woman's belly and thighs he had been using his belt freely. but as Hugo rushed into the room he was in the process of up-ending the bottle between her thighs to fill her receptacle with wine.

The noise of the door slamming against the wall caused Dmytryk to turn unsteadily, his pointer swaying comically from side to side with his movement. He gaped foolishly at Hugo, champagne from the bottle he held cascading on to the carpet.

'Help me!' the upside-down woman gasped. 'He's got a gun – he's going to kill me!'

If Dmytryk had a gun with him it was not on his person – that much was obvious – and Hugo saw no point in taking chances now that he had recognized the trussed woman. It was Peg Foster, whom he had first seen enjoying ill-treatment at the hands of another man. He grinned and closed the door behind him in case any curious person passed by outside.

'This is the third time we meet in unusual circumtances, Prince,' he said casually.

'Go away!' Dmytryk answered irritably, 'I have nothing to say to you.'

He sounded more than half-drunk and Hugo was certain that Peg had deliberately got him into that condition before enticing him upstairs.

'Help me,' she pleaded. 'He's crazy!'

Hugo ignored her and addressed himself to Dmytryk.

'I do not think that your fiancée would approve of this private party of yours,' he said, with a shrug, 'Miss Gilbert is a person of high moral standards.'

171

Dmytryk glanced from the bottle in one hand to the belt in the other and shook his head doubtfully. He reeled towards a chair and almost fell into it, legs sprawling out in front of him and his stilt aiming upwards at the ceiling.

'She must not see me like this,' he mumbled.

'It would not be easy to explain the presence of Miss Foster naked and upside-down,' Hugo agreed. 'Unless you can claim that vampirism runs in your family.'

'Get me down from here!' Peg implored him. 'Call an ambulance – I'm hurt!'

'No ambulance!' Dmytryk insisted. 'There must be no scandal.'

'But your victim needs hospital treatment,' said Hugo, going along with Peg's game.

'Be a good fellow,' Dmytryk muttered, 'drive her to a hospital yourself. I'll pay for her treatment, but you must keep me out of it.'

Hugo stepped close to Peg to ascertain how best to release her. The join of her thighs was level with his chest and he had an excellent view of her groove, over which her dark-brown curls were plastered flat with spilled champagne. The cord by which she was hanging was a part of the four-poster decorations and the weight of her body had pulled the knot tight.

'Hurry up!' Peg moaned from somewhere down near his groins, 'I'm in agony!'

'All in good time,' he answered, climbing up to stand on the bed and get a closer look at the knot, and then to Dmytryk, 'have you got a knife?'

'It is unnecessary to kill her,' the Prince observed lugubriously. 'Flog her to make her scream and then rape her and enjoy yourself – that's what I do. It is wasteful to kill whores after you've used them.'

'Who are you calling a whore, you fat slug!' Peg complained viciously.

'I think I see how to get you down,' said Hugo, 'I'll lift you on to the bed and if you take your weight on your arms that will give me enough slack in the rope to get the knot undone.'

172

First he untied the silk stocking which bound her wrists behind her back. He got down from the bed, put his hands under her upside-down hips and lifted her until he could swing her across like a pendulum and she had her fore-arms on the bed. During this manoeuvre he could hardly help noticing that for a woman of average build she had extremely well-developed breasts. Head-down as she was, they hung towards her chin and, in the process of arranging her so that she could balance her weight on her arms, he felt her melons thoroughly.

Up on the bed again, he told Peg to lean her weight against him while he tackled the knot. The cord had pulled very tight and it took him some time to unpick the tangle. When it came loose at last, she collapsed against him and he overbalanced, landing on his back on the bed, Peg on top of him and his head between her thighs. On a whim he stuck out his tongue and settled the question of whether the champagne Dmytryk had poured into her had been *sec*, *demi-sec* or *brut*.

She lay still for a few moments, legs apart, as if to let him sample her flavour, then rolled off him. Hugo got up and examined the red weals on her thighs and belly more closely. Dmytryk had lashed her savagely and she would have some nasty bruising to show for it, but that was all.

'We must get you to a doctor at once,' he said loudly while he felt her between the legs and winked at her. 'There's not a moment to lose or you'll be scarred for life.'

'Oh my God!' Peg moaned as she winked back at him. 'It's the end of my film career!'

Hugo thought that was overdoing it, even for the benefit of an idiot like the Prince, since she had never been in a movie – unless she had been the star of an illegal film for exhibition at salesmen's conferences only.

'You must be brave,' he said dramatically. 'Plastic surgery can do wonders these days, but it is the internal injuries we must worry about,' and he fondled her heavy breasts to see if he could detect any such injuries.

'I'll pay for everything,' Dmytryk groaned, his eyes

173

closed. 'Get her the best treatment and send the bills to me.'

Hugo helped Peg to sit up on the bed and then to her feet. Uttering loud moans of pain, she slipped her flame-red frock over her head. Her hand-bag lay on the dressing-table and into it she stuffed her silk underwear and ruined stockings.

'Lean on me while I get you to my car,' said Hugo.

'He's crippled me – I can't walk!' Peg sobbed noisily and convincingly. 'You'll have to carry me.'

Hugo picked her up and they both looked at Dmytryk, who was slumped naked in his chair. His once-proud part had shrunk to hang sorrowfully under his plump belly between hairy thighs. He opened his eyes to stare up at them.

'No scandal, please,' he mumbled. 'Get her out the back way. I'll pay her compensation as long as there's no scandal.'

'Damned right you will!' Peg spat. 'You've maimed me!'

Once outside the bedroom Hugo set Peg on her feet and she showed him the back-stairs. They met no one on the way down and only two couples neither of them knew when they walked round the side of the garage away from the house to Hugo's Buick. He helped her in with a pat on her bottom and drove smartly away.

'I don't know where the hospital is,' said Hugo, grinning at Peg. She had taken a silver compact from her bag and was busily checking how badly mussed her hair was from hanging upside-down.

'We'll go to my place,' she said. 'Make a left turn at the next corner.'

Chapter 11

Peg at home

By the time Hugo parked outside Peg's apartment on 3rd Street he had remembered that Lily was waiting for him in Chester's bed-room and he laughed to think that he might never now learn exactly how she expected him to help her get into films. Far more interesting than that was his meeting with Perversity Peg in circumstances both bizarre and appropriate.

His first sight of her had been at Oskar's party – the first Hollywood party he had attended. On that occasion she had been face-down on Oskar's bed, her wrists tied to one of its posts and all he had been able to observe then was that she had curly brown hair and a handsomely-shaped bottom. At Chester's party she had been hanging by her ankles and he had been able to see that her balloons were larger and rounder than average and that the tuft between her thighs was a dark shade of brown. Seen upright and clothed, she proved to have a pretty face, large brown eyes, a square chin and a sulky mouth.

Her apartment was in a modern building and expensively furnished. She offered Hugo a drink, and if she was suffering any discomfort from the Prince's beating, she gave no sign of it.

'You've been a big help, Hugo,' she said, handing him a glass of whisky and ice-cubes.

'You know my name,' he observed, raising his glass to her.

'I know everybody's name – everybody that matters, that is.'

'And I'm one of those who matter?'

'I should say so! According to Oskar you're the hottest property in Hollywood right now. He told me you're taking over from Chester Chataway as the movies' Great Lover, like he took over from Valentino years ago. So that makes you very important and I like to be friends with top movie people.'

'And from what I've seen, they like to be friends with you.'

'They surely do,' she agreed, putting her glass down, 'Listen – can I ask you for one more favour?'

'Yes, if you'll answer a question or two for me,' Hugo said.

'Sure – I've got no secrets,' she said at once, and rummaged in a cabinet drawer and brought out a Kodak camera.

'I need a few pictures while the marks are still clear,' she explained, smiling at Hugo. 'I don't think the Prince will give me any trouble, but a snap-shot or two is insurance.'

'But I know nothing about photography, Peg!'

'You don't have to – I'll tell you what to do.'

Along one side of her living-room were long windows onto a south-facing balcony. Peg gauged the strength of the late afternoon sunshine and did things to the camera settings before handing it to Hugo.

'You don't have to get it right every time,' she said encouragingly. 'We'll shoot the whole film and one or two will be good enough to scare the hell out of Dmytryk.'

She hoisted her red frock over her head and threw it on the nearest chair before positioning herself close to an open window and sideways on to it, so that the sun-light illuminated the front of her body. Hugo stared with pleasure at the slenderness of her arms and shoulders which made her round breasts look even larger than they were, the graceful curve of her belly down to the walnut-brown fleece between her thighs. He thought her belly-button

176

especially pleasing, for it was perfectly round and protruded gently outwards from within a little circular ridge of flesh.

'When you've seen enough, maybe we can get on with the pictures,' she said, her voice friendly. 'Stand about there and turn the lens ring until you've got me in clear focus.'

He experimented for a moment or two and told her he'd have to stand much further back to get all of her in.

'I know that – I want close-ups of the marks. Take me in sections – got the idea?'

There were four red weals across her belly from Dmytryk's belt. Hugo focussed on them, the view-finder showing him that the top edge of his picture would just take in the red-brown nubs of her breasts and the bottom edge would cut across her dark tuft. He took three shots, then asked Peg to move her feet apart while he focused on her thighs. She had three angry-looking welts across them and Hugo snapped away, cutting her off at the knees and belly-button.

Asking Peg to move her feet apart had nothing to do with the photography – Hugo wanted a more complete view of her dark-brown curls and the long furrow beneath them. When he'd taken enough pictures for her felonious purposes, he amused himself by using up the rest of the film on shots of her luscious bundles and the plump join of her thighs. His tail was stiff in his trousers when he handed the camera back and sat down again.

'Thanks,' said Peg, giving him a warm smile. 'Pour yourself another drink while I make myself decent.'

He was sitting on the sofa when she came back from the bed-room wearing a full length negligee of pale green satin with a black sash tied round her narrow waist. She took the drink he had poured for her and sat down beside him.

'Why are you being so helpful to me?' she asked. 'What's in it for you?'

'I dislike Dmytryk intensely,' he answered, giving her his professionally charming smile. 'On the other hand, I have never yet found it possible to dislike a pretty woman. And you promised to answer a question for me.'

177

'Sure,' she said easily, 'what do you want to know?'

'When Ambrose Howard was shot he was naked and covered in Chanel Five – the perfume you're wearing now. And there were cords lying beside him. Is it possible that you and he were playing an exciting little game together – a game which involved cords and a revolver?'

'You mean did I shoot him?' she asked, unperturbed.

'No, I don't mean that at all, Peg. I'm sure you didn't shoot him. But in the excitement of the game – perhaps in the moment of climax – the revolver may have gone off by accident.'

'Is that what you told Switzer?' she asked.

'Is he a policeman? I've told it to nobody. Nor do I intend to. I've heard several different versions of how Ambrose came to be shot, some more plausible than others. If it was an accident, then that's the end of it.'

Peg crossed her legs and her thin satin negligee slipped from her knee and bared her to halfway up her slender thighs.

'Maybe it was an accident,' she said, 'but he wasn't playing games with me that night, so I can't help you.'

'But you've been questioned?'

'Everybody whose phone number was in Ambrose's book has been questioned. How about you?'

'We'd only just met and I was staying in a hotel. Obviously he had no number listed for me.'

'I said I'd got no secrets,' said Peg, 'I'll tell you what I told Dectective Switzer. Sometimes Ambrose called me to go over to his house and play with ropes and stockings and ribbons and all sorts. But on the night he was shot I was with somebody else and we played games from eleven at night till five the next morning. I had to tell Switzer his name because he threatened to arrest me for obstruction if I didn't, but I don't have to tell you.'

'Thank you for answering my question,' said Hugo, turning on the full power of his charm. 'If Dmytryk gets difficult about compensating you, tell him I'll back your story if you have to go to Norma Gilbert with it. You'll have no trouble then.'

178

'What are you after?' she asked. 'A cut?'

'A what?'

'A percentage – you're trying to deal yourself in on my action, right?'

'No, no, no!' Hugo exclaimed, outraged by the suggestion.

After a moment he laughed and reached out to take hold of the two ends of Peg's sash and pull them slowly away from each other. The knot came undone and her negligee fell open to show him her magnificent melons and the dark curls showing just above her crossed thighs.

'Is that what you're after?' she said, her thin eyebrows arching upwards. 'Why didn't you say so before? I'd love to get acquainted with you that way.'

She took his hand and rubbed it slowly over her soft belly, then stood up and led him to the bedroom. Her bed was low and broad, with a redwood headboard that had uprights to which wrists could be tied. The fitted bed-cover was made of long-haired Angora, silky and white, and while Hugo was half-deciding to buy one like it for his own bed, Peg moved behind him.

'Put your hands behind you,' she said over his shoulder.

'I must undress,' he said, 'you are almost naked already.'

'I'll take care of that for you. Hands behind your back.'

Without understanding what she had in mind, he put his hands behind him and heard a click as she snapped steel handcuffs on his wrists.

'I thought you used cords,' he said, feeling her hands sliding quickly down his legs. He looked down and was just in time to see her fasten another pair of handcuffs round his ankles.

'But that makes me completely helpless!' he said in surprise, 'I can't move a step without falling over!'

'Right!' said Peg, pushing him violently in the small of the back.

He fell forward, his legs struck the side of the bed and he pitched onto his face on the soft cover. At once Peg jumped on his back and he gasped as her knees dug into him. She crawled the length of his body, put a hand under his chin, twined the other in his hair and pulled. It was so painful that Hugo scrabbled forward with his knees, tears in his eyes, until he lay completely on the bed and Peg pinned him face-down with one bare foot on the back of his neck.

'Now I'll have the truth out of you,' she said, a note of cruelty in her voice.

Hugo had no time to say anything. Peg was behind him again, her hands fumbling under his waist for his belt-buckle. She jerked his trousers open roughly and dragged them and his shorts down his legs to expose his bottom.

'Let's see if a good slippering loosens your tongue,' she said and Hugo groaned as she leathered his bottom with one of her slippers, hard enough to hurt him.

'Not talking yet?' she demanded after a dozen blows. 'How do you like this, then?'

She pulled the cheeks of his bottom apart and stabbed a finger-nail sharply into the knot-hole between them. 'Ah, that makes you jump! It's only the start of what you'll get if you don't come clean.'

'What do you want? Tell me, for God's sake!' Hugo gasped as her sharp nail jabbed into him again.

'You're making it tough on yourself,' she warned him, and she forced her hand between his thighs until her nails touched his soft dependants.

'No, don't!' he moaned in alarm. 'I'll give you anything you like!'

'I guessed that would loosen your tongue,' she sneered, 'I'll shred them if you don't tell me!'

Before he could answer, her weight was off the back of his legs and her hand slid under his belly to grip his handle and pull at it so fiercely that he rolled over on his back at once. While he lay gasping from the pain, Peg seated herself across his thighs and stared at his exposed parts.

'I'll have you begging for mercy,' she breathed harshly, her brown eyes dark with unspeakable emotion. 'Why are you pretending to be helping me? Who put you up to it?'

'No one! I told you I hate Dmytryk!'

Peg ran her thumb-nail up his stem from root to tip, making it jerk as if she had slit it with a blade.

'Not good enough,' she said.

'I thought you'd let me make love to you if I helped you,' Hugo said quickly, seeing her nail poised for another pass.

She snorted in outright disbelief and scratched his plums. Hugo squirmed on the bed-cover, unable to escape her attentions.

'It's the truth!' he exclaimed. 'When I saw you upside-down I wanted you.'

'So you're just another pig who thinks he can stick it into any woman he wants,' she said questioningly. 'Well, you had your paws all over me when you were getting me loose and your snout was between my legs when you thought I wouldn't notice. There's no difference between you and Dmytryk – you're a couple of slobs.'

'But I don't want to beat you, Peg! I want to make love to you the way a woman should be loved – I swear it!'

'You think you can side-track me with love-talk?' she said ferociously and dragged his shaft upright to sink her finger-nails into it. 'It won't work – I know you're up to something and I'm going to have it out of you!'

Her nails sank in deeper and at the same time those of her other hand nipped into the loose skin of his pendants. Holding him like that, she began to jerk and down brutally.

'You won't hold out against this!' she said vindictively, her hands moving so fast that Hugo's throbbing part became a blaze of agonising sensation.

Unbearable pangs ripped through him and he shrieked in the tormented discharge wrung from him by Peg's vicious attentions. His back arched off the bed and he shook like a man touching a live wire, his elixir gushing from him in excruciating ecstasy.

It took him some time to recover, and by then Peg had wiped him dry and unfastened the handcuffs from his wrists and ankles. He lay where he was, across her bed, exhausted by the mental anguish she had put him through. She brought him another glass of whisky and ice and sat by him on the bed, her legs tucked under her and her green negligee open to show her body.

'You really had me thinking you intended to torture me

181

to death,' he said, 'I admire your skill, Peg, though it is not for me.'

'Maybe not,' she answered easily, 'but it got you going pretty fast – some men take a lot more punishment than that before they squirt off. You were a push-over. There's hardly a mark on you.'

'I'm pleased to hear it! Not long ago a crazy woman almost bit it off and the marks of that have only just faded.'

'Anybody I know?' Peg asked, laughing at him gently.

'Mildred Gilbert – Norma's mother. Do you know her?'

'That old battle-axe! How did she get her claws into someone like you?'

'Not her claws, her teeth,' said Hugo with a smile. 'It's hard to explain now, even to myself. She came to my apartment because she thinks her daughter may have shot Ambrose and she wanted my help in keeping someone else quiet.'

'But she knows damned well her daughter didn't do it!' Peg exclaimed indignantly. 'She shot him herself!'

'Do you know that for a fact or are you saying it because you don't like Mildred?'

'I'm sure enough that I told the police. I hope they give her the third degree till she confesses and then fry her in the electric chair! What kind of mother tries to frame her own daughter – answer me that!'

'But Mildred has an alibi and the police must have checked it. She was with Dmytryk all night, or so she says.'

'Banging her own daughter's fiancé? That's about right for Mildred Gilbert, stealing everything she can from Norma. She's been doing that for years and Norma didn't find out till she moved out on her own and got her own accountant and attorney.'

'That may be so,' said Hugo. 'but it doesn't mean that Mildred shot Ambrose.'

'It shows what kind of woman she is! No wonder she wanted to play around with you if she's been shacking up with Dmytryk to spite Norma – he's as exciting as a barrel of cold mush!'

'How much compensation will you ask him for, Peg?'

'I don't see it's any of your business,' she answered, frowning at him. 'But I'm asking fifty thousand dollars for not telling the press how he got me drunk and tied me up and thrashed me before he raped me. He's broke, and he'll stay broke until he marries Norma Gilbert. I figure that fifty thousand is the most he can raise against his expectations.'

Hugo smiled and reached up to clasp Peg by the waist and pull her down close to him.

'I like you,' he said. 'You have an uncomplicated approach to your work and your clients. You should be in movies.'

'That's what Ambrose used to say,' she answered, nestling against him. 'He said I had the looks and instincts to be a star and I could act better than most he directed.'

'He was a perceptive man and I'm sorry he's dead,' said Hugo, slipping a hand under her open negligee to play with her big soft bundles, 'did you know him well?'

'He'd call me maybe once a month when he wanted a change from the movie stars he usually fooled around with.'

'And you perform the same service for Oskar Brandenstein – was it Ambrose who introduced you to Oskar?'

'That's right – it was when Oskar started to make big money at Ignaz International. Ambrose took me to Oskar's house-warming party in Beverly Hills and left me there with him as a kind of gift. That was pretty nice of him, I guess.'

Hugo doubted very much whether Ambrose had left her with Oskar out of kindness. He wanted to get Oskar involved with Peg and her dangerous games in the hope he would go too far and hurt her – and so open himself up to pressure from her – or from Ambrose working through her. That suggested that Ambrose saw Oskar as a threat to his own position as Ignaz's top producer-director. But had Ambrose been so devious?

There was the question of why he had invited Hugo back to his house the evening they had dinner together and arranged it so that he made love to Connie and Thelma. At the time Hugo had thought Ambrose was just an ordinary run-of-the-mill pervert with a taste for foursomes and swapping partners. But now he asked himself if there was more to it than that and thought one possible answer was to separate him from Oskar, who had brought him to Hollywood. If so, then it looked as if Ambrose was more afraid of being displaced by Oskar than anyone had guessed.

'You've got a nice touch,' Peg said softly, obviously enjoying having her breasts felt. 'At least you're not trying to twist them off my chest.'

'It grieves me to think that these superb bobbles should be abused and tortured by men who cannot appreciate their merits. Did Ambrose treat them brutally?'

'Never,' she answered comfortably, snuggling close to him. 'He never beat me – he liked to be tied up and spanked.'

'And Oskar – does he enjoy that too?'

'Not him -- he always wants to tie me up and slap me around before he sticks it in.'

'The same as Dmytryk, in fact?'

'Sort of, but Oskar uses his hands and you saw that Dmytryk is a lot nastier. Maybe he does that trick with the champagne bottle all the time in his own country, but it was new to me -- and I thought I'd seen everything. I was wondering just where he'd jam his pecker in when you rescued me.'

'Would you have minded which entrance he picked?' Hugo asked.

'It makes no difference to me,' she said. 'That's my job.'

Hugo sat up on the bed to take off his clothes, but Peg had other ideas and, while he was hauling his shirt over his head, she took advantage of his temporary blindness to wrap her legs round his neck and throw him sideways, as if they were wrestlers in a ring. Hugo thrashed about on the bed to get his arms out of the shirt-sleeves, hampered by his trousers down round his knees and unable to see what was happening while Peg bounced him about with surprising strength. By the time he had his head and arms free he found himself face-down, his mouth pressed against her

184

walnut-brown curls by the pressure of her thighs round his neck.

'Kiss me!' she ordered.

He flicked the tip of his tongue over the petals of soft flesh between her legs until he could force it a little way inside. Her legs released him and opened wide, and he got his hands between them to curl her petals back and use the flat of his tongue on her exposed bud. She flopped about on her back as her excitement got the better of her.

'You're not getting off easily – not after what you did to me,' Hugo warned her.

He knelt upright between her thighs, put his hands under her and lifted her legs and bottom right off the bed until she was balanced precariously on her shoulder-blades, her feet hanging down towards her face and her bare bottom in the air.

'There is something both comical and at the same time appealing about a woman upside-down,' he said, his hand roaming at will over the cheeks of her bottom and between her legs. 'Now here are two interesting openings and I shall put a thumb in each – like that!'

'Oh!' she cried out. 'Oh, Hugo!'

'Into which shall I plunge?' he asked, and although his question required no answer, Peg gurgled, '*Either! Both!*'

'Or neither,' he taunted her.

He shuffled sideways and jerked her sharply backwards with his thumbs. Her legs flailed through the air and she landed on her back, her negligee crumpled under her shoulders, and bounced on the springy mattress. Before she knew what he had in mind, he got rid of his trousers, straddled her head and flung himself on her, his face between her thighs. He used both hands to peel her open and rubbed his tongue roughly on her pink nub.

Her hot and wet mouth closed over Hugo's spike and her breasts were like pillows under his belly as he and she excited each other frantically. Her body convulsed under him when she reached her crisis and a moment later he cried out loudly and spurted into her sucking mouth.

Later on, when they lay side by side and rested, he asked her about Mildred Gilbert again.

'You still haven't told me anything to suggest that Mildred shot Ambrose.'

'Haven't I? Let me tell you something – I heard her threaten to kill him, only the week before. And she meant it.'

'Where was this?'

'At his house. She didn't know I was there, that's why she spoke her mind. He called me over and we were fooling around in the bedroom when the door-bell rang. Ambrose was all trussed up and his pecker was standing up like a broom-handle, so he said not to answer it, but it kept on ringing. I had to untie him and he put his dressing-gown on and went down to see who was there. It was none of my business, but when I heard shouting I crept to the top of the stairs and listened. It was Mildred Gilbert and she was telling Ambrose she'd spill the beans to Ignaz if Norma didn't get the lead in the big new movie he was casting.'

'What beans – what does this mean?'

'She'd tell Ignaz what she knew.'

'I see. And what was that?'

'As far as I could make out, what she had on him was that he'd played around with Norma and got her pregnant. She mentioned some doctor who'd taken care of it, but I didn't catch his name properly. She said if the story got into the newspapers Ignaz would fire Ambrose.'

'Did her threat seem to worry him?'

'He laughed at her and called her a jealous old bitch. And he told her if the story got out Norma's career would be finished as well as his, because the fans wouldn't stand for Little Miss Sweetheart getting an abortion – and as Mildred depends on the thirty per cent of Norma's salary she collects as her manager, she'd better keep her mouth shut.'

'Thirty per cent!' Hugo exclaimed in horror.

'That's when Mildred got vicious. She told Ambrose she'd get him. She said she'd get him in a way that wouldn't hurt Norma or herself.'

186

'Such as?'

'She said she'd kill him.'

'Oh, Peg – can you be sure she said that, or was she just abusive?'

'She said she'd kill him. I heard the words plainly. They were shuffling around in the hall and I guessed he was pushing her out of the door. So I went back to the bedroom and waited for him to come up.'

'That spoiled the evening, I imagine.'

'Pretty much. Ambrose was furious and in no mood for fooling around with me. We finished a bottle together and got into bed and slept.'

'Do you honestly believe Mildred to be capable of carrying out her threat? Or was it no more than angry words?'

'Sure she's capable of killing – look what happened to the chauffeur who tried to put the squeeze on her.'

'I know nothing of this. Please tell me what happened.'

'A couple of years back she hired a French-Canadian boy to do the honours for her. He got the foolish notion that he could shake her down for a lot of money by threatening her with a picture he had.'

'A photograph, you mean?' Hugo asked immediately.

'I guess so. It was supposed to be a candid camera shot of Mildred with her panties down and twiddling herself. It was never found, afterwards.'

'Afterwards? What happened?'

'Mildred had the chauffeur drive her up the coast to San Francisco. It was late and they were travelling fast – the limo went over the edge with him in it. They found Mildred by the roadside with her clothes torn and scratched up some. She said she'd been thrown out when they went over the side and knocked unconscious.'

'The chauffeur was killed, I take it?'

'Burnt to a crisp,' said Peg, yawning.

'It could have been an accident. Who told you about the photograph – someone reliable, or just the usual Hollywood scandal-mongers?'

187

'It can't do any harm to tell you now – Ambrose told me one night when I was over at his place.'

'He had a great interest in photographs of women in unusual poses,' Hugo said thoughtfully. 'I wonder if the one of Mildred was taken by her French-Canadian boy or given to him by Ambrose to make trouble for her?'

'If it was, then it gave her plenty of trouble. The investigation into the chauffeur's death went on a long time before it was dropped as an accident. I even heard it said that Mildred paid a lot of money to get it dropped.'

'Perhaps,' said Hugo, 'but in the short time I have been here I have learned that there is no such thing as the truth – only different versions of it, according to what is most convenient for whoever is telling it. You would prefer Mildred to be guilty of shooting Ambrose, yet she claims she was with Dmytryk all that night.'

'So she's a liar. She's got something on that slug to make him give her an alibi. But after what I told Switzer, maybe the police can crack the alibi.'

'Maybe,' Hugo said doubtfully, his hand clasped comfortably between Peg's warm thighs. 'Let's go for dinner somewhere and come back here afterwards.'

'I've had enough fooling around for one day,' she answered, 'and I've got weals across my belly to prove it.'

'And I've had enough of your games to last me a long time,' said Hugo. 'What I had in mind was to dine you well and then make love to you as romantically as they do in the movies.'

'But there's always a fade-out as soon as the girl gets kissed,' Peg objected. 'Nobody ever gets to make love in movies – not even the biggest stars.'

'I can show you what might happen after the fade-out,' Hugo offered, smiling at her and stroking lightly between her thighs. 'You can pretend to be Greta Garbo in the moon-light and I'll be me, kissing you until you melt with passion.'

'That sounds good,' said Peg, 'only can I be Joan Crawford? They say I look a lot like her and her movies are terrific.'

188

'Darling Peg, with me you can be anyone you want to be and I shall make love to you tenderly until you fall asleep in my arms.'

It was in Hugo's mind that Peg knew a great many of Hollywood's odder secrets and that she could be a most useful friend for him to have.

Chapter 12

A lesson from Desma

Oskar Brandenstein had arranged for Hugo to have lessons from Mrs Desma Williams, a language coach he recommended highly, and Hugo had gone so far as to agree an hour a day with her. But he had allowed himself to be diverted by events after only the first lesson. He now realised with great alarm that the shooting-schedule for *Sinner and Saint*, as the Mary Magdalene movie was now provisionally called, would require him to appear before the camera before very long. In a great panic he telephoned Desma Williams, apologised profusely and persuaded her to give him an appointment for five that evening.

She lived in Bonanza Drive, up in the hills north of Hollywood Boulevard, in a white-painted clapboard house that stood on the steep slope up from the road. Hugo parked his white tourer outside and ran up the steps to knock at her green front door. The first time he had seen her he had been astonished by her appearance – she was as tall as he was and twice his circumference. Her smooth face put her in her mid-thirties and her straw-coloured hair was cropped as short as a man's, as if to make up for the over-abundance of the rest of her.

That first time Hugo was there, she had been wearing a knee-length smock of white linen. Today she wore a loose green frock, printed with giant red poppies, and under it her breasts were immense pumpkins and her belly was like a water-barrel.

'Come on in,' she said in her beautiful contralto voice, holding out her hand to him. In contrast to the rest of her body, her hands were not pudgy at all – they were narrow-backed and had long slim fingers.

'I've behaved disgracefully in missing so many lessons,' said Hugo, turning on his charm, 'I am more grateful than I can say to you for seeing me at short notice, Mrs Williams.'

'Call me Desma,' she said, 'I like to establish a bond of friendship and trust with my students – I find it helps.'

She led him into her pleasant living-room, waddling on legs set widely apart, her water-melons rolling freely under her bright smock. She saw that Hugo was staring at her, though trying from politeness not to, and she grinned at him.

'When you get to be my size you stop fretting about trying to look glamorous,' she told him. 'What you've got is what you've got and you might just as well be comfortable with yourself as uncomfortable.'

'You are a very natural person, Desma,' said Hugo. 'That's unusual – at least in my experience so far.'

She waved him to a chair and lowered herself slowly onto a pale brown sofa designed for two people but which she almost filled by herself.

'If you mean that Hollywood is full of phonies,' she said 'you're not saying anything that hasn't been said a million times already. Easy money attracts crooks, con-artists, pimps, whores and get-rich-quick merchants. But you'll also find some real people here if you look for them, even if at first sight they don't seem exactly like the folks back home.'

'I have met some already,' said Hugo, thinking of Thelma.

'Good – when you meet real people you should make them your friends. But you don't need me to tell you that. Now, let's see what we can do about your accent – you said on the telephone that you start shooting soon. Read something for me,' and she handed him the morning newspaper.

'Anything in particular?' he asked.

191

'Anything you please. Start reading and keep going till I tell you to stop.'

Of the stories on the front page, one was headed NEW CLUE IN MOVIE SLAYING, and Hugo started to read it aloud, using his voice to the best advantage. The story was typical newspaper rubbish, as he knew from reading it over breakfast that morning, but the subject was too interesting to him not to choose it. The reporter's name was given under the headline as Padraig O'Leary, Special Crime Correspondent, and his story gave a summary of how *International celebrity film director* Ambrose Howard of Ignaz International Studios had been found shot dead in his home on Glendale Boulevard after a neighbour reported hearing a shot fired at half past midnight.

The vital new clue mentioned in the headline proved to be a possible sighting in Mexico City of Luis Hernandez, chauffeur to the slain director, who had been missing since the crime was discovered. Captain Bastaple of the LA Police Department was quoted as saying that he had sent one of his best men to Mexico to make contact with the local police and that he expected news hourly that Hernandez had been apprehended. All of which sounded most unconvincing to Hugo. He thought it more likely that, caught between pressure from the newspapers to do something and pressure from Ignaz International to do nothing, the bold police captain had made the obvious move of sending Detective Switzer on a wild goose chase round Mexico City.

If by some incredible stroke of misfortune the detective did capture the chauffeur and get him back to Hollywood, great indeed would be Captain Bastaple's embarrassment when Ignaz told him that Hernandez must not in any circumstances be allowed to talk about his dead employer's personal affairs and, in particular, the photographs he had taken of him with the stars.

'You can stop now,' said Desma. 'You speak English correctly enough, but the intonation is wrong. That's what we have to work on. Every language has a rhythm of its own and your teacher did not understand the rhythm of English.'

'Will it be difficult for me to learn, do you think?'

'You're an actor and you've been trained in the theatre to have a ear for dialogue. You'll pick it up easily enough. Can you give me two hours a day for the next ten days, say?'

Desma's thighs were so fat, Hugo observed, that she had no choice but to sit with her knees apart. She was bare-legged and wore white sandals with heels and ankle-straps.

'Two hours a day for ten days is impossible,' he said, smiling at her to show his goodwill, 'I'll come here as often as I can until we start shooting, but some days it will be at very short notice.'

Desma ran a hand through her straw-coloured hair and the raising of her arm made her squashy melons roll in a way that gripped Hugo's attention and indicated that they were not restrained in any way under her bright smock.

'There is one other way I've found works,' she said, 'but it will cost you more than a course of two-hour lessons.'

'The cost is not important, only the outcome. What is this other way?'

'Twenty-four hours straight. We'll both be exhausted at the end of it, but you'll be speaking English as if you'd learned it at your mother's knee. What do you say?'

Her clear blue eyes stared at him inquisitively as he thought about it and a moment later she showed that she had his measure by leaning back casually with her fine-fingered hands clasped round one slightly raised knee. Hugo gazed along the pale expanse of exposed inner thigh as her position lifted her loose frock above her knees.

'You're staring at me as if you want to eat me alive!' she commented.

'Some such thought was in my mind, Desma,' he confessed.

'I thought you were here to talk business, not for a social visit,' and she leaned back further, her clasped hand pulling her plump knee a little higher, so that Hugo could see halfway up her thigh.

193

'There's no reason why we can't make it both,' he said, turning the force of his dark eyes and irresistible smile on her, 'I'll stay here with you for the next twenty-four hours and at the end of that time I expect to be speaking English perfectly?'

'As well as I do myself,' she agreed, smiling back at him. 'But you'll be a wreck by the time I've finished with you.'

Hugo's pointer had been upright since he had glimpsed her massive domes rolling about inside her smock. He wanted to know what it felt like to handle their superabundance and put his face between them. He had never in his life made love to any woman the size of Desma Williams and he found it hard to imagine how it would be to lie on her barrel-belly and slide his stem up between her great tree-trunks of thighs. *Satyriasis*, he said to himself with an inner grin of acknowledgement to Theodor Prosz for telling him the word that best described his permanent state of mind.

Desma hauled herself to her feet and went over to a writing-desk by the wall, letting him see the way the ponderous globes of her backside rolled up and down as she walked – a sight that made him sigh in anticipation of getting his hands on them and sinking his fingers deep into their rolypoly flesh. She came back with a recording-machine which she set on the coffee-table between them.

'You read well enough,' she said, 'but I want you to talk into this so we have something to analyse together. That way you'll be able to hear where you're going just slightly wrong.'

'What shall I talk about?'

'Anything you can keep going on for five or ten minutes. I know – go on from what you read in the newspaper and give me your views on the shooting of Ambrose Howard – that's something everyone in Hollywood has views on.'

'Did you know him?' Hugo asked.

'Yes – everybody knew him. He used to send me his young hopefuls to teach how to speak English properly.'

'And naturally, they are all film stars now,' said Hugo, giving her his charmingly impudent grin. 'Just as I will be.'

194

'Most of them are working in films,' she answered, 'but only one has become a big star so far – Thelma Baxter.'

'I know Thelma well. She needed your help, did she?'

'If you know Thelma well then you've slept with her,' Desma said with a grin. 'She came to Hollywood after she'd won a beauty competition in her home town. She has a natural gift for comedy on the screen and she did very well in silent movies. When talkies came in she was in trouble – she had an accent that set your teeth on edge. But a few lessons in pronunciation and voice control made her what she is now. She was the first student Ambrose sent me. I'll switch the machine on now and you start talking.'

'Thelma told me how she found Ambrose dead in his bathroom,' Hugo began. 'She thought the killer was still in the house and went looking with the revolver she picked up from beside the body and so spoiled whatever finger-prints were on it. She may have caught a glimpse of someone disappearing into the darkness, but she may have imagined it – just as she may have imagined that she saw a woman disguised as a man. She believes that Ambrose was shot by Norma Gilbert, though her reasons do not seem to be very convincing.'

'Norma Gilbert the *Sweetheart of All the World?*' Desma said and smiled softly.

She was half-lying on her sofa, her yellow-haired head resting on its high back, one foot on the floor and the other up on the cushions. Her raised knee made her red and green frock fell down her thigh to reveal an abundant expanse of smooth pale flesh.

'In this belief Thelma is not alone,' Hugo continued, his eyes shining as he stared at the inviting inner thigh being shown to him, 'Miss Gilbert's mother thinks her daughter is responsible, although I am not clear why. However, she is an unbalanced woman and her opinions are not reliable. This assumes, of course, that Ambrose was murdered. Dr Theodor Prosz believes that it was suicide in an alcoholic depression. Mr Stefan Ignaz pretends to believe the same thing and the studio publicity department is promoting the theory far and wide.'

'I never heard anything so outright stupid!' Desma interrupted him. 'Ambrose Howard kill himself? Not in a million years!'

There was a flat gold wedding-ring on the hand with which she was stroking her bare thigh absent-mindedly. Hugo's stalk jumped eagerly in his trousers.

'Prosz gives the dread of impotence as the reason for Ambrose's depression,' he said, parting his own legs to draw Desma's attention to the bulge in his trousers.

'Then he's a liar,' she said, her hand disappearing from Hugo's sight under her frock.

She must be touching the softness where her massive thighs joined, he realised. He had half a mind to move across to the sofa with her and put his own hand up her clothes, but he was enjoying her tantalising little game and there was no reason to cut it short – they had twenty-four hours.

'Yes,' he said, 'Dr Theodor Prosz is a liar and a pervert, though both pass without comment in Hollywood. Gale Paget thinks that Prosz is the killer. Nurse Bell says he was with her that evening, but she is totally unreliable where the doctor's interests are concerned – she lies for him as readily as she whores for him.'

'You seem to know a lot about the shooting,' said Desma. 'None of these people have been named in the newspapers. What's your interest?'

'I knew Ambrose briefly and I liked him. I've been asking questions, that's all.'

'Did you get any answers to your questions?'

'I've been told a great many lies, that's the only thing I can be sure of. The ordinary rules of law and logic do not apply in this town, it would seem. Those who were involved with Ambrose are using his death to project their own anxieties, fears and insecurities outwards. Mildred Gilbert blames Chester Chataway because he deflowered her daughter when she was a child, though secretly she fears that her daughter shot Ambrose. Chataway blames Prince Dmytryk because he is engaged to be married to Norma Gilbert, and Chataway has been infatuated with Norma since the day he took her virginity. Dmytryk claims that Stefan Ignaz is the killer because he hates him. Prosz is using the death too as a model of his own future suicide when the cocaine fails him – to him the contemplation of Ambrose naked and dead and drenched in perfume is a sort of foreplay for his own eventual fatal climax.'

'Foreplay,' said Desma, 'I like the sound of that. Come and sit by me while I rewind the tape and we'll work through it.'

She did not, as he expected, remove her white-sandalled foot from the sofa when he went round the coffee-table. Instead, she hitched herself further back into a corner of the sofa and pressed her lifted knee against the back-rest, to make room for him to sit between her sprawled legs. The wide separation of her thighs pulled her smock up almost to her groins – a finger-breadth higher and her underwear would be on show.

The tape recorder on the table was whirring loudly as it rewound. Hugo ignored it and put his palm flat on Desma's bare thigh and stroked quickly upwards.

'Foreplay,' he told her with a smile that made her clear blue eyes gleam. 'In twenty-four hours we can enjoy a lot of foreplay together, Desma, and as many climaxes as you find pleasing.'

She was not another Gale, he saw, to bare her secrets to him instantly and snatch her pleasure almost in sight of the doorman. Desma would want to approach her crisis slowly and spin it out. He slid his hand under her poppy-strewn smock, being careful not to raise it and so discover too quickly the secret of what sort of underwear enveloped her mighty bottom. His palm lay on the bulge of her belly and her flesh was very warm and very pliable under his fingers.

'Listen carefully,' she said, switching the recorder on.

For the next twenty minutes she took him through the recording, explaining where small changes would improve his pronunciation and speech-rhythm, having him try it, bit by bit, until she was sure he had it right. By then Hugo had made a discovery that made his heart beat faster – his

197

fingers roving down the dome of her belly to between her enormous thighs found no underwear at all.

As soon as Desma was satisfied with his first lesson, Hugo flicked up her smock and saw, between her fat thighs, a broad expanse of thick dark hair that extended well up her belly – its colour very unlike the straw-yellow hair of her head. He played with the long fleshy lips under her thatch and opened them and touched her secret button. She grew wetter and wetter, her clear blue eyes gazing fondly at him all the time. After five or ten minutes she started to utter cavernous sighs and her giant wobblers heaved under her smock like an earthquake. Her long fingers reached for his trouser-buttons and undid them deftly.

'I'm ready for you,' she murmured, moving her body round a little until she could rest her short-cropped head on the arm-rest of the sofa, still with one foot on the floor and one on the sofa-cushions with her knee raised, offered him access to her pleasure-ground.

For Hugo the position was an awkward one as he tugged out his hard peg and spread himself over her. With one leg over the side of the sofa and his other knee on the cushions as the pivot of his actions, he pushed firmly up into Desma's capacious burrow. The sensation of being engulfed by her warm and wet flesh was so exciting, and the long wait through the lesson while he massaged her belly, had so aroused him that he knew his golden moments were going to arrive very soon.

He gripped Desma's heavy melons through her smock and sank his fingers deeply into them while he stabbed into her belly. Her fingers lay along his cheeks, pulling his face close to hers so that she could kiss him.

She held him in a long, strange, sucking kiss that pulled his tongue into her mouth and drew the breath from his body at the instant his belly clenched and spouted his passion into her. Her belly heaved under him as his breath fled.

'I'm going to have to slow you down, Hugo,' she said when he could breath again. 'You're too quick on the draw for me. Sit up now and make yourself decent – we've got work to do.'

Her matter-of-fact tone surprised him, but he concluded that she was slow to arouse – perhaps because of her bulk. He climbed off her and sat upright while he tucked his wet and shrinking hilt away and fastened his trousers. Desma pulled her bright smock down over the dark bush between her legs but otherwise stayed sprawled across the sofa.

'Carry on talking,' she said, 'give me more to work on.'

'Shall I read you something?'

'No, I want your own words and sentences. Tell me more about the shooting – that's a subject you seem fluent in.'

'As you wish,' he said, smiling at her in contentment now he was sure that she would let him make love to her as often as he chose, 'Stefan Ignaz is the prime suspect on my list. Besides Prince Dmytryk, Theodor Prosz suspects Ignaz and is spreading the tale that it was suicide as a cover. Connie Young is convinced that Ignaz did it, and Oskar Brandenstein hints at it so heavily that he might as well put an advertisement in the newspapers.'

Hugo thought it impolitic to add that he had met a madam and one of her whores who also thought Ignaz responsible, on the strength of drunken gossip by a client.

'There are various reasons given for why Stefan Ignaz wanted Ambrose dead,' he continued, 'some to do with money and all to do with sex in one way or another.'

'Sex in one way or another,' said Desma with a chuckle. 'Movie people do it to each other in all sorts of different ways, some of them nice, some very nice and some weird.'

'So I have discovered,' Hugo told her with a grin. He put his hand on the inside of her raised thigh again and stroked it slowly while he talked into the recorder.

'The evening I had dinner with Ambrose we shared two famous film stars between us, changing over halfway, so to speak,' he said. 'That alerted me to his well-developed appetite for the joys of women. But in the past few days it has emerged that he made love to almost every major star in Hollywood – and had souvenirs and pictures to prove it.'

'He had that reputation,' Desma agreed, 'but like everything else round here it was exaggerated. Sorry – I didn't mean to interrupt. Go on.'

'It was not exaggerated by much, to judge by certain photographs I have seen,' said Hugo.

He reached right up under her loose frock to grasp one of her great bouncers and his stalk began to stir again in his underwear.

'The money theory is that because Ambrose had proof of his frolics he was able to make demands on Ignaz – a stock-holding, a seat on the board of Ignaz International – whatever it is that he is supposed to have wanted. The sex theory is that Ambrose extended his conquests to include Mrs Ignaz – and for a reason I do not propose to divulge, I know this to be true. Some believe that there was a witness to the shooting.'

'No,' said Desma, forgetting that this was a lesson and not a conversation. 'If anyone had seen Ignaz shoot Ambrose Howard he would have been eliminated straight afterwards.'

'Unless, delicious thought,' said Hugo, his entire arm up under the smock to feel Desma's big bundles, 'unless when Ignaz arrived to remonstrate with the lover of his beautiful young wife, he found her naked in the hated rival's bed-room, tying a pretty velvet ribbon round Ambrose's tail, as laurel wreathes were once placed on the heads of ancient Greek athletes at the Olympic Games.'

He paused while Desma laughed so heartily that her melons shook in his hands like huge jellies.

'Imagine the scene,' he resumed, when the quaking ceased at last, 'shouting and confusion and Ambrose snatching his revolver from the bedside drawer to protect himself against imminent attack. Ignaz is then in fear of his own life and seizes the gun from Ambrose and chases him into the bathroom, jams the muzzle to his bare chest and pulls the trigger. Virginia Ignaz lies shocked and naked on the bed – Ignaz forces her to put her clothes on and drags her away before Thelma can arrive on the scene. Thus, you see, there is a witness who will not speak, for it is against her own interests for her husband to be arrested and tried for murder.'

'Stop there for now,' said Desma, 'we'll work through that passage. I must say that I love your imagination, Hugo – if the Police Department were half as bright as you they'd have the killer in the cells by now.'

While the tape was rewinding she sat up, took the hem of her smock in both hands and hauled it up and over her head. Hugo stared in delight at her massive bare bobbles as she leaned back again in the corner of the sofa, his hand lying fondly on the coarse tuft between her legs.

'An incentive to get the lesson right first time,' she explained.

Once again she played through the tape, stopping it frequently to comment on different phrases and to make him repeat them her way. She gestured with her hands while she taught and this caused her ponderous breasts to roll about her chest in a manner that aroused Hugo until he found it difficult to concentrate. As a result, nearly half a hour passed in trial and repetition before Desma was ready to accept that he had grasped the lesson.

'We're not trying to break any records,' she said, her blue eyes staring at him appraisingly. 'Play with me till I tell you.'

Hugo threw off his green suede jacket and his open-necked shirt, stripped off his trousers and underwear, his shoes and socks, and knelt naked between Desma's splayed thighs. He pressed his chest against her fat and rough-haired mound and lay forward up her domed belly to use both hands on her pumpkins. He took their pink nubs between fore-fingers and thumbs and stretched them rhythmically. Desma sighed loudly and held his wrists to encourage him to continue, her flat gold wedding-ring immediately beneath his eyes.

'Not that it matters, but where is Mr Williams?' he asked

'In San Bernardino,' she sighed, her fingers rubbing at his wrists to make him play harder with her. 'He ran off with my sister Cordelia.'

'Her name is as unusual as yours, Desma. Where is your family from?'

'Seattle,' she murmured, her eyes closing in delight. 'My father was a teacher and crazy about Shakespeare. My real name's Desdemona, but I've been Desma since I was a little girl. You can't imagine me ever being little, can you?'

'I adore you the way you are now,' Hugo exclaimed, his spike prodding against the sofa cushion as he joggled her breasts and rubbed his chest into the soft flesh between her thighs, 'there's so much of you to make love to – I hardly know where to start! I want to do it to your gigantic bundles and in your belly-button and up the hot hollows under your arms and between the cheeks of your bottom and everywhere I can get hold of handfuls of you!'

'Twenty-four hours won't be long enough,' she gasped, her hands clasping his face again to pull him up her body and get his mouth to hers. Hugo let go of her breasts and reached down between her spread thighs to open her wide with one hand and guide his trembling shaft into her with the other.

'Can you do all that to me?' she asked as he sank deeply into her soft warmth, 'or will you go flat as a bust balloon after the second time round?'

'All that and more,' Hugo promised, rocking to and fro in a strong and steady rhythm that made her gasp in pleasure and press her open mouth to his mouth.

This time there was no mistake – he kept himself in check and slid in and out for as long as was necessary to push her up the long slope of delight to her climactic peak. She groaned and cried and sobbed loudly into his open mouth, sucked at his breath and heaved so furiously under him that he was reminded of a cowboy movie he had seen, where rugged hero Buck Jones clung one-handed to the back of a wild bronco and rode it to a standstill. The breath rushed out from Hugo's mouth and the passion from his loins as he rode Desma bareback on her sofa.

'Better,' she said when she regained the power of articulate speech, 'you're improving, Hugo.'

And so the lesson continued, Hugo speaking his exposi-

202

tion of the mystery surrounding the death of Ambrose Howard into the tape recorder in instalments and Desma criticizing each section in detail and showing him how it should sound. After a couple of hours of intensive learning interspersed with love-making, she put her smock on and went into the kitchen to cook dinner while Hugo rested full-length on the well-used sofa.

She cooked a simple and sustaining dinner of large and half-raw steaks with green salad and a bottle of Californian wine. Hugo was sceptical when he saw the label and relieved when it proved to be drinkable. He put his shirt and trousers on to sit at the table and eat with proper decency, so pleasing Desma, who was gazing at him with open affection now that he had twice made her sob in ecstasy and gave every indication of continuing to pleasure her after dinner.

'You put the case against Ignaz well,' she said as they ate. 'He didn't shoot Ambrose, of course, but the DA could give him a hard time in court.'

'How can you be sure that it wasn't Ignaz, Desma?'

'The obvious person did it – the only reason she wasn't arrested right off is because someone is protecting her, and Ignaz is the only person with influence enough for that.'

'Norma Gilbert, you mean? She admits she was with Ambrose.'

'No – the obvious person is Thelma Baxter,' said Desma, taking him by surprise. 'She *says* she heard a shot and went to see what had happened – and there was Ambrose dead. If you want my opinion, she fired the shot herself and then made up her story before she started to raise the alarm. Her finger-prints were on the gun, after all.'

'She explained that,' Hugo said thoughtfully.

'She explained a hell of a lot when you think about it,' said Desma, 'but one thing she hasn't bothered to explain is that she and Ambrose Howard were married.'

'I don't believe it!' Hugo exclaimed, 'they couldn't keep that quiet!'

'They could and they did. When Thelma first came to Hollywood and was playing bit-parts she and Ambrose fell for each other like a landslide. They were married in San Francisco and they kept it secret because they both thought Thelma's career in movies would go better if she was thought to be on her own. Understand what I'm saying?'

'You seem to be telling me that she might have less chances to lie on the casting-couch if she was known to be married to a director – is that it?'

'Especially with Stefan Ignaz, who is an extremely moralistic man in some ways and would never fool around with someone else's wife. And any girl who wants a contract with Ignaz International has to show Ignaz what she can do on her back first. So Thelma and Ambrose lived in separate houses and pretended they were having a big affair.'

'In a way, that's all they were doing,' said Hugo, 'but why should Thelma want to murder Ambrose six or seven years later – tell me that! It certainly wasn't jealousy – I was there with her when he made love to Connie Young.'

'Thelma's not jealous of Connie Young,' Desma said, 'she wasn't even jealous of the dozens of others he was sticking it into. Thelma likes to play around herself and she never grudged Ambrose his fun. But when he got serious and asked Thelma for a quiet divorce, that was it – she exploded!'

'He wanted to marry someone else? But why should he, when he had this very convenient arrangement with Thelma?'

'Ambrose was forty-four on his last birthday and he wanted children before he got too old. He found the girl he thought ideal to have them for him – pretty, clever and very young. He asked her to marry him and then told Thelma.'

'My God – who was the lucky girl?'

'Norma Gilbert, of course. He'd been diddling her for years and he was fond of her, though I'm sure he wasn't in love with her. Norma's movie career is in a slow patch right now - she's a couple of years too old to go on being the World's Sweetheart and she wants to get right away from her mother.'

204

'She's done that already,' Hugo pointed out, 'she lives in her own house and she will soon be married to Dmytryk.'

'Mildred Gilbert still dominates her mentally and Dmytryk is too much of a wet rag to protect Norma. More likely he'd gang up with Mildred to rob Norma after the marriage, but the engagement is only a bluff to stand Mildred off for a while, though I guess the Prince doesn't know that. The fact is that five years off having a couple of babies for Ambrose would suit Norma very well and he could guarantee her come-back.'

'But I've never thought of Thelma as the killer!' said Hugo. 'Are you certain that she and Ambrose were married?'

'I was a witness at the wedding, and so was my sister.'

'Even so, that doesn't prove that Thelma shot him.'

'Ambrose wasn't a poor man,' said Desma, 'Thelma inherits everything now he's dead – there's no family to make a claim. If she's innocent, why hasn't she announced they were married and claimed what's legally hers? She's kept it quiet, even from the police.'

'Poor Thelma,' said Hugo, 'I feel sorry for her. Are you going to tell what you know?'

'None of my business,' said Desma. 'If you ask me, Ambrose got what he deserved. I wish I'd had the guts to shoot my husband when I found him climbing off my sister.'

After dinner they started the lesson again in the living-room. Desma took her seat on the sofa, sitting upright this time, and Hugo hitched her colourful smock up round her belly and pushed her knees far enough apart for him to sit on the floor between them. He rested his cheek against the warm flesh of her inner thigh while he spoke into the recorder and listened to what she had to say, before putting his hand on her dark thatch and making love to her again.

About midnight they moved to her bedroom and lay naked, side by side, the tape recorder on the bed down by their feet. By then Hugo had made love to her five times, the latest into the deep and saucer-like depression of her belly-button while he attended to her concealed bud with his fingers so successfully that she sobbed in ecstasy for longer then he thought humanly possible. Like the bronco in the rodeo movie, she was at a standstill, lying limp, her body shiny with the perspiration of ecstatic convulsions and almost comatose with satisfaction. Her eyes turned towards Hugo in silent adoration as he wiped her wet belly with a corner of the sheet and lay down beside her. He saw that the time was right to get answers to questions she would have ignored earlier.

'There's a photograph of Lily Haden naked in your writing-desk, Desma,' he said softly, stroking her splayed-out breasts hypnotically, 'I saw it while you were making dinner. Does she have one of you?'

'You've guessed, haven't you?' she murmured, her blue eyes half-closed while his hands smoothed her soft flesh.

On a sudden impulse Hugo straddled her barrel of a belly and forced his bent knees into her arm-pits, his shaking stem hovering above the fat breasts he was playing with.

'Yes, I've guessed, Desma,' he said, 'but I would like to hear you tell me.'

'Very young girls find me attractive,' she sighed, her pink buds standing firm under his circling palms. 'It's because I'm so big, I guess – it makes me look friendly and comfortable. They feel they can tell me all their little problems while they hug me and hide their faces in my bosom.'

'And you find Lily very attractive,' said Hugo, 'so you stroke her – and then you bring her in here to undress her and lie on the bed and play with each other.'

'Not just Lily,' she sighed gently, 'Norma too – she's been coming here to play for years. And lots of others – the word spreads among them. I think I've fooled around with almost every star in Hollywood – the girls, that is.'

'You are a very surprising woman,' said Hugo, rubbing his trembling spike along the satin skin between her big balloons, 'does Norma Gilbert still visit you now she's grown up?'

'She was here in this bed with me the night Ambrose was shot — that's how I know she didn't do it.'

'But she was with him first that night and he made love to her,' said Hugo.

'He upset her by refusing her a part she wanted badly, so she came to me for comfort and I gave it to her.'

'I haven't had the pleasure of comforting Norma yet, though I've come close to it,' Hugo told her, his fingers gripping deeply into her great bundles to lift them and press them together round his hard stem. 'But I've comforted little Lily in the back of Chester Chataway's Rolls-Royce and I've comforted you, Desma – and now I'm going to comfort you again!'

Chapter 13

Party games at Oskar's

The announcement that the role of St Mary Magdalene in the epic of that name, on which shooting was shortly to begin at Ignaz International Studios, would be played by Norma Gilbert, surprised Hugo at first. On reflection he came to the conclusion that Norma had appealed over Oskar's head to Stefan Ignaz. How she had persuaded the mogul himself that she was right for the movie was not easy to imagine – it would require a great deal more than the removal of her knickers to convince Ignaz that she would be good box-office in the part. Hugo hoped that the right decision had been reached, the success of the film being essential to his own Hollywood career.

Oskar's party to celebrate the announcement was a rerun of his previous party with an even larger cast than before, and with the added prestige of the presence of Stefan Ignaz and his wife. Hugo arrived at the Beverly Hills house as requested, splendidly dressed in a white double-breasted dinner jacket he had bought only the day before and found himself treated as a celebrity.

As he moved through the house looking for his host, his hand was shaken warmly by a score of men he'd never seen before and his cheek kissed by a host of pretty girls equally unknown to him. Those he did know were even more effusive in their greetings – Chester thumped him on the back and wished him well – Thelma and Gale threw their arms round him and presed their bellies against his while they kissed him on the mouth, so that his pommel was upright before he had been in the house five minutes.

Stefan Ignaz was in the main sitting-room, seated on a white satin sofa, Norma on one side and Oskar on the other, holding court amid an obsequious throng of stars, employees, would-be stars and would-be employees. He was adorned with even more gold than when Hugo had met him in his office – three heavy rings on each hand, two bracelets on his wrist and a thick watch-chain across his evening waistcoat.

Norma looked deliciously ravishable in a frock of stark black velvet, low-cut to display a heavy diamond necklace against her perfect skin. Her light-brown hair had been dressed upwards and her make-up had been applied to make her appear twenty-one instead of seventeen. This, and the unusual semi-exposure of her breasts, was evidently a plan by the studio to make her look grown-up at last, in readiness for the movie.

She smiled graciously at Hugo and extended a pretty hand towards him. He bowed and kissed it delicately, amused by the thought that the last time he had seen that hand it had been clasping his stalk as he and she lay naked on the black bear-skin of her den. Perhaps there was a glint in his eyes to betray his secret thought, for Norma's lips parted in a silent gasp and she squeezed his fingers before he released her hand.

Oskar had kept his lion-tamer style of dress for the party, with only slight modifications – his roll-top sweater and his riding-boots were black, his breeches soft white doe-skin. He glared affectionately at Hugo through his monocle and greeted him loudly in German, as if to stress their bond of shared culture among the barbarians. Stefan Ignaz gave Oskar a brief stare of disapproval and reverted to the avuncular manner he had adopted for the evening.

'Now we are complete,' he said, beaming at Hugo. 'Now I have both wonderful stars and the brilliant director of the greatest movie ever to be planned and produced in Hollywood. Come and sit by me, Hugo, so that I can make you and my beautiful little Norma good friends. Oskar – will you please get a drink for him.'

Hugo took the seat vacated by Oskar and smiled dutifully. Virginia Ignaz was nowhere to be seen in the sitting-room, but he intended to make her acquaintance before the party ended. After seeing the photograph of her naked and in the after-glow of ecstasy with Ambrose, he was looking forward with keen anticipation to seeing her in person and touching her hand – and, who could say, perhaps laying the foundation for a friendship that would allow him in due course to touch more than her hand.

'It will be a great pleasure to work with so celebrated a star as Miss Gilbert,' said Hugo, when there was a pause in Ignaz's flow, 'I am glad she is to play Mary Magdalene.'

'You are very kind, Hugo,' Norma murmured across the width of Ignaz's chest that separated them, 'I have heard so much about you from Oskar – I'm looking forward to working closely with you.'

Ignaz detected the warm under-tone in her seemingly innocent remark and looked shrewdly at her and then at Hugo.

'I like my players to get on well together,' he said. 'Especially when they are as important to me as you two. I'll leave you to get to know each other better while I go find Virginia – she wants to make your acquaintance, Hugo.'

Hugo slid up to Norma on the sofa and smiled at her.

'Congratulations,' he said, 'I always believed that you'd get the part. I'm sorry I haven't been able to call you but I've been on an intensive language course.'

'You could have called me from Desma's,' she answered, 'I was waiting to hear from you after the way we parted, Hugo.'

'The course was extremely intensive,' he told her, 'I didn't want to risk losing my concentration.'

'You can't fool me,' she said in a tone of voice which Hugo found unnecessarily offensive. 'You didn't want to risk Desma going off the boil while you talked to another woman.'

'Fortunately there was no bungling fiancé to crash in at the most important moment,' he retorted.

'Then there should have been,' Norma said sharply, 'Desma was absolutely destroyed after you finished with her! She was in bed for two days sleeping it off -- I went round to see her and she was a wreck! She couldn't keep her eyes open.'

'And she certainly couldn't keep her legs open,' Hugo retaliated. 'That must have been a big disappointment for you.'

'How dare you say such a thing!' Norma exclaimed, her cheeks scarlet.

She got up quickly and walked away. Hugo got up too and made for the bar at the end of the room – Oskar had never returned with the drink Ignaz had ordered. He chatted for a few moments to Gale Paget, who introduced her husband, a powerfully-built man of twenty-one or two who said that he was a professional football player. Apparently he toured a lot with his team and was only allowed to attend parties on very special occasions. He was effusive and cheerful and much impressed by his beautiful wife and the world of film-making.

He's not very intelligent, was Hugo's conclusion, but has a strong enough back to satisfy Gale when his training schedule allowed. But from the way she stared shamelessly at Hugo, he had every confidence that she would call on his services again as soon as she was deprived of her husband's. He smiled back at her to indicate his readiness to oblige and strolled on to look for Mrs Ignaz and introduce himself. But she was nowhere to be seen. Was it possible, Hugo asked himself, that she was upstairs?

He remembered Prince Dmytryk's drunken tale of his uncle's rampage with Vanda Lodz and his discovery of the spy-holes in her house. The moment seemed right to put Dmytryk's claim to the test and with this in mind, Hugo made his way up the curving staircase, being careful not to notice the couple coming down with arms round each other's waists. But Peg Foster had no inhibitions about her way of life and she grinned broadly and winked at Hugo as they passed on the stairs. The man pretended not to see Hugo, who recognised him as one of Ignaz's company executives.

It was interesting to speculate which of this couple had tortured the other -- Hugo's guess was that the man had wanted to be the victim. It was even more interesting to consider why Peg had been invited to the party -- she was there to make mischief from which Oskar might benefit. Her companion separated himself from her at the bottom of the staircase and walked away quickly. Peg called after Hugo and, when he paused and turned near the top of the stairs, she trotted back up to kiss his cheek.

'His Royal Highness came through with the money,' she said with a grin. 'If you want to fool around with me for half an hour I'm all yours.'

'Thank you, Peg,' Hugo answered, his hand on her shoulder, 'I'll take you up on that in a while.'

'Any time, tiger,' she said, still grinning as she turned away.

Dmytryk's description of the way into the viewing-gallery was hazy in Hugo's mind, but he recalled a mention of a cupboard at the end of the upper floor, and it was easy enough to find that. The cupboard had shelves laden with linen and towels, but the back, when he pushed at it, turned out to be a door which opened on to a wooden staircase. There was even a light-switch which turned on a bare bulb at the top of the stairs.

Hugo pulled the cupboard door shut behind him, then the secret door, and climbed the uncarpeted stairs until he emerged into a square and windowless room. It was stacked with old steamer trunks, valises, cardboard boxes that overflowed with bundled letters and files, several ancient-looking hat-boxes that probably dated back to Vanda Lodz herself in the twenties, and other assorted junk, all piled higgledy-piggledy on the floor.

If Dmytryk had been speaking the truth about spy-holes, there had to be another way out of this room. Hugo circled the walls, knocking and pressing until he noticed, well below eye-level and concealed behind a trunk, a flat metal bolt recessed into the wooden wall.

The bolt slid back stiffly to let him push a section of wall open and step over the trunk into the long roof-space of the house. It was dimly lit from small windows at either end and it looked as if it had been undisturbed for years. A dozen once-colourful Indian blankets, now dull with dust, lay on the open floor, stretching away from Hugo in two parallel rows, spaced well apart. On one or two of them there were tasselled cushions, dusty and faded.

Hugo walked slowly to the first viewing-point. Set into the floor by the blanket was a square metal plate about a hand's breadth across and in its centre was a little hinged disc, no bigger than a thumb-nail. He shook the worst of the dust from the blanket, turned it over and knelt on it to bring his eye close to the plate before silently flicking the spy-hole open.

It was no surprise to find that he was looking down into a bedroom, that being the whole purpose of Vanda Lodz's unusual architectural feature. Nor was it a surprise to find that a broad bed stood directly beneath him, for it was the antics of her friends in bed that the strange Miss Lodz had wished to observe. What did surprise Hugo was who he saw in the room and what they were doing together. For one thing, they were making no use of the commodious bed at all.

There stood the enchantingly beautiful Virginia Ignaz with her short mane of golden curls and her classically beautiful face. She stood with her feet apart and she was holding her elegant chocolate-brown taffeta frock up round her waist with both hands. Her flimsy knickers had already been discarded and lay on the bed, so that she displayed to her companion a secret Hugo already knew from Oskar's photograph – that the smooth pink lips between her silk-stockinged legs were bare-shaven and unconcealed.

Naturally enough, the person honoured by·this view of her most intimate charms was not her husband. Nor, to Hugo's intense astonishment, was he any of the scores of

213

handsome young men at Oskar's party, though Virginia could have had any one of them by snapping her fingers.

It was the thin, dark-suited, Dr Theodor Prosz with the fluffy moustache who knelt, fully clothed even to jacket and bow-tie, on the carpet in front of the beautiful Virginia. His normally pale cheeks were flushed red, as which man's would not be with the emotions of so entrancing an experience. But even as Hugo stared at the scene below, it was made obvious to him that the good doctor's colour had another cause, for Virginia Ignaz dropped her skirt and slapped his cheeks hard with short swings of her jewel-ringed hands.

Theodor Prosz did not react at all, not even to flinch from the blows. Virginia said something to him, though Hugo could not hear the words, and smacked his face double-handed again before raising her frock to display her pink-petalled glory once more. Hugo's stalk was very stiff and he was envious of Theodor's luck. In the doctor's place he would have taken Virginia by the elegant cheeks of her bottom and kissed her between the legs as a preliminary to lifting her on to the bed.

To kneel on the floor with an eye to the spy-hole and rump in the air was an uncomfortable position, Hugo found – hence the presence of the blankets to lie full length on. He could hear the murmur of conversation between the couple below and although he could not make out what they were saying, the expressions on their faces were a useful guide – Virginia Ignaz's was haughty, Theodor Prosz's humbly adoring. It was perfectly clear to Hugo that she was humiliating Theodor for her own pleasure and that he was very content to be used in this way.

Holding her frock up round her waist, she moved closer to the kneeling doctor and spoke sharply. At once he leaned forward and pressed his mouth to the pouting lips between her thighs. Hugo watched entranced, unaware that he was holding his own stalk tightly through his trousers. From his vantage point he saw Virginia's eyes shut slowly as she became aroused by the tongue that was invading her alcove. He wondered why she had chosen Theodor Prosz

214

and concluded that it was because the doctor's living depended on the goodwill of Stefan Ignaz – which meant that Virginia could make him do anything she liked without any fear that he would betray her.

That brought another thought in its train – if Virginia had wanted Ambrose dead, could she dominate Theodor enough to do it for her? Gale Paget was very certain that Prosz had pulled the trigger, though the motive she suggested was not entirely convincing. But suppose that the motive was not Theodor's but Virginia's, and he was merely the instrument? The girl Hugo had slept with at Big Ida's claimed she had heard of a quarrel between Ignaz and Ambrose over Virginia – perhaps Ignaz had also threatened Virginia with divorce. One way she might avoid that was to remove Ambrose permanently from the scene!

Down below in the bedroom matters approached a satisfactory conclusion for the beautiful Virginia. Her head was well back, her closed eyes and open mouth towards the ceiling. Her trembling hands pulled her rustling frock higher, showing her smooth and flat belly, as she rubbed herself against Theodor's lapping tongue. *Oh yes*! Hugo gasped out loud, staring down at her face as it set in an ecstatic mask. He saw her sway on her feet and then recover slowly, until the breasts under her chocolate-brown frock heaved and fell in three or four long and deep breaths to calm her.

In another moment or two she stepped back from her kneeling partner and flicked the display handkerchief from his breast-pocket to wipe herself carefully between the legs. Theodor knelt unmoving and stared at her in mute adoration. She threw the handkerchief into his face and addressed a few words to him with a look of intense scorn, snatched her knickers from the bed and walked out of the room.

Poor Theodor, Hugo thought, chuckling to himself, *you played that all wrong – you should have got hold of her when she was too far gone to resist you and pulled her down on the floor*.

But as events quickly proved, Hugo was misjudging the doctor by attributing his own desires to him. Theodor showed that he wanted other satisfactions by jerking his trousers open and pulling out his long and swollen stem. From the carpet he picked up the burgundy silk handkerchief Virginia had used to wipe herself, wrapped it round his staff and rubbed quickly with both hands. Virginia's domination had evidently aroused him almost to the limit, for in only seconds he shuddered and gushed his passion into the handkerchief.

Hugo closed the spy-hole and, for the first time, he began to wonder about Vanda Lodz and how much time she had spent up here watching her guests entertain themselves below. Did she come up here alone to watch and perhaps enjoy solitary pleasures, or did she invite someone to be with her and attend to her needs when she became aroused? Hugo decided that he would trace where she was living and go to see her when he had the time – she would be in her forties now and he would like to make her acquaintance.

He moved to another of the viewing-posts, shook the blanket and lay down to flip open the little disc. He was looking down into the master-bedroom and the bed beneath him was Oskar's great four-poster. The only view he had was that of the top of the canopy. When the legendary Miss Lodz designed her house, she had taken care that no one should be able to spy on her.

Hugo was about to close the viewing-window and move on when a woman got off the bed and moved out away from the canopy into his field of vision. Her naked back was to him, but from her heavy hips and bottom he was sure that it was Mildred Gilbert. She turned round to speak to whoever was on the bed and he saw her pendulous breasts and the broad patch of brown hair between her thighs.

She was smiling and talking to her companion in a very friendly way – he must have pleasured her well, Hugo thought, waiting for the man to appear. But he stayed where he was on the bed and Mildred stood naked before the mirror to examine her make-up, conversing over her bare shoulder. Could it be Chester Chataway? Hugo asked himself gleefully. Had the famous Chickenhawk become the plaything of a tough old hen?

216

Finally the man slid off the bed and stubbed out a cigarette – and it was Prince Dmytryk, his tassel limp between his fat thighs. Mildred was fully dressed by now and she threw an arm round Dmytryk's meaty shoulders and kissed him warmly, her other hand gripping his dingle-dangle in a very proprietorial way.

Hugo closed the spy-hole and thought about what he had seen and the implications. No man in his right mind would make love to Mildred if he could have her daughter instead, and Dmytryk presumably could, by virtue of their engagement. Mildred must be useful to Dmytryk for him to gratify her. The only way in which she could be useful was to keep him supplied with money, so that he could keep up appearances until he married Norma.

More than that – Peg Foster had just told Hugo that Dmytryk had paid her off for the imaginary injuries he had inflicted on her upside-down. It was a fair guess that Mildred had supplied the cash and was collecting her reward down below on Oskar's bed.

A faint sound brought Hugo's eye back to the little spy-hole. The feel of Dmytryk's dangler in her hand had reawakened Mildred's interest in his capabilities. She was down on her knees, fully-dressed, his stem in her mouth and her eyes turned up to look at his face, her expression soulful, in so far as Hugo could identify it. Her arms were round Dmytryk and she was kneading the heavy cheeks of his bare bottom with great enthusiasm.

Dmytryk was smiling a trifle wanly and trying to look as if he was enjoying what was going on. Clearly he had no wish to continue his intimate encounter with Mildred, but at the same time he had excellent reasons not to annoy her by refusing her desires. Serve the silly fellow right, was Hugo's thought as he stared down with a malicious grin at the Prince's predicament.

Whether Mildred sensed her companion's reluctance or not, she was not a woman to be denied. Her cheeks hollowed as she sucked vigorously at the fleshy lollipop in her mouth and no doubt her tongue was active, for the lollipop-stick was straightening itself and getting longer.

Hugo's grin grew broader and he began to entertain hopes that Dmytryk would fail to respond as Mildred wanted him to and that she would fly into a temper and bite his stalk as badly as she had bitten his own. But in this he was underestimating the Prince, whose face grew slowly dark red and whose breath now rasped loudly enough for Hugo to hear up in his hiding-place. *Uhh, uhh, uhh!* Dmytryk groaned, his hands clutching at Mildred's shoulders to balance himself on shaky legs.

At this point Mildred stood up, leaving Dmytryk's shiny wet pointer jerking up and down, put her hands on his bare chest and ran him backwards under the shelter of the canopy and presumably flat on his back on the bed. For Hugo the end of the scene was lost and though he could see the canopy vibrating to movement on the bed, there was no way of knowing how Mildred had chosen to take advantage of her reluctant companion.

The money Mildred gave Dmytryk came from Norma's earnings, for she had no other source. Whichever way you looked at it, Hugo concluded, Norma Gilbert had been exploited all her life – financially by her mother and, most probably, by Ignaz in the contracts he offered for Mildred to sign for her daughter while she was under-age. Sexually, Norma had been exploited by Chester Chataway and Ambrose from a tender age – and who could guess how many others had put a hand up her clothes to feel her little toy? Including Stefan Ignaz, who personally tried out all his female stars, according to Gale. But could Gale be believed?

Even now that Norma was of age she was still being exploited by her mother and her fiancé working together. If she had any inkling of that, she might well agree to marry Ambrose – and any hint of that would be reason enough for Mildred and Dmytryk to get Ambrose out of the way by shooting him, and then give each other an alibi for the night in question. But had Ambrose asked Norma to marry him and had she agreed?

For that there was only Desma Williams' word, and she believed that Thelma had shot Ambrose in a fit of jealousy

218

– or at least she said that was what she believed. She also claimed that Norma spent the night of the shooting at her house. In fact, she must have told this to the police when they checked the stories of everyone who had known Ambrose well. Perhaps Norma *had* spent the night in Desma's bed, being comforted and fondled by the big-ballooned language coach – and perhaps the story had been cooked up between the two of them after the event.

In Hugo's opinion everyone he talked to lied without hesitation, and he could think of no way to establish the truth of whether Ambrose had proposed marriage to Norma or not. If he had, and word got around, then it seemed probable that Connie rather than Thelma would have been hurt and angry enough to shoot him. But the LA Police Department had not objected to Connie leaving for Europe, which meant they were satisfied with her account of where she was when Ambrose was shot. It occurred to Hugo that he had never even asked her, but he suspected that her answer would have been that she was staying at Santa Monica with the Callans. He did not doubt for a moment that they would lie to shield Connie.

All things considered, looking through the spy-hole had extended the range of possible motives for the shooting of Ambrose and confused Hugo further. To be sure, the sight of Virginia Ignaz holding up her frock to show her pretty plaything had been pleasing, but her choice of the person to oblige her suggested that she was being extremely cautious since her affair with Ambrose. That offered Hugo little chance of progress towards his desire.

To see Prince Dmytryk being put through his paces by the cannibalistic Mildred had been amusing, but the implications for Norma Gilbert of that episode were not pleasing. She deserved better, Hugo decided, and went to search for her. He found her in the book-lined study with Oskar. She was lying full-length on the dark green velvet chaise-longue, her ankles crossed prettily, while Oskar was striding up and down as he held forth on the psychological motivation of Mary Magdalene.

219

'Come in, Hugo,' he said heartily. 'Are you enjoying my party?'

'I'll leave you two to talk,' said Norma, sitting up at once.

'Don't go,' Hugo said in his most sincere tone of voice. 'There are things I must say to you – important things.'

'I'm sure I can't think of anything I want to hear from you,' she replied, but she stayed where she was.

Oskar ran a hand over his bald head and glanced from one to the other.

'It is better if I go,' he said. 'You two must reach an understanding if you are to work together with me. I will not tolerate bad temper, hysteria or temperament on my set, so if there is to be a fight between you, please have it now when it doesn't matter.'

He strode across the study and out. A moment later there was the sound of a key turning.

'He's locked us in!' Norma exclaimed, her expression one of shock.

'What of it?' said Hugo. 'Listen to me please, Norma – I was very rude to you earlier this evening and I wish to apologise sincerely.'

'You accused me of something unforgivable,' said Norma, not making it clear whether it was the accusation of Sapphism or the act of Sapphism that was unforgivable. Hugo filled two glasses with French cognac from a bottle standing on a silver tray on Oskar's desk and sat on the chaise-longue by her.

'You and I need to make a great success of this movie,' he said, handing her one of the glasses. 'Your career and my career need it, even if for different reasons.'

'Speak for yourself,' said Norma, 'you need a big success because you're unknown. I've been the World's Sweetheart since I was fourteen. To me this is just another movie to add to the twenty-eight I've made already.'

Hugo raised his glass to her and smiled while he spoke plainly.

'You're too old to play little girls now, Norma. And the world out there has changed. This is 1932 and there's not much public demand for sweet-faced and innocent little virgins any more.'

'You're being insulting!' Norma exclaimed, her face red.

'No, I'm being frank. And I mean to go on being frank while we are working together. Drink your cognac.'

She took a long sip and stared at him as if bewildered by being told what to do. Her expression was so childlike and vulnerable that Hugo had to remind himself that he was dealing with an accomplished actress.

'Your life is in as much of a mess as your career, Norma,' he said pleasantly. 'You've managed to get engaged to an unsuitable person without escaping from your mother's clutches. If you're ever going to become a film star and not just a former child star you'll have to get rid of both of them.'

'I won't let you talk about the Prince like that!' she exclaimed. 'At least *he* behaves like a perfect gentleman to me, which is more than I can say about you!'

'I was behaving in a very gentlemanly way towards you on a bear-skin rug when that idiot interrupted. And you were receiving my courtesies like a perfect lady, if I may say so.'

'Stop grinning at me like that!' Norma said, her cheeks flushed. 'What you tried to do to me was unspeakable! Dimmy would never try to take advantage of me the way you did!'

'A man who does not make love to the girl he has asked to marry him is a strange fiancé indeed! He must be a strong believer in pre-marital chastity between the betrothed. Happily for him, this belief does not extend to his future mother-in-law and so he does not become frustrated through abstinence.'

'What did you say!'

'You know what I said, Norma, and I do not think that you are so surprised as you pretend. Not half an hour ago Dmytryk was upstairs on Oskar's four-poster bed with your mother, both stark naked.'

'How do you know?' she demanded, her face scarlet.

'I opened the wrong door and caught a glimpse by

chance,' said Hugo, with a diplomatic disregard for the exact truth.

The baby-faced *Sweetheart of All the World* lost her temper and described her mother and fiancé in words which were not often spoken in what passed for polite company in Hollywood. Some of the words were new to Hugo and he made a mental note to find out at a suitable moment what exactly they meant. He listened with attention to Norma's fluency until she burst into tears. He put his arms round her and her head on his shoulder and rubbed her back soothingly until she stopped.

'I've been a fool, Hugo,' she said, sounding desolate. 'But I'm a girl all alone in the world. There's no one to turn to now that Ambrose is gone.'

'We've been through this conversation before,' said Hugo, determined not to let her try her emotional wiles on him again, even though he knew it to be second nature with her, 'Dmytryk interrupted us before we had time to resolve it.'

'I never want to see that fat pig again!' she screamed suddenly, pulling the diamond ring from her hand and hurling it across the study. 'Mother can have him if she wants him! He's no good -- she'll soon be banging the chauffeur again!'

'Your mother will make a suitable Princess for him,' said Hugo. 'As for you, dear Norma, I intend to become your lover and remain so while we are working on the movie together. After that we shall see.'

She raised her tear-streaked face to stare at him doubtfully.

'Are you always this frank?' she asked.

Hugo took her back into his arms to kiss her warmly and slip a hand down the top of her low-cut black velvet frock to clasp a small breast.

'Oh Hugo, you mustn't try to rush me,' she sighed, apparently forgetting that she had lain naked on her own hearth-rug while he kissed her belly. Hugo wondered how many layers of false modesty and deception there were to peel off before he came to the real Norma Gilbert. Or was

222

there no real person concealed inside the layers? He pressed his mouth on hers to silence her while he felt for the fastening down the back of her bodice and opened it. She sighed into his mouth as he peeled her frock down to her waist and fondled her bare breasts with both hands.

'Not here, Hugo,' she said, 'someone might come in and see us!'

'Here and now,' Hugo insisted, 'I want you and I mean to have you, Norma.'

He was certain that they would not be interrupted, for the excellent reason that the door was locked and the key in Oskar's pocket. But it seemed unnecessary to say so while he was trying to establish an ascendancy over Norma. She was still protesting when he flipped her on her back on the chaise-longue and put his hands under her black velvet frock, to stroke up her bare thighs above her silk stockings until his fingers were under the lace edging of her knickers.

'Not here,' she pleaded, 'take me to your apartment, Hugo.'

He did not bother to answer her. His thumbs were caressing the silky floss on her little mound and his stalk was trembling against his belly. He raised her legs straight up in the air, peeling her skirt back to her hips at the same time, until he had uncovered her lacy black knickers. He had already bared her breasts – her expensive frock was bundled round her waist – and he stripped away her knickers to expose her completely. She was staring up at him wide-eyed and it occurred to him that she may never have been handled so firmly before – the men who had enjoyed her had treated her like a little girl who has to be coaxed into taking her knickers down.

He knelt upright on the chaise-longue to rid himself of his evening jacket and pull out his thick and quivering stem. Norma gasped loudly when he took hold of her ankles and stretched her legs upwards and outwards in a great V, so that he could stare down and gloat a little over the pleasingly-shaped lips which he meant to penetrate as he slid into her flat little belly. He lifted her bottom and slipped his bent knees under her until he could rub the heavy head of his mace against the blonde floss that adorned her plaything.

'Hugo, Hugo, this is not the time or place!' she moaned. 'Have you no shame at all?'

'The right time to make love is when you feel like it,' Hugo gasped, 'and the right place is wherever you are at the time. And besides, this is unfinished business between us.'

He pushed his stem relentlessly against her petals until they parted and let him slide into her. The moment she was broached, Norma abandoned her show of reluctance and went along with the moment. She sighed and moaned pleasurably to Hugo's rhythmic plunging and gave a soprano wail of ecstasy when, all too soon, his passion detonated in her belly.

Hugo shuddered and gasped, rapturously happy that he had at last enjoyed the delights of the young woman desired by millions of men round the world. Making love to Connie and Gale and Thelma had been marvellous, but to have *All the World's Sweetheart* writhing to the stabbing of his spurting tail was the supreme pleasure of his life so far and convinced him, if he needed any convincing, that he was going to be a very important star before long.

'Good, good, good,' he gasped through the throes of his delight. 'From now on you're my girl-friend and nobody else's, Norma — do you hear me?'

'Yes, Hugo, yes,' she murmured, smiling contentedly up at him as she became calmer, 'do you want to be engaged to me?'

'No, I want to enjoy you. You're coming with me to my apartment now and by morning you'll be as destroyed as Desma.'

'But we're locked in,' she said. 'How do you intend to get out — phone the Fire Department?'

'Through the window, of course,' he answered, easing his tail out of her. 'There's no point in pretending to be shy now — by the morning you will be clinging round my neck and begging me to stay with you forever.'

His show of conviction seemed to work well — Norma lowered her eyes modestly and nodded agreement.

Chapter 14

Hugo is taken by surprise

Connie had been gone for less than two weeks before her prediction came true. Captain Bastaple of the Police Department called a press conference one morning and announced that, after exhaustive investigation and with the advice of the Coroner's Department, he was satisfied that the well-known film director Ambrose Howard had died by his own hand. This could have been established immediately and saved a lot of police time and trouble if the neighbour who found the body hadn't picked up the suicide weapon and smudged the dead man's finger-prints.

Howard's reason for taking his own life had been evident all along, the Captain asserted – heavy depression brought on by worries about his health. Dr Theodor Prosz had been his medical adviser for many years and had testified to his patient's depressed state of mind. So had Howard's close colleagues at Ignaz International. The Police Department wanted to talk to Luis Hernandez, the dead man's chauffeur, when he was traced, but there was no reason to think that he could add anything to what they already knew.

In answer to a question from a sceptical journalist why the chauffeur had vanished, Captain Bastaple said the investigation had established that Hernandez owed large gambling debts to local underworld racketeers and was unable to pay them off. It was coincidence that he had left town on the night his employer had killed himself.

Asked if he would care to make a statement on the story

going around that the police had found a collection of pornographic photographs and female underwear in the Howard house, the Captain said that these were the usual dirty-minded rumours that surfaced whenever a film star or studio executive met with an accident or died suddenly. The late Ambrose Howard was a man of good reputation in the community and had been well-known for his voluntary work for film industry charities.

When Hugo read this farrago in the afternoon newspaper he telephoned Thelma at once and found her in a cynical mood.

'What did I tell you?' she said. 'The little bitch has got away with it. She's bribed Bastaple.'

'You're wrong about Norma. It was Ignaz who shot him – I've seen a photograph that proves it.'

'What does it matter?' she said wearily. 'It's all over, Hugo. Let it drop.'

'Is it true that you and Ambrose were secretly married, Thelma?' he asked her.

There was a long pause and he could hear her agitated breathing down the telephone before she answered.

'Who told you that – Desma Williams? It's all water over the dam, but yes, we were. At least, we went through a marriage ceremony together when we were crazy for each other. But I always had a sneaking suspicion that Ambrose had a wife back in England somewhere. It didn't matter then, and it sure as hell doesn't matter now.'

'But if he had a wife already, your marriage would have been invalid. That means he wouldn't need a divorce if he wanted to marry somebody else – but that would have been invalid too, unless his English wife died recently. Thelma, I'm confused.'

'Give your brains a rest,' she said. 'Why don't you come over here – I've got the blues and I need cheering up.'

'Yes, I will,' he promised, 'I'll cheer you up till you fall asleep exhausted. Tell me one thing, Thelma – did Ambrose say to you that he wanted to marry Norma Gilbert?'

By way of answer to that question Thelma slammed the

226

telephone down and cut him off. Hugo decided that it would be inadvisable to drive over to see her until her rage cooled – a rage which strongly suggested that the answer to his question was *yes*.

Not that it made any difference – he was clear in his mind that neither Thelma nor Connie had shot Ambrose, however much he had distressed them. Norma may well have lost her temper with Ambrose but Hugo was sure that she was no more responsible for the killing than her deranged mother. As for Dmytryk, he was just a princely slob on the make and stood to gain nothing from the death of Ambrose.

Nor for that matter did Theodor Prosz. And though Virginia Ignaz dominated him sexually, Hugo regarded him as incapable of any act more enterprising than putting his hand down Nurse Bell's knickers. Chester Chataway's brain was addled enough for him to shoot anybody in a jealous frenzy, but Lily was certain he didn't know about her and Ambrose, and Hugo was inclined to believe her. The hard fact was that when all the improbables had been eliminated, only Stefan Ignaz was left.

He sat thinking for a minute or two before deciding to go and talk to Oskar. Naturally, neither of them wanted to accuse Ignaz openly of murder, but it seemed reasonable to think that the investigation would be reopened if the Los Angeles newspapers saw copies of the photograph of Ambrose and Virginia Ignaz naked together. The natural thirst of newspapers for scandal would drive them to harass Captain Bastaple for further statements. Though the next part was hazy in Hugo's thinking, he felt that if the newspapers were persistent enough, the finger could somehow be made to point at Stefan Ignaz. It all depended on persuading Oskar to distribute copies of the photograph anonymously.

He drove to Oskar's house, rehearsing the argument in his mind. But when he rang the door-bell, nothing happened, even after several rings and a long wait. He was turning away from the door in disappointment when it opened and there stood Patsy, bare-foot and wrapped in a sage-green bath-towel.

'Oskar's out and it's the servants' day off,' she said, by way of explanation. 'Come on in.'

'My God, have I dragged you out of the bath?' Hugo asked, giving her his charming smile, 'I'm surprised you bothered to answer the door.'

'I wasn't going to, but curiosity got the better of me, so I peeped out of the window and recognised your white Buick.'

Without thinking where he was going, Hugo accompanied her up the pink marble staircase, a friendly arm round her waist. Her body felt very warm and soft through the towel and he was unable to resist sliding his hand down to squeeze her bottom.

'Where's Oskar – at the studio?' he asked.

'He's out somewhere in Orange County looking for a good spot for the crucifixion in his movie. He won't be back till late tonight.'

She led him into the bathroom and Hugo's resolve to track down Vanda Lodz when he had time was strengthened by what he saw. The bath was circular and made of green and amber-veined onyx. It was sunk into the white-carpeted floor and big enough to hold half a dozen people all together. Patsy shed her towel, went down two steps into the scented water and lay full-length with her head resting on a green cushion on the side of the bath. Hugo sat down on the carpet and stared in admiration at her slim body gleaming pearly-pink through the water.

'Some bath, this,' she said, a grin on her pretty face. 'You don't mind if I carry on where I left off, do you? Did you come over to talk to Oskar about the movie?'

'No, it's something else I want to talk about,' he said.

'I was going to lure you upstairs and rip your clothes off at the party,' said Patsy, setting out on a different tack, 'but you disappeared early. What happened? Oskar said he left you in the study, but I couldn't find you anywhere.'

Hugo shrugged off the question and smiled at her as he started to shed his clothes.

'You missed a stand-up fight between Jesus Christ and Chester Chataway over his girlie-doll!' she said, watching with close interest while he undressed. 'Both of them were drunk as skunks or they'd have murdered each other.'

'Who is playing Jesus – do I know him?'

'Sherman Gibbs – you must have noticed him – the one with the blond beard and long hair. He's only a bit-part player, so I guess you haven't heard of him. The Chicken-hawk went looking for Lily and found her with her panties in her hand and Sherman wearing nothing but his shirt and socks. So he took a swing at him and Sherman swung back and the fight spilled out of the bedroom and down the stairs and into the main party. Everybody was cheering and clapping, except Lily, and she was sobbing her little heart out. It was better than a floor-show.'

'My God, who won?'

'It was pretty much a draw – it stopped when they were both too tired to get up off the floor. Some of the men carried them upstairs and locked them in separate rooms to sleep it off.'

'I'm sure Lily was doing no more than trying to persuade Gibbs to help her get started in movies,' said Hugo, grinning. 'She's so disillusioned with Chester that she'll try anyone.'

A moment later he was naked and stepping down into the water, his hard stilt waving in front of him. He sat beside Patsy with an arm round her shoulders and kissed her while he played with her breasts under the warm water. She reached for his handle at once – something Oskar must have taught her to do, since she had never displayed that sort of interest when she had been Hugo's girl-friend.

'You men fall for Lily Haden's little girl routine, but she's not as green as she looks,' said Patsy. 'It won't be long now before we see her name on the screen credits.'

'I see – so whose heart was softened by her tears?'

'This is going to knock you sideways, but I swear it's true. Half an hour after the fight I came up to my room to freshen up my make-up. I opened the door and the lights were off, so naturally I thought there was nobody there.

229

But when I walked in I saw Lily lying on the bed with her clothes up round her waist.'

'Not Sherman Gibbs if he was locked in – who then?'

'You're not going to believe this – it was Mrs Ignaz with her.'

'Yes, I can believe it,' said Hugo, after a moment's reflection. 'Virginia is feeling so guilty about Ambrose that she's anxious not to give her husband grounds for suspicion of any other man just now, and so she's enjoying what might be called alternative pleasures. I saw her involved in something just as surprising earlier on that evening. What was she doing when you interrupted her?'

'She had her hand down Lily's panties, so you can make your own mind up what she was doing. As soon as I saw who it was I got out of there fast!'

'Did she see you?' Hugo asked, stroking Patsy's smooth belly and down to her thighs, which she parted at his touch, 'Virginia Ignaz would be a bad enemy for anyone starting in films.'

'She was too busy fingering her girlie and whispering to her to notice me,' said Patsy, 'but Lily spotted me.'

'Can you be sure, if it was dark?'

'She turned her head on the pillow to stare at me – and she had the nerve to wink!'

Hugo laughed and bent his head towards Patsy's bobbins – their little pink tips were just out of the water – and he flicked at them with his tongue. Her free hand found his wrist and pressed his fingers between her thighs.

'Well why not?' he asked. 'If all it takes to get into movies is to let the owner's wife play with you a little, what's wrong with that? Virginia Ignaz is extremely beautiful and it must be very exciting to have her feel you.'

'Oh!' Patsy exclaimed as his fingers opened her petals. 'The water went into me – it felt so nice!'

'I have something that will feel even nicer inside you.'

'Prove it!' she murmured, her mouth close to his.

That hasn't changed, Hugo thought. When she was with him before she always wanted to get the act of love over as soon as possible. It held no great interest for her, it was

230

something she exchanged for favours – meals when she had been broke, a luxurious home and a bit-part in a movie now that she had charmed Oskar.

He slid on top of her, sending waves of scented water rolling across the bath, and her fingers steered him into her warm nook. A long push sank him to the limit and her legs came up out of the water to cross over his bottom and hold him tight.

'Nice, very nice,' she whispered. 'Do it slow and gentle, Hugo – really make love to me.'

Now that *has* changed, he thought. He cupped her face in his hands while he kissed her lingeringly and slid in and out with easy strokes.

'Oh, Hugo, yes,' she murmured, 'that feels so good – you were the first and you'll always be the best for me.'

'The first what?' he asked, stroking her soft little dumplings lovingly. 'You had lovers before me.'

'Only one or two – and they never made me feel anything. But the night you got the phone call from Oskar you loved me so wonderfully that you made something happen – it was like an earthquake that wiped me out . . . it was my first climax, I guess.'

Hugo pressed tender little kisses to her eyes and cheeks and lips. Patsy's recollection of the event was not exactly the same as his own, which was of an altogether more casual incident. But if it made her happy to recall it that way, then why not?

'We should have ignored Oskar's invitation and stayed where we were in bed and made love again,' he said to please her, his steady thrust bringing him ever closer to his crisis.

'Don't say that!' she gasped, her belly pushing upwards rhythmically against him under the water. 'Then I wouldn't have met Oskar and got into movies!'

'So everything worked out for the best!' Hugo exclaimed, his voice shaky as he stabbed hard and fast and felt his eruption beginning.

Patsy's wet hands were on the back of his head, forcing his mouth hard to hers as she gasped and whimpered in ecstasy and thrashed about under him, sending the water cascading over the sides of the onyx bath.

'I love you!' she was sobbing through the spasms that shook her slender body.

She was still trembling when he slid out of her and took her in his arms stroked her back. After a while her eyes opened and she looked at him adoringly.

'It's true,' she said, 'I do love you, Hugo. I've been thinking about you a lot lately. There's never been anyone like you for me. When my climax started just now I realised how I felt about you.'

'Are you sure?' he asked, hoping to pass the moment off lightly. 'Maybe you're tired of Oskar's experiments in bed and want someone more traditional for a change.'

'It's not that,' she said, shaking her head seriously. 'To tell you the truth, I love the crazy things Oskar makes me do. He made me have four climaxes in a row one morning before we got up and it was fantastic! But what I feel for you is altogether different.'

'I shall make you do it five times here and now,' said Hugo, not sharing her interest in her climax, but still hoping to avoid the inconvenient issue she was raising.

'Oh, yes!' Patsy said at once. 'And each separate one will be sensational because I truly love you. You don't believe me, I know, but you will. There's nothing I wouldn't do for you, Hugo.'

'I am very touched,' he said, regretting that he had got into the bath with her in the first place, 'but to be honest, Patsy I hardly know what to say.'

'You don't have to say anything you don't want to,' she told him, her hand stroking his cheek, 'but I know things will work out right for us.'

'You're not thinking of leaving Oskar, are you?' Hugo asked anxiously, 'I mean, after you've done so much to be on good terms with him, you mustn't risk being dropped from the film now. It's your big chance – you know that.'

'He won't drop me,' she said confidently, 'he can't – not after all I've done for him.'

'Don't be too sure about that,' Hugo told her, his hand

stroking lightly up and down her wet flank. 'You may have had some agreeable times together but Oskar's an outright egotist. If you move out, he'll move your friend Sylvie in right away, or some other girl.'

'That's not what I meant. He has other girls besides me and I don't mind. He's taken Sylvie out with him today and I'm sure he'll give her a good crucifying when he finds a spot he likes. But he can't get out of making me a star now that I got rid of his biggest rival for him.'

'Rival for what? Who do you mean, Patsy.'

'I'll prove how much I love you,' she said, her cheek pressed to his and her arms round him to hold him close. 'You're the only person in the whole world I'll ever tell this to – I shot Ambrose Howard for Oskar when he asked me to.'

'My God!' Hugo exclaimed in stunned disbelief. 'Why?'

'So Oskar would get to direct the Bible movie. He's flat broke and owes hundreds of thousands.'

'But even so – a civilised man does not have another killed to pay off his debts! I simply refuse to believe you, Patsy.'

'There's more to it than paying off the sharks. Oskar's number one now at Ignaz International. He told me the Bible movie is a fool-proof script for a box-office smash and it's going to put him right on top of the heap. If Ignaz can't give him everything he wants, he'll be able to write his own ticket at MGM or Paramount.'

Hugo pulled away and sat up in the cooling water, hardly able to take in what Patsy was saying.

'It was for *money*?' he said. 'Ambrose died because Oskar is *broke*?'

'He was in the way,' said Patsy, a smile on her pretty young face at his consternation. 'Oskar is a very talented and very ambitious man and nobody is going to be allowed to stand in his way. Surely you can see that?'

'Very clearly,' Hugo said, appalled by what he was hearing, 'Was Ambrose in your way, too?'

'I didn't know him, but he must have been, because now he's gone I'm heading for the top. Oskar's promised me I'll

233

be bigger than Connie Young and Gale Paget inside a couple of years.'

'Starting with a bit-part in *Mary Magdalene*?'

'It won't be just a bit-part,' Patsy assured him, 'Oskar's building it up and having lines written for me. I'm going to be second lead to Norma Gilbert. And in my next movie I shall play the lead opposite you.'

Hugo crawled out of the onyx bath-tub and sat cross-legged on the white carpet with a towel wrapped round him. Patsy turned over in the water and stared at him, her arms on the green cushion and the cheeks of her rounded bottom just breaking the surface. The hair bristled on the back of Hugo's neck as he recalled that there had been no more than four days between the time he brought Patsy to Oskar's party and the shooting of Ambrose – in that brief space of time Oskar had grasped her capabilities and involved her in his murderous scheme. To Hugo that suggested two things, both of them unwelcome – that Patsy was without any sense of right and wrong whatsoever, and that Oskar was a far more dangerous person than he had ever guessed.

'How did you shoot Ambrose, Patsy?' he asked, curious even then to know the details.

'Oskar had it all planned out. He drove me over to Glendale Boulevard about half past eleven that night.'

'He drove you there himself?'

'He said we couldn't risk a taxi driver remembering afterwards that he'd set down or picked up near the house. Oskar dropped me off five minutes walk away and waited for me at the all-night diner further down the street.'

'But how did you get Ambrose to let you in? Norma Gilbert was there less than an hour before and he had quite a lot to drink. I'd have thought he was fast asleep by the time you got there.'

'No, he wasn't asleep, but he was pretty drunk. He opened the door wearing a towelling robe and just stared at me without saying anything.'

'And let you in – a complete stranger, late at night?' Hugo asked, his eyebrows rising up his forehead.

'That's where Oskar was brilliant – he made me go there wearing a Yacht Club blazer and cap and white trousers. I didn't understand why, but he said it would get me in. And he was right.'

'But Oskar didn't see the photograph of Norma dressed like that till after Ambrose was dead,' said Hugo, puzzled by what Patsy was telling him, 'but he must have seen it to send you there in those clothes! But how was that possible?'

'I don't know anything about photographs,' said Patsy, 'I just did what Oskar said and it worked like a dream. I stood there smiling and the man dragged me inside and upstairs into his bedroom. He kissed me a couple of times and give me a good feel through my trousers – there was a strong smell of whisky on his breath and I don't think he knew who I was, or cared.'

'In his confused state he thought you were Norma Gilbert come back to make up after a quarrel they had before you arrived,' said Hugo.

'He thought I was a movie star!' Patsy said triumphantly, 'Oskar never told me that!'

She slid out of the water, as sleek as a seal, and pushed Hugo's feet apart so that she could sit between them on her haunches and hold his limp equipment in both her wet hands.

'There's only one way I can think of that Oskar could get hold of that picture of Norma,' said Hugo, 'he bribed the chauffeur Hernandez to give him anything that he could use against Ambrose. The picture makes it look as if Ambrose is doing it to a boy – if Ignaz saw it he'd have fired him. And if the police had seen it they could have sent him to jail, because Norma Gilbert was hardly likely to admit it was her. But go on, Patsy – what did you do in the bedroom?'

'Not much – he felt me up for a while and took his robe off but he'd had so much to drink that he couldn't get his pecker to stand up.'

In spite of the steady manipulation of her hands, Hugo was experiencing the same problem, for the first time in his life. To distract Patsy's attention he asked her about the black ribbon.

'He had a drawer full of ribbons by the bed,' she said obligingly, 'pink, green and mauve and all colours. He wanted me to tie a black bow round his pecker because of the sad state it was in. Like yours is now – don't you want me anymore?'

'I was right!' Hugo exclaimed. 'The ribbon had nothing to do with Peg Foster. Moran must have emptied the drawer when he was destroying evidence before the police arrived.'

'Maybe,' said Patsy, neither understanding nor caring what he meant. 'Why don't you want me anymore, Hugo?'

'To tell you the plain truth, I'm afraid of you,' he answered, his smile nervous.

'But why? I'd never hurt you – I love you! I'd do anything for you, Hugo, anything at all – just ask me!'

'Tell me the rest of your story first and then we will talk about us,' he promised.

'If you like. There was a gun in the drawer under the ribbons, and after I'd tied him a black velvet bow and he was busy admiring it, I slipped the gun into my blazer pocket. I don't know why – that wasn't in Oskar's plan. But it seemed safer that way.'

'But what was Oskar's plan – what were you going to do to Ambrose?'

'Put him to sleep,' Patsy answered calmly. 'Oskar gave me a little bottle and said all I had to do was to pour it into his glass when he offered me a drink. Without him seeing, that is.'

'And when he was asleep – what then?'

'Nothing – Oskar said there was enough in the bottle to make sure he'd never wake up again. I had to wait for him to fall asleep and then tidy up any trace that I'd been there. Oskar was waiting for me down the street and the plan was for us to be back here before Ambrose stopped breathing. Oskar had written out a list of people he was going to phone through the night to give himself an alibi, though he

236

didn't expect to need one because the police would think Ambrose had done himself in with an over-dose.'

'It sounds like a watertight plan. Why did you change it?'

'I couldn't help it. There was a Scotch bottle by the side of the bed but it was empty and Ambrose wanted to fool around right away. There was no choice but let him have me and fix the drinks afterwards.'

Hugo stared at Patsy's smooth and pretty young face, astonished that it could be so untroubled while she was relating horrors. Her hands were still massaging his unresponsive part slowly and she was staring down at it.

'Did he have you?' he asked.

'It didn't work out that way. Maybe the fool ribbon did the trick, because his pecker stood up at long last. He mumbled something about *second time round* and dragged me into the bathroom. Was that anything to do with the photograph you were talking about?'

'Yes, he had a photograph taken of himself diddling Norma Gilbert in the bathroom. In his drunken state he mistook you for her and expected a repeat performance.'

'Some performance!' she exclaimed in indignation. 'Maybe I'm stupid, but I had all my clothes on, and I didn't guess what he was up to when he told me to put my hands on the bath and bend over. He dragged my pants down round my knees and I thought he wanted an ordinary stand-up. But he shoved his pecker into me so hard it made me scream – I guess you know what I mean.'

'He forced his way in from behind.' said Hugo. 'It seems to have been a caprice of his. But not of yours.'

'I struggled like hell to get free! He was hurting me and I was screeching at him to stop it. He'd got hold of me by the hips and he was slamming into me like a maniac. I broke loose by feeling behind me and grabbing his dinkies and giving them a good hard yank till he squealed and pulled out. He'd made me so furious I hardly knew what I was doing – I got the gun out and pulled the trigger.'

'How close were you to him?' Hugo asked.

'We were close enough for the gun to touch his chest

when it went off. The shock turned him round and his legs folded under him. He slid down the side of the bath and sat on the floor propped up against it. That made me think he was still alive, but not when I knelt down and looked close. His eyes were open but there was nobody there.'

'Well,' said Hugo doubtfully, 'you have already told me you went there to kill him – now you are turning it into self-defence against unnatural rape. Why do you try to deceive me, dear Patsy?'

'I'm only trying to make you understand,' she said. 'Sure I meant to give him the dope. And I wanted him to die when I shot him – but there's a big difference. If he'd made love to me the proper way and I spiked his drink afterwards, that would have been in cold blood. But the way things worked out, he hurt me and drove me into such a rage that I wasn't really responsible for what I did, even though I killed him. Do you see what I mean?'

'I hear what you're saying, but it would require the combined talents of a lawyer and a theologian to determine your degree of blame.'

'Who'd want to blame me?' she asked. 'He was asking for it. A lot of people are very happy that Ambrose Howard is dead, Oskar says.'

'Who, for instance?'

'Mr Ignaz, for one – his old lady had been fooling around with him. And Chester Chataway, for the same reason – Lily takes her panties down for anybody in movies, including Mrs Ignaz. And that dopey prince that Norma Gilbert is going to marry – he was jealous because Ambrose had his girl more times than he did himself, And that's only a few – I could name half a dozen others who are pleased he's gone.'

'I see that Oskar has acquainted you with the background to Ambrose's life-long hobby. But don't you think that it's wrong to kill people, Patsy?'

'How many chances shall I get to be a star?' she countered. 'I'd been around Hollywood for three months when I met you, and I was down to my last twenty-five cents. The only meals I had in a week were the ones you bought for me. Then I meet Oskar and he guaranteed me a career in movies if I did one easy thing for him. Any girl would have accepted – you said so yourself.'

'When did I say any such thing?' Hugo demanded.

'When I told you about Lily Haden letting Mrs Ignaz have her. You said – *if all it takes to get into movies is to let the owner's wife play with you, what's wrong with that?* That's all I did really, let someone play around with me – it was his own fault that he hurt me and got shot.'

Hugo reached out to stroke Patsy's fair hair.

'What am I going to do with you,' he asked, realising how pointless it was to try to make her understand why what she had done was wrong.

'What you're going to do with me is make love to me,' she said softly, her lips brushing against his. 'You're hard again – and about time!'

Troubled though his conscience was, Hugo's cherished part had no such qualms and was behaving entirely naturally by standing hard and ready in Patsy's hand. She ran her hand lovingly up and down it and nature won out over conscience. Relieved of the need to think of moral consequences, Hugo dropped the fluffy green towel from round his shoulders and put his hands between Patsy's thighs to play with her brown-fleeced pouch, still very warm from the bath.

Her eyes closed and her breathing quickened as he aroused her rapidly, both his thumbs in her open little pocket. He had reached the conclusion that there was nothing to be done about her confession. The police investigation was officially closed – pressure by Stefan Ignaz had achieved that, not because he was guilty, but because he was afraid that whatever the police turned up might damage his business and cost him millions of dollars.

'I love you, Hugo!' Patsy gasped, her thighs quivering as her golden moments approached.

To go to the police now and repeat what Patsy had told him would cause chaos. Assuming that Captain Bastaple took the story seriously, Patsy and Oskar would be arrested and charged. Without Oskar, Ignaz International's movie of Mary Magdalene would be held up for months at the very least, perhaps shelved for years. Hugo's career in Hollywood would never get off the ground – Ignaz would have no time for an actor who cost him a fortune by getting his top director tried for murder. The contract for three thousand dollars a week would be worth no more than waste paper.

'Ah, ah!' Patsy moaned, shaking uncontrollably in spasms of ecstasy, her hand clasped tightly round Hugo's spindle.

She was still trembling and sighing when he laid her on her back on the white carpeting of the bathroom floor and spread her thighs apart to kiss the loose and slippery lips between them. A moment later he had his belly on hers and his stem deep inside her.

'Hugo . . .' she sighed, her fingers entwined in his curly dark hair to pull his face down to hers. She smiled up at him as he began to move firmly in her, and he smiled back and then kissed her.

It was in his mind that if Patsy had committed murder for Oskar for the sake of a film part, then there was nothing at all she wouldn't do for the man she thought she loved. Hugo felt more than ever confident about his own future in Hollywood and set to with a will to pleasure her beyond her wildest dream.

Confessions d'Amour
Anne-Marie Villefranche

Confessions d'Amour is the culmination of Villefranche's comically indecent stories about her friends in 1920s' Paris.

Anne-Marie Villefranche invites you to enter an intoxicating world where men and women arrange their love affairs with skill and style. This is a world where illicit encounters are as smooth as a silk stocking, and where sexual secrets are kept in confidence only until a betrayal can be turned to advantage. Here we follow the adventures of Gabrielle de Michoux, the beautiful young widow who contrives to be maintained in luxury by a succession of well-to-do men, Marcel Chalon, ready for any adventure so long as he can go home to Mama afterwards, Armand Budin, who plunges into a passionate love affair with his cousin's estranged wife, Madelein Beauvais, and Yvonne Hiver who is married with two children while still embracing other, younger lovers.

"An erotic tribute to the Paris of yesteryear that will delight modern readers."—*The Observer*

Ironwood
by Don Winslow

The harsh reality of disinheritance and poverty vanish from the world of our young narrator, James, when he discovers he's in line for a choice position at an exclusive and very strict school for girls. Ironwood becomes for him a fantastic dream world where discipline knows few boundaries, and where his role as master affords him free reign with the willing, well-trained and submissive young beauties in his charge. As overseer of Ironwood, Cora Blasingdale is well-equipped to keep her charges in line. Under her guidance the saucy girls are put through their paces and tamed. And for James, it seems, life has just begun.

Folies D'Amour
Anne-Marie Villefranche

From the international best-selling pen of Anne-Marie Villefranche comes another 'improper' novel about the affairs of an intimate circle of friends and lovers. In the stylish Paris of the 1920s games of love are played with reckless abandon. From the back streets of Montmartre to the opulent hotels on the Rue de Rivoli, the City of Light casts an erotic spell.

Education of a Maiden
Anonymous

This infamous tale of sexual coming-of-age in Victorian England is an amorous adventure unduplicated in the annals of erotic literature. Here, volumes I and II are published together, allowing readers to follow their lusty narrator from his first 'innocent' experimentations with his sisters to his final initiation into 'the mysteries of the coition of the sexes.'

Best of the Erotic Reader, Vol. III
by Anonymous

Assembled from more than a century of famous and infamous works of lascivious literature, readers are taken on an excursion to Paris in the 1920s and 50s, Victorian England, 16th century France, and the flesh-pots of New York. *Best of the Erotic Reader, Vol. III*, is a lusty reader's best companion.

Blue Angel Nights
Margarete von Falkensee

This is the delightfully wicked story of an era of infinite possibilities—especially when it comes to eroticism in all its bewitching forms. Among actors and aristocrats, with students and showgirls, in the cafes and salons, and at backstage parties in pleasure boudoirs, *Blue Angel Nights* describes the time when even the most outlandish proposal is likely to find an eager accomplice.

Order These Selected Blue Moon Titles

Souvenirs From a Boarding School ..$7.95

The Captive $7.95

Ironwood Revisited $7.95

The She-Slaves of Cinta Vincente ...$7.95

The Architecture of Desire $7.95

The Captive II $7.95

Shadow Lane $7.95

Services Rendered $7.95

Shadow Lane III $7.95

My Secret Life $9.95

The Eye of the Intruder $7.95

Net of Sex $7.95

Captive V $7.95

Cocktails $7.95

Girl School $7.95

The New Story of O $7.95

Shadow Lane IV $7.95

Beauty in the Birch $7.95

The Blue Train $7.95

Wild Tattoo $7.95

Ironwood Continued $7.95

Transfer Point Nice $7.95

Souvenirs From a Boarding School ..$7.95

Secret Talents $7.95

Shadow Lane V $7.95

Bizarre Voyage $7.95

Red Hot $7.95

Images of Ironwood $7.95

Tokyo Story $7.95

The Comfort of Women $7.95

Disciplining Jane $7.95

The Passionate Prisoners $7.95

Doctor Sex $7.95

Shadow Lane VI $7.95

Girl's Reformatory $7.95

The City of One-Night Stands $7.95

A Hunger in Her Flesh $7.95

Flesh On Fire $7.95

Hard Drive $7.95

Secret Talents $7.95

The Captive's Journey $7.95

Elena Raw $7.95

La Vie Parisienne $7.95

Fetish Girl $7.95

Road Babe $7.95

Violetta $7.95

Story of O $5.95

Dark Matter $7.95

Ironwood $7.95

Body Job $7.95

Arousal $7.95

The Blue Moon Erotic Reader II ...$15.95

ORDER FORM
Attach a separate sheet for additional titles.

Title	Quantity	Price
_____	____	_____
_____	____	_____
_____	____	_____
_____	____	_____

Shipping and Handling (see charges below) _____

Sales tax (in CA and NY) _____

Total _____

Name _____

Address _____

City _____ State _____ Zip _____

Daytime telephone number _____

❏ Check   ❏ Money Order   (US dollars only. No COD orders accepted.)

Credit Card # _____ Exp. Date _____

❏ MC   ❏ VISA   ❏ AMEX

Signature _____

(if paying with a credit card you must sign this form.)

Shipping and Handling charges:*

Domestic: $4 for 1st book, $.75 each additional book. International: $5 for 1st book, $1 each additional book
*rates in effect at time of publication. Subject to Change.

Mail order to Publishers Group West, Attention: Order Dept., 1700 Fourth St., Berkeley, CA 94710, or fax to (510) 528-3444.

PLEASE ALLOW 4-6 WEEKS FOR DELIVERY. ALL ORDERS SHIP VIA 4TH CLASS MAIL.

Look for Blue Moon Books at your favorite local bookseller or from your favorite online bookseller.